I0691624

SHARP PRACTICE

Iponymous Edition
First edition published 2014
By Iponymous publishing Limited
Swansea United Kingdom SA6 6BP

All rights reserved
© Mike Adlam, 2014
Moral rights asserted

The rights of Mike Adlam to be identified as author of this work has
been asserted in accordance with Section 77 of the Copyright, Designs
and Patents Act 1988. This book is sold subject to the condition that
it shall not, by way of trade or otherwise, be lent, resold, hired out or
otherwise circulated without the publisher's prior consent in any form
of binding or cover other than that in which it is published and without
a similar condition including this condition being imposed on the
subsequent purchaser

A CIP record for this book
Is available from the British Library

Design and typesetting: GMID
www.gmid.co.uk

(EBook) ISBN 978-1-908773-59-3
(Physical Book) ISBN 978-1-908773-60-9

www.iponymous.com

A word from Mike Adlam

There are many links in the chain of events that has brought this book into your possession, but, for me, the most significant is that it was only written thanks to the life-saving surgery and treatment I received at the hands of the Queen Elizabeth Hospital liver unit in Birmingham.

In spring of 2007 I collapsed with cancer of the liver and my wife, Rhian, was told by my Swansea doctors I wouldn't live; that was the only thing they got wrong. When I refused to die, they referred me to Birmingham and just over a year later I was given a full liver transplant at QEH. A week later I walked out of hospital, albeit bent double.

While awaiting my transplant - there is a grim period when you can only live in hope that an organ will become available – I did a sponsored jump off Langland Cliffs on the Gower Peninsula and raised a couple of grand for Cancer Research UK. Since my survival I have been contemplating ways of making a more permanent donation to the battle with Cancer. As a result, I have convinced my publisher that we should donate ten percent of profits from all sales of Sharp Practice to the Queen Elizabeth Hospital liver unit.

In return he has convinced me that I should write a further book about the hapless Mr Tony Stamford to complete a trilogy. Ten percent of proceeds from the sales of all three will then go to support the ground breaking research and life-saving surgery that the QEH unit carries out. I hope you enjoy Sharp Practice all the more knowing you have contributed to such a worthy cause.

1

It was a passably bright spring mid-week morning when I finally walked out of Her Majesty's Open Prison, Standford Hill, Isle of Dogs. It did little to lighten my mood, particularly given the flat monotony of the surrounding Sheppey countryside. It was as if the place had been specifically located to give departing inmates a parting shot of tedium. The warden on the gate, an oaf called Haskins, saw me off with a smug 'Cheerio, Doctor Stamford!' which seemed to carry 'and let that be a lesson to you' with it. I resisted the urge to point out I was a surgeon and therefore a Mister, not a Doctor, and nodded a curt farewell to my gaoler, consoling myself with the thought that he had the rest of his career to spend in the place. I hefted the black bin liner which contained my immediate worldly possessions over my shoulder and headed for the mini-cab that I had booked straight after breakfast. I was not in need of cash – I had the best part of six hundred quid nestling in my pocket, thanks to my labours in the prison kitchens.

'Maidstone', I ordered in a tone which suggested that a meandering tour of the Kent countryside would not elicit a tip.

To be honest, I was a little surprised at my lack of elation. I had spent the last fortnight picturing myself falling to my knees and kissing the earth beyond my prison walls, and then dashing madly up Rowletts Way to freedom. As I gazed numbly out of the taxi window at the fleeting countryside, I concluded that I had spent too much time in anticipation. My driver soon gave up any attempts at chirpy Kentish conversation and I settled back in peace to review the last nine months.

It had started as eighteen months, but had been reduced to nine thanks to my 'good behaviour'. I was never aware of behaving particularly well, any more than I was ever aware of any opportunities to behave particularly badly. I was offered the opportunity to buy 'some pills' on one occasion, but declined on the basis that my benefactor struck me as even less qualified than many of my former colleagues to prescribe such things. He assured me it was 'good gear' and that he 'done 'em reg'lar' himself, so perhaps I was a little unfair in this judgement.

Other than that, life in Standford Hill Open Prison had been tediously uneventful which, given my condition on arrival, was an absolute boon. Readers of my earlier memoires will recall that, at the time of my incarceration, I was in the grip of a mental breakdown engineered by my ex-wife, her psychopathic lover and her arch-bitch of a lawyer. Finding myself in a controlled environment in which I was regularly fed, encouraged to wash myself and routinely obliged to sleep, was a situation any psychiatrist would have rushed to prescribe.

It was three months before I was actually aware that I was detained in a prison and, even then, it only dawned on me gradually, because people had given up trying to be sociable, or even talking to me. Even the prison chaplain ignored me. The real breakthrough came when I bit into a forkful of meat pie and found the filling was still frozen.

'What the fuck is that!' I exclaimed in disgust, spitting it into my palm for inspection.

'Good God, it speaks!' came the reaction from a fellow prisoner who had tried more than most to elicit a response from me over the weeks since my arrival. Before I could retreat back into my shell of bewildered introspection he introduced himself and more or less forced me into a rather stilted initial conversation.

'Hi, my name's Peter Chisholm, what's yours?'

'Anthony Stamford,' I mumbled.

'Stamford? Stamford. Well, Standford Hill Prison – sounds like you were made for this place. What do you do for a living Anthony Stamford?

'I'm a surgeon.'

'A surgeon? Really? We don't get many surgeons in here.' He leant conspiratorially across the table.

'You want to keep that under your hat, they'll be queuing up outside your cell to show you their in-growing toenails...'

'I'm not that kind of surgeon.'

'That won't stop 'em, mark my words. What kind of surgeon are you anyway?'

'I'm a colorectal surgeon.'

'What, bums and things?'

I nodded.

'You could put it like that.'

'Hmmn, well there's a few round here who might try to book an appointment against your will, if you know what I mean. The sort you don't want to bend down in front of if you drop the soap in the showers.'

I gazed at him blankly, so he changed the subject.

'I hope you don't mind my asking, but what has brought a practitioner of colorectal surgery to such a sorry pass?'

'What do you mean?'

'Well I don't imagine you are in here for misdiagnosing piles. I mean, you'd have had to have done something pretty terminal to land yourself in here for a medical fuck-up, unless you copped a manslaughter charge or something. It wasn't that was it?'

I shook my head.

'No I didn't kill anybody.'

'What was it then? Don't tell me...embezzlement. You got caught cooking the books, over-ordering the wet-wipes or fiddling the new scanner appeal, eh? Come on, spill the beans...'

I shook my head again, irritably.

'No, nothing like that either.'

'Okay, so are we talking something non-medical?'

'What is this – 'What's my Line'? What's it got to do with you?' I hadn't intended to be so abrupt, but these questions were making me feel uncomfortably pressurised.

'Well aside from the fact that I have hours of monotony to fill, nothing I suppose. Don't worry, I won't ask again.'

I glanced up at his slightly injured tone, but he was still gazing at me rather than turning away in a sulk. A voice inside me pointed out that I had some time to go in this place, even if I was currently too confused to know quite how long. Besides, compared to some of my fellow inmates, he seemed quite personable. Perhaps it was time to dip a toe back in the stream of human affairs. I took a grip on myself and relented a bit.

'I was prosecuted for fraud.'

'Fraud? Sounds interesting,' he looked at me quizzically. 'Want to talk about it?'

'No, not really...' Memories of the events leading up to my

arrest were pushing forward and the reeling panic and confusion of my breakdown were threatening to overwhelm me again. I began drawing deep breaths to try and fight back the panic. It clearly showed in my face and his reaction was surprising. He reached across the table and grabbed my wrist. I tried to pull away, unaccustomed at this intrusive contact, but he held me tight. At the same time he spoke quietly, but urgently.

'Anthony, Anthony, listen to me! You are okay. You are having an anxiety attack. Just stay calm and it will pass. Trust me.'

I wasn't about to put my psychological welfare in the hands of a complete stranger, but there was something about the certainty of his manner, and besides, he ploughed on regardless.

'Listen to me, do you like sex?'

'What?'

'Just answer me, do you like sex?'

I nodded.

'What's your favourite position?

'What do you mean?'

'From the front or from behind, what's your favourite position?'

'I don't know...I like both, I suppose...'

'Good, come on concentrate! If I told you there was a woman waiting for you in your cell, who would she be?'

'What d'you mean?'

'Who would you most like to fuck right now?'

'Well I don't know. Marilyn Monroe, maybe?'

'Marilyn? You're pulling my leg, she's been dead for fifty years! Are you sure you're not in here for necrophilia? What about Madonna? She used to look a bit like her and she spends a lot of time in Britain and, last time she was in here, she asked me specifically if there were any horny surgeons she could shag. What about Madonna?'

I sat staring at him in disbelief. Not because I was struggling to trust his account of Madonna's sexual preferences, but because the anxiety fugue was receding, or at least failing to take over. He tightened his grip.

'Come on, concentrate. You've got her in your cell, right, and you want to get that stupid pointy bra off, remember that? Good. So how do you get it off?'

'What d'you mean?'

'How d'you get her bra off? Do you reach round and unhook it, or do you just yank it up? These are Madonna's tits remember!'

I didn't know why on earth we were talking about Madonna's breasts, but somehow I knew it was a lot better thinking about them than sliding backwards into the dark chaos of a fugue.

'I unhook it I suppose...'

'Excellent, a gentleman to the last! So now she pulls your head down for a closer inspection and you reach up for a proper handful. How does that feel?'

'I don't know...'

'Course you do, use your imagination. Don't tell me you're gay for Christ's sake!'

'No, of course not!'

'Right well get on with it then! You've got the finest pair of tits of our generation in your hands and she's gagging for it. What d'you do?'

'Well, I suppose I'd give them a bit of a squeeze and caress them first.'

'And then what d'you do?'

'Are you serious?'

'Not really, but how's that panic attack feeling?'

I paused to ask myself the same question and, to my amazement, I was feeling shaky but the worst of it had passed. Somehow, in a few seconds he had dispelled a condition which Professor Tanquist of the astronomically expensive Tanquist-Berg Clinic in Putney had taken weeks (or was it months?) to fail to cure. As I relaxed, he relaxed his grip.

'How do you feel now?'

'I don't know, a bit wobbly, but back on terra firma I suppose. How did you do that?'

Chisholm grinned.

'I don't know exactly, but a late business acquaintance of mine used to get attacks like that and it worked on him. I guess it relies on some sort of misdirection – getting the punter to think of something they find more interesting. For most blokes that has got to be sex; for most women too I expect, come to think of it.'

'Is it a permanent cure?'

'I don't know. It wasn't for him, but then he was selling kit to Angolan mercenaries on the side, so he had a lot of anxiety to deal with, particularly when he sold them a batch of empty grenades and they chopped his head off.'

'They did what?'

'They chopped his head off, bastards, decided to make an example of him.'

'Good grief, you must have felt dreadful!'

'Too right I did, the stupid sod owed me a packet. I broke my golden rule and gave him credit and the fucker went and got himself killed by a bunch of psycho niggers.'

This was all getting too much to take in, so I was not sorry when dinner ended and we headed off in different directions. However, I had taken the first step on the road back to some sort of normality and, better still, found someone who seemed willing and able to help me along it. Furthermore, my interest had been piqued by a glimpse of a world dramatically removed from the orderly, well-scrubbed corridors of St George's Hospital, or the oppressive prison walls of Standford Hill prison.

It was therefore a bit of a blow when he announced just over a fortnight later that his time was up and he was due out the following week. Nevertheless his companionship had, despite a few minor relapses, carried me out of the dark, anxious world of stress psychosis, into the daily routine and reality of prison life, and then beyond that into an exciting, glamorous world of ruthless international finance I could barely imagine or believe.

It transpired that my new companion was a banker with offices in London, New York and Zurich who was completing an eighteen month 'stretch' for brokering a shipment of commodities which had turned out to be weapons when inspected by customs officials during a routine search on the high seas. According to Chisholm, he had been sitting quite innocently minding his own business in his Mayfair offices one morning, when detectives from the Serious Crimes Squad turned up for a chat. For some reason they had refused to accept his assurances that, as far as he knew, the shipment was comprised of much needed medical supplies for the refugee camps in Kenya, and had invited him to assist them with their enquiries instead. An even less trusting judge had ignored his suggestion that he was the victim of a highly sophisticated 'mule' deception and had invited him to spend three years in Standford Hill.

As my confusion lifted and my thought processes clarified, part of the entertainment his company provided, lay in trying to assess quite where the plausible autobiography of Peter Chisholm stopped and The Secret Life of Peter 'Walter Mitty' Chisholm started. Still, to his credit, he was a fine storyteller and I never managed to catch him in an inconsistency. As we said our farewells on the day of his departure, I asked him if he might fancy meeting for a drink when I joined him on the 'outside'. True to form he took my arm confidingly.

'A word of advice old boy: if you shit in your own nest, leave it for the cuckoos to clear up. Fuck Britain, I'm off to Zurich to lick my wounds. If you're ever out in that neck of the woods, feel free to look me up. Adios old boy, adios.'

With that he shook my hand and hurried out of the door. When I took a glance down at my palm there was an old, rather stained business card nestling inside it. I slipped it into my trouser pocket.

*

Any further reminiscences regarding Peter Chisholm were cut short by my arrival in Maidstone. To my, admittedly, jaundiced eye, Maidstone was a dump, but it did contain two things that made it worth a slight detour en route to London: a branch of Barclays and a department store. I really didn't know how I planned to pick up the torn threads of my life, but I was certain of one thing, it wouldn't happen dressed in the clothes I'd been arrested in. They were part of my old life and, as far as I was concerned, they were going to stay that way; I needed to make some urgent improvements on the sartorial front. However, before I could go shopping, I was desperate to ascertain my financial situation.

The cab dropped me outside what seemed to be the central branch of Barclays. I had considered taking a look at what one of the bank's ATM's might divulge, but decided that I might need more than just an account balance. I went in and was shown to a seat by a strikingly ample young lady, in order to wait for an 'advisor' to become free.

As I awaited my turn, I fished out a letter nestling in my inside pocket. It purported to be from 'Tubby' Timothy Rosewall, the overweight junior solicitor who had supposedly helped me put together my case against my late enemy, and former good friend, Hamish Carmichael, to the GMC. In fact, I knew perfectly well it was from Rosewall's boss, my ex-best friend and solicitor, Roger Caraway, who had jumped ship and joined my money-grabbing, late wife's crew. Trust Roger to hide behind an underling's shirt-tails, the two-faced little shit.

To explain, just before my arrest for fraud, whilst in the grip of a weapons-grade anxiety fugue, I had foolishly signed a document giving Caraway and my wife's bitch of a solicitor, Amelia Harper (aka to me, Cruella) powers to handle our divorce settlement. What on Earth possessed me to sign it, beyond the fact that I didn't know my arse from my elbow at the time, I cannot imagine! Anyway, that's what had happened, and now I was desperate to discover what the arrangements described in Rosewall's letter really amounted to.

The quickest way to do that was to stop at an ATM and check the balance on the account that the devious bastards had opened up on my behalf, and in which they had supposedly deposited my share of the division of the family's cash and assets. These purported to be broken down in Rosewall's letter along with the Barclays Visa debit card and its PIN number which he had sent me separately, but I did not trust my enemy's underling. I wanted proof and I wanted it from an accountable human being, not a hole-in-the-wall machine.

I sat mentally peeling the Barclays uniform off the ample queue lady, despite never having much admired the work of people like Rubens – perhaps nine months in Standford Hill had had hidden cultural benefits after all, or perhaps I was just more desperate for a shag than I cared to admit. Finally, I was shown through to a pleasant enough young man who looked like he would be more comfortable in rugby kit than in his Barclays suit. His lapel badge proclaimed him to be Nick Evans. The knot of his tie hung loose in a half-hearted gesture of individuality. I sympathised after my recent prison attire. He gestured me to a chair.

'Good afternoon, Mr Stamford, how can I help you?'

'Well, er, I would like to know the balance on this account, please.' I passed over the bank card.

'Certainly, let's have a look.' He rattled the account number of the card onto his keyboard and then blinked and paused. He turned and inspected me more closely. My appearance clearly did not match my bank balance. He groped for a delaying tactic whilst he figured out if he was dealing with a card thief or an eccentric millionaire he couldn't afford to offend.

'I, er, see you don't actually bank in this branch.'

'No, is that a problem?'

'No, of course not sir, it's just that I would usually ask to see some ID.'

'Oh...right.'

Shit, I hadn't thought of that! I had switched to internet banking the moment Coutts, my former bank, had made it available and, even before that, I had rarely seen the inside of their Cadogan Place branch, thanks to ATMs. My brother Jeremy had always dealt with the day-to-day finances of Stamford Holdings and left me to get on with the medical world; I was out of touch. I pulled Rosewall's letter back out of my pocket.

'Well, I have this letter...' I passed it across the desk. He gave it a cursory glance out of politeness before handing it back.

'I'm sorry sir, we need something with a photograph on it like a driver's licence or a passport. This letter doesn't even bear your address.'

As he said this, I was sure I detected as slight shift in his tone. He glanced rather pointedly at the bin liner containing my possessions. I suddenly became very self-conscious. One benefit of prison food was that I had shed nearly a stone and a half during my confinement. But prison pallor, and a lack of the sort of exercise that rushing round hospital corridors had once provided, meant that this had not produced a fit and healthy appearance. Furthermore, I had left prison in the same clothes I had arrived in. A wash and press in the prison laundry had simply left them looking like I'd bought them in a car boot sale. It dawned on me that, viewed objectively, I probably didn't look like someone who would even qualify for a bank account, let alone someone who should be enquiring about one for which he had no ID.

'Oh, I see. I'm sorry... it's just, I've been away for a while.'

There was more truth in that than I had intended and it still didn't do anything to explain why I was carrying no ID. I was panicking, the last thing I needed was to end up back in court charged with attempted bank robbery! Fortunately, young Evans seemed to take pity on me; I was almost certainly not the first ex-con to pass through their doors on his way back from the Isle of Sheppey.

'Yes of course sir, well, if I can explain, you need to take this enquiry to your own branch in Richmond.'

'Richmond?' I echoed, before realising that this was information I was meant to know.

'Yes sir, and given that, from the look of it, this account has not been open long or seen much traffic, it may be advisable to take some ID and a proof of address this time.'

Proof of address? I didn't even have an address. The bastards had sold Thurleigh Road. This was getting worse by the moment.

'Right, okay, I'll make sure I do that. Thank you very much for your advice.'

I stood, suddenly quite desperate to get out of there. I grabbed my bin liner and nearly forgot to shake his hand before beating what felt like a pathetically confused retreat. I had been out of prison less than two hours and I had already experienced a vivid glimpse of just how hard it was going to be getting my life back on the road.

*

I was attracting more unwelcome attention as I fought to control the violent coughing fit induced by gulping down my first large whisky in the best part of a year. The lunchtime denizens of Drakes Bar looked briefly affronted at my gasping and spluttering, but then soon returned to their office politics. Yet again, my new found freedom was falling short of expectations.

I hadn't intended to stop for a drink as I hastened away from the bank, but as I approached this welcoming hostelry, I was struck by the thought that my nerves could benefit from a little bracing and, indeed, it was about time to relax and enjoy one of the many little pleasures denied to those that reside at Her Majesty's pleasure. I hadn't, of course, planned on choking on my first swig and, by the time I had sipped my way through the remains of the scotch (now with added soda) seated on my own in a corner, I had concluded that I was missing the companionship of prison. It was time to move on. Perhaps it was the jailbird aura which I was now convinced was clinging to me, but I clearly didn't fit in with Maidstone's lunchtime business crowd.

I finished my drink and left the pub with a grunted 'thanks' to anyone who would listen. I headed on up a sort of dismal, urban carriageway called Fairmeadow, which is presumably what it was until the town planners got hold of it. One of the local yokels assured me that the blighted boulevard led to my ultimate Maidstone destination, The House of Frazer.

*

I had spent my whole career in too much of a rush to bother with shopping. Now, for the first time in years, I was free to indulge in some serious 'retail therapy'. It was rapidly becoming apparent that life back on the 'outside' was going to need some adjusting to, and getting re-equipped for it promised to be a pleasant, unpressurised way of going about it after my stressful, earlier encounters with daily life.

In preparation for this occasion, I had spent hours in my cell, listing and relisting all the items a man might select in pursuit of a new wardrobe for a new life. Now, armed with a shopping list longer than The Dead Sea Scrolls, I headed for the men's department with real purpose in my stride.

Ten minutes later, I had filled a basket with underwear, nightwear, shaving kit and smellies, and was starting on my choice of casual gear. I was just adding a couple of Ralph Lauren polo shirts to my shopping basket when the price tag caught my eye: seventy pounds! Seventy pounds for a polo shirt? Jesus Christ, what was it made of – the eyelids of Mongolian silk worms? Alright, I probably hadn't bought a polo shirt since my student days, certainly not since my wedding day, but seventy pounds for crying out loud!

It suddenly hit me that six hundred pounds wasn't going to

begin to cover the shopping spree I had been planning. In fact, it probably didn't pay for what I'd collected so far! How was I going to explain that to the middle-aged shrew I'd deposited my first basket with? I surreptitiously dropped my current purchases down behind a rack of chinos and headed for the escalator.

*

By the time the train crept into Victoria Station I was ready to go back to prison. I was still wearing the same clothes I had left the place in and poorer to the tune of nearly one hundred quid, thanks in no small part to the extortionate train fare. It had occurred to me on the train that I was actually homeless. Sure I still owned half of the family home in Dorking, but it was let out to some crackpot religious organisation, so I could hardly turn up on the doorstep looking for lodgings. I could of course drop in on Jeremy for a dose of fraternal hospitality, but our relationship had always been based on brotherly competitiveness and I really didn't want him to see me like this. Besides, my appearance would probably get my cow of a sister-in-law, Esther, thrown out of the Epsom Women's Institute.

I re-knotted the top of my bin liner and braced myself. As I stepped down onto the platform I was appalled at how different London looked through the eyes of a down-and-out. Where once it had looked bold and exciting, now it looked cold and forbidding and that was only the station concourse! I told myself to get a grip and headed for the barrier. As my ticket vanished into the machine and I walked out into another sort of freedom, I reached up and touched my chin. There was a hint of new growth after my morning shave, but I still had a few days before it would count as a beard and a few more after that before it became matted. I reminded myself for the hundredth time that there was no need to panic, at least not yet.

My flight from Maidstone had at least provided me with a chance to properly contemplate my situation. I had headed for London because my money was in Richmond and the nearer I could get to it, the sooner I could get my hands on it. On a limited budget I couldn't risk the cost of a hotel and it was now getting pressing to find someone who might put me up for the night. I couldn't afford hotels until I was sure of my financial position and there was no way I would make it to Barclays in Richmond by five o'clock. Presumably Roger the Rat or Tubby Timothy had chosen that branch because it was round the corner from their fucking offices! My shopping was now scaling down to basic survival needs. I took the Tube for Oxford Street.

I found my way into Burtons on Oxford Circus and emerged half an hour later dressed in jeans and tee-shirt with a navy jumper and a worsted jacket over that. A pair of brown leather shoes completed a sort of poor man's Harvard look. At least I didn't look like a latter day Magwitch anymore!

Next stop, a mobile phone shop. I still had the phone I had on me when I was arrested, but the battery had died after a few months in Standford Hill. I resisted the urge to empathise with an insentient object and headed for Orange across the road. After a queue to rival the dinner queue in prison, I was beginning to understand why long term jailbirds were so quick to re-offend – at least they didn't have to pay anything when they got to the front of their queues!

Just as I was toying with the idea of grabbing a monitor and hefting it through the shop window to get attention, an enthusiastic young man approached and tried to explain the benefits of apps and touch-screens. I eventually convinced him that I had no intention of buying anything more technologically advanced than the cheapest pay-as-you-go on the premises and got him to switch my SIM card into it. At last, more or less respectably dressed and telephonically equipped I headed for the nearest Starbucks.

*

The gastronomic indulgence of Gentleman's Shortbread, washed down with hot chocolate, was beginning to wear off. I had been in need of the good things in life more than I realised. I was going through my list of female London contacts with a singular lack of success. Out of the twelve I had tried, only three had answered the phone. They had all assured me that they were delighted to hear from me and would love to meet up, but unfortunately they all had things to do that Wednesday evening. Was it just paranoia or did I detect an underlying disinclination to have anything to do with a former whistle-blower and jail bird?

Whatever their reasons, it didn't much matter. I still didn't have a roof over my head. Finally, with a hesitancy now tempered by desperation, I typed CVR into my new Samsung.

The initials stood for Caroline Vaughn-Riggs a consultant anaesthetist of my long-standing acquaintance.

My hesitancy was not due to any hostile reception I might expect from her – I knew that, if she was free, I could rely on Caroline for unstinting and luxurious hospitality in her Hampstead home. That was not the cause of my hesitancy. Nor was my hesitancy fuelled by fear of rejection – Caroline was quite open about her liking for me. No, my hesitancy, thanks to nine months of sexual activity confined only to routine self-abuse after lights-out, was prompted by lack of match practice. I knew, as did any leading London, or indeed international physician, that in presenting myself at the door of Caroline Vaughn-Riggs, I was facing up to the daunting prospect of shacking up, albeit temporarily, with a nymphomaniac doctor who kept a nurse's uniform in the cupboard.

2

I was awoken by a series of extremely unpleasant sensations arriving in quick succession. The first was a blinding light in my right eye as the lid was pulled back. The second was pain in my right wrist as I tried to yank my hand over to shield my eye and found it wouldn't move. The third was my mouth being suffused with warm liquid as my jaw was gripped and forced open. My mouth was then abruptly rammed shut and my nose pinched, leaving me with no option but to swallow or suffocate. I swallowed in desperation and my jaw was released.

I had another go at moving and found that all my limbs were secured. As my vision adjusted to the light, I peered down and realised that they were also naked, as was the rest of me. In fact, it would appear that I was lying naked, spread-eagled and cuffed to some sort of bed or couch. This was not how I remembered going to bed. My captor had just administered God only knew what kind of poison.

'Don't worry, it won't hurt you,' came a less than reassuring voice.

'What was it?'

'Just fifty mils of Viagra ground up and suspended in warm water so you couldn't spit it out.'

'Viagra?'

'Certainly darling, you didn't think I'm going to let you get away with that pathetic five minute effort you came up with earlier, do you?'

This was clearly rhetorical so, rather than replying I

concentrated on my surroundings. This was not the room I had gone to bed in. That had contained a double bed. It had also contained the soft, tasteful furnishing and decor one might expect to find in the bedroom of a well-to-do, Hampstead, lady consultant. This room was utterly different. The walls were, as far as I could tell despite the spot lights shining down into my eyes from above me, white and clinical. Was I in some sort of operating theatre? For a moment I was transported back to an old nightmare in which my late wife and her cronies had disembowelled me in front of my eyes. Thankfully, before memories of that became too intense, my captor spoke again.

'I expect you're wondering where you are?'

'Too bloody right! There are laws against kidnapping, you know!'

'Don't worry, you're in the Copulating Theatre adjoining my bedroom.'

'The what?'

'The Copulating Theatre. Isn't it fabulous? I designed it myself.'

'How did you get me in here?'

'Easy, you were in such a rush to shoot the sheriff that you didn't notice the bed splits in two. The part you're on now wheels like a hospital bed. A couple of diazepam dissolved in your post-coital glass of Scotch did the rest, which reminds me, it may take a while for the Viagra to kick in, but don't worry I've already thought of that. Now what is this I hear about my old lover Mr Anthony Stamford getting himself disbarred for being a naughty boy?'

As she spoke Caroline stepped into the circle of brighter

light cast by the spots. I recalled that her favourite role-play used to involve her dressing up in a nurse's uniform. As far as I ever got involved in the hocus-pocus of psychiatry, I had always tended to assume that this was some sort of reverse role-play after a hard day bossing patients and underlings around. If I remembered rightly she obediently administered lingering blanket baths and was quick to submit to a bit of gentle spanking if she spilled anything or otherwise failed in her administrative duties.

Now it appeared that her sexual horizons had widened considerably. Her uniform was no longer pinched from the NHS, unless they were now handing out short, low-cut tunics made of black latex off-set by white lace stockings with Red Cross badged garters. Her hair was drawn up into a tight bun under her white nurse's cap which also bore a Red Cross logo. More worryingly, it wasn't just her costume that had changed, it was her whole demeanour.

There was an underlying note of menace in her question and it was impossible to ignore the fact that I was securely tied up and that she was now holding a handful of kit which, whilst difficult to distinguish individually, clearly comprised an assortment of items made of chain and studded leather. She dumped this on the bed between my widespread legs.

'I don't know what you mean...' I stammered feebly.

'Come off it', she rolled her eyes, 'I've heard all sorts of rumours about fraud and blackmail and philandering. It's the philandering part that interests me of course, particularly now it has fallen to me to administer a suitable punishment.'

'Now hang on! I've already done nine months in prison for

that and I'm not into all this S&M bondage stuff...'

'You never mentioned that when you used to tie me up and, besides, you were sent to prison for fraud, not philandering, so it falls to me to come up with a punishment that fits the philandering part of your crime.'

I gulped in dread at the relish with which she pronounced her judicial duty, then gazed in horror as she selected a black leather hood from between my legs and checked to see if the zip worked. There were two slits to fit over where the eyes would be, but what was making my blood run cold was the large rubber phallus that protruded from the mouth area. My brain began to curdle at the prospect of what she intended to do to me wearing that. I almost gasped with relief when she walked round the bed and fitted it over my head instead.

*

My wrists and ankles were painfully numb and sore as 'Nurse' Caroline freed me from the straps, but that was as nothing when compared to my 'fifth extremity' which felt ready to drop off. She had administered regular doses of strong black coffee laced with heaven knows what stimulants to keep me awake, whilst the Viagra had served to keep the old chap standing to attention, no matter how exhausted I became. When I questioned the legality of this abuse she simply replied: 'Trust me, I'm a doctor.' Eventually, I passed through some sort of pain and exhaustion barrier into a state of otherness usually associated with extreme Eastern mysticism. Finally, thank God, the Viagra wore off.

Having satisfied herself in a number of highly inventive ways that there really was no life left in my wilting, tortured member, she went off to make breakfast.

'So you're not working today?' I ventured over croissants and a generous dollop of Bonne Maman fruit preserve. Caroline was pouring fresh coffee.

'Certainly, later this evening.'

'Oh, caught with a late one, eh?'

'Everyone's a late one darling. I don't suppose you've heard, what with your enforced absence and everything...'

'Heard what?'

'I'm no longer an anaesthetist, at least not a practicing one.'

'Really, how do you pay for all this then?'

'How d'you think?'

I paused to consider how I thought.

'You don't mean you, er...'

'Screw for a living?'

I helped myself to another croissant while I adjusted to her surprising forthrightness.

'Yes, well, I suppose you could put it like that...'

'Indeed I do, except it's not described like that on my tax return.'

'Right, I see. So does that mean I owe you any money?'

'No, that was a Get out Of Jail Freebie.'

'Thank God for that!'

'Why? A wealthy man like you could afford it, surely.'

'I don't know. That all depends on how badly my late wife and her boyfriend have ripped me off.'

'Late wife?'

'She died crashing the Aston Martin they stole from me.'

'Not that beautiful Aston you used to drive to work?'

'The very same, and I won't know what else they've ripped me off for until I get to Barclays in Richmond.'

'Can't you get a balance from a cashpoint?'

'I don't know if it will show all the details.'

'Do you have to go all the way to Richmond? Won't any old branch do?'

'I tried that in Maidstone, but they just referred me to Richmond because it was a new account.'

'So what happens if they have ripped you off?'

'I don't know. It depends to what extent. I was sent a letter in jail from my old solicitor, but he had switched to her side at some point before they put me on trial...'

'Put you on trial?'

'Yeah, I accused Liz's lover of manslaughter because he cocked up an op he asked me to assist with. The GMC and the police threw it out and he threatened to sue me for defamation. My supposed solicitor and best friend told me he could fix up a negotiated settlement, but, when I turned up for the meeting, it turned out to be a sort of bizarre mock trial at which my family took it in turns to tell me what a lousy father, shitty husband and out-and-out bastard I was.'

'That's seems a bit one-sided...'

'It was, and I was in the middle of some sort of breakdown at the time so I didn't stand a chance. I tried to fight my corner at which point they confronted me with evidence of the nest egg my father had left me and had me arrested for fraud because I hadn't declared it in the divorce settlement. That's how I ended up in prison.'

'What did this letter say?'

'Nothing helpful, it simply said that all sales and division of assets and monies had been completed and that I was to apply to his office for a full account of the settlement on my release from prison. I don't even remember giving any instructions, though I've got a faint memory of signing some sort of agreement at that phony trial. Quite what it said is completely beyond me, so God knows what I agreed to.'

'So what are you going to do now?'

'I don't know. I suppose I'd better head off down to Richmond and find out what I'm really worth, then think about starting a new life. What are you up to?'

'Oh, I don't know. I expect I'll call a few girlfriends and see if anyone fancies a coffee. I'm due at Gary's at eleven to have my hair and nails done then I'll be working most of the afternoon. Will you want to stay again tonight?'

'Well, it's kind of you to offer, but it rather depends on whether I'll actually be able to get some sleep if I do...'

Caroline laughed.

'There, there, poor darling, you'll sleep soundly enough tonight. I'm working right through. You happened to call on my night off last night and I was feeling playful, but you're welcome to one of the spare rooms until you're sorted out.'

'Well, in that case, I don't mind if I do – nothing against the exquisite pleasures of the freebie of course...'

'Of course not, just not fully up to speed yet?'

'If last night was anything to go by, I'm not sure I ever was...'

'Don't worry darling, stay a week or two and I'll lick you into shape, if that's quite the expression I'm looking for.'

'Great. Thanks, I'll look forward to it.'

'Think nothing of it.'

Caroline was smiling as I got up to go and collect my things, but there was a steely glint in her eye.

*

'No, I don't want to talk to Mr Timothy fucking Rosewall. I want to talk to Mr Roger fucking Caraway, so get on that fucking telephone right now and tell him Mr Anthony Stamford is in reception or I'll take the bloody thing off you and strangle you with the cord!'

I was standing, red-faced in the elegant reception room of the offices of Roger Caraway and Partners.

'Really Mr Stamford! I am not paid to tolerate such abusive language and, if you do not calm down immediately, I'll be calling the police, not my colleagues...'

This was not the response to help the situation.

'Call them! I don't give a shit. I've just come from prison thanks to your thieving, two-faced boss, so there's nothing you can threaten me with. Just make sure you tell them to bring two sets of cufflinks, because I'll be explaining to them what a crook he is!'

'Look, will you please calm down! Making a scene like this will solve nothing...'

'No it won't, but it will make sure everyone else in the building knows what a cheating little shit Roger Caraway is and it won't take long for that to do the rounds at Richmond fucking Golf Club, will it?'

'Alright, alright, just let me see if he's in...'

'Of course he's in. There's a new BMW parked in his space which I probably paid for. Call him and tell him I'm on the way. I'm not hanging around here arguing the toss anymore!'

This outburst was calculated on the basis that my former best friend would not want me disturbing his carefully cultivated clientele, but the anger was nevertheless real enough. There was always the possibility that the woman would carry out her predictable threat to call the police, but that was offset by the prospect of their current clients being treated to the spectacle of a former client being bodily removed.

I had just marched from the Barclays by the station to Roger's plush offices on Richmond Green in double-quick time. The walk had done nothing to abate my fury. I had spent the last nine months calculating and re-calculating what I reckoned would be my share of the proceeds from my divorce from Elizabeth and what I had just heard came nothing near my expectations. I knew I was going to get ripped off – I had signed over the right to handle arrangements to my enemies – but I was not expecting this!

According to the original list drawn up by my late wife and her bitch of a solicitor Cruella our joint savings and assets came to over five million quid. True, in my confusion, I had agreed to considerably less than half of this at our final showdown, but I still reckoned that I should have come away, extremely conservatively, with at least one million eight hundred thousand. According to the nice young lady at Barclays in Richmond, I was now worth just over one million one hundred thousand! That was a shortfall of seven hundred thousand and

I was not going to write that off without a fight. I knew Roger would do his best to hide behind Tubby Timothy's coat-tails, hence the guerrilla tactics.

'Wait, please! He's got a client with him, but he shouldn't be long...'

I paused. So he definitely was in, the BMW had been a calculated guess.

'Alright, I'll wait, but if you try to palm me off with young Rosewall, I'll put that coat stand through the window, understand?'

The woman nodded, stunned by this violent caesura in her genteel working day, but relieved that I was crossing the room to take a seat. Ten minutes later a late middle-aged couple emerged through the door that led to the offices. She nodded to me.

'You can go in now Mr Stamford. Mr Caraway's office is at the end...'

'I know where his office is, thank you,' I snapped, just to let her know I was far from mollified. With that, I rose and headed through the door and down the corridor to the office dead ahead of me.

*

Roger was looking sulky and more than a little nervous as I barged in without knocking.

'Look Tony, this really isn't on...'

'Don't you 'Tony' me you fucking little weasel!' I retorted, planting my knuckles on the front edge of his desk. 'I want some answers and they had better be convincing.'

'What d'you mean?'

'I mean where in hell did this pathetic figure come from?' I waved the bank statement I was clutching in my fist across his desk at him.

'I take it you're referring to the final settlement figure MS Harper and I arrived at?'

'The very same, and I'm telling you now it bears no resemblance to the figure I've spent the last nine months in prison arriving at!'

'I don't imagine it does. You were in no position to be aware of fluctuations in prices and market values while you were in prison. I'm afraid we found ourselves disposing of your family assets in extremely unfavourable market conditions. The recession hasn't, unfortunately, lifted during your absence.'

'I don't give a damn about the recession or the market conditions! You and that Harper woman have conspired to rip me off in cahoots with Liz, Annette and that bastard Carmichael!'

'No-one has conspired to rip you off. Liz is dead and her share of the estate was willed to Peter and Annette as her next of kin.'

'Is that so? Then how come I'm left with just over a million quid out of an estate worth more than five million?'

'Because you are basing your expectations on an early and over-generous estimate...'

'Sure, very generous when it was in Liz's interest to make me out to be loaded!'

Roger shrugged.

'An estimate is just a calculated guess and usually on the generous side. Don't pretend you didn't realise that. Anyway, I have a full inventory of what was disposed of and what it realised. I'll print it out if you would take a seat.'

I paused. He was defeating me with reasonableness, but I wasn't going to trickle out of his office having just gone to the trouble of storming in.

'Very well, but get on with it,' I agreed. I sat down on one of the chairs occupied by the previous couple and drummed my fingers on his desk. Roger fiddled with his mouse then sat back and waited as his printer clicked and hummed into life. He stared at the ceiling as intently as I was staring out of the window. A few moments later he got up and collected a couple of sheets of paper from the tray. He glanced over them, and then handed them to me.

The document was, in effect, the list of monies and assets that my wife and her solicitor had originally drawn up. Against the original values they had estimated, someone had now entered the amounts that had been realised along with each party's share. Even at a glance I could see that our savings and cash at bank had been equally split, which I knew was all legal enough.

'What have you done to my bloody pension?' I demanded to keep my blood on the boil.

Roger shrugged.

'We have been very fair with your pension. We ascertained its value and deducted half from your cash to create a clean break. We felt a one-off payment would suit both parties more than on-going payments...'

'Bollocks! You simply figured that there was no way of knowing if I would ever work again having succeeded in getting me thrown in prison and destroying my career in the process!'

Roger shrugged again.

'Think what you like. We were well within our remit given the powers you signed over to us.'

'Yes, well whatever I signed, I did so whilst not in sound mind. I was in the middle of a nervous fucking breakdown for God's sake!'

'Can you prove that? I have a letter here from Professor Tanquist at the Tanquist-Berg Clinic stating that you discharged yourself shortly after the GMC hearing and another from the prison authorities stating that your behaviour in prison was withdrawn, but not outside the parameters of behaviour expected of first-time inmates.'

'That's because I was having a fucking breakdown! I didn't know the time of day!'

'Perhaps not, but you've got to ask yourself who's going to be believed – a professor of psychiatry and a governor of Her Majesty's Prison Service, or a man convicted of fraud and deception.'

I sat stunned. Yet again, adjusting to my new-found place in the world was proving shockingly hard to grasp. Roger took my silence as an invitation to continue.

'You've got to remember that the estimate included things like your Aston which is now in a scrap yard. Furthermore, no-one foresaw what a tough negotiator you brother would turn out to be. He only coughed up a hundred and fifty thousand to buy out your share of Stamford Property Holdings. I've never seen anyone play the cloth-eared elephant with such determination. You could always ask him for an improved offer, but I wouldn't hold out much hope for your chances.'

I found myself nodding, unconsciously, in agreement. My brother Jeremy was the businessman in the family and would not have been impressed with the trouble all this must have put him to. If he had made himself a tidy little packet out of this, I couldn't see him feeling generously disposed towards me as a result. We weren't big on brotherly love.

I stood up.

'So that's it then. I should have known you'd have an answer for everything – you're a bloody solicitor.'

'I'll take that as a compliment and I should add that, as far as I am concerned, our friendship is over and I would strongly advise you not to come here or try to contact me again.'

'That depends on whether or not I decide that I still have a claim against you.'

'Well if you do, you had better be prepared to handle the consequences...'

'Meaning?'

'Meaning that I, along with your daughter Annette, find it very hard to believe that your Aston Martin just happened to develop a fault resulting in a fatal accident on the day it was collected from Dorking. Particularly since Annette has subsequently discovered that you visited the garage to say your farewells to it a short time before.'

'What are you trying to say?' I gasped as I felt the blood literally draining from my face.

'I'm saying that that is one hell of a coincidence and I'm not the only one that thinks it. I had a long chat with that copper Newcombe who arrested you and he was far from convinced. In fact it took some persuading to convince him that I didn't know more than I was letting on. I've still got his card and if I hear anything from you again, I might just call him and make sure he knows about that visit. Now fuck off and count yourself lucky you're getting anything.'

*

I blundered down the steps from his office. The world was reeling and closing in on my head. I had tried to retort but no words would come and the harder I tried the more reality bent away from me. I left Richmond and headed back into Town. I wandered round the West End stopping with increasing frequency at the various hostelries that presented themselves along the way. I kept moving on as my company was solicited by assorted bar-flies and members of the gay community. It was years since I had stepped this far outside the closed social milieu of the medical world and frankly, I was not fit to cope with the experience. As the fugue abated the drink took over, leaving me just as confused.

I finally found my way back to Hampstead – I had nowhere else to go – although it was not until late evening that I arrived back at Caroline's front door. By then I was well and truly inebriated, but I managed to fumble my key into the lock without causing any undue disturbance. With elaborate caution I wove my way upstairs to the spare room she had allocated to me. I folded my clothes with drunken fastidiousness and then dropped them on the floor before collapsing onto the bed.

This last action seemed to produce instant wakefulness. I found myself gazing up at the darkness as my mind filled with the elusive question that had been tormenting me for the last few months. In fact, it wasn't the question that was elusive, just the answer.

The question was, had I murdered my wife and her lover Hamish Carmichael, by cutting through a brake hose on the Aston Martin they had cheated me out of? The answer was lost to me in the sea of confusion and bewilderment I had been swimming in since my ensuing breakdown. Even now, greatly recovered as I was, I still could not retrieve any clear memory of my true actions as I knelt down by the wheel arch of my beloved DB6 to say goodbye. Did I, as I would like to think, produce a camera and take a final snap or two of the beautiful car I was about to lose to my wife and her lover and leave it at that, or did I then produce a mini-hacksaw and cut a notch into the brake pipe hiding in the wheel arch? I still couldn't say. Was I nursing a harmless revenge fantasy, or was I locked in denial as the perpetrator of a calculated murder? I knew that a symptom of my breakdown was amnesia which could take a long time to wear off, but what would I discover about myself when it did? Is that why I couldn't remember – because I was not willing to face the truth that would emerge?

Over the last few months I had gone a long way to rationalising this problem. I was a surgeon so I was hardly unaccustomed to death. At times it could be argued that I had even caused it, or at least failed to prevent it, so I didn't have the horrors usually associated with an encounter with the Grim Reaper. At the time when this episode occurred I had just discovered that my wife was screwing the man who I had recently been led to believe was my best friend. Perhaps it was not an excuse to impress a judge, but I was almost unhinged with jealousy and rage at the time. Certainly sufficient to make me act out of character. If I had killed them, it really was a case of what the French call *le crime passionnel*.

Furthermore, I had been methodically tricked into playing the part of a heartless, philandering husband and ended up in prison serving a quite disproportionate sentence for fraud with my career in tatters. Even if I had killed them in a moment's crazy vengefulness, my God I'd paid a heavy price for it! In other words I had concluded that, if I really was guilty, then my revenge was perhaps excessive, but to some degree justifiable and more importantly I had paid my dues to society.

Finally, as I stared into the darkness, I arrived at the startling fact that insomnia, or even the guilt of homicide, were the least of my problems. What I was currently trying to blot out was the awful realisation that I was not the only one questioning my innocence. I had barely been out of prison for twenty-four hours and the past I had hoped my incarceration would help to bury had reared its ghastly head again.

3

'You're looking rather fragile this morning.'

I nodded glumly. I wasn't improving my soggy Weetabix by shoving them round the bowl, but the thought of shoving them down my throat made me nauseous. If my arrival at the office on Richmond Green had been marked by a Napoleonic bravura, my departure had resembled the defeated generalissimo's retreat from Moscow. Now I was sitting in Caroline's kitchen viewing the world through a haze of bewildered, hungover depression. She finally lost patience and consigned my breakfast to the organic waste disposer.

'I take it from your demeanour that the meeting didn't live up to expectations?'

'You could say that.'

'I know. I just did. Well, are you going to sit there all day feeling sorry for yourself, or are you going to tell me about it?'

This was a much more imperious Caroline than I remembered from her medical days. I winced mentally.

'You wouldn't want to know...'

'Why don't you let me decide that, unless you intend to sit there with a face like a slapped arse until you starve to death. Am I right in assuming that your financial situation has not turned out to your liking?'

'Sure, but it's more complicated than that...'

'Well come on then, a problem shared is a problem halved. Are you broke?'

'No, not really. It's not that.'

'What is it then?'

I looked up to meet her enquiring gaze.

'I can't explain.'

This last reply was truer than she had reason to suppose. Rather to my surprise, she seemed to accept the rebuff without further probing.

'Okay, then why don't you go and get yourself shaved and showered and looking as presentable as possible.'

'What for?'

'I've got a business proposition to put to you so I'm taking you out to lunch.'

'But I'm not a businessman...'

'Right now you're not anything, so shut up and go and get ready before I change my mind.'

'Oh, right.' With uncharacteristic obedience I rose and headed upstairs even more bewildered than I'd been five minutes earlier.

*

I pushed the remains of my 'Fusilli with Salmon, Asparagus and Cream' away from me and sat back feeling somewhat revived. We were sitting in Hampstead's Villa Bianca and I now had a more-or-less square meal inside me thanks to a starter consisting of two large Bloody Marys. It had taken two to wash away my hangover and leave me with the semblance of an appetite. They had also left me with a far more benign view of the world and my place in it.

I picked up the glass of Pinot Bianco I was using to continue the good work begun by the B.M.s and raised it in a toast.

'Well, here's to the most accommodating hostess in the world. I can honestly say I have never received hospitality that went so far beyond the call of duty.'

Caroline raised her glass of Perrier to acknowledge the toast.

'Cheers! Do you now feel sufficiently revived to hear my proposition?'

'I most certainly do, though I am still not sure about the 'business' aspect of it.'

Caroline shrugged impatiently.

'Don't worry about that, it was just a turn of phrase, you pay accountants to handle all that. It's just that I can see an opportunity that might very well turn out to be to our mutual advantage.'

I raised my eyebrows.

'Go on.' Right now I was interested in hearing about anything that might turn out to my advantage.

'Well it strikes me that, from what I've seen so far, you are going to need accommodating on a more than temporary basis?'

'Well, I would appreciate a few more days while I get myself sorted out...'

'Because you haven't got anywhere to live?'

'No, not really...'

'So you're homeless and I take it you've lost your licence to practice?'

'No, well yes...I mean I let it lapse while I was in prison.'

'So you have to apply for a new license. Do you realise that you are then going to have to convince a Fitness to Practice tribunal that you haven't brought yourself and the medical profession into disrepute.'

'How do you know that?'

'Because I phoned the GMC yesterday and asked them.'

'Did you say you were calling on my behalf?'

'No, why?'

'Because I haven't told them I've been in prison. I was done for fraud, not medical misconduct so why should it matter to them?'

'Oh for goodness sakes Tony, you are meant to be an honest, upstanding member of the community. The young man I spoke to told me that the police report every doctor they charge with a criminal offense to them, regardless of its nature. There's no way of pretending it never happened.'

I sat back stunned as the reality of what she had said sank in. The warm glow of alcohol had turned to something more akin to heartburn. Again, I was being slapped in the face by the ramifications of a moment's foolishness. My father's 'nest egg' was turning out to be a cursed gift – a sort of Stamford version of The Monkey's Paw. Not only had the money gone to pay the fine the court imposed along with my prison sentence, but now my failure to declare it stood to end my career completely! Finally I turned back to Caroline.

'So how does any of this amount to a business opportunity?'

'Well, unless you plan to fritter away what money you do have left on hotel bills, you're going to need somewhere to stay while you sort the GMC out and, assuming you do get your license back, I suspect you are going to need a line of medical work that doesn't involve the NHS. I doubt if that pig Chaudhuri will have you back after bringing the good name of his beloved St George's into disrepute and he has a lot of influence with his fellow Medical Directors in the Health Service.'

A vision of my obese former Medical Director swam, unwelcomed, into my mind.

'You don't sound too enamoured of the great man?'

'He offered me an internal examination in an empty side-ward one afternoon and got quite forceful when I declined. I had to hit a nurse call button to discourage him and I was a doctor. Apparently the nurses used to hide in the toilets if they heard he was on his way. It's said that was why they kicked him upstairs into admin. Anyway, after that I found all sorts of things began getting difficult. Nothing I could pin on him of course; just little things that all added up – leave applications getting mislaid, that sort of thing. It was part of the reason I decided to quit in the end.'

I nodded sympathetically. I was happy to listen to anything unpleasant said about that slimy bastard.

'Anyhow, I digress. The opportunity I have in mind is based around the fact that you need somewhere to live and a way to earn a living. True?'

'I guess so.'

'And, at least for the time being, that will have to be done without a medical license?'

'So you say.'

'Well, I don't know if it struck you during our little session, but you might have noticed that the Copulating Theatre is equipped to pretty much resemble a real operating theatre?'

'It was more like a torture chamber...'

'That was just the S&M lighting I thought you'd enjoy, but the couch you were on was a genuine hospital bed. In fact, it's a second hand maternity bed with adjustable stirrups and everything.'

'How is this relevant to me?'

'It's relevant because I happen to know a lot of women around here whose husbands work in the City. Wealthy, bored women who would like a bit of pampering to make them feel better about their husbands 'staying late in the office' with their secretaries.'

'So what are you suggesting? I set up shop as some sort of paramedical gigolo?'

'No, not at all. It would be entirely up to you what services you choose to provide and, with your qualifications, that could be anything from massage to corn removal. Just so long as you stay away from the sort of services that require a medical license until you've got one. The point is that I have a smart, hygienic room that is currently standing unused throughout most of the day because I work evenings. You could rent it from me say from ten 'til five and then I could take over from six with my male clients. It would suit me if your services were more above board than mine because the last thing I need is to be accused of running a bawdy house.'

'But I don't know any of these women...'

'Don't worry about that, I do. Give me a week and I'll have them running up the drive. They'll be queuing up to have handsome surgeon Mr Tony Stamford as their Personal Medical Adviser, particularly now you've been to prison.'

'I beg your pardon?'

'Don't you remember what happened after your arrest?'

'I hardly remember being arrested, it's all a total blur.'

'Well, the papers had a field day, particularly the tabloids who christened you 'Sex-Mad Surgeon Stamford'. Someone got hold of a video of you 'bonking' a hooker after some shindig up in Scotland and even I was impressed by the number of St George's female doctors and nurses who claimed you had bedded them. It died down soon enough, but I assure you your reputation precedes you. Women love bad boys.'

I nodded trying to take this in.

'You mentioned rent. What sort of money are you talking about?'

'Well, while I was researching this yesterday I had a look on Google and the going rate for a studio flat in this area is about three hundred pounds per week and renting a consulting room costs about a hundred and twenty-five a week. How about I throw in the equipment for free and we share the cost of a secretary/ receptionist to give the whole thing an air of respectability. She would set us back no more than four hundred a week. She can finish at five and I'll carry on using my mobile for my clients.'

I did a quick mental calculation.

'So I would be paying you six hundred and twenty pounds per week. That's an awful lot of Personal Medical Advising...'

'Tony, we are talking about wealthy women here. Women who think nothing of paying two hundred quid for a frock! You could charge two or three hundred quid for a morning or afternoon session without them batting an eyelid. That, if I'm not very much mistaken, works out as two to three thousand per week and that's only for a five day, seven hour per day, week. You're used to much longer hours than that.'

I nodded. She certainly had a point. I had spent my life in a profession that didn't know which way the hands went round a clock. Furthermore, a spell spent as a Personal Medical Adviser would keep the wolf from the door while I tried to get my license back. God knows what reception I could expect from the sanctimonious sods at the GMC! I decided to play a little harder to get.

'Well, it's a very tempting offer, but I'd be starting from scratch doing something I've had no experience in...'

'Right now that applies to almost anything you decide to do, but I tell you what, why don't I give you a month rent free to settle in and get established? In four weeks time, if it's not happening, we call it quits and you owe me nothing. Fair?'

I paused for effect, and then tilted my head in partial acquiescence.

'Okay, six hundred pounds per week all in and you've got a deal.'

I leant across the table and offered my hand. Caroline tilted her head calculatingly then grinned and accepted it.

'Okay, you've got a deal, but only if you promise to tell me the real truth about what went on between you and Elizabeth.'

I laughed.

'I'm sorry, you'll have to buy my memoirs for that.'

Caroline passed on a dessert for the sake of her figure. I passed on it for the sake of a last Bloody Mary, and then magnanimously called for the bill. As I paid it I wondered quite what rent she would have settled for if I had pushed harder, but, to be honest, I didn't give a damn. Three days after coming out of prison I was accommodated, fed and earning a quasi-medical living! Most important of all, for the first time in more than a year, I was feeling a stirring of the old, confident, self-assertive Tony Stamford again.

*

Caroline had not exaggerated the potential demand for my services as a Personal Medical Adviser. Almost overnight the downstairs bedroom that had led through into the Copulating Theatre was split in two to provide a reception room and separate consulting room, with the theatre itself functioning as my examining room. I was open for business. Caroline continued to use it for her more 'personal' evening services as she had done before. Within a week of this cosmetic building work reaching completion I was fully booked and, by the end of the month our new receptionist, Jill Pellow, had started a waiting list. A month after that I took Caroline out for lunch to discuss the situation.

We sat down in the airy restaurant of the Freemasons Arms and shared a Mediterranean Mezze. The buzz of lunchtime chatter kept our conversation private.

'So at the moment you are handling ten clients a week, two a day, five days a week?'

I nodded, choosing to ignore the smirk that flitted across her lips as she used the word 'handling'.

'That's right.'

'And what kind of services are you providing at the moment?'

'Well, much as you'd expect. The sort of routine check-up a

G.P. would do, the Stamford Diet which basically involves eating a balanced diet with an eye on the calories and the Stamford Fitness Program which involves a thrice weekly swim at the pool of their choice and however many daily sit-ups I see fit to prescribe. I make it all sound personal to them and then deal with individual problems such as corns and varicose veins as the need arises. Oh, and a regular gynaecological examination seems to be getting quite popular.'

Again I noticed that fleeting smirk.

'I see. Well it seems a pity to be turning business away if you're happy to handle more. If you're managing two clients a day easily enough, why not increase it to three or four even? Four a day would entail two one and a half hour sessions, morning and afternoon, with an hour off for lunch. Do you think you could handle that?'

'Sure, but what would my existing clients think about having their hours cut?'

'They can take it or leave it. They're women for goodness sakes! They'd rather share than give you up to a rival.'

'Well shouldn't I offer them a reduced rate?'

'Has anyone complained about your charges to date? Money is not the object. If I were you I'd be more inclined to think about upping the rate, and working Sundays if you're feeling that accommodating – don't bother about Saturdays, they're for shopping.'

'Really?'

'Sure, make hay while the sun shines...'

'And what do you hope to get out of it?'

'Well I got you started and paid for the building alterations so how about paying me a cut on each client you handle above the basic ten a week?'

'What sort of cut are you thinking about?'

'How about twenty percent?'

'Jesus Christ, that's a bit steep! How about ten?'

'Fifteen and we've got a deal.' This time Caroline held her hand out, but I took it without any hesitation. I was enjoying the good life again.

*

Less than a week later the reason for Caroline's eagerness began to make itself apparent. I was just finishing Jocelyn Mowbray's weekly gyno check-up (she had been the first to enquire about the existence of this service – and the first to notice the stirrups). I was trying to ignore it, but the experience was clearly having a visible effect on her. Her breathing had quickened and her cheeks were flushed. When she bit her lip and her pelvis twitched noticeably I paused.

'I'm sorry Mrs Mowbray, am I causing you any discomfort?'

'No, no, doctor, please carry on!'

Quite thrown by this – I was locked into 'objective medical examination mode' – I hesitated further.

'Are you quite sure you wish me to continue?'

'Of course I am man, get on with it will you!' She demanded. She thrust herself against my probing fingers to make the order explicit.

It was a moment of choice, a professional fulcrum. If I acceded to her demands, who knew where this would lead, and how often? Unfortunately, my 'objective medical examination mode' was proving hard to maintain, thanks in no small part to the fact that Mrs Mowbray was a reasonably attractive forty-something who still clearly went to the gym. I instinctively fell back on the age-old failsafe of my profession.

'Are you aware that I make a modest charge for this sort of extra service?'

I felt her muscles tighten, she clearly liked this prostitution of my ethics.

'How much?'

'Well thirty pounds if this satisfies your requirements...'

'How much for a fuck?' she gasped.

'Would a hundred pounds be acceptable?'

'Get on with it!'

*

The deviousness of the female mind should never be under-estimated. An atheistic man of science I may be, but there's no denying that the parable of Adam and Eve in The Garden of Eden set the shape of things to come. In hindsight, it was no coincidence that Caroline chose to negotiate a cut of my takings a few days before my new business venture sky-rocketed!

Within twenty-four hours of my encounter with Jocelyn Mowbray, the extra consulting slots I had instructed Jill to announce were full and, more significantly enquiries, nay requests, for my 'extra services' were flooding in. Within a fortnight I had ordered Jill to turn away all new business for the time being and keep all current customers restricted to one visit per week. That didn't stop repeated attempts to obtain emergency appointments.

I rapidly began to appreciate where Caroline's original confidence in the project had stemmed from and furthermore the power of the female social network that spread throughout the coffee houses, tea rooms and ladies' gymnasia of Hampstead Heath. She had been running a comprehensive PR campaign behind my back. There was never any hope of my arrangement with Jocelyn Mowbray remaining a secret. In fact, I am now convinced Jocelyn was acting as a sort of sexual scouting party. More than once I found myself wondering if my ex-wife Elizabeth had availed herself of similar facilities on Wandsworth Common whilst I worked late at St George's.

I will not deny that this was all very flattering to my male ego. I made a point of offering all applicants a free initial 'consultation' to ensure I had the pick of the crop, and the crop was pleasingly varied. I made sure to include Ruth Benowitz, Sharleen Clarke and Nisha Kapoor amongst the Claremonts and Montagues.

At first I was sustained by the variety and novelty of the situation, but as the emphasis swung ever more from consultation to concupiscence, I began to find my work-load increasingly hard to sustain, my output was noticeably drying up. I convened another Saturday morning business meeting with Caroline, this time at Pizza Express on Heath Street which I had taken to frequenting to keep my carbs up. Caroline finished eating her Napoletana as I explained the problem. She sat back with her old air of medical detachment.

'Are you using Viagra?'

'Of course I'm using Viagra! I'm taking so much I rattle when I fuck!'

'Okay, okay, keep your voice down!' Caroline cast a nervous glance round at our fellow diners, then resumed.

'So what's the problem...isn't it working anymore?'

'The Viagra's working alright but it's the pain. There are serious soreness issues on top of the physical fatigue. I'm beginning to suffer from chronic back ache in the lower lumbar region.'

'I see,' she dabbed her lips with her napkin to hide a smirk and just about recaptured her consultative manner. 'Well, we don't want you running out of steam do we? Perhaps you need a little time off. Why don't you tell Jill to write to your clients telling them you are shutting down for a few days?'

'A few days? It'll take more than that for the blisters to heal and I reckon I ought to see an osteopath in case I've done something permanent to my back...'

'Oh don't be such a baby. I see as many clients as you and you don't hear me complaining...'

'Fine, well in case it passed you by at medical school, us men are physiologically different from you women. We can't keep it up forever and we aren't used to the pain of child-birth you seem so fond of enduring. I'm taking a week off and that's that!'

Caroline glared at me in silence for a moment before she broke the silence.

'Very well, if you need a break, go ahead and take one, so long as you continue to pay your rent.'

With that she threw her napkin on the table and made an abrupt exit.

*

I sat there taken aback and feeling more than a little hurt. Perhaps I was being a little melodramatic, but I felt I deserved a little more sympathy than that. I certainly did not take kindly to being treated like an employee begging for leave, let alone some sort of immigrant sex worker. We were meant to be business partners, even if the business was of a somewhat 'irregular' nature and perhaps not entirely above board in our dealings with the tax man. Come to that, it was hard to say quite how our 'business' would be viewed by arbiters of public decency such as the police. True we weren't hanging around street corners and there were no red lights in the windows, but whichever way you looked at it money was getting paid in return for sex and put like that, it all looked rather squalid.

Suddenly, I found myself questioning my current purpose in life. I had never had much interest in politics and philosophy. I was vaguely atheist and more concerned with making money than worrying about futile questions like 'Why are we here?' or 'Is there a God?'. I had seen very little evidence of a benign and loving God in hospitals around the world and what alleviation of human suffering I had seen seemed to be the product of science and the efforts of my fellow man.

Now, if I wasn't exactly experiencing a 'road to Damascus' episode, I was certainly beginning to feel like I was falling short of my true potential as a human being. I tried reassuring myself that my situation was only a stop-gap whilst I got my licence back and generally sorted myself out. I reminded myself that

I certainly hadn't started out with the intention of earning a living as a gigolo, indeed I had rather been naively duped into it, but none of that made me feel any the better about my current employment. It was time to get my act together and move on.

This was clearly not something I needed to rush into. Up to now I had been swept along by my burgeoning career as an unlicensed sex therapist, or whatever I had become. Now my thoughts returned to regaining my legitimacy in the real medical world and for this I needed to do some research. I finished the bottle of wine I had been sharing with Caroline, paid the bill and went outside to hail a cab, first stop Comet to buy myself a laptop.

4

I stared at the screen of my new state-of-the-art computer in something approaching disbelief. I was sitting in my bedroom working my way through the list of adjudications handed down by the GMC's Fitness to Practise panel over the last couple of years. Given some of the cases I had seen so far, I really couldn't foresee any problems getting my license back. What I had just read regarding a certain Dr Percival was a case in point:

4. On 30 October 2009, you held a consultation with Patient A, during which you:

a. required Patient A to undress,
Dismissed following successful Rule 17(2)(g) application on behalf of Dr Percival

b. carried out a physical examination of Patient A including:
i. groin area,
Dismissed following successful Rule 17(2)(g) application on behalf of Dr Percival
ii. buttocks,
Admitted and found proved
iii. thighs,
Admitted and found proved

c. failed to obtain Patient A's informed consent,

Dismissed following successful Rule 17(2)(g)
application on behalf of Dr Percival

d. did not ask Patient A whether she required a chaperone to
be present whilst the examination was taking place;
Admitted and found proved

5. During the examination outlined at paragraph 4 above
you touched the Patient A's labia majora;
Dismissed following successful Rule 17(2)(g)
application on behalf of Dr Percival

6. Following the examination outlined at paragraph 4
above, you smelt your fingers;
Dismissed following successful Rule 17(2)(g)
application on behalf of Dr Percival

7. Your actions in relation to paragraphs 5 and 6 above,
were sexually motivated;
Dismissed following successful Rule 17(2)(g)
application on behalf of Dr Percival

And that by reason of the matters set out above your fitness
to practise is impaired because of your misconduct.

That was the charge. I skipped on to the end, confident of the
good doctor's iniquity, only to discover that the panel had
upheld his innocence because they found the patient was lying
following a diagnosis she disagreed with! Come off it! Who

were they kidding? If ever I'd heard a case of my profession looking after its own, this had to be it! This was encouraging: surely, if he could get away with it, my misdemeanour which had no medical implications and had happened during a period of great mental and emotional strain, would be viewed as insignificant?

Before I moved on, I paused to consider what I had learned so far. I was struck by the careful choice of the things that Percival admitted to. While Percival was smelling his fingers I was smelling the presence of a crafty lawyer. I already knew to my cost how words could be selected, twisted and manipulated to paint a highly distorted picture of events far beyond the wildest imaginings of a simple surgeon. It was the machinations of my late wife's devious lawyer, to wit Amelia Harper, that had landed me in prison. Given that I was no longer best chums with my erstwhile lawyer, Roger 'two-faced' Caraway, I decided it was time to recruit a replacement. I fished out my wallet and emptied my assorted credit and business cards onto my bed. Buried amongst them was a membership card for the Medical Defence Union. It went against the grain, but I had to admit I needed help. I couldn't afford to cock things up this time.

*

'So Mr Stamford, am I right in thinking that you did not inform the GMC of your imprisonment?'

'I was not aware that I had to, besides I was in the grip of a mental breakdown. For the first six months in prison I hardly recognised my own name let alone where I was or why I was there.'

'Hmmn, yes I see. Can anyone testify to that?'

'I don't know. I don't suppose so. It was a prison not a hospital. I didn't cause trouble and I did what I was told so I was ignored.'

'Right, yes, unfortunate – most unfortunate.'

Mr Emrys Penrice-Pugh removed his gold-framed spectacles, fished out a silk handkerchief and began polishing them vigorously. After several moments, during which time he seemed to be becoming utterly absorbed in the task, I ventured to ask why. He looked up startled as if this analysis was self-explanatory or he'd forgotten that I might even expect one.

'Paragraph fifty-eight.' He nodded at the booklet entitled Good Medical Practice which he had given me on arrival. As I began leafing through the pages in search of his reference he re-donned his glasses, squeezed his eyes shut and began reciting:

'You must inform the GMC without delay if, anywhere in the world, you have accepted a caution, been charged with or found guilty of a criminal offence, or if another professional body has made a finding against your registration as a result of fitness to practise procedures.'

There was nothing wrong with his memory even if his nervous system could do with some attention. He was small, twitchy and Welsh, like a Valley's teacher in an expensive suit; the sort who spoke the lingo and dressed as a druid at weekends. Still he had a good memory.

'Surely, they can't hold that against me?'

He opened his eyes to fix me with a surprisingly emphatic stare.

'I'm afraid they can, Mr Stamford. I'm afraid they can!' He

snatched up his handkerchief, whipped off his glasses and began polishing again. However, this time he spoke as he worked. 'Not that you should allow yourself to become disheartened, Mr Stamford. Should they choose to be obstructive, we can always lodge an appeal. There you have it Mr Stamford, we can always appeal the buggers!'

'And you think that would be successful?'

'Perhaps, they love an appeal at the GMC. An appeal keeps their wheels turning you see.'

'And that will get my license back?'

'I can't say. The purpose of the appeal will be to persuade them to overlook your failure to notify. As to whether they will then see fit to lift your suspension, that will depend how they view your case in the light of Paragraph fifty-seven.'

Jesus wept! We were going through the paragraphs backwards!

'And what does it say in Paragraph fifty-seven?' I didn't bother leafing through Good Medical Practice. He re-donned his glasses and shut his eyes again in order to recite:

'You must make sure that your conduct at all times justifies your patients' trust in you and the public's trust in the profession.'

'Well I don't see how my offence could possibly have any bearing on that...'

Penrice-Pugh raised his hand dramatically, and quite strikingly given his diminutive stature.

'Probity, Mr Stamford! The issue here is probity. You see the average citizen has little or no grasp of the finer workings of medicine and, as a result, will overlook or simply fail to grasp many cases of incompetence or even neglect. Probity, or lack of it, on the other hand, stands out like a sore thumb. Dishonesty is something anyone can understand and therefore stands to bring the profession into much greater disrepute. In a word, the GMC view it very unfavourably.'

'Oh, I see.' This was not what I wanted to hear at all. 'So assuming they are persuaded to overlook my failure to notify them, what happens then?'

'I'm assuming you would wish to resume your career at the earliest opportunity?'

'Obviously.'

'Well then we will have to hope they do not invoke the five year rule.'

'What's the five year rule?'

Penrice-Pugh tossed his much abused glasses on the desk, apparently impatient at my ignorance, then sat back and joined his fingertips as he selected a point on the ceiling to lecture.

'The five year rule describes the period of time a disbarred doctor must wait before he or she is permitted to apply for the reinstatement of his or her licence to practice.'

For a moment the room seemed to sway around in a sickening reminder of the unhinged, disorientated sensation I had experienced during my breakdown. I gripped the arms of my chair trying to steady myself.

'Would you like a glass of water Mr Stamford?' Even Penrice-Pugh had registered that his words were having an unexpected impact and switched from his point on the ceiling.

'No, I'm alright, thank you.' This was not at all true, but I needed space to gather my wits. 'So you're saying I've got to wait five years to get my licence back?' I gasped.

Penrice-Pugh nodded.

'Very possibly Mr Stamford. It all depends on whether the tribunal decides to view their earlier decision as a suspension or a disbarment. If it is the former then we may apply for your case to be reviewed, but, if it is the latter then the five year rule will undoubtedly be enforced.'

This was dreadful. I was already dissatisfied with my current mode of employment. The thought of another five years was more than I could bear! A vision of myself being pursued, naked and exhausted, around Hampstead Heath by a bunch of ravening harpies flashed into my mind and sent it reeling in horror. I couldn't survive another five years, I was already worn out!

*

'That'll be twelve pounds sixty please guv.'

'Keep the change.' I gave the man thirteen quid in the hope that the amount would bring him bad luck. The bastard hadn't shut up about the state of the economy since I got in his cab on Chancery Lane. I got out and shut the door more firmly than usual as I stalked off up the drive to the house.

I had left Penrice-Pugh, or Pompous Penrice as I'd mentally rechristened him, on the understanding that I would contact the GMC to establish my current status before instructing him further and that I would not be expecting a bill for this preliminary consultation. I had recovered from my initial shock at the delay I was facing and assured him that I would contact him if I needed his services with regard to an appeal and then left. I was in no mood for further lecturing.

I was striding through reception on my way upstairs to my room when Jill Pellow called me back.

'Oh, Mr Stamford!'

I turned and retraced my steps. Forty-something, immaculately turned out, Jill was certainly worth turning back for, though I was always careful to keep things on a strictly professional footing.

'Yes Jill, how can I help you?'

'A man called for you, Mr Stamford.'

'Oh really, did he leave a name?'

'Yes,' she glanced at her computer monitor, 'he said his name was Detective Sergeant Newcombe.'

'Newcombe? I see. Well, thank you, Jill.'

Newcombe? Newcombe! What the fucking hell did he want? I felt a desperate need to steady myself on something as I fought to remain casual.

She continued: 'He said he just wanted a chat. He left a business card for you to contact him.' She held it out for me to take it. I forced myself to turn back, fighting to keep my composure.

'Right, thanks Jill.' I accepted it and turned away quickly, wondering what on earth she was making of my expression. I headed for the stairs as fast as dignity would allow.

*

I sat on the edge of my bed staring blankly at the card, Penrice-Pugh and the GMC completely forgotten. This was bad news, possibly on an epic scale. I knew who Detective Sergeant Newcombe was alright, it was what he wanted that was filling me with dread.

Newcombe and his side-kick Shipley were the police officers who had arrested me for fraud having been tipped off by Cruella who, in turn, had been tipped off by my daughter Annette as revenge for my treatment of her mother Liz. I believe the popular sociologists' term for our kind of family is "dysfunctional". Anyway, the pair of them had been called in to investigate my allegations of malpractice against my wife's lover and had somehow turned their investigative gaze onto me instead. Now, it would appear, they, or at least Newcombe, were back on my trail again!

I searched my mind for a simple explanation without success. To the best of my knowledge Detective Sergeants were not in the habit of making social calls on their former "customers". I was hardly au fait with latest police practice but, according to the occasional police drama I had seen on TV, which, apart from my arrest for drunk-driving and subsequent arrest for fraud, was the only contact outside of work that I had ever had with the police. They were concerned with capturing criminals, not rehabilitating them. No doubt they kept tabs on those they had reason to believe might reoffend, but I couldn't see myself falling into that category. No, whatever Newcombe wanted, he hadn't popped round on the off-chance I would put the kettle on.

Furthermore, they must have been at some pains to track me down. On my release from prison I had been asked for a forwarding address, but avoided giving one by explaining that I would be staying in a hotel, as yet unchosen, until I sorted out my financial affairs. This was true and motivated by nothing more than an overwhelming desire to put the whole experience behind me. Since then, I had kept records of my "business activities", or at least those I felt would be suitable for declaration to the tax man, but still had some months to go before I needed to hire an accountant and become formally self-employed. To the best of my knowledge nobody from my past knew where I was or what I was doing and yet they had still traced me.

No doubt they had sophisticated methods, and come to think about it, there was an operational bank account in my name, so I was hardly under cover. But why had they bothered?

Perhaps it was something stupid like I had left some property in the police station they took me to at the time of my arrest. I was far too out of it at the time to have noticed. But then they would hardly send senior officers on an errand like that! No, this was something pretty serious and the recognition of that made me cringe. There was only one thing that I could think of that was worth sending Detective Sergeant Newcombe in pursuit of me for and that was the one thing I had been shutting out of my mind for over a year now; the possibility that I had murdered my wife and my one time best friend, and then bitter enemy, Hamish Carmichael.

I sat on the bed with my head in my hands and tried to force my memory to penetrate the blur that surrounded that final farewell to my Aston, but still the haze of confusion refused to clear. In fact, as always, I felt the old waves of anxiety immediately start to gather and tug at my grip on reality. This was no good. I tried to brace myself by reminding myself that even if I had cut the brake pipe, the bastards had deserved it. If Carmichael had succeeded in running me off the road at Knockhill race track he could very easily have killed me and his late night assault on me, in my own house, could very easily have left me dead on the floor of my den! Furthermore they had sexually betrayed me, fleeced me of most of my money and left me to rot in prison!

No! No! Forget that! That was going to get me nowhere. Going back over all of that for the umpteenth time was pointless. I needed to focus on the here and now, assess the current situation and act. Okay, so Newcombe was looking for me again and I didn't know why. True, I had reason to suspect the worst, but then isn't it human nature to do that, particularly when there is a guilty conscience involved? The truth was I didn't know what he wanted.

I picked up his card and stared at it again. What should I do: up sticks and head for the hills? It seemed pointless. He'd found me once with no apparent effort, so he'd find me again. More importantly I couldn't picture life as a fugitive. I wanted my life as a respected, successful surgeon back, not a life spent skulking in the shadows or on the run. I could still afford a decent lawyer even with the pittance that thieving bastard Roger had coughed up. If this turned out to be a murder charge, this time I would fight it on the grounds of diminished responsibility. Given my past character I might even get off! Whatever, I had survived prison once, I'd survive it again. I fished out my mobile and dialled the number on the card.

*

We met in a pub down in the town near the Royal Free. I don't recall the name or the décor, just the sickening tension that knotted my stomach. Newcombe was still the burly, ponderous Mr 'Plain Clothes Plod' I remembered, but he bought me a pint which, in my desperation, I prayed was a good sign. We settled down in a fairly secluded corner and, to my relief, he dispensed with niceties and got to the point.

'I'm sure you are wondering quite why I have requested this meeting Dr Stamford, so I won't beat about the bush.' He picked up his pint and took a leisurely pull. I was so keen to hear his explanation that I did not bother to correct his misuse of the title 'Doctor'.

'Yes, please, get on with if you don't mind.'

He placed his glass very deliberately down on a beer mat then raised his gaze to my face. My last remark had sounded jittery to me so God knows how I was coming across to him! His next remark made it clear.

'If you don't mind my saying so Dr Stamford, you seem a little tense for someone who has done his time and squared his debt to society...'

'Do I indeed? Well perhaps I do not feel very comfortable being pursued by someone who, as far as I am concerned, has no further reason to intrude on my time.'

Newcombe raised his eyes non-committally as he took another pull of his pint. He lowered it and wiped away a drop of foam with the back of his hand.

'Hmmn, I imagine in your circumstances I would feel much

the same, particularly now the boffins have had a chance to look again at the remains of your Aston.'

'What do you mean?'

'Well, the more I looked into the circumstances surrounding your relations with your wife in the period leading up to her most unfortunate demise, the more I found myself wondering if it was purely coincidence that she should die in a car that she had rather deceitfully obtained from you. True you were in prison at the time of the automotive mishap that brought about her unfortunate end, but it struck me that you are a clever man and murder does not necessarily require the perpetrator's presence at the scene of the crime. Indeed, prison would have been a perfect alibi. This thought niggled at me to such an extent that, to be perfectly honest, I reopened the case on an unofficial basis. Call me obsessive, but, well I'm sure you've been there yourself with a diagnosis that was eluding you. Anyway what the boffins found when they took a closer look at the Aston's brake pipes makes most interesting reading...'

'What are you saying?' I knew perfectly well what he was saying. The elusive memories that my breakdown had kept hidden from me were flooding back: the cathedral gloom of the workshop, the filtered light, the wheel arch, the mini hacksaw. My body felt icy as if my blood had, quite literally, run cold. My breath felt so constricted I could hardly speak. I fought back a sudden urge to make a dash for the door.

But then why was he talking to me in a pub on Hampstead High Street instead of in an interview room in Hampstead police station? I told myself to get a grip. Perhaps he hadn't got solid evidence. Perhaps he wanted to trip me up or scare something out of me, but then wouldn't that be best achieved in said police station? This didn't add up. I fought to stay calm and stared him back in the eye. He held my gaze for ages with an expression that suggested infinite patience, but I knew I was now standing in a minefield and I wasn't going to budge first. Suddenly he brightened and spoke as if everything that had just passed was utterly inconsequential.

'Anyway, you'll be relieved to know that, for the time being, I've been instructed by my superiors to let the matter drop, or perhaps it would be more accurate to say, put it on ice.'

'What do you mean?'

'Well, it's one thing for the boffins to establish that those pipes were sawn through, but it's quite another thing to establish that you were the perpetrator, although we can put together a solid case for opportunity and motive. The problem is that my superiors, and the organisation I have recently been seconded to, have other bigger fish to fry and it seems you might be uniquely well placed to help us heat up the deep fat fryer.'

He smirked at what he clearly imagined was a clever play on words. I couldn't imagine for the life of me what my circumlocutory host was leading up to but, if I wasn't mistaken, he seemed to be hinting at some sort of deal. That, or he was trying to trick me into a confession: by showing interest in a deal was I admitting that I needed one? Caution, Anthony, caution!

'I don't know what on Earth you are talking about.'

He continued as if I hadn't spoken.

'I believe that while you were incarcerated you made the

acquaintance of one Peter Chisholm?'

'I may have done. I believe I remember meeting someone of that name...'

'And you engaged during meal breaks in conversations about his past history?'

'How do you know?'

'Because all your conversations were recorded using directional digital audio equipment...'

'Are you saying you were spying on me?'

'In a manner of speaking, but it would be more accurate to say we were spying on him.'

'Why?'

'Because all those wild yarns he told you about mercenaries and gun running are true. The only areas in which he was economical with the truth concerned his criminal involvement with them. Furthermore, now he's back at liberty, we have reason to believe that the temptation to return to his old ways is likely to prove too much for him, despite the Mr Nice Guy image he is currently at pains to foster.'

I stared at him for a moment in disbelief. Peter? The Peter Chisholm I had met in Standford? The Peter Chisholm who had done more than anyone including the astronomically expensive Professor Tanquist to rescue me from my breakdown? Was he asking me to believe that this man was really some sort of heavy-weight master criminal? Never! A bit of a bullshitter maybe, a right Walter Mitty come to that, but not a down-and-out crook! My scepticism must have shown in my face.

'Hard to believe, eh?' he continued, 'but you've got to remember you only met him in a prison canteen dressed in prison clothing. He looks very different sitting behind his antique desk in his swanky offices in Geneva wearing an Armani suit and a silk shirt.'

He paused to let this sink in. What if it were true? It was only my assumption that no-one could have got up to the sort of adventures that Peter had described to me, but then, as a surgeon at St Georges Hospital, Tooting, I had to admit that I had led a somewhat sheltered life compared to some people. Even Hollywood's wildest imaginings had to have started out with some basis in fact, and someone had to have taken part in those dramatic war scenes I had watched over the years on the News. Still, what had this to do with me? Peter had been released some time before me and I had no plans to renew our acquaintance. That was until now. Now, I had the sickening feeling all that was about to change. I braced myself.

'Okay, what's all this leading up to?'

Newcombe renewed that stare, which I must confess had taken on an almost hypnotic quality. Finally he spoke:

'At your final meeting before his release I believe he gave you a card?'

I nodded, there was clearly no use in denying it.

'I believe he also suggested that you might care to drop in on him should you ever find yourself in his part of the world?'

I nodded again.

'Well we would like you to do just that.'

'Who's 'we'?'

The people I am seconded to. I cannot say more than that. Let's just say people who wish to see Chisholm serve a sentence which reflects his real crimes, not just a few months for a tax evasion technicality and, more importantly, people who wish to see him behind bars where he can't cost anymore innocent lives.'

'And how do you imagine I can achieve that?'

'That will become apparent at your briefing should you agree to go ahead.'

'And if I don't?'

'Well then there's always the matter of that investigation sitting on ice.'

'Are you trying to blackmail me?' I demanded.

'He held my toughest stare calmly.'

'I hardly think 'trying' is an appropriate word under the circumstances,' he replied.

*

I sat on the edge of my bed with my head in my hands. What the fuck was I going to do? I was a surgeon, not some sort of secret agent for God's sake! Worse still I was being asked to stitch up the only man who had shown me any kindness in years. Newcombe had rather smugly suggested that we meet in the same pub at noon the following day for my answer. I needed time and I clearly didn't have much of it. So what were my alternatives? It was still only a few months since I had emerged from prison and I had no intention of going back if I could possibly avoid it; particularly given that this time it could be for an awful lot more than nine months.

Suddenly the television sparked into life. I had turned it on when I got home and left it to wait for the World News to come on line at seven o'clock. With no preamble Zeinab Badawi launched into the latest news from the political crisis in Syria:

'Good evening, the situation in Syria has taken a dramatic turn for the worse as the UN General Assembly passes a resolution demanding the resignation of President Assad and there are reports of further high-level resignations from his government. US President Obama indicates that Syrian use of chemical weapons could trigger US military intervention...'

Apparently, things were really hotting-up with rioting in the major cities and refugees flooding over the borders into neighbouring countries like Turkey and Lebanon.

They cut from the studio to Jeremy Bowen in a flak jacket standing next to a Red Cross tent with gun fire booming in the background and artillery flashes lighting up the night sky. Behind him a column of desperate looking people shuffled through a makeshift checkpoint. He explained, in that half-shout war reporters use on such occasions, that the refugee problem was reaching crisis proportions in neighbouring countries with shortages of food, medical supplies and trained doctors and nurses.

We then cut to a female representative from Medécins Sans Frontières who said much the same from a studio in Beirut, though in a much sexier voice. Finally we turned to a politician in Badawi's studio who told her that, while there were real concerns in Westminster that the situation could develop into revolution, there were no immediate plans for Western intervention and it was hoped that a peaceful settlement could still be reached. When pressed about reports coming out of the country regarding attacks on civilians by government forces he explained smoothly that it was hard to be clear at present how true these claims were, given the current chaos and the propaganda battle raging between the various political factions.

I hit the mute button and sat staring unseeingly at the screen. I had just heard something that seemed to be a possible answer to my problems. It was so unexpected that I needed a moment to make sure I wasn't hearing things; then another moment to convince myself that it wasn't an utterly preposterous idea seized upon by my fevered and desperate imagination. I sat and let it take form.

I had just been told in no uncertain terms that there was a place in the world that was crying out for doctors. I was a doctor and yet, for various bizarre and extremely unjust reasons, no-one in my vicinity wanted me. In fact the only people who wanted to employ my services were people whom I viewed with considerable distrust, animosity even and they wanted me to do something I had absolutely no desire to get involved in. All I wanted to do was roll my sleeves up and get back to pursuing my profession.

Well here was my chance and better still, from a practical point of view, it was taking place in a part of the world that had to fall well outside the remit of Newcombe and his mysterious chums. Even if they found me there, it was doubtful if they could, or would even be bothered to extradite me. Whatever their current plans for Peter, things move on and, by the time they had got their hands on me, I would probably be surplus to requirements anyway.

The more I thought about it, the more it appealed. No

more sore John Thomas and a bit of rewarding hard graft in a sunny climate. By the time I returned I would be free to re-apply for my License to Practice and, if Newcombe still wanted a piece of me, I would scream and shout 'blackmail!' No doubt the idea contained a thousand snags, but given my current circumstances I would simply have to deal with them later.

Okay, so what was I to do? The first thing that struck me was that the man was expecting my answer in approximately sixteen hours time so I needed to get a move on!

I stood up and looked around my room for a bag to pack, then realised that that was not a particularly good idea. I needed to leave without it looking like I had fled or that I wasn't coming back. That ruled out climbing out of the window and shinning down a drain pipe. It also ruled out walking past Jill carrying a case or even an overnight bag. I needed to leave no clues as to where I had gone or for how long.

So that was it. I was just going to drop everything I had built up since leaving prison and yet again, start afresh? I shrugged mentally. I didn't have much choice, and perhaps it wasn't such a bad thing. Only hours earlier I had been listening to Penrice-Pugh throwing the dampeners on my future prospects simply because I was dissatisfied with my current lifestyle. Perhaps this was the catalyst I needed to really set about changing things.

I reached over and pulled open the drawer of my bedside cabinet. Inside lay my passport, driving licence and old GMC registration card alongside the two thousand pounds contingency fund I had taken to keeping since my release from prison. If I had learned one thing from the past two years it was to never to believe that you've got life taped.

5

I lowered my copy of the Times and casually peered around me for anyone who might give me cause for concern. Unsurprisingly, no-one new had added themselves to the assortment of passengers on the upper deck of the Dover–Calais ferry which was now helping me put some distance between myself and the long arm of the British Law. In fact, several passengers were beginning to round up bags and kids as the ship prepared to enter the embrace of Calais harbour. The only creature evincing any interest in me was a haughty Gallic seagull who had perched on the nearby railing, clearly in the hope of being offered some titbit, but too proud to ask. I stood up, shouldered my overnight bag and began making my way down to the lower decks to join the other steerage passengers.

My departure from London had been straightforward enough. I had called a cab on my mobile and watched from my bedroom window until I saw him pull up outside, then hurried downstairs pausing only for a quick word with Jill:

'Oh, Jill my dear, if that gentleman who called round earlier comes back, could you just say you haven't seen me since this morning?'

She looked as if she was about to ask why, then decided against it. Wise woman, ignorance is bliss. Trusting her to tell a fib on my behalf was something of a gamble, but then I calculated that she knew very well what was going on as regards Caroline and my business activities and therefore needed our discretion nearly as much as we needed hers. I was also gambling that he hadn't staked the place out.

'Certainly Mr Stamford, are we expecting you back today?'

'I'm not quite sure yet. I'm expecting a call from some friends in Manchester. I might be popping up there for the last few days of my holidays if they can get time off; if so, I'll see you when I get back.' I had no intention of going anywhere near Manchester, but a red-herring could do no harm just in case Newcombe returned and Jill was persuaded to change her mind.

I told the cabbie to take me down to Hampstead High Street and at the last minute jumped out at the underground leaving him clutching a very generous twenty pounds rather than wait for the change. I bought a ticket to Tottenham Court Road where I emerged in order to buy myself a change of clothes, an overnight bag and pair of weak, over-the-counter reading glasses. That was as far as I was prepared to go without risking a possible accusation of disguising myself. I changed in a pub toilet and caught the tube back to Euston. I strolled through to St Pancras and took the train to Dover. Just over two hours later I embarked on the ferry.

As I trudged off the gangplank onto Calais's terra firma, feeling more like a refugee than a tourist, I consoled myself with the thought that I had bought myself time without, so far, doing anything which would confer fugitive status on me. Perhaps my chosen route was a little more circuitous than simply taking a plane or jumping on Eurostar, but I could always argue that I disliked flying and loved boats. I headed for the station and bought a ticket to the capital.

*

My flight from Blighty had been rather too precipitous to dignify with words like 'escape'. I had no idea what, if anything, I was escaping from, or where this trip to Paris was intended to lead on to. I had simply been responding to my sense that I needed to buy time. Nevertheless, a notion had begun to nag at me on the ferry and, when I threw open the curtains of my room at the Hotel Central and gazed out at the sunlit Rue Champollion the following morning, I discovered that it had begun to crystallise and take real shape overnight. I threw on my new blazer, slacks, open necked white shirt and sandals, then decided to skip the hotel breakfast and headed downstairs to find a St Germain pavement café.

I swallowed the last of my croissant and apricot preserve and knocked back the rest of my coffee then pulled out my phone and called up Google. I found the address I was looking for and switched to Google Maps. Despite Haussmann's triumph of orderly street planning, Paris's elegant boulevards swam before my eyes as I tried to focus on my route and shut out the enormity of what I was contemplating. Finally, I paid the bill leaving a generous pourboire to avoid being pursued down the street by a stroppy garcon, then set out on my chosen route.

By the time I reached the Bastille my feet were definitely beginning to drag and it wasn't thanks to the distance I had covered. Did I really want to do this? Did I have any idea what I was letting myself in for? This was the sort of thing I might have volunteered for in my twenties or thirties if I hadn't been so busy skiing and sailing, or studying, qualifying and earning a living to feed my family and maintain my lifestyle. I must be fucking mad!

Then another voice started muttering about where that had all got me and the good a complete change in direction would do me. I needed a new start and a chance to really shake off my recent past; not just Standford Prison, but the rather sordid lifestyle I had found myself drawn into in my attempts to rehabilitate myself. That wasn't me! How on Earth had I allowed myself to be drawn into the life of some sort of high-class male whore? A wave of self-disgust drove me forward and an even more persuasive voice added that, right now, the new start I had in mind could also put some useful miles between myself and the persistent Detective-Sergeant Newcombe, or whatever his real occupation now amounted to. Even as this internal debate continued to rage, my legs carried me inexorably round the corner of Boulevard Beaumarchais and down to Rue Saint-Sabin.

I don't know what I had been expecting, but it definitely was not this! I found myself confronted by a concrete monstrosity with odd round windows in an otherwise completely nondescript Parisian street. Perhaps I was expecting something grander, more commanding and international in style. Then again, I was looking for something different and perhaps this odd building symbolised it! With no further hesitation I threw back my shoulders and marched through the front doors of Médecins Sans Frontières, Paris.

*

Quite why I ever imagined I could simply turn up in the reception of a large international organisation and expect to be offered a job, voluntary or not, is now a matter of some puzzlement to me. Nevertheless that is precisely what I did and, unsurprisingly, I got stopped in my tracks. I was not turned away so much as wrapped up in the bureaucratic tape that working for any large organisation involves. This was the last thing I needed.

It all started simply enough with a somewhat indifferent enquiry from the rather stunning young girl with the nose piercing behind the desk:

'Puis-je vous aider, monsieur?'

At least I had prepared for the language barrier.

'Ah, oui mam'selle, je suis un docteur et je veux travailler pour Médecins Sans Frontières, s'il vous plait.'

I congratulated myself privately on my recall of my 'O' level French. Unfortunately, my French had rusted considerably since my last stay in Paris and that was pretty much all I did recall.

'D'accord, monsieur vous avez besoin de compléter cette questionnaire.'

What did she say? That was altogether too quick. The snooty little cow clearly had no intention of cutting this particular 'Anglais' any slack! I was trying to remember the French word for 'slowly' when she handed me an official-looking form. Yes, of course, there was bound to be some paperwork. I hadn't thought of that and, more importantly, I hadn't stopped to consider that it would be written in French. I retreated to a seat to study it.

A few minutes later I returned to the desk. I had spent as much time couching my next request as I had trying to translate the form.

'Excusez-moi, mam'selle. Est-ce qu'il y à quelque personne qui peut m'aider?'

'Pouquoi?' The Parisian contempt for foreigners was annoying, despite the gorgeous green eyes that conveyed it.

'Parce que je ne comprends pas!' I snapped, waving the document to indicate that it was more than simply life in general that was baffling me.

She took a moment to suggest with a sly glance that I really ought to calm down and get a grip and, while I was at it, think about taking the time to master a respectable grasp of her language before turning up in her reception and expecting her to help me with it. Having conveyed all this she muttered:

'Un moment,' then clicked a switch on her keyboard and rattled something swift and incomprehensible into her headset. She then nodded me back to my seat and sat back to inspect her fingernails. A minute later a young man entered the room and approached me.

'Good morning Monsieur...?'

'Stamford, Tony Stamford...'

'Ah very good, would you please come with me Monsieur Stamford?' He relieved me of my form and led me back the way he had come.

'Your young lady in reception is very beautiful...' I ventured as we headed down a corridor, assuming a good looking girl would be the ideal ice-breaker with any Frenchman. He nodded.

'Sure Céline is very beautiful, but she is très fière... she is very, er, proud. Many strange people come to our door and Céline is good at keeping them to a distance.'

He said this with an innocent smile, but I could not help

wondering if I was considered to be one of the strange people. Before I could attempt any more small talk, he stopped at a door, opened it and popped his head round the corner. Satisfied the room was empty he beckoned me in. It was clearly some sort of interview room, designed with utility rather than comfort in mind. He gestured me to a straight-backed chair in front of the solitary desk, then walked round and sat down behind it. He arranged my application neatly on the desk and laid a pen on top of it. On closer inspection I would have put him in his early thirties, maybe twenty years my junior, but he assumed the role of interviewer effortlessly.

'Now Monsieur Stamford, my name is Jean-Luc Garon and I am an administrator with MSF. I understand you would like to volunteer to work with us?'

I nodded.

'Ok, perhaps you would like to tell me what kind of doctor you are?'

'Of course; I am a general surgeon, specialising in proctology.'

'I see, and you are English?'

'Yes.' I made an effort to conceal my impatience with this self-evident question.

'Then perhaps you would explain to me why you do not make your application in our office in London where there is no language problem?'

Shit! He'd gone straight to the hardest thing to explain away. I could hardly say that I might just possibly be on the run from the British Police, though I wasn't quite sure. He was staring at me politely, but expectantly and there was no hint of a smile now.

'Well, to be honest, this was a bit of a spur of the moment

decision. You see I've just split up with my wife and I just feel like a really clean break after all the stress and acrimony of the divorce...'

I knew this sounded weak, but it was the best I had been able to come up with during my walk over there.

'I thought a trip to Paris would do me good, but I've come to realise that I need something more fulfilling, more challenging, to give me back a sense of purpose in life.' That sounded better to me, but apparently not to Monsieur Garon.

'I see, but do you not think it would be easier to do this in your own country? After all, the application process here is not so simple. It can take maybe a month. Do you plan to stay in Paris that long?'

'If needs be. England holds nothing but bad memories for me at the moment.'

'Monsieur Stamford, this is MSF, not the French Foreign Legion. We are seeking people who are motivated by the wish to help others not themselves.'

This rebuke was delivered evenly, as if inviting a response, so I pressed on sensing that I had slipped past the immediate danger.

'Of course, I didn't mean it to sound like that. What I am trying to say is that I have come to realise that I need more than just a holiday. I need a real challenge, something I can get my teeth into. Something that will make me really appreciate how insignificant my own problems really are. What better way of doing that than to use my skills to help people who are really suffering?'

'I see. Can I take it you have visited our website and made a study of the conditions we expect our people to work under?'

'Yes.' I lied. I couldn't afford to lose momentum now.

'And you are aware that you may be working in conditions of great pressure?'

'Of course, I've dealt with my fair share of knifings, shootings and car crashes...' Even as I said this I could hear how glib it sounded. Monsieur Garon clearly agreed with me.

'I am sure you have Mr Stamford, but have you dealt with them in a makeshift surgery in a jungle, or a war-zone where there is every possibility that you may be the next victim? Have you dealt with them after days with no sleep and little food? We take great pains to protect our staff, but they work in places where such perils are constant...'

'Yes, yes, I realise that. I am not stupid and I have observed the kind of environments you work in on the news over many years. To be honest, I have never worked in a war zone, but I have been in perilous situations in my sailing and mountaineering days. At the end of the day, my skill as a surgeon comes from within, not from the environment in which I employ it. If I lack the sort of experience you are talking about, then everyone has to start somewhere and I'm asking you to give me that chance.'

I must have said something right in all of that because suddenly he was regarding me with a much more thoughtful expression. He sat back and played absently with the pen. Quite unexpectedly he appeared to make a decision.

'Very well, Mr Stamford, perhaps there is a way for us to usefully employ your skills. There is someone who it would be necessary for you to meet before such a thing could become possible. Perhaps you would not mind returning here tomorrow? I will text you with the exact time of an appointment if it can be arranged.'

*

I shoved aside the plate of empty mussel shells and continued mopping up the juice left in the bowl with crusty slices of baguette. I was considerably hungrier than I had realised and picked up the menu to study the rather delicious choice of crêpes on offer.

I had left the interview with Monsieur Garon with my stomach churning. It had all turned out to be a lot more stressful than I had anticipated. The language barrier aside, I had simply failed to appreciate how much of my recent life I wanted to hide and, I suppose, the fact that offering my services for free did not provide immunity from scrutiny. It had taken an effort to hide my displeasure at being called back the following day; whether my guilt was imaginary or not, I could almost feel Detective-Sergeant Newcombe breathing down my neck.

Now, a good meal and a couple of Ricards later I was feeling somewhat more fortified and less pissed off. What did I expect? My recent past really was nothing to boast about, regardless of whom I chose to blame for it. Furthermore, I had done nothing but act on impulse over the last twenty-four hours so, all things considered, I had coped quite well. In fact, come to think of it, they could have shown me the door but somehow I had wangled myself a second interview. I wondered who that would turn out to be with, but concluded that there was no way of finding out and resigned myself to waiting for the next day. That set me thinking about what else I could do to improve my chances in the meantime.

I ordered a chocolate crêpe to sustain my improving mood and Googled the MSF website on my phone. In retrospect, something I should have done before I walked through their doors. As I sipped my Ricard I applied myself to really understanding what they were looking for.

They certainly made no bones about the risks and discomforts involved in working for them, but then you would expect them to discourage fools and dilettantes. I asked myself with unexpected honesty quite why I felt that I did not fit such a description. I was quite surprised at my own answer: true I needed to buy time whilst I ascertained Newcombe's intentions but, more than that, I really did need a clean break and a real purpose in life. Even before Elizabeth decided to take a lover and rob me blind, I was in a rut. Sure I was living the life of a wealthy, successful surgeon with a pretty good social life, in fact a lifestyle many would have given their right arms for, but I had begun to feel that I had run out of things to aspire to. I guess that's why I had fallen under Ham's spell so easily. There was something dangerous, even feral, about the man that had attracted me like a moth to a candle. Sure I was furious when I discovered he was screwing my wife, but deep down I guess I wasn't that surprised. This realisation made me pause before I resumed my self-analysis. I thought on.

Okay, so my motives in joining MSF weren't purely altruistic, but then I suspected nor were those of the majority of MSF applicants. Did it matter if you were looking for thrills in foreign lands, or suffering from some Mother Theresa complex, provided you could cut the mustard and handle the pressure? What was true was that I had always excelled at my profession and could save a lot of lives while I sorted myself out and got through this mid-life crisis, if that's what my current desire for change amounted to.

I returned to the immediate future. What could I do to improve my chances of recruitment in less than a day? The one thing that stood out was my lack of French. They even stated on their website that speaking the lingo was a distinct advantage, though not an absolute prerequisite. Were they just being politically correct? My crêpe arrived so I savoured it as I wrestled with this potential discouragement. True, there was no nationality more snobbish than the French when it came to their precious language, but surely they couldn't turn away someone with my qualifications? Particularly given that a field surgeon's vocabulary didn't need to contain much beyond a handful of basic technical terms like 'scalpel', 'cut' and 'suture'. Probably not, but there was no harm in doing everything I could to make the right impression. Could I enrol on some sort of rapid learning course in the time remaining? Again, probably not, but then would that really be where I would want to go to improve my smattering of French with a bit of medical terminology? Definitely not, so I picked up my phone and went back into Google.

6

I waited for the surgeon to discard the ligature scissors in the instrument tray before I lowered my mask and spoke sharply above the strains of Mozart's Don Giovanni which were thankfully fairly sotto at that moment.

'Vous essayez de suturer une plais, non reprise une chaussette!' I remarked.

This roughly translates as 'You are trying to stitch a wound not mend a sock!' a rebuke my good friend Gaston Racicot had once suffered at the hands of a tutor during his student days and confessed to me during a drunken evening at the Folies Bergère. He looked up as if I had fired a gun, and then yanked down his mask as a wide grin of recognition spread across his broad features.

'Antoine, Antoine Stomfor!' he roared – he pronounced my surname 'à la française' and always called me Antoine as part of his mission to turn me into 'un vrai Français'. He deserted his patient and strode round the operating table to where I had been hiding behind the anaesthetists, seizing me in a bear-hug and planting a couple of smackers on each of my cheeks. It had not been difficult to beat hospital security with a lordly air, a wave of my GMC membership letter and a surprisingly good memory of the layout of the place. It wasn't hard to find some kit in the scrubs room. I endured Gaston's Gallic embrace with my usual British reserve which only provoked him to hug me all the more. Finally, he released me to arm's length in order to inspect me like a mother inspects a wayward son.

'Antoine, my good fellow, what are you doing here?' he demanded.

'Just checking to see if your surgery's improved,' I replied airily. I was dressed in the scrubs and mask that I had purloined from the changing suite of an operating theatre in the Pitié-Salpêtrière Hospital, one of Paris' leading teaching hospitals where Gaston and I had first met some fifteen years earlier. At the time I was presenting a paper on possible links between colonic and ovarian cancer which Gaston and his gyno team had expressed an interest in. That first encounter led to a week-long introduction to the pleasures of Parisian nightlife.

'How dare you, you insolent English dog!' he roared. 'I expect you will be saying you wish me to take you out on the town and buy you a meal to demonstrate my hospitality also?'

'Well, now you mention it, something like that had crossed my mind...'

'Okay, well you will have to wait until I have finished here. Go to the café in the basement I will join you in an hour.

*

'So, Antoine, tell me what is the real purpose that brings you to Paris?'

'Like I told you Gaston, I'm trying to improve my French.'

'Yes, but why? What do you need of our beautiful language at this time in your life?'

We were in a trendy place called Le coq Rico and communication was difficult since we were expected to share our table with a rather drunken birthday party. The place specialised in chicken dishes and obviously thought it should give its customers a taste of the food's previous lifestyle by cramming us into a noisy room the size of a chicken coop. Gaston had explained that he hoped the intimacy would help get me immersed in the language, which might have worked if I could hear myself think. Right now we were trying to communicate in the lacuna left by our two companion nurses who had just signed that they were heading to the loo, presumably in search of some peace and quiet. I thought about my answer for a moment then decided on partial truth.

'Because I am about to join Médecins Sans Frontières.'

'You are what?'

'I am about to join Médecins Sans Frontières. I fancy a change.'

'A change? MSF, a change? You are kidding me! What about you wife and kids? MSF est très dangereux!' Gaston was almost shouting above the clamour.

I shrugged.

'Perhaps, but Elizabeth is dead and I haven't seen my kids in two years.'

'Antoine, this is terrible! You say your wife is dead...?'

'She died in a car crash with her lover so don't feel bad about it.'

Gaston paused and looked at me for a moment. Then spoke as tentatively as the din would allow:

'Maybe I hear something on the grapevine. Is it the case that you have been to prison?'

I nodded.

'Sure. I got caught lying about an inheritance during my divorce settlement with Elizabeth which turned out to be a prisonable offence.'

'But this is no reason to be joining MSF – this is crazy! There is no need for you to risk your life. With your experience I could make a job for you here if British hospitals do not wish to know you...'

I shook my head.

'Thanks for the offer pal, but it's not easy to find a job with a criminal record and besides, it's not just that...'

Gaston raised his eyebrows questioningly so I pressed on, curious to hear the answer myself.

'It's just I need to prove myself. I've got the qualifications to prove I'm clever, and my colleagues and my work record tell me I am good at surgery. My wife and all the women I have ever known tell me I'm a decent lover. They can't all be acting and they keep coming back for more. I've got two kids, so I've done my bit for the propagation of the species and I've earned enough to spoil the bastards something rotten. It's just I feel I still haven't done enough.' I paused to see how this was going down, but he was clearly unconvinced so I pressed on. 'I have never faced real fear or real danger. True, my wife's lover attacked me, but even that felt like play acting. I don't know whether we would have had the balls or ability to actually kill each other. I came out on top, but I didn't see it through when I had the opportunity...'

'But that is because you are a doctor, a saver of lives not a taker. You will not be taking lives if you go to MSF either, so what will you prove?'

'Nothing, but I will be seeing the reason for saving them close up and unvarnished by the sterility of a hospital operating theatre with its neat rows of instruments and instant anaesthetic. I need to get hands on and dirty. I need to see the suffering I am trying to save my patients from...'

'It seems to me you need a good rest mon ami. I think you wish everything to happen too soon when you have been through some very bad experiences. Also I do not understand how I am going to make you speak French in just one evening?'

'Well you could stop speaking English for a start.'

*

I was in bed with Nurse Sylvie the following morning in the spare room of Gaston's garret apartment near the Arc de Triomphe when the text arrived summoning me to a meeting back in Rue Saint-Sabin at eleven o'clock. The noise obviously disturbed my companion who arose with a delightful lack of self-consciousness and disappeared from the room leaving me to get my head together whilst I acknowledged the message. Apparently I was due to meet a woman called Suzanne Moreau who was described as a Directeur des Opérations à l'Etranger. This obviously called for a touch of the old Stamford charm. I decided to resist Nurse Sylvie's seductive powers and practice my spoken French on her instead. She returned a couple of minutes later bearing a couple of cups of coffee and everything else to boot. I changed my mind.

Two hours later, and I was sitting in reception at MSF for the second day in a row. Sylvie had delivered a note from Gaston, along with my coffee, wishing me luck with MSF given his failure to dissuade me the previous evening. He had had to leave for work, but was adamant that I should stop off back in

Paris on my return. I had paused to reflect that I could have done with a few friends like him back in England before sinking back into Nurse Silvie's embraces again.

I was idly comparing the profile of snooty receptionist Céline's breasts with my recent memory of Nurse Sylvie's when young Jean-Luc Garon appeared and invited me to follow him. This time, when he knocked the door of the meeting room and beckoned me in, the room was occupied by a woman. She looked up from behind the desk where she was studying a sheet of paper and gestured me to the interview chair. Jean-Luc retreated to the back of the room.

As I sat down I was already trying to glean some reaction to my application, but Madame Moreau remained firmly neutral, both in her appearance and her manner. Her hair was fair and short, but not cropped. Could I detect any softness in those brown eyes or were they just magnified by her horn-rimmed spectacles? Their steadiness suggested the latter. She placed the piece of paper on the desk between us.

'Good morning Mr Stamford and thank you for attending our offices a second time. We are both busy people so I'm sure you won't mind if I get straight to the point.'

Shit, this didn't sound too good! I shrugged my acceptance though I suspected that she would have carried on regardless. She had the easy European English of a person accustomed to operating at an international level and, given her job description, was clearly no push over. I decided to major on my surgical skills and leave the charm on the back burner.

'Good. Then I'm afraid I have to tell you that we will not be proceeding with your application.'

'I beg your pardon?'

'I'm sorry, did you not hear me? I said we will unfortunately not be proceeding with your application. My colleague Monsieur Garon here has contacted your former employer, a Doctor Chaudhuri at St Georges Hospital in London, who tells us that your employment was terminated thanks to your imprisonment. He does not explain any further. Jean-Luc has also spoken to your medical organisation the GMC who tell us that your medical licence is currently suspended.' She nodded at the piece of paper. 'They sent us a facsimile to this effect this morning.'

'Yes, but surely the GMC are a British organisation. Why should you be governed by their rules?'

'Because we rely on their goodwill, and the goodwill of many other such organisations, to carry out our work. We cannot investigate the history of every doctor who makes an application to us, or sit in judgement over him, so it must be sufficient for us that your former employer and your governing body do not, as yet, allow you to practice medicine in your own country. Do I take it that that is the reason for making your application here instead of London?'

'Yes, I guess so, but I wasn't trying to mislead anyone, it's just that I want to get back to doing my proper job and it seems impossible. I'm a surgeon, not a bloody criminal, for God's sake!'

Madame Moreau held up a placatory hand.

'I am sure you are Mr Stamford and I would like to help you, but we have a strict code of practice developed from many years of experience. I am sure, if you are patient, you will get your licence back when the rules permit and then I will be glad to personally welcome you to our organisation. I am sad to say there is nothing in my experience to suggest our need for qualified medical people is likely to cease in the foreseeable future.'

I sat there speechless. The bloody woman was turning me down! Hadn't they looked at my qualifications and surgical experience? They were meant to be in the business of saving lives, but were rejecting me on the basis of some petty, trumped-up, unrelated misdemeanour that I had already been unfairly punished for. I wanted to explode, but something in her cool, steady gaze told me I'd be wasting my time and probably end up in an arm-lock courtesy of the young, fit-looking Jean-Luc. I decided a dignified retreat was my only option. I rose and nodded so stiffly that it almost turned into a waiter's bow.

'Very well Madame, then I'll thank you for your time and take my services elsewhere.'

For the first time she allowed herself a glimmer of a smile.

'I wish you the very best of luck, Monsieur Stamford.'

*

I was sitting at a table in a bar not far from my hotel. I had agreed before leaving for MSF to meet Nurse Sylvie back at Gaston's apartment, but my sex drive had nose-dived along with my career prospects. I fished out my phone and texted her a curt apology, then signalled to the patron for another Pernod. He somehow managed to pour and deliver it without once taking his eyes off the widescreen TV that dominated the bar. The horse racing was still as incomprehensible as it had been on my arrival and we were the only two people in there so the atmosphere was hardly vibrant. Occasionally he picked up his mobile and engaged in a terse conversation with someone whom I assumed was his book maker. All I had gleaned so far was that we were watching the events taking place at a race course called Longchamps.

I watched the Pernod cloud up as I added water from the carafe and then pushed it aside. I was on my third and it wasn't working. Self-pity is misnamed, it only really works with someone else to share it. The oaf behind the bar clearly limited his functions in life to taking my money, spending it on the horses and possibly beating me up if I didn't leave a tip.

A voice was also whispering in my ear to the effect that, with Newcombe possibly hot on my trail, I needed to apply myself to the thorny question: where next? I signalled for l'addition and threw enough in the saucer to satisfy 'Monsieur Miserable' then headed back to my hotel. On arrival in my room, I turned on the television and flicked through the channels until I found a news programme. I watched it with half an eye as I laid out my belongings on the bed and reviewed them in the light of an idea that had begun to take shape in my mind.

Okay, so MSF didn't want me. To hell with wounded pride, it was probably exactly as Madame What's-Her-Name had explained: they had their protocols and, no doubt, they had all sorts of odd-bods turning up at their doors volunteering their services. In her eyes I was just a disbarred doctor with a criminal record. How was she to know that I wouldn't try to steal the scalpels?

The news programme finished and I hadn't heard my name mentioned or seen my mugshot fill the screen. Why did I imagine that was even likely? I was getting paranoid. I gave myself a brief lecture on the need to calm down and focussed on my belongings. The paperwork that had got me to Paris would suffice to keep me on the move, but I calculated that I would be wise to top up my wash bag with extra toothbrushes and paste. I discarded my shaving cream canister and made a mental note to buy a brush and plenty of bars of soap. If I bought some scented stuff I could also do without my deodorant.

Next I inspected my clothes which amounted to little more than I was standing up in. The only other garments were the ones I had changed out of during my departure from London. They didn't strike me as particularly well designed for where I was headed to, so I deposited them in the bottom of the wardrobe where a maid would assume they had been forgotten. I needed to be travelling light and dressing light, so I added tee-shirts and chinos to my shopping list. On the same principle, I made a note to invest in plenty of changes of socks and pants and several pairs of trainers.

Finally, satisfied that I had thought of everything, I closed my bedroom door and headed downstairs to pay my bill.

*

I was sitting in the departure lounge at Charles de Gaulle waiting for my flight to be called. How the hell they had the nerve to call these places 'lounges' was beyond me. The place was heaving with business types, students, and holiday makers with mewling brats, along with the usual drunks and odd-balls that seem to inhabit such places. It didn't help that I couldn't shake the feeling that Newcombe's hand could descend on my shoulder at any minute. I checked my watch yet again.

My impatience was not, in fact, entirely provoked by my fear of a last minute arrest, nor indeed by my earlier realisation that I needed a clean break and a new sense of purpose in my life. It was largely the product of a far more profound realisation which had come to me on, of all places, le Métro on my way to the airport. I was gliding along with several stops still to go and no further need to concentrate on my route so I allowed my mind to drift. As always I found myself wondering how I had come to this and where it was all leading, and, as usual, arrived at the conclusion that it was all beyond me.

As I tried to dismiss these pointless musings I found myself thinking about the operation that Ham had fucked up and the trouble it had led me into. However, it wasn't the trouble that was catching my attention. It was the operation itself. I found myself reliving the drama of the scene, the panic, the stress, my recognition of the mess Ham was making of it and my intervention. I found myself recalling the clamp he'd misplaced, and the split aorta, and the frenzied activity as the kid went into cardiac arrest followed by the sense of limp exhaustion as we lost him. I found myself gripped by the drama and excitement of it. I found myself missing it all desperately.

It wasn't quite a revelation, it was more like a rediscovery as if I had suddenly seen back through the mists of my breakdown to a world I had loved and been master of. A world where I reigned supreme and colleagues turned to me for my help and expertise; a world where I would work every unsociable hour, every day of the week if necessary, in order to dwell in that moment of absolute focus and harmony when my knowledge and experience fused with my surgical gifts.

Suddenly my desire to join MSF and my bitter frustration at their rejection made absolute sense. I needed to operate, and operate at a level which demanded the very best of me. To hell with fixing corns on Hampstead Heath! I needed to feel the adrenaline again, to feel the rush and the pressure and to know I could cope. I needed to know if I still had the gift.

7

The seat belt light came on and the pilot's reassuring tones informed us that we were now approaching Beirut's Rafic Hariri International Airport and that he hoped we had all enjoyed flying Middle East Airlines. It was a mystery why I had chosen to bestow my surgical gifts on the victims of the Syrian conflict, except that the country was clearly in desperate need of international aid as the civil war escalated. Perhaps, somewhere in the back of my mind it didn't represent the extreme geographical relocation required by some MSF operations such as Haiti or the Congo. It was still nearly Europe if I changed my mind. Moreover, from a practical point of view, I still stood a chance of keeping tabs on Newcombe whilst still keeping well out of his clutches. Anyway, I couldn't hang around at Charles de Gaulle forever and the girl on the Middle East Airlines desk had offered me a cancellation on the next flight to Beirut.

The flight had provided me with an opportunity to clear my thoughts and reflect further on my treatment at the hands of Madame Moreau and her organisation. To be frank I had been more than a little pissed off at what I felt to be her high-and-mighty attitude, no matter how much I told myself that she was no doubt obeying regulations that she couldn't side-step whoever the applicant was. Let's face it, if she could find out that quickly about my recent difficulties, then she would also know that she was dealing with a senior surgeon from a top London hospital and one of the world's leading proctologists. Was she telling me that MSF could afford to turn their noses up at that level of expertise and experience? I thought not!

So what was behind her attitude then? I recalled that little smile that crossed her lips as she ended the meeting. It also struck me that she had wished me luck, not forbidden me from ever darkening their doorstep again. So perhaps this wasn't a rejection after all ... perhaps it was some kind of test! It was almost certainly true that they didn't accept just any old Tom, Dick or Harry and, no doubt, my imprisonment weighed heavily against me, but more than that, working in a war zone was clearly one hell of a challenge and the last thing they needed was to saddle themselves with deadbeats and the faint-hearted. Perhaps this was the medical equivalent of joining the SAS where they put you through your paces first to ensure you were tough enough.

Fine, if that was their game, then they would soon find out that they hadn't got the measure of Tony Stamford, or perhaps they had! Perhaps they had spotted an inner determination in me and decided to put it to the test, after all they had nothing to lose and this way they weren't disobeying any protocols, very shrewd. Okay, so perhaps I was on the receiving end of a bit of gamesmanship here, but so what? I had already decided that my overarching objective was to get back in a set of greens and start operating again and, moreover, do it in an environment which gave me a true sense of purpose and achievement. It didn't particularly matter to me under whose auspices I was attaining those goals. If MSF wanted me to turn up and offer my services at the front line instead of back in Paris just to prove I wasn't easily discouraged, then so be it!

I sat back, satisfied that I had almost certainly cracked their inexplicable attitude, though a little voice in the back of my mind warned me that the test was not necessarily over yet. How was I to know when they would be satisfied that I had the mettle to make a front-line surgeon? That was a tougher nut to crack. Finally, I concluded that only time could answer this but one thing was certain: I wasn't going to all this time and trouble to be snubbed again. This time I would play my cards much closer to my chest and make a proper assessment of the lie of the land before I approached anybody. Not long after that, the stewardess announced our imminent arrival at Beirut and I turned my thoughts to where I was going to stay.

The first thing that struck me as I descended to the tarmac was the heat. Thanks to a stop-off at Frankfurt we had arrived in the early hours of the morning and it was still hot enough for me to break into an instant sweat as we filed out of the air-conditioned plane. This was going to take some getting used to. For the first time I thought about my future relationship with the local insects and the possible diseases I might need to inoculate against. I decided that could wait until I had got some proper sleep behind me.

As I stood waiting for my bag to appear I Googled a list of Beirut hotels on my phone and chose the Hilton Habtoor Grand. Given that I was headed for something akin to a desert war zone, I was not in search of luxury, though a bit of extra pampering before eschewing my creature comforts could hardly come amiss. More importantly, I was in urgent need of the kind of technology which would bring me up to date with the current refugee situation in the east of the country. That meant a room with a TV that received Lebanese local news.

From there I should be able to figure out where the refugees were coming into the country and even, possibly, where the main medical agencies were operating from.

*

The following morning I took an early dip and then sun-bathed for an hour, plastered in factor thirty, to start acclimatising to the already scorching sun. After a second hour spent stoking up on the hotel's endless selection of 'International Breakfast Cuisine' I retreated back to my room, put on a tee-shirt and shorts, and then tuned into a local news channel.

There was no disputing the fact that there was a crisis going on involving refugees and violence, but that's where my grasp of the situation stopped. I can only imagine that I had been expecting English subtitles! Anyhow, I found myself getting increasingly confused, not enlightened, as images cut from crowds of people shouting, running and even firing off weapons, to scenes in hospitals where harassed medical people were being asked for comments as they attended to the sick and wounded. This was hopeless. Was this happening in Lebanon or Syria? It had better be Syria! I was happy enough to help with a refugee crisis, but I hadn't come here to get my arse shot off! No doubt a grasp of the lingo would have made perfect sense of it all, but that was the one thing I lacked. I clicked off the set for some peace and quiet and strolled out onto the balcony to review the situation.

I settled down on a sun lounger with my phone and selected the memo pad. I had already decided to check my inoculations, so I keyed that in. Next on my list I added an interpreter; it was already apparent that I was going to get nowhere without one. On the subject of going places, it was clear that I would still be needing transport so I added a vehicle. Thinking back to the images I had just been viewing, I typed in 4x4 beside it. I followed that up with the word Supplies, then realised that such a generalisation was virtually meaningless and probably not necessary. The country was half the size of Wales for God's sake! If things went according to plan and I hooked up with a relief agency, they would have supplies I could buy or scrounge. Failing that, it was less than a day's drive in any direction to go and collect some.

That set me thinking again about my interpreter. What I really needed was some sort of general factotum, an interpreter, cum driver, cum cook, cum general handyman and mechanic looking at the state of the roads. Some knowledge of small arms might also come in useful looking at the crowds on the news footage. In fact, the more I thought about it, the more I concluded that an assistant was my first priority. I couldn't think of anything else to add to my list and there was clearly nothing more I could glean from the TV so I turned it off, collected my wallet and headed downstairs in search of someone who could set me in the right direction.

*

'Excuse me! Could you spare me a moment? I need a bit of advice.'

The concierge turned and bowed his head enquiringly.

'Indeed, how may I be of assistance sir?'

'Well, I'm looking for a chap who can sort me out while I'm staying in Lebanon.'

The concierge nodded his understanding.

'I see sir. I'm sure that can be arranged. How long might you require his services for?'

'Well, I don't really know. It could be days or weeks and I should add it could turn a bit rough.'

'Rough?'

'Well hopefully not rough...I don't know. I've never done this sort of thing before. I'm new to the country and need a general handyman, ideally good at French as well as English.'

'A handy man who is also good at French, of course, I see sir. That should provide no problem. May I ask your room number and a time when it would be convenient for me to bring you a choice of young men who might suit your requirements?'

I looked at my watch. It was nearly one o'clock already and I fancied a bit of sightseeing before I moved out of Beirut.

'Well I've got to go out for a while, so how does six o'clock sound? I'm staying in room three-six-seven.'

'Six o'clock will be most acceptable sir.'

Satisfied that I got the ball rolling as regards priority number one, I asked him to call a cab to take me in search of a vehicle hire company.

*

I stood marvelling at my own naiveté as the young man paraded up and down my bedroom with his hand posed seductively on his hip. I turned to the concierge who was clearly expecting some gratuity for his efforts on my behalf.

'I, er, don't know how to put this, but I don't think I explained my requirements very clearly to you earlier...'

'I assure you sir, this young man will meet any requirements you may ask of him...'

'Yes, but I should explain, my requirements are not of a sexual nature.'

The concierge's eyebrows shot up as he attempted to picture, no doubt, quite what form of depravity I might have in mind which was not of a sexual nature.

'Perhaps I did not make myself clear, but all I need is a driver and translator to act as a guide and helper while I am here. I am a doctor and I plan to help the people being driven here from the war in Syria.'

I watched with some irritation as understanding dawned on the man.

'I must apologise most sincerely sir. I quite misunderstood the nature of your requirements...'

He was too bloody right there, but before I could decide whether or not to spare his blushes, the second young man he had brought for my delectation spoke up.

'Pardon me sir, but I would be most delighted to be the driver and servant for this gentleman.'

I had been so startled by his colleague's camp posturing that I had paid him little attention. Looking at him now, aside from the earring and a definite hint of blusher and lipstick, there was nothing particularly effeminate about him. There was no lisp when he spoke and, thinking about it, he didn't mince like his colleague as he entered the room. The concierge gestured for him to shut up but I intervened.

'What is your name, young man?'

'My name is Talal, sir.'

'And you say you would be happy to work for me as a driver?'

'Indeed sir.'

'And you understand that I am not interested in having sex with you and we may be going to places where there is military activity and there may be some danger?'

'I understand this sir. I was doing military service when Israelis attacked my country and killed my friends.'

'I see, right.' To be honest I wasn't aware that Israel had been at war with Lebanon, but now he mentioned it something rang a bell. 'Okay, Talal, well if you're sure you are up to the job and can spare the time perhaps you would like to meet me tomorrow morning and we can discuss the terms of your employment.'

*

Talal was waiting for me when I arrived in the coffee lounge at eight the following morning which I took to be a good sign. The earring was gone along with the make-up and he was generally more 'toned down' in a white shirt, jeans and trainers. He was a bit older than I had taken him for the previous day so, as the waiter deposited two cups of coffee and departed, I said:

'Okay Talal, you said yesterday that you saw action in the war with Israel, so how old would that make you?'

'I am twenty-four, sir.'

104

I did a quick mental calculation. I had Googled the Israeli/ Lebanese War the evening before with this eventuality in mind and his answer made sense. I had also checked, given his previous mention of National Service, that Lebanon was using conscription at the time, they were. Things were adding up so far.

'Fine, so what made you leave the army?'

Talal didn't hesitate.

'Money sir, I earn better money as I am working now.'

'Really?' Talal's attitude was hard-nosed to say the least! 'But don't you find yesterday's method of earning it a little... unconventional?'

Talal grinned.

'You should see what goes on in army barracks sir, besides, I have wife and kids to look after.'

'Oh, right, I see.' To be honest, I didn't see at all, but then I reminded myself that Middle Eastern sexual mores were reputed to differ considerably from the West. I also reminded myself that until recently I had also been earning a living largely thanks to my willingness to accept money in return for sexual favours. I decided sexual ethics were best left out of this arrangement.

'I explained yesterday that there could be some risk involved in this undertaking. How do you feel about this given your wife and children?'

Talal grinned again and shrugged.

'Allah perhaps will decide not to care for me, but he will certainly care for my beautiful children, and soon they will be big enough to care for themselves.'

Talal sat back quite clearly satisfied that there was nothing more to say on the subject. In the face of such fatalism there didn't seem to be anything I could add so I cut to the chase.

'Yes, well, I'm sure you're right, in which case do you have a figure in mind for your services?'

A flicker of calculation lit up in his eyes and I braced myself for some ruthless Arab negotiating.

'This must depend on how long you wish for my services.'

'Yes, of course, I don't suppose you have an hourly rate as such... well, let's say how much would you charge if I took you on for a week and then we could see how we went from there.'

Talal had obviously given this some thought already.

'Very good, sir, then I would charge six hundred thousand of our Lebanese pounds.'

He said this rather speculatively, but I had also done some thinking and more importantly, Googled current exchange rates so I wasn't fazed by the apparently astronomical figure. This equated roughly to two hundred and fifty pounds sterling which I had also discovered was more-or-less the British minimum wage. Either Talal did not share his countrymen's reputed fiscal acumen, or he was keener than he cared to admit to quit the buggery business! Given my own experience of heterosexual harlotry, which was almost certainly less physically discomforting than his, I didn't blame him. Still, this was coming out of my pocket, so I didn't want to start getting charitable. I leant across the table and offered my hand satisfied that, as far I could reasonably tell so far, I had got myself a bargain.

*

Talal slid out from beneath the somewhat battered, flat back Toyota Hilux that his cousin was standing proudly beside. He hurried over to me wiping his hands on an oily rag, nodding slightly as he approached.

'She is not too bad for an old woman. Maybe her brakes are not so good but Fadi says he will fix that. It is not so important away from the city where there is little traffic. Otherwise she is good, with no oil leaks, and her steering is also good.'

I nodded my appreciation.

'How much?'

'Fadi will take one hundred and fifty U.S. dollars if you pay with cash, no cheque.'

I could have bet he would. Still, it was a big improvement on the six hundred and thirty I had been quoted by Europcar on my shopping trip the previous day. Talal had clearly spotted from the outset that I was not going to be an easy touch.

'Okay, I guess it will do for our needs.' I counted out the money and handed it to him. 'Why don't you sort out the paperwork and then we can go and find some lunch while he sorts out the brakes.' Talal nodded and hurried off.

The rest of the day followed a similar pattern. We collected the Toyota and took her for a spin down the coast to check that cousin Fadi had made the necessary repairs, then we returned to town and spent the rest of the day rounding up kit and supplies some of which, to be honest, I would never have found, or even thought to buy on my own. By the end of the day we were equipped with non-perishable food such as coffee, dry fruit, nuts and a rather tasty dried meat called pastirma from a market. We bought sleeping bags, mosquito nets and a tent, along with a kettle and camp stove. We called at a pharmacy to sort out a basic first aid kit and stocked up on industrial quantities of insect repellent. He even took me to a doctor to check my jabs. With a final stop to pick up a map from a sort of Lebanese newsagents we headed back to the hotel.

This time, with Talal acting as interpreter, it was possible to make some sort of sense of the conflict. We sat glued to the television in my room ignoring the beer and sandwiches I had ordered on our way up. The situation was clearly on a knife edge with reports of Syrian troops and planes pursuing their own people across the border as they fled the civil war. It seemed only a matter of time before the situation escalated. A lot of these incidents were occurring in a place called the Bekaa Valley which I had already heard mentioned on the news back in England. Now, sitting in Beirut with this happening only fifty miles up the road, it all seemed a lot more real. I like to think I'm as brave as the next man, but Zeinab Badaw in her air-conditioned studio didn't capture the half of it.

One piece in particular caught my eye. It was a straight-to-camera report by a harassed-looking young woman in a flak jacket. She would have caught my eye in her own right, but what really grabbed me was the MSF logo on the lorry parked behind her.

'Where is that place Talal?' I muttered, so as not to drown out her report.

'It is a town called Arsal,' he whispered back without taking his eyes off the screen.

As the young woman walked to her left and the camera panned round to show a wider view of the street you could be forgiven for a joke about the aptness of its name. The place was a dump.

'What's going on there?'

'It is confusing but some important people in our government do business with Syrian government so they do not wish to help the refugees too much. The townspeople wish to help them so they fight with our government soldiers. The soldiers say refugees hide Syrian spies.'

'Do you think that's true?'

Talal shrugged.

'Who knows? Maybe, but it is dangerous place.'

I thought for a moment. If I was serious about getting a taste of frontline medicine, this was the sort of place where I needed to be and, from a practical point of view, this was the sort of place where I stood a realistic chance of sliding back into surgery underneath the MSF radar. I made a decision.

'Come on, finish your beer. We're on our way to Arsal!'

8

We finally left Beirut at seven the following morning after some last minute shopping and a healthy breakfast to sort us out for the journey; there was no telling when we would next eat and what it would be when we did. Again Talal had demonstrated common sense the previous evening by pointing out that it was foolish to risk breaking down in the middle of nowhere in the middle of the night. When I conceded the point he shot off to say farewell to his beloved wife and beautiful children. Given that this took him all night, he no doubt devoted some time and effort to the prospect of Mrs Talal adding to his brood. Still, if Arsal was as dangerous as we had been led to believe, I could hardly begrudge him the opportunity.

We made good time driving against the steady influx of office workers and farm trucks still bringing produce into town. Our biggest delay was an overturned pickup that had spilled melons everywhere. The delay was principally due to the fist-waving and gesticulating that such disasters necessitated. Once everyone's mother and deceased relatives had been roundly abused the protagonists formed a co-operative and cleared up the mess.

With the city behind us things changed. Suddenly the traffic thinned slightly and became much more official. Military and police vehicles were commonplace, interspersed with official-looking vehicles and relief agency cars and trucks. I had never seen a country at war, or on the brink of it, but this is how I imagined it to feel. Buses packed with what I took to be refugees were heading towards the city, their faces gaunt with fear and hunger. Talal chattered on, pointing out remarkably uninteresting features of the barren landscape as I wallowed in culture shock.

Finally, he informed me that the collection of windowless, block-built huts, shimmering in the developing heat haze up ahead, was our destination. As we got nearer, it became apparent that Arsal was a bit more substantial than first impressions allowed for. The place began to unfold through the shimmer revealing a number of taller edifices at its centre. Soon we were driving through ramshackle huts populated by goats, small children and old woman who gazed impassively at us as we rattled past on the bumpy highway into town.

By now, I was suffering a form of schizophrenia as one half my mind reassured me proudly that I was finally proving that I had the guts and determination to look life squarely in the eye, whilst the other half was screaming what the hell did I think I was doing stuck in a war-torn shit hole in the back of beyond! Before I could resolve the dilemma we rounded a bend and came to an abrupt halt. The road was almost blocked by pickups parked outside what appeared to be a mosque that someone had not got round to finishing. Workmen were digging in the road alongside the building as a crowd looked on impassively. Talal glanced at me enquiringly.

'You wish to learn what is happening?'

I paused. Why not? We had to start somewhere and I wanted to get the lay of the land before offering my services. I nodded.

'Sure.'

We got out and Talal went ahead to engage some official-looking characters in conversation. Alone, I wandered across the road and into the building.

The first thing that struck me was the smell. As a coloproctologist, I reckoned I was accustomed to the smell of human faeces, but I had never experienced anything like this. It was like an all-pervasive, inescapable miasma which left you not wanting to inhale. As I fought the urge to gag, my eye was drawn to a corner of the room from where the hum of flies was audible. Beneath the black cloud an old man squatted, defecating.

I got a grip and forced my mind to accept what my eyes were telling me. There were at least twenty people living in this room if the small piles of belongings marking out each sleeping area were anything to go by. People and families were sleeping, packed side by side, on the perversely ornate, tiled floor. The corner of the room where the old man squatted was their only latrine.

Talal stuck his head in through the entrance, clapped one hand over his nose and beckoned me over with the other. With some relief I followed him back outside. He led me over to join a couple of men dressed in short sleeved shirts and slacks who were standing back from the throng surveying the work in progress. As I approached they clasped their hands together and nodded their "salam alaykums" then the taller of the two stepped forward, shook my hand. It appeared the natives were friendly! The shorter, plump man preferred to remain in the background. As the tall man stepped back, Talal explained his enthusiastic welcome.

'These gentlemen are of the Ramzi Foundation Mr Stamford,

sir. I am explaining that you are a doctor from England who has come to help our people.'

'What the hell's the Ramzi Foundation?' I muttered out of the side of my mouth. The shorter man interrupted.

'The Ramzi Foundation is a Lebanese NGO dedicated principally to providing aid to disadvantaged women and children Doctor Stamford. However, under current circumstances we have extended our remit to all victims of the current situation.'

Shit, the man spoke better English than I did! It seemed petty to correct him on the doctor/mister distinction.

'I'm sorry, I didn't realise that you spoke...'

'No matter, it is not important. Let me just say how grateful we are that you are giving up your time and expertise to help these people.'

'Yes, well that's nothing...' I replied feebly.

'On the contrary, sir, it is a very generous gift and I thank you for it on behalf of them all.'

I stood lost for words. The man had left me speechless, but cured my schizophrenia! I no longer doubted why I was there. I suddenly felt more worthwhile than I had ever done in my life. I was used to being looked up to, respected and lauded, but that was for my qualifications, status and even talent; here I was being praised for my actions as a man. Before they began to wonder if they were dealing with an inarticulate idiot, I got a grip and switched to practicalities.

'Good, well, is there anything I can do to help here?'

Short of fetching a mop and bucket, there was clearly no immediate call for my help, but my new acquaintances were too polite to remark on this. Instead the taller of the two turned and pointed on down the road into town.

'The refugees are coming from the east and that is where you will find the doctors are working, sir. May I ask, do you belong to any particular organisation?'

A simple 'no' would have sufficed. I was quite sure that anyone was free to volunteer their services here and these men had no jurisdiction over me anyway, but another answer sprang unexpectedly to my lips.

'Yes, I'm affiliated to Médecins Sans Frontières as it happens.'

The man broke into a wide smile.

'Excellent! Your organisation does much wonderful work here. Your services will be most welcome. Now, if you will excuse us...'

We all exchanged another handshake and they disappeared round the side of the building to supervise the digging. Talal and I climbed back into the Toyota. It was bizarre, but I felt better than I did on learning I had passed my Fellowship of the Royal College exams and I had really done that, this was a lie! Still, I had qualified it with the word 'affiliate' and it was only a lie as things stood at the moment. It was up to me now to figure out a way to turn it into the truth.

*

I sat in the passenger seat of the Toyota picking thoughtfully at the dried fruit and meats Talal had rustled up. It was mid-afternoon and the heat was sweltering. Across the square a selection of MSF vehicles were drawn up in a defensive semicircle around the entrance to the building they had commandeered as a temporary hospital. I could see why they had set up a quasi-stockade. The place was like the Wild West. There were vehicles of all shapes and states of repair parked haphazardly wherever space could be found. People of all nationalities hurried about organising anyone who seemed willing to be organised. The latter tended to stand huddled in groups looking lost.

In amongst the chaos a few real nutters stood out. My attention was drawn in particular to a lanky, long-haired individual in a white coat who was sporting a stethoscope and a head mirror and was apparently directing operations by shouting and waving a clipboard at anyone who would look at him, like a paramedical John the Baptist. It was not difficult to understand why anyone serious about getting things done needed to adopt a certain aloofness. This was all familiar territory to me. I was a member of a profession who in years gone by had adopted Latin to keep the ignorant masses at bay!

Unfortunately, a diagnosis was not a cure and understanding the need for security was not going to get me past it. My plan, insofar as it could be called that, was to look for a chance to demonstrate my surgical abilities and consequently make myself useful, if not invaluable, irrespective of my recent professional difficulties. That depended on first getting past an unobtrusive, but highly effective security system that had evolved over years of working in crisis situations. Just like in any other hospital, the system relied on recognition. People knew each other or, failing that, they knew the uniform. Those ubiquitous white tee-shirts with the red and black MSF logos looked casual enough, but I was willing to bet they were jealously guarded.

This was not going to be easy.

I concentrated my attention on the vehicles forming the semicircle. They all carried MSF logos too, but some were clearly marked as ambulances. I watched as patients were carried out of the building and loaded into the backs. I assumed that these were patients who had survived initial trauma and were on their way to Beirut or Tripoli for proper hospitalisation.

The others ranged from cars and vans to the odd truck. It was the vans that caught my interest. As one arrived another would depart, on what I judged to be a roughly hourly basis. These carried goods not people. The MSF supply lines were working smoothly and the departing vehicles were leaving with as much as they had arrived with. Clearly they had no waste disposal or laundry services on site which was hardly surprising given the distant sound of explosions and the occasional glimpse of fighter planes away to the east. They probably didn't want to get too settled.

I watched an MSF orderly throw another couple of sacks into the back of a van then walk round to the front and drive off. I turned to Talal.

'See that van pulling out over there?' He nodded as he swigged more water. 'I want you to follow it. Keep your distance. There's no rush, I just want to see what route he takes.'

Talal leant forward to start the engine, no doubt relieved at the opportunity to get some breeze through the cab. He turned to me and grinned.

'Yes sir, certainly, maybe we will get the chance to steal some tee-shirts too!'

I glanced sideways at his cheery grin and smiled myself. My

companion was turning out to be a far shrewder retainer than I had expected.

*

I waited until the distant speck heading down the highway towards me grew into a recognisable MSF van then I stepped into the middle of the road and raised my hand signalling it emphatically to stop. Our Toyota was slewed half-on, half-off the road in a manner that clearly suggested I had broken down. I had already seen two vans sail past thanks to excessive timidity on my part or a 'stop for no man' policy on the part of MSF. This time the driver was going to stop, or go off the road to avoid me. I assumed, given his employers humanitarian principles he wouldn't simply run me over. Thankfully, my assumption proved correct. The van slowed and came to a halt in front of me.

The driver leant out of the window, obviously less than pleased at this interruption to his busy schedule.

'Qu'est-ce qui se passe?' he demanded brusquely.

'Mon téléphone est cassé,' I replied. 'Ma voiture est cassé et maintenant mon téléphone est cassé aussi. Merde!' As I explained my double predicament I waved my mobile in my left hand to hold his attention. I scrambled round his bonnet to the driver's window, pressing it with my hand as if to prevent him driving off. 'Avez-vous un téléphone que je pourrais utiliser pour appeler un garage?' I clasped my hands together in supplication and spoke slowly to emphasise that I was a foolish Anglais. He looked at me with contempt for a moment, and then relented. He fished out a mobile and prepared to dial. He wasn't sufficiently trusting to hand it over.

'Avez-vous un nombre pour téléphoner?' he demanded.

I shook my head and shrugged helplessly.

'Non, monsieur.'

He tutted a bit more contempt and went into his address book or the internet because shortly after he began speaking rapidly in what I took to be Arabic. He ended the call and spoke in French again.

'Vous y êtes. Quelqu'un sera ici en une heure.'

'Une heure? Ici? Merci bien Monsieur, merci bien, vous êtes très gentil...'

My benefactor had clearly had enough of being très gentil because he cut me short with a rev of his engine and sped off up the road. I waited until he was a dot in the distance then strolled back to the Toyota and tapped on the side. Halal popped his head up and grinned.

'Any luck?'

He didn't reply. Instead he rose, solemn-faced on the back of the pick-up and began a strange rhythmic gyration which I distantly recalled was meant to resemble Egyptian dancing. As he jerked his chin and arms back and forth in a serpentine motion he reached into a sleeve, produced an MSF tee-shirt and dropped it to the floor. He reached down the front of his shirt and produced a scrub suit which he similarly deposited. I stood staring at this pantomime in disbelief for a moment and then the absurdity of it hit me and I began to laugh.

Encouraged by my reaction, Talal gave it all he'd got, squirming and wriggling and tossing garments in all directions.

I laughed until tears ran down my face and my sides ached. I laughed harder than I had laughed since before my breakdown, or my imprisonment, or indeed when I thought about it, since before my marriage. Standing there under the blazing desert sun, watching Talal clowning around, my recent cares and worries and fears and ambitions seemed to fade into insignificance and I felt strangely young and carefree again. Now all I had to do was use this disguise to infiltrate myself into the MSF compound!

The unwelcome thought of that brought me back to Earth with an abrupt bump and, besides, Talal was out of stolen garments to fling around. I clapped my hands, signalling an end to the hilarity.

'Excellent, Talil! Well done! Okay, collect them up and hang onto them until we get back to town. We'd best get out of here before the tow-truck turns up.'

Talal climbed off the back of the Toyota and we got into the cab, our robbery complete. My initial plan had been to commit the robbery myself whilst Talal created the diversion, but he had pointed out that he was better suited to clambering on and off the back of our Toyota than I was. Furthermore, I would be stuck if the back door of the van door was locked. When I asked what difference it would make if he were to discover that rather than me, he had simply grinned, produced a slim-bladed knife and informed me that you learned many things in the army.

*

We spent the remainder of the day hunting in vain for accommodation. Everywhere was full to bursting with many townsfolk taking refugees into their own houses. I could probably have pulled rank using my newly acquired MSF credentials, but I didn't want to attract attention unnecessarily. Instead we drove out just past the town's limits and pitched camp in the pup tents Talal had had the foresight to buy. As I lay on the mat separating me from the stony desert floor, listening to gunfire in the distance and Talal's snoring next door, I reflected that if it was some sort of contrast to my pampered western existence that I was in search of, then I had come to the right place. Finally, I dozed off.

The following day I prepared to test out my first disguise. I was determined to make sure that, when the time was right, I didn't cock things up by not knowing my bearings. I could possibly get away with the uncertainty you would expect from a new arrival, but I would still need to show some familiarity with MSF procedures. The more I could blend in, the better.

The night before I had selected the best of the garments Talal had pinched and had used a pint of our precious water and some toilet soap to give them a good scrub. Now I chose the best of the tee-shirts. For the time being, I was content to pass myself off as a porter. The last thing I needed was to have a scalpel thrust unexpectedly into my hand! I decided to join the team unloading the vans and get a look at the layout of the building from there.

I left Talal to try and find us better accommodation and made my way back into town on foot. I cut down between two of the delivery vans I had been observing the previous day and carried straight on into the building. I then mimed having forgotten something and followed a porter straight back out to the van he was unloading. I waited as he was given a package, then collected one myself and followed him back in. He headed down the room passed rows of stainless steel emergency beds containing patients in various states of disrepair. I counted six tightly packed beds on each side of the room. There was no telling whether they were pre or post op and I suspected that there was no distinction beyond immediate physical need. Some had clearly been treated and were awaiting shipment out to Beirut or Tripoli, others had yet to make it through triage. Ahead of us a bed was being wheeled by a man and woman dressed in scrubs.

The stony desert floor had finally won out the night before and I had given up trying to sleep and gone to watch the latest arrivals. Many came in on foot, some of them carrying stretchers. Others arrived on push bikes and in cars. A lot of the wounded arrived in vans and trucks. All were trying to get across under cover of darkness. Townspeople were driving out in their own vehicles to help bring in stragglers. Now the brunt of that night time influx had been absorbed and some sort of order had been restored. Staff members of all sorts were walking round pale with fatigue, but with an air of achievement. If things went according to plan, I would soon be one of them. Rather than lose myself in images of future surgical heroics, I turned my attention to the practical aspects of my surroundings.

My fellow porter followed the bed to the end of the ward and on into a reasonably wide central corridor. I guessed this place was a former school with one big classroom at the front and offices at the rear. The bed ahead was being manoeuvred round a tight angle into a room on the right, no doubt a makeshift operating theatre. On my left was a smaller room containing a couple of beds attended by a nurse or doctor, a recovery room more than likely.

As we passed the 'theatre' I could see an operation in progress even as the new bed was being manoeuvred into position. The place had an air of frantic calm. We carried on down the corridor to a second door on the left which my new colleague proceeded to unlock. This was clearly the stock room which, in combination with the others I had seen, constituted a serviceable if cramped arrangement. It was the nearest I could get to the action for the time being. Rather than risk getting drawn into a potentially difficult conversation with my co-worker, I dumped my box outside the room, headed off back out of the building and went in search of Talal.

9

The plane flashed and glinted in the first rays of early morning sunlight as it circled above the distant vehicles racing along the barren road towards us. The poor devils hadn't managed to reach the town before the pitiless sun revealed them to their pursuer. Suddenly it switched from leisureliness to breath-taking speed as it completed its turn and swooped down on its prey, its cannons spitting fire. This was its third pass at the unprotected convoy.

No doubt thanks to his military background, Talal was taking this all rather matter-of-factly, but I felt sickened. This was not war, it was vindictiveness. To be honest, my nearest encounters with military action up to then had consisted of a stint in the T.A. at school, war gaming in my den at home, old World War Two newsreel footage and Hollywood recreations from John Wayne to Apocalypse Now, that and the memorable shots of the Argie planes screaming down 'bomb alley' in San Carlos Bay. Nothing I had ever seen on film captured the casual savagery I was witnessing now. There was no camera man, or even a heat haze at that time of day, to stand between me and the cold-blooded murder I was watching.

The pilot came up behind the convoy and opened up with cannon fire as if a missile was too expensive and impersonal to waste on this motley rabble. I found myself holding my breath as he bore down on the trucks. Vehicles shunted each other as drivers slammed on their brakes and passengers ran to get away from the road. People stumbled and fell, dead or wounded, it was impossible to tell at that distance. One lorry caught fire, slid off the road, overturned and exploded, as the pilot veered away and then turned his plane back to Syria satisfied with his morning work. Jesus Christ, what difference was I going to make against this sort of unbridled barbarity?

Vehicles were racing out from the town, this time unopposed. I had already witnessed a violent confrontation the day before after recceing the hospital. The townspeople had clashed with government troops who were trying to prevent them helping refugees suspected of sheltering a spy. Thankfully the troops had moved on. I was getting my first taste of war's true destructiveness – the Syrians' war already had their Lebanese neighbours at each other's throats. I hadn't been foolish enough to imagine that TV and film ever captured the full reality of battle, but this was something I could never have imagined.

The pair of us had been up since four o'clock but, compared to the previous night it had been pretty quiet until now, certainly not busy enough to provide good cover for me to slip into the hospital unobtrusively. Suddenly, things were looking a lot more promising. To my surprise my stomach was knotted with tension.

'What d'you think Talal?'

Talal was watching the incoming traffic intently.

'I think you will not get better opportunity, sir.'

'Hmmn, I agree. How do I look?' I was now dressed in the best set of scrubs he had been able to put together.

'You look like the very finest surgeon in Arsal, sir,' he grinned.

Damn! Stupid question, I was showing my nerves.

'Right, well we'd best get on with it, let's go.' We climbed into the Toyota and headed back into town.

*

Talal parked in a side-street just off the square and I simply walked round the corner into the melee of arriving refugees and on into the 'hospital'. This was now something else again! The previous day I had seen the place coping with the tail end of an influx, now it was operating at full action stations. People were almost running between the extra beds which were being squeezed in along the walls. Surgical staff were moving from patient to patient selecting those most in need of immediate treatment and, no doubt, by-passing those they considered beyond help. This was a living lottery. I reminded myself that I was there to save those I could, not waste time on those I couldn't. I began casting round for a suitable candidate.

I was hopelessly spoiled for choice but one candidate, parked on a bed against the right hand wall, seemed to stand out in particular. A woman dressed in scrubs was already in attendance which suggested her patient was worth trying to help. There were drips already up and she was checking a blood pressure machine which implied that she was a nurse who could assist me rather than a doctor already in command. It was only as I approached that I could see the patient was a woman. She was lying on her side with her back to me. She wore the traditional black robe which had already been largely cut away along with the clothing beneath it. As I approached I prepared a suitably authoritative opening question.

'Qu'est-ce qui se passe ici?'

The nurse glanced back at me, clearly unimpressed by my command of French.

'This woman's been shot in the back. The bullet's gone clean through on the right hand side, but she's in a bad way. I've covered both wounds to stop the sucking. She looks cyanosed, but it's hard to tell with her complexion, and her b.p. is through the floor.'

I was hearing an American or Canadian accent but right then I didn't give a shit, at least I was hearing English!

'Sounds like a pneumo or haemo thorax, perhaps both. Okay, let's take a look. I'm Tony Stamford by the way.' The woman stepped back immediately to make room for me.

That was it, I was in! It was as easy as that! Nothing beats sounding knowledgeable. I stepped forward to make an examination, all trace of nerves gone.

'Sure, I'm Ariane. I think she may be in labour by the way.'

'I beg your pardon?'

'I think she might be in labour. I had to put her on her side to dress the bullet hole, but if you turn her over she's heavily pregnant. It's possible she's wet herself, but I think her waters have broken. '

'I see. Well the gunshot will have to come first.'

As I spoke I moved round the bed and bent down for a better look. Her lips were definitely tinged with blue and her breath was shallow and difficult. Her pupil dilated when I lifted her eyelid, but she showed little awareness. I straightened up and turned to Ariane.

'We'll lose her if we don't improve her breathing soon. We'll worry about the baby after. Where do you keep the syringes? Oh, and I'll need some gloves.'

She gave me a puzzled glance then bent down and picked

up a medical bag from the floor with the MSF logo stamped on the side. My heart sank. These were clearly standard issue for emergency triage. Even if I had forgotten mine I should still have known where the kit was kept.

'What size needles do you want?' she enquired.

'Biggest you've got.'

As she ferreted in her bag I checked the occlusive dressing on the woman's back. It was clearly not the first time Ariane had dealt with this kind of trauma. Assuming the wound was positioned centrally underneath it, the bullet had narrowly missed the lower inside of her right scapula. It was properly in place so, assuming the other one was as well, we were definitely looking at a collapsed lung and, looking at the queue for surgery at the end of the room, we couldn't wait to get proper drains inserted.

'Will twenty gauge do?'

'They'll have to. Here can you help me turn her onto her back.'

Ariane nodded and moved round opposite. Gently we eased her into the supine position. The exit wound was slightly higher, about two inches above the right nipple, as if she was stumbling or diving as the bullet hit. It was about four inches to the right of the sternum. There was no way of judging the scale of the damage without removing the dressing, but I doubted she would be breast-feeding her baby on that side if it lived. Again Ariane had done a neat, air-tight job so I concentrated on getting the needles in.

I moved her right arm up above her head and inspected the 'safe triangle' as it's known. Fortunately the wounds were over to the right. The woman had clearly been eating for two and was distinctly on the plump side. I would just have to hope that the needle was long enough to reach through this extra layer into the pleural cavity.

I unwrapped the first syringe then withdrew the plunger and set it aside. Dry as my mouth was I had managed to work up a dribble of spit which I now trickled into the syringe. With my left index finger I felt through the fat until I could feel the gap between the ribs, then used the tip as a guide as I slid the upper apical needle in. I need not have worried about my patient's extra poundage, almost immediately the spit began to bubble as air came hissing out. I detached the syringe and used the tape Ariane passed me to hold it in place.

I turned my attention to the basal drain. I selected a spot lower down her side so that I could angle the needle slightly up into any blood that had collected and let gravity help the drainage. I pushed the needle in up to the hilt and slightly withdrew the plunger, nothing. Okay, fat or no fat, it was in as far as it would go so either there was no haemothorax, or I was looking in the wrong place, or the needle was in too far. I said a quick prayer to Asclepius and pulled it out a centimetre, still nothing. I tried again and this time I got blood – an instant syringeful. Ariane handed me an emesis bowl which I placed under the syringe. I withdrew the plunger completely and held the syringe in place as blood came gushing out. The bowl filled rapidly and she handed me another. That began filling too, and then the flow slowed and stopped abruptly. I eased the needle further out and it started again. Good, it was possible the bleeding had stopped and I was simply draining the residual blood. What I wouldn't have given for an x-ray! Ariane took the second bowl to empty in the bucket someone had kindly left at the end of the bed and handed me back the first. By now the flow was down to a trickle and I was constantly adjusting the needle to keep it going. I gestured for Ariane to take over and straightened up to reassess my patient.

The difference was astonishing, not because the bluish tinge had gone and her breathing had returned, but because her face was now contorted with pain and her knees were drawn up as she feebly pushed and strained. She was having contractions. I was a surgeon not a midwife, but I had been present at the birth of my children and I knew that expression. Even as I watched, the effort drained out of her and she simply lay groaning, too weak to try any further. I turned to Ariane.

'We need to get her into surgery fast. She's not strong enough to give birth in this condition. She needs a caesarean or we'll lose her and the baby.'

Ariane nodded her agreement.

'Sure. The bleeding's stopped, d'you want me to check out where she is on the waiting list?'

'Great, and make sure to emphasise that this is an absolute priority.'

'Okay, give me a minute.' She hurried off towards the corridor at the end of the room.

I picked up a wrist. The pulse was worryingly weak, but I was even more worried about the weakness of my story. I didn't even have a stethoscope round my neck! There was only so far I could go pretending I had forgotten my medical bag. Still, I had at least done enough to prove I had a degree of surgical competence and she hadn't seen anything that had persuaded her to challenge that. I would just have run with the thing as far as I could and hope I succeeded in proving a point.

That set me thinking. I was a general surgeon not an obstetrician and I had never performed a caesarean in my life. Was I up to this? Obviously, I knew the general principles. Moreover, as a proctologist I had removed countless tumours and growths in the past and a foetus was certainly easier to locate and isolate than any of those. On the other hand no one gives a shit when a cancerous growth is destroyed. A baby and quite possibly the mother were at peril in this case and that turned it into a completely different kettle of fish. Then again, this wasn't St George's with a state-of-the-art gynie unit on call. I was probably as qualified as anyone else round here to do the job. Furthermore, I needed to impress someone a lot more senior than Nurse Ariane and, if I didn't run with this opportunity, I might not get another. Just as I reached this conclusion the lady in question returned with some good news.

'Mr King is just clearing his current patient and says under the circumstances we can go straight in.'

With that she kicked the brakes off the wheels and began to drag the bed out from the wall. I looked round for someone to help her, but there was no-one in evidence. When I looked back she was staring at me expectantly. I cursed myself as I grabbed the bed head and began heaving it round. Yet again I had shown a lack of awareness of what was expected of me.

'Sorry, just checking the best route through.' I added lamely.

*

Ariane mopped the woman's brow and squeezed her hand encouragingly as we waited for the previous patient to be wheeled out of theatre and down the corridor past us. There was nothing else we could do. I racked my brains for the name King, but nothing came to mind. Surgical medicine is a surprisingly small world thanks to the internet, but then he could belong to any country and branch of medicine in the world. Shame, a bit of professional recognition would not have come amiss. There again, at least he wasn't going to turn out to be a hated former rival from med school!

We got the nod and wheeled the bed into the same room I'd noted the day before. I was barely through the door when I knew things were wrong. Everyone in the room was staring at me except Ariane who was staring intently at something in the opposite corner, clearly embarrassed. A tall man in scrubs with his mask pulled down was standing in the middle of the room, his hands on his hips. He got straight to the point:

'Who the fuck are you?'

This was said in an unmistakable Australian accent with unmistakable Australian bluntness. I had expected to have to introduce myself, but not in the face of such overt hostility. I stepped forward and drew myself up in affront.

'My name's Tony Stamford...'

'And what makes you think you can invite yourself into my operating theatre without so much as a by-your-leave?'

'Well Nurse Ariane here said you were ready for us to...'

'I'm not talking about that! I want to know what the fuck you think you're doing here in the first place. Who the hell do you think you are inviting yourself in here when you're not a member of this mission?'

'Yes I am, it's just I came out at short notice and you haven't been notified as yet...'

'Nuts, I know every surgeon on this mission, including the reserves, and you're not one of them. I don't know you from Adam and I don't know how you got in here, but you can bloody well get out.'

'But...'

'No 'buts'! Out now, or I'll have you thrown out!'

I stood my ground a moment longer, but there was clearly nothing to be gained by defying this quite uncalled for aggression. Besides I had noticed a couple of hefty male nurses appear and were they were now positioned either side of me. With a last defiant 'You are making a serious mistake', I turned on my heel and strode out of the room.

*

'Come on Talal, pack up, we're out of here!'

Talal glanced up from his iPad, took one look at my expression and set about breaking camp. I have always prided myself on not taking out setbacks on my staff, but right then, it was as much as I could do not to kick him into action. Fortunately, no doubt thanks to his military training, he knew when to shut up and get on with things.

I had arranged to phone him once I knew what was happening at the hospital, but I'd left in such a temper that I had stormed all the way back to camp. The walk had done nothing to calm my growing indignation. How dare they throw me out like that? Who did this King fellow think he bloody well was? Hadn't I amply demonstrated that I knew what I was doing, that I wasn't just some bum or crank off the street? Were they seriously telling me that they didn't need all the help they could get? The questions simply kept piling one on top of the other. Why hadn't that bloody woman in Paris spelled it out clearly instead of smirking in that idiotic fashion and encouraging me to waste all this time and money on a wild goose chase? I glared at the shimmering heat haze and the shimmering heat haze glared back. A small voice in the back of my mind pointed out that she hadn't encouraged me to do anything, but I was in no mood to listen to that. Ungrateful bitch!

Talal interrupted my thoughts with a tactful cough.

'Where is it you wish to go, sir?'

'I don't know Talal, Beirut will do.'

In my anger I hadn't even thought that far ahead. I suppose it had never occurred to me that they would really turn me down, at least not in such a peremptory, high-handed fashion. Perhaps they wouldn't have let me jump straight in without checking me out and assessing my capabilities, but they could at least have given me a chance; particularly in the light of my handling of the haemo-pneumothorax!

To my displeasure another little voice made itself heard. What if I had been King? What would I have done if a surgeon I had never heard of had walked into my theatre in St George's and announced that he was going to operate on a patient under my care? Seen like that, I had to admit that his reaction had not been that unreasonable, in fact, it had been pretty much word-for-word what I would have said or shouted.

Before I could talk myself round to admitting that, in my desire to rebuild my career and my life, I had acted altogether too hastily and, indeed, even foolishly, I climbed into the Toyota and slammed the door.

'Drive!' I commanded the waiting Talal.

*

The Toyota rounded a bend. Ahead of us stood the unfinished mosque we had passed a couple of days previously on our way into town. The workmen were still there, although there was no sign of the two men we had spoken to. Some progress had clearly been made, a large tarpaulin had been rigged up above the building to serve as a temporary roof and there was now a row of what looked like army latrines where the men had been digging. People were being fed out of the back of a couple of vans bearing incomprehensible, squiggled, Arabic logos. Talal slowed to skirt round them.

'What do the signs on those vans say, Talal?' This was the first time I had spoken since we quit camp.

'Those are the emblems of the Ramzi Foundation that is undertaking this work, sir.'

'Really? You have a good memory for names.'

'It is not difficult sir. When you were looking in the building the tall gentleman gave me his business card.'

Talal reached into the breast pocket of his shirt and held up the item in question with a distinct air of self-satisfaction.

'Why did he do that?'

'I told him you are a doctor who is going to help the refugees and he said he was looking for doctors for this Ramzi Foundation.'

'He didn't mention that to me.'

Talal shrugged.

'That is not the Arab way, sir. He would not wish to interfere with plans you already had made, but he would trust in Allah to guide you to him if things did not work out as you desired. He asked me to give you this if that turned out to be the case.'

10

I lowered the iPad I had been working on as a particularly well-formed posterior swayed invitingly past. I was back in Beirut sitting at a poolside table in the Hilton Habtoor Grand again. I excused my brief lapse of concentration on my need to rest my eyes given that I had been staring at the screen virtually non-stop since my return three days earlier. This was laudable indeed, considering that the burka had clearly lost out hopelessly to the bikini amongst the hotel's cosmopolitan female guests.

My temper had cooled considerably since my abrupt departure from Arsal, but my pride was still smarting painfully. That, however, was no bad thing in that it had awakened in me a determination to steady down and plan things carefully this time.

I liked to think that my earlier rush to join MSF had been prompted by my desire to return to my calling, but there was no denying that it had also been prompted by my need to escape the clutches of Detective Inspector Newcombe. Now, I reminded myself that I had no need to worry about that. There was, to the best of my knowledge, no extradition treaty between Britain and Lebanon and even if there were, it would involve endless red tape. I would know what I was being charged with well before Newcombe could slap the cuffs on me. There really was no reason to rush into things beyond my lingering desire to show those hoity-toity bastards at MSF what Tony Stamford was really made of! That needed some careful thought and planning.

The trip to Arsal had turned out to be far from the monumental waste of time I had cursed it for as Talal and I began our drive back to Beirut. For a start, he had proved himself to be a very capable lieutenant rather than the willing man-servant I had recruited him to be. For another, it had provided me with a look, albeit a very brief one, at the workings of an international relief agency. What had struck me was that, from what I had seen, it would be far from impossible for me to set one up myself. Alright, it would be an impossible task to set one up on the scale of MSF – that had been built up over decades – but that was not what I had in mind. I just wanted something modest, a small field hospital, to prove my worth on and perhaps provide me with some sort of rehabilitation in the eyes of the medical world. Ideally, bang opposite the MSF building in Arsal town square.

What had also struck me was the surplus of non-MSF people who apparently always turned up in the wake of MSF. Alright, a proportion of them were undoubtedly not quite the full bottle of plasma, like the paramedical John the Baptist I had seen in the square, but there were no doubt others, such as myself, who were excluded by MSF due to circumstances irrelevant to their medical skills. I doubted if MSF were half so choosy in their early days but, in fairness to them, as organisations grow they always become more bureaucratic. Surely, with a bit of careful vetting, I could soon sort out a team that could be welded into an effective medical-surgical unit?

The third thing that had struck me was that all this would cost money and, thanks to Talal's grasp of the lingo, my Arsal visit had already put me in contact with an apparently wealthy Lebanese charitable foundation. This was unquestionably a long shot, but then why had the tall one given Talal his business card unless he saw something in me that might fit with his plans? If he was serious about helping to relieve the current crisis, he would surely want to listen to a proposition that would provide him, or his backers, with a fully operational field hospital? It was as this idea had taken root that I set up my poolside office to start drawing up lists of equipment staff and medication from which I could begin to figure out the sort of budget such a project would require. As a result, I was now poised to put my proposals to the test.

As the sylph-like body that owned the well-formed posterior dove gracefully into the far end of the pool I glanced at my watch, stretched, and began shutting down the iPad. It was time to get ready for my meeting with Dr Azzi and his silent companion.

*

Talal guided the limousine to a gentle halt outside an imposing building just off Nejme Square in the heart of Beirut's Central District. This, according to Talal in his latest role as my uniformed guide and chauffeur, was the business and government heart of the Lebanese capital. When I had queried the cost of our current transportation he had grinned and explained that cousin Fadi had sorted us out for a most reasonable consideration. I left him to park the limo and headed through the modern revolving doors into the elegant, thirties reception area. Before I could reach the desk a smart young man in a suit and tie appeared.

'Dr Stamford?'

'Yes, indeed.' I didn't bother to correct him regarding my medical title.

'Good afternoon sir. I am secretary to Minister Khoury. Would you come this way, sir?' With that he led me into a rickety-looking lift of the sort popular in Parisian hotels of the nineteen-thirties.

To be honest, I was a little at sea here. I had asked Talal to call the number on the business card the tall man had given him. According to the card the man's name was Doctor Azzi and he was a director of the Ramzi Foundation. Somehow I hadn't expected him to be operating from a government building containing a Minister. Still, no doubt all would become apparent in due course. As we rode up I tried fishing for a little more information.

'So this is a government building then?'

The young man nodded.

'Indeed, sir.'

'Does it house any particular ministry?'

'Yes sir.'

'Do you mind my asking which one?'

'No sir.'

At this point the carriage arrived at its destination with a slightly alarming clang. I gave up trying to learn more. The young man led me down a carpeted corridor and knocked at the end door. He opened it and guided me in.

Azzi rose from the table around which he had been sitting with his earlier plump companion and a man I had never seen before. He hurried over for another handshake.

'Dr Stamford, sir, you do us a great honour to spare us some of your most valuable time. Please allow me to introduce you to these gentlemen who are most eager to discuss the proposals you have sent us.'

This time the plump one stood up and moved in for a handshake as Azzi went on:

'This gentleman is our most esteemed founder and patron Sheikh Ibrahim Rezek. I'm afraid he speaks little English and therefore did not partake in our conversation the other day.' In contrast to our first meeting, the man was now dressed in full Arab costume, unlike Azzi who was sporting an ill-fitting, navy business suit.

'Please also let me introduce our Minister for Internal Affairs Mr Khoury.'

The other man remained seated behind the table. He nodded a curt greeting. 'You are very welcome to my country Dr Stamford.'

I nodded back.

'How do you do, nice to meet you.' I turned back to Azzi. 'I hope you don't mind my asking, but how does the Minister fit into all this?'

Azzi fixed me with an expansive smile.

'Please, before we turn to discussing business matters, allow me to offer you a cup of coffee...'

Before I could accept or refuse, he clapped his hands twice. The young man re-entered the room carrying a silver tray and deposited it on the floor between us. The silent sheikh picked up the elegant coffee jug and proceeded to pour a shot into each of the little cups as Azzi handed round a bowl of popcorn. As we sipped at the toxic brew I did my best to further assess my hosts.

Azzi, I decided, was pretty much an underling, but who was he answerable to: the Minister or the Sheikh, or both? On balance I reckoned the Sheikh. They had been together in Arsal and they were sitting together on the same side of the table opposite Khoury when I walked in.

For the time being I could see no reason to doubt the Doctor's description of the Sheik's role in this. I was no expert when it came to Arab apparel, but his clothing was clearly expensive and he had a taste for heavy gold jewellery. Good, let's hope his ostentation extended to funding the building of hospitals!

That left the Minister, Khoury. He sported a heavy moustache à la Saddam Hussein. In fact, he reminded me of pictures of the Dictator when he went on trial: tired and wasted. He wore a grey, silk suit and a collarless, white, silk shirt buttoned to the neck. I sensed that, whatever his agenda, he was the one that ultimately needed convincing. It was he who now brought the ceremonials to an end and got down to business.

'Dr Stamford, please let me extend the good wishes of my Ministry to you. I have read with great interest the document that you were kind enough to e-mail to Dr Azzi and I am pleased to inform you that my Ministry views it with true enthusiasm.'

'Good, I'm most flattered, but would you mind telling me what my proposal has got to do with your Ministry? With all due respect, it is an initial outline intended only for consideration by the representatives of the Ramzi Foundation.'

The man inclined his head in acknowledgement of my firmness.

'I apologise if you feel our involvement is a little premature Dr Stamford, but let me explain. Relations between my country and Syria are most severely strained at present; indeed, we are dangerously close to being on a war footing. Under the circumstances, no proposal such as yours could possibly come to fruition without prior approval from this Ministry. It seemed best for all parties concerned if this was made clear from the outset.'

'I fail to see why Sheikh Rezek and the Ramzi Foundation should not be free to fund a humanitarian project without government approval.'

'Sheikh Rezek would not wish this. He is a loyal patriot and sees no conflict in doing humanitarian works and acting in support of his government. Besides the Sheikh tells me that, due to his other humanitarian projects, he is only able to make available approximately half the funds your figures indicate are required to finance this undertaking.'

'Yes, but what happens when the project is called upon to go to the assistance of people his government disapproves of? I've already seen it. Your troops were fighting their own countrymen in Arsal the day I arrived there because they thought they were sheltering a spy! My organisation works on purely humanitarian principles. It has to remain independent of all partisan considerations.'

This was a bit rich, given that I didn't actually have an organisation, but it had a certain hauteur I rather liked. Besides I had gone to some trouble to create a plausible looking letterhead for myself by cutting and pasting in MediCal International, the name of the pharmaceutical company my late wife Liz worked for not so long ago. It had a medical ring and, if a bored clerk in Beirut bothered to do a check, there was a good chance the name Stamford would still be recognised by the computer sufficiently to convince him I had a real organisation behind me. So far no-one had shown the slightest inclination to question my credentials. My satisfaction with this reply was short-lived.

'In that case Dr Stamford, as attractive as your proposition undoubtedly is, I fear it is not something my department is able to consider. Now, if you'll excuse me for a moment...'

With that he rose abruptly and disappeared through a door I had not even noticed. I couldn't believe it! Surely he wasn't going to dismiss it out of hand? Come to that, what gave him the power to do so? I looked at Azzi in search of support, but he immediately looked away. No support there! Worse still I was sitting on a pile of bloody cushions. It's no easy matter standing up and exiting in high dudgeon from a cross-legged-on-the-floor position if you're not used to it, certainly not with any dignity. Since no-one had invited me to leave, I decided to sit and fight.

A couple of minutes later a toilet flushed and he reappeared. He sat down and looked at me questioningly. I wasn't sure if he was expecting a response, or surprised I was still there, so I pressed on:

'But surely humanitarian considerations should take precedence over temporary political disagreements no matter how serious?'

'I wish it were so, Dr Stamford, but just imagine if you will, the loss of life and misery that could be inflicted if an enemy agent succeeded in using your hospital to penetrate our security and, as a result, succeeded in planting a bomb here in our capital?

How would you address the suffering this terrorist would inflict on my people? The citizens of Beirut and Damascus have endured such hardships many times in our recent history and it is my duty to prevent them suffering more.'

The man had a point. Damn, what would an MSF representative have said in reply to that? I suppose they would just have gone ahead anyway and defied him to stop them, assuming they even found themselves talking to this man in the first place. But then they had the resources, they didn't need his help or funding. More importantly they weren't facing the possibility of a lengthy prison sentence if this bastard kicked them out of the country! So much for principles, perhaps it was time for a bit of good old British diplomacy.

'Yes, I see, you have a point. So what are you proposing? Some sort of vetting of patients as they enter or exit the hospital?'

Khoury paused to study me with his soulful eyes, as if to check that the bacillus was still on the slide, and then turned his attention to some intricately patterned drapes.

'I'm afraid it would not be quite as simple as that Dr Stamford.'

Damn he'd got me and he knew it!

'Then perhaps you would be kind enough to tell me what you have in mind?'

'Well we would wish for a secure facility to be attached to the building for the questioning and detention of any suspects...'

'What, some sort of prison wing?'

'No, no, nothing of the sort, just some sort of unit where we could carry out adequate vetting procedures away from the important humanitarian work you would be addressing.'

Jesus, what was I being asked to sanction here? Visions of a silk-carpeted interrogation unit sprang to mind! Still, he had a point about his need to counter the terrorist threat and at least we'd have the facilities to sew their thumbs back on when he'd finished with them! I nodded cautiously.

'Is that it?'

'Not quite.'

He turned to face me and his expression made it clear that his next demand was absolutely non-negotiable.

'If, as sadly seems most likely, the situation escalates to the point where our people are taking significant casualties, I would expect Lebanese citizens and especially Lebanese soldiers to be given priority over all other casualties.'

'In other words you are asking me to set up a military field hospital for you?'

'If you wish to put it like that and only if the situation demands it. Surely that is not too unreasonable a request?'

I paused for a moment to gather my thoughts. Ethics were all very well but, keen as I was to give MSF a poke in the eye, I was not in a strong position in the wider scheme of things. My ultimate objective had to be to stay out of Newcombe's clutches until he and his mysterious paymasters lost interest in me. Still, I wasn't going to give in without a fight.

'I'm sorry Minister, but what you are asking me to do is out of the question. My organisation would expect the same degree of autonomy and political independence as Médecins Sans Frontières, no more, no less.' I sat back to let him chew that one over. He didn't take long, in fact, no longer than it took to fix me with another baleful stare.

'Well, I hope you will forgive me (this was said in a tone which suggested that he really didn't give a shit either way), but I have done a little research into your background. Your record is indeed exemplary as a surgeon of the world-renowned St George's Hospital in London. However, my colleagues in our external security services have been unable to find any records of your employment with this pharmaceutical company MediCal International, though I understand your dead wife was employed by them. Nor can they find any record of your more recent employment with St George's Hospital. Furthermore it would appear a warrant for the apprehension of a doctor called Anthony Stamford, fitting your description exactly and quite recently released from prison, has been discreetly circulated across the main European security services. It is not for me to judge the correctness of this warrant, but I cannot see any immediate reason why I should harbour such a man who is of no apparent use to me, can you?'

My God, the bastard had gone straight for the jugular! I sat there mentally squirming as his cold eyes bored into me demanding an answer I didn't have. He left me gaping for a moment and then snapped: 'I tire of this nonsense! You have skills I require, I have the power to protect you from those you are currently fleeing from. If you disagree with my assessment and are unwilling to put your services at my disposal, I will have you immediately deported to London for your security services to greet you off the plane! Is that understood?'

I nodded dumbly.

'Yes Minister Khoury.'

*

The toilet flushed and he emerged again. Did Lebanese ministers associate victories with bowel movements? I was still sitting dazed by my ruthless recruitment. To my bewilderment his tone and tack had changed entirely. He sat down and lit a cigarette from an ornate silver box sitting centrally on the table in front of him. Then he leant forward and placed his elbows on the table almost confidingly. Finally he spoke.

'Dr Stamford, no matter what you might think given the current military activities you will have observed during your time here, my government is eager to avoid a military confrontation with our Syrian neighbours. Nevertheless we feel obliged to take sensible precautions in the event of such an unfortunate outcome. As you will observe from a most elementary examination of our country's geography, our key cities are situated to the western side of the country. This is undoubtedly due to the historical convenience of travel by sea to our foreign trading partners. As a result an attack from the east is not, at present, discouraged by the sort of significant body of people that would be represented by a large town or city. This causes us grave concern and we wish to find a solution. Our strategists believe that the town of Arsal could be developed into just such a discouragement at a time when the Syrian government is torn with its own internal strife. As part of this development it would be a most important priority to build a well-equipped hospital to provide for the needs of a considerably larger population.'

Not being of a military or political bent, I was in no position to pass judgement on the scheme, but I could see the sense of it. What better time to consolidate a border, or even expand a bit over it than when your neighbour was locked in civil war. I wondered just how Napoleonic this man's plans really were. Still that was none of my business.

'Yes, I can see the sense in that, but it's really not my field. I'm always keen to see a hospital being built of course,' I ventured.

He took a long drag on his cigarette and continued as if I hadn't spoken.

'It seems to me that, with the correct financial backing, it should be quite possible to use your experience and medical knowledge to develop this 'field hospital' you wish to build into the much more extensive facility that I believe will be needed to meet the needs of such a city, perhaps something not so different from your very own St Georges.'

'I beg your pardon?'

'There is no need. I have made this decision already and the contract is already being drawn up by my legal department.'

I sat back stunned. This was unbelievable! A moment ago I was about to be shipped home in chains; now, if my ears were to be believed, he was asking me to set up a state-of-the-art, money-no-object, modern European-style hospital for them! There had to be a catch.

'Do you mind my asking why you have not offered this project to a more mainstream hospital contractor, perhaps someone here in Beirut?'

Khoury inclined his head in acknowledgement of my caution.

'That is simply answered Dr Stamford. The need for secrecy

is paramount until as close to the time when plans for the new Arsal are unveiled. If the matter is put out to tender, our plans will be public knowledge within days if not hours. It is therefore felt advisable by my colleagues and me to put the planning and development of the project in the hands of a number of non-Lebanese consultants and agencies sworn to absolute secrecy. At the stage when plans are drawn up and all aspects of the operation such as medical suppliers and staff are in place, then we can call in suitable builders for the physical construction of the facility and indeed of Arsal, the third city of Lebanon!'

I noticed a distinct rise in the pitch of his voice and a definite gleam in those soulful eyes as he reached this conclusion. I couldn't help wondering which street in the new Arsal he planned to have named after himself. Still, who was I to complain, even if the thought of Lebanon's third city being designed by the Minister for Internal Affairs and his cronies made me wince.

As Azzi showed me to the door I watched my new boss disappear off to the loo again.

*

I was back beside the pool at the Hilton Habtoor Grand again and not a single gluteus maximus amongst the gorgeous selection on display was succeeding in distracting me from the lists of supplies and people I had spent the morning drawing up. I had left Khoury and Co on the understanding that we would reconvene in three days time, by which time I would have revised my estimates upwards to allow for the building of a modern, medium-sized hospital with the capacity to be rapidly expanded as the medical needs of Arsal grew. I was not to be concerned with the cost of land as a large area to the north-west of the town had already been compulsorily purchased from a local farmer. Khoury had explained this with that casual coldness of his that suggested that no money had changed hands.

My current indifference to the local totty was not the product of a new found love of logistics, but rather the swooning sensation that gripped me every time I tried to believe my luck! Suddenly, from what was threatening to become a position of all-time low, I found myself in charge of the construction of a bloody hospital! They hadn't even haggled about the two hundred grand I had tentatively suggested would suffice to employ my services. This had surprised me given the Arab reputation for barter, but Khoury had simply nodded and stressed in return the need for absolute secrecy. I even had the nasty feeling that I had under-priced myself!

The flip-side of my euphoria was the intrusive thought that I had never overseen the building of a hospital before, but I quickly put it aside by reminding myself that I had virtually lived in them for the last thirty years. I knew what they looked like and how they ran. Beyond that, I was used to managing medical people and now my recruitment radius would range well beyond the misfits and weirdos hanging around Arsal town square.

To get around my ignorance of the finer aspects of hospital design and construction, I had recommended to Khoury that, once I had drawn up a rough outline of the facility showing where the wards, clinics, operating theatres and admin rooms went, the real design work should be put in the hands of an international turnkey hospital architecture firm. I had read about these people in a Sunday supplement. Apparently, they could build and deliver a ready-made hospital on the moon for a fee – on reflection, a challenge not dissimilar to Arsal.

Naturally, I would be on hand to make amendments and oversee things as work progressed, but the idea was to erect a ready-made hospital overnight, giving no clues to its intended use. No doubt the press could be persuaded to suggest it would turn into a barracks or suchlike while the ground works were being put in place. When it opened it would simply be full of medical, instead of military, people and equipment and lost amongst all the other building work going on in the area. I stressed that turnkey hospitals didn't come cheap, but he seemed quite unfazed by that.

This solved the problem of my ignorance in the field of hospital construction, but left me concerned that I could end up looking badly under employed. Thankfully, by now, my juices were flowing and I found the answer to that staring me in the face. In order to recruit and train staff whilst the hospital was being built, why didn't I open a small facility along the lines I had described in my original proposal? I could divide my time between overseeing construction and saving the lives of refugees and war victims. I even had my eye on a site just across the square from MSF. With a cursory nod Khoury agreed this sensible arrangement and we all stood up for more hugs and kisses.

*

Now, sitting poolside, my one real bug-bear was medicinal and equipment supplies. When I had cautiously brought up the question of where the medicines, drugs and anaesthetics, as well as all the equipment would come from, Khoury had immediately turned back to his 'need for secrecy' hymn book and suggested I might want to look to 'outside suppliers' such as MediCal International with whom I clearly had 'most cordial relations'. Shit! The 'most cordial relations' I had with them amounted to the fact that my late wife had taken a job with them to assert her independence from me. I had already used their name in a somewhat misleading fashion, so I really didn't need to attract their attention any further. To really rub it in, he even went as far as to imply that my 'international connections' had played a significant part in my being offered this post.

In truth I had no experience of the wider world of medical supplies beyond what I read in the newspapers and the trade press. I knew it was all pretty ruthless with the big boys like Pfizer and Roche constantly at war with the non-branded merchants and the counterfeiters, but that didn't help at all. In fact, it left me with an overwhelming sensation of not knowing where to begin.

As a surgeon back in London, I was constantly bombarded with sales letters and brochures, most of which I ignored, preferring to rely on my own experience and listen to colleagues about what worked best, and relying on reps who had proved themselves over the years. Furthermore, I was only really familiar with the latest developments in the drugs I used as a colo-proctologist. I had a host of other specialists to refer to for anything else. I still relied largely on the trusty Harvard Apparatus surgical kit my mother had bought me as a graduation present. Everything else was disposable.

Now I was faced with a sea of equipment and pharmaceutical suppliers offering an ocean of medication and kit. Google offered page after page of companies some of whom, on closer inspection turned out to be suppliers of herbal remedies and kinky enema kits! I discovered a website which promised an insight into the NHS 'procurement process', but soon vanished into a fog of jargon explaining Standard, Planned and Blanket Purchase Orders.

It rapidly dawned on me that I needed help, but where from? Khoury had made it clear that secrecy was more important than cost and that tied in with buying outside Lebanon. Unfortunately, with Newcombe possibly on my trail clutching a summons for murder or manslaughter in his paw, I needed to steer well clear of Europe and even, possibly, America. The Far East was an option, but I didn't speak the language and had no contacts beyond the odd conference I had attended, usually with an eye to a bit of extra-marital research with my female co-attendees.

The longer I stared at my laptop screen, the more intractable the task seemed to become.

11

'Noch ein Bier, Sir?'

'Nein danke.'

I shook my head to reinforce my extremely limited German and took a break from the tension that was gripping me to watch in admiration as the cute Swiss waitress retreated back into the shade of the Bar Nocciolina on Zurich's Bleicherweg, a rather nondescript street in the capital's financial district. It was sunny and warm, even hot by European standards, but positively cool compared to Beirut. It was midday and I was sitting at a table on the pavement outside appreciating the contrast.

I tore my eyes from her retreating arse and asked myself for the hundredth time what the hell I thought I was doing here; it was an act of desperation which made my approach to the Ramzi Foundation look like the nec plus ultra of business stratagem. The truth was my attempts to source supplies for the Arsal clinic, let alone the proposed hospital, had run into an unyieldingly solid, brick wall. Poolside in Beirut I had finally come to the alarming conclusion that I had bitten off considerably more than I could chew. The more I researched the world of medical supplies, the more I began to appreciate that it was an arcane world in which I had no experience or clout. All I had learned was that organisations like the NHS had whole teams of people employed to monitor prices and employ short and long term strategies to negotiate deals on anything from paracetamols to brain scanners. That was a million miles away from what I did for living!

Thanks to Newcombe I didn't dare show my face in the countries where I was most likely to find what I needed, assuming I managed to work out what that was and how to buy it. Unfortunately the world of medical supplies left me no choice. The big players were based in America, Japan, or here in Switzerland. I was currently gambling like hell on getting away with a fleeting visit. Before I became entirely overwhelmed by this grim thought, I forced myself to focus on the problem that had brought me here. If I couldn't do the job, I had to find someone who could and I had two days before I was due back in front of Khoury to report on my progress. Khoury struck me as the sort of man who prided himself on kicking down brick walls and expected everyone else to.

Even as my heart sank at the thought of Khoury's displeasure, it occurred to me that Rome wasn't built in a day. The three day deadline was only for an initial progress report. All I needed was to be seen to have done something. In fact, the last thing I needed to do, and the last thing he would respect me for, was to run around like a blue-arsed fly every time he snapped his fingers! I needed to calm down and put myself in his shoes.

He was undoubtedly an ego-maniac with definite visions, if not delusions, of grandeur and he would respond to people who operated on a similar scale. Instead of claiming to do all the donkey work myself, it would make more sense if I went back and announced that I had identified and appointed a European broker to handle his vision's purchasing requirements. This sounded big. I could throw around names like Roche and Bayer on the pharmaceuticals front and Siemens and Drager on the equipment front. He would lap it up. But where was I going to find this broker? Suddenly, the idea began to fade before my eyes. I had never even known who was in charge of purchasing at St George's and I worked there for years!

That was back in the relative safety of Beirut. For the hundredth time I checked my watch and then glanced around for any suspicious characters before pulling out my wallet to check the address on the battered business card that had brought me to this street in Zurich. Finally, I threw some francs on the table and gathered my laptop for the short walk down the street to the address it bore. As I did so, a taxi pulled up at the curb beside me and a businessman type sporting a somewhat inappropriate sunhat and sunglasses got out. To my amazement he threw his arms open wide and exclaimed:

'Tony Stamford as I live and breathe! How the devil are you, sir?'

Before I could reply, he seized me by the arm and steered me forcibly into the back of the taxi, rattling off something in German as he followed me in. Moments later we were accelerating off down Bleicherweg leaving the Bar Nocciolina and the address on the business card rapidly behind.

I turned to my kidnapper as he peeled off the hat and glasses and I found myself facing someone very different from the man I had shaken hands with as we said our farewells on the landing back in Standford Open Prison. The ill-fitting prison fatigues were now replaced by a very expensive navy suit, silk shirt and crested tie and he was sporting a haircut that would have cost Warden Haskins a month's salary.

'Well Peter, you're looking much bonnier than last time I

saw you!' I exclaimed to cover my surprise. 'How did you know I was here?'

Chisholm grinned.

'Contacts old boy, contacts and lashings of the filthy lucre, I pay a chap in customs to tip me the wink if anyone who might be interesting comes through. Their computer pinged you, probably due to your current popularity with Interpol, and my secretary passed me the email.'

I tried not to let my alarm show in my face.

'So they know I'm here?'

'Sure, but they will have let you through to see where you go. Hopefully Jamila here will give them the slip.' He nodded at our rather gorgeous driver who was currently steering us down a narrow back street as if her life depended on it.

It struck me that Peter's security arrangements didn't come cheap, but then nor did the cologne he was wearing.

'So you're not actually based back there, then?'

'No, not since I last saw you. I decided it was time for a change, too many bad memories et al. We're based over at Oerlikon on the other side of town where the rents don't carry a health warning. We keep the Lindenhof address for image. Here, fancy a schnapps for old time's sakes?'

With that he opened the briefcase that had been sitting on the floor and produced two tot glasses and a bottle.

*

We had barely sat down when a call came through, so I took the opportunity to take a discreet glance at my surroundings. The decor was pleasing if somewhat disconcerting. The building itself was modern and, from my host's floor, offered an elevated view of an airport in the distance. The office was modern too, boasting several desks bearing computers with large wall-mounted screens, all filled with rows of inexplicable words and figures. People in casual office clothing were sitting in front of them talking rapidly into headphones. I didn't merit a second glance.

In contrast to this, the non-electric parts of the walls and other surfaces were adorned with an eccentric collection of odds and sods of what I judged to be African and Asian origin. There were masks and spears and hookahs, and a mannequin dressed in what I imagined to be the costume of an Indian prince. Chisholm replaced the phone and rose again:

'Sorry about that. Here come through here, it's more peaceful.' I followed him through a door into what was clearly his private office. This was kitted out with a western sofa, chairs and coffee table but hung with sumptuous silk drapes which I took to be Chinese in origins. My host was clearly a well-travelled man. He gestured for me to take a seat on the sofa and sank into an armchair opposite. We both waited as a svelte, young, black woman came in. It was Jamila, our recent driver bearing coffee and biscuits. As she handed him his cup he muttered something to her. As she departed he grinned.

'Always had a taste for foreign treasures, old boy. So, what brings you to Zurich?'

I had anticipated this question during my flight and decided to play my cards fairly close to my chest. Up to now the Peter Chisholm I had known was, to be blunt, a jail-bird with a fabulous line in what would probably turn out to be bullshit. Thankfully, what I had seen so far went some way to allay this concern: there really was no way that I could see that he could have known I was coming to see him, or even that I was in Zurich, without me having been spotted at the airport. That really was pretty sophisticated and therefore expensive surveillance!

Furthermore, my surroundings and the equipment and artefacts they contained could not be conjured up out of nowhere. This had not been laid on for my benefit. In fact, the more my surroundings sank in, the more encouraged I felt. The significance of the little things began to strike me more forcibly. His tales had mostly come from Africa and, insofar as I was able to judge, so had his ornaments. Those computer screens full of figures didn't mean much to me but they looked strikingly similar to the one's that cropped up in the background on Newsnight when Paxman was grilling someone about 'World Markets'. They looked precisely like the sort of kit an international commodities broker might employ. I turned to him with my well-rehearsed reply.

'Well, a medical conference actually. I was planning to look you up if I had the time...'

'And my cock's a carrot! Are you trying to tell me that you got off a flight from Beirut sporting a tan like Tutan-fucking-khamun and, on the way to some conference, just happened to park yourself in a café virtually opposite my old offices? Come on you devious bugger, spill the beans or fuck off. I'm a busy man!'

This was said with a grin that qualified its bluntness, but

threw me nevertheless. For the second time since I had known him he had shown himself able to read me like a book and I found it most disconcerting. I wasn't accustomed to being so flatly contradicted, particularly with such over-familiarity!

'Well, I...er...'

'Well, you want or need something, is that it? Don't look so alarmed, that's why people come to me. I don't waste my time on people who have nothing better to do than chew the fat. Come on out with it, what do you want?'

Somewhat to my chagrin, I realised that I had no choice but to put up with this badgering jocularity. I needed him more than he needed me, or at least he was a past master at giving that impression. I made my mind up.

'Okay, Peter, point taken! You're right, there is something I hope you can help me with.'

'Pray tell.'

'Well I've just picked up a contract to oversee the building of a hospital in Lebanon.'

'Really, I thought you were a surgeon not a bricks and mortar man?'

As he said this he produced a mobile and pressed a couple of buttons, nothing more.

'I am and that's the problem. The building side of things is easy, you can buy ready built and furnished hospitals off the shelf these days so I don't need any expertise for that. What I didn't expect was how complicated the equipment and medication side of things would turn out to be. It's not a field I've ever worked in. I've never touched a bedpan in my life.'

There was a knock at the door and his svelte secretary re-entered. She swayed over to Chisholm with a litheness that would not have shamed Grace Jones, murmured something in his ear, and then exited with equal felinity. Phew.

'Haven't you got any old chums at the place you used to work?'

I re-focussed with an effort.

'St George's? No, not really, we just used to let the admin department know our requirements and they passed it through to purchasing.'

'I see.' Chisholm paused to study me a little harder, and then seemed to make a decision. 'Tell me more.'

'Well they want this place built yesterday. They expect me back in Beirut tomorrow with a clear outline for how it's all going to happen.'

Chisholm greeted that with a dismissive wave of the hand.

'Yes, well they would, wouldn't they? That's par for the course. Tell me, who exactly are these people and what exactly do they want?'

'Well, my initial contact was with a charity called the Ramzi Foundation, but the organisation with its hand on the purse strings is the Lebanese Ministry for Internal Affairs, this is all mega hush-hush of course,' another dismissive wave from Chisholm, 'my contact there is a man called Khoury. They are talking about turning a village called Arsal into a large town or city overnight as a base from which to supply their eastern defences against Syria.'

My host leaned forward and picked up an iPad of some description. He played with it for a few moments.

'Is that A-R-S-A-l?'

'That's it.'

'It's not showing on Google Maps, not that that means much.'

'Well it exists. I was there a few days ago... in the Bekaa Valley. It's such a shit hole it probably doesn't appear on maps...'

'Ah ha, got it, there's a few pictures in Images. Christ, I see what you mean. They're going to have their work cut out turning that into a town, let alone a city, still, it's surprising what you can do with an army for cheap labour. Okay, so they want a hospital to go in their lovely new town or city and they want it fast so off-the-peg will do?'

'That's about it. Oh, and I've agreed, while they're putting in the ground works, to set up and run a field clinic to deal with current refugees. It seemed like a smart way of getting supply lines up and running and getting staff recruited.'

Chisholm nodded his approval.

'Hmmn, makes sense. Have you agreed a fee for all this?'

'Yes thanks.'

Chisholm raised his eyebrows at being told, in effect, to mind his own business, but accepted my reticence.

'Do you mind my asking if you have your agreement in writing?'

'Well no, not exactly, not at present, it's early days...'

'So what's to prevent matey-boy getting you to build his hospital then assigning your body to the sands of Araby?'

'He wouldn't do that!'

'Why not?'

'Well, because I am Tony Stamford MRCS. I am not a total bloody nobody you know!'

Chisholm threw back his head and laughed mockingly, and then grew serious.

'Oh come on Tony, Jamila just told me that you haven't worked for the NHS since you came out of Standford so you can bet your life your chum Khoury knows that too. He's a senior man in a national security ministry. He'll know your 'o' level results. I'm not saying he hasn't got your best interests at heart, but you don't get to be a senior man in anyone's national security ministry without listing Homicide under Hobbies and Interests on your C.V. Why shouldn't he save himself your mystery fee and guarantee the project extra security at a stroke?'

I sat there speechless. I really couldn't think of an answer to that. Chisholm continued:

'It seems to me, my old China, that you need a lot more than a bit of advice on where to buy your toys from. Take it from me, you can't trust these ragheads further than you can throw 'em.'

I found my voice.

'So what do you suggest?'

'Well it's probably not as bad as I am making it sound if you handle it properly...'

'You mean you think I should go ahead with this deal given what you've just said?'

'Sure, why not? It sounds bloody lucrative. There's no reason not to do business with these people provided you know what you're doing.'

'And what makes you think I don't?'

'Well, what you've just said really, plus what I know about you from our conversations in prison. Let's face it, St Georges Tooting, with all its protocols and sanitation, is hardly life on the front line. NHS hospital politics is not Beirut real politic; Tooting sounds like somewhere out of Thomas the Tank Engine not a constantly war-torn Middle-Eastern state. Back in Blighty, you medicos are deliberately sheltered from the harsh realities to allow you to get on with mending the whinging masses...'

'Rubbish, we deal with death and disease and disfigurement on a daily basis!'

'True, in a sterilised, anaesthetised environment. When did you last see a man made to dance on his stumps or a pregnant woman bayoneted against a telegraph pole?'

'Well certainly not in Lebanon...' I retorted feebly.

He shook his head.

'Perhaps not since you've been there, but just you wait until it really kicks off. Besides that is not my point. I am simply trying to make you appreciate that you are moving in a world here where the rules you take for granted simply do not apply. Furthermore, you are likely to get no warning as to when the people you are dealing with have stopped applying them.'

'So what do you do about that?'

'You never let yourself become 'exposed'.'

He gestured the inverted commas with his index fingers.

''Exposed', what do you mean?'

'Well, in simple terms you never get in a position where they owe you money. If they don't owe you anything they have no reason to kill you so you insist on everything up front.'

'Will they fall for that?'

'If they want their hospital, they'll bloody well have to. If they can't or won't front up the cash, it's either because they haven't got it, or don't intend to pay it. Either way they aren't worth doing business with and it's best to walk away now. If, on the other hand, they come up with the filthy lucre, we can take them for a right little waltz round the block.'

'What do you mean?'

'Well the trick in these situations is to stay light on your toes. These deals almost never come to fruition; war is too fickle. One minute Armageddon is kicking off and the country is on standby, then the politicos reach some agreement and everyone's stood down while pacts of peace and love are signed. Fucking nuisance to people in my line of business, but we survive by getting cash up front and ducking and diving...'

I held my hand up.

'Hold on a minute Peter, before we take this any further, do you mind my asking exactly what is your current line of business?'

He stopped in mid-sentence, clearly surprised by the question.

'What do you mean?'

'Well you just used the word Armageddon. You said yourself that I am out of my depth and this sounds like I'm about to sink further. You described yourself to me back in prison as an 'international commodities broker'. Do you mind my asking what commodities you deal in?'

Chisholm leant back in his armchair and stared, unseeingly at a porcelain vase on the table as he considered his reply. Finally, he took out his mobile again and redialled, then looked up to stare me straight in the eye.

'Okay Tony, good question and I don't have time to answer it right now. If we are to be partners in this thing, and I recommend strongly for your sake that we are, then I think it's only fair that I answer it properly. In fact, I reckon it wouldn't be a bad idea if I filled you in a little more on my background and also on the new direction I decided to take during my stay in Standford Hill. I think you might find it rather interesting under the circumstances. How about dinner this evening?'

It was my turn to pause.

'I'd like that very much if I weren't due to catch a plane to Beirut at eight.'

He broke into a grin.

'Lesson one, Tony, brinkmanship: when it comes to negotiating, particularly with Ragheads, the longer they wait, the more they want.' He paused to savour this bon mot a moment and then repeated it: 'The longer they wait, the more they want.'

His secretary entered like a stalking panther.

'Ah, Jamila, be a love and book us at table at the Glockenhof for eight and book a room for Tony while you're at it.'

He turned to me.

'You go ahead, Jamila will call a cab for you. I've still got a bit to do here, but I'll see you in the terrace bar at seven. In the meantime, send your chum Khoury an email telling him you have identified several suppliers and are locked in high-level negotiations and won't be back for at least a week. That should get the bugger jerking off!'

12

We were sitting enjoying a postprandial glass of wine in the civilised elegance of the Hotel Glockenhof's garden restaurant.

'Don't get me wrong old boy, I ain't suffering from a crisis of conscience and the hospitality of Her Majesty's open prison, Standford Hill did absolutely nothing to show me the error of my ways. In fact, if anything, it proved the rightness of them. What on Earth's the point of a prison run by a bunch of lily-livered pansies? How's that going to straighten out the bad boys? Still, what d'you expect from a nanny-state with that wet little spiv Cameron and his Old-Etonian arse bandits in charge?'

'First time I've heard the current Conservatives called wet.'

'That's because you don't know any different.'

'Is that why you live abroad?'

'Too right, and the tax of course. Why should I hand over my hard-earned cash so that those jumped-up little pricks can squander it on the Great Unwashed?'

As a lecture in unbridled, dog-eat-dog capitalism my companion's diatribe was hard to beat. As a Tory by birth I was not unaccustomed, or even opposed to such views, but I always found them a little hard to square with my membership of one of the caring professions, let alone the salary I had been used to earning from the said 'nanny state'.

'So, if you are not a reformed character thanks to the UK penal system, what has made you decide to mend your ways?'

'Amend, not 'mend' old boy, and the answer is old age.

Those tossers from Customs would never have caught me behind a desk in my younger days. In the good old days I'd have been with the ship and jumped for a getaway boat from the deck. Besides, if they'd caught me, I'd have escaped. Instead I've just spent a couple of my valuable remaining years sitting in nick boring all and sundry with tired old anecdotes. I won't be doing that again in a hurry.' Peter paused and grinned. 'Even then, the crew managed to dump the really naughty kit and I only got nabbed for tax evasion. How's the Schnitzel?'

'Fine thanks. So nowadays you're only interested in business ventures that profit from war instead of actually conducting war?'

'Bingo! Couldn't have put it better myself and there's nothing like medicine for that, the two go hand in hand.'

'I wouldn't say that...'

'Oh come off it man! Read your history books. War has always been the cauldron for medicine, particularly in your line of business. Surgery started on battlefields going right back to the Romans and probably before.'

'Alright, I take your point, so if you are interested in helping set up this hospital and supplying it, how do you see that working in practice?'

'I'm not interested in setting it up, just supplying it. If we're going to walk away from this rich and healthy, it's imperative that I stay completely invisible.'

'Why?'

'Because the first thing your Mr Khoury is going to do is to try and get to me direct and cut you out.'

'Given what you've said, I'm not sure that wouldn't suit me down to the ground.'

'Oh come on now Tony, where's your sense of adventure? With me unapproachable you'll be safe enough; as long as everything has to go through you you'll be flavour of the month. You told me back in Standford that your wife had dumped you and you'd lost your job, here's your chance to make a really fresh start. You were keen enough until I told you there could be a few risks attached.'

I shrugged.

'Perhaps I don't share your Boys Own outlook on life, but maybe you're right. I could certainly do with the lolly. What sort of split would you be looking at?'

'I dunno, how about seventy-thirty after costs?'

'What seventy to me?'

'No way, old chum, t'other way round...'

'You have got to be kidding! You sit in your comfy office in Zurich making a few phone calls, or getting your minions to, whilst I run around a war zone in peril of being double-crossed and murdered by a thug from Lebanese Security and you want the lion's share? What d'you take me for, a raving simpleton?'

'Far from it, a little unworldly perhaps, but hardly a simpleton, let me explain the way these things are viewed in the grown-up world. Sure, you are taking a more immediate physical risk than me, but then one of us could be run over tomorrow. Danger's too random to be quantifiable in business terms. Investment risk is the real yardstick. It can be assessed on tangible criteria based on supply and demand and probable returns. In business the one putting up the cash is always seen as the main risk taker. As an old pal of mine used to say, money talks, bullshit walks.'

'So what cash are you being asked to put up here?'

'Well this is going to need at least a four man buying team for a start, but, assuming I'm willing to absorb that, there's no way any European or American drug companies are going to give credit to a company supplying a hospital in a potential war zone, so I'm going to have to upfront the cost of the meds and bandages etcetera, etcetera.'

'Surely it's up to Khoury to do that, you said yourself that we wouldn't give him credit...'

'We won't, but he is hardly going to hand over large amounts of money to you and me without the goods in plain view. He's going to want everything checked and inventoried before money changes hands and he'll demand that takes place in Beirut. That suits us because it keeps me out of the picture.'

'What's to stop him relieving me of it unpaid at that point?'

'Because he won't get any more if he does, which is where I'm taking the big risk. I am betting on him needing a steady stream of deliveries, not just a one-off, and I am also gambling on his lovely new hospital not being blown off the map the day after it opens. All I can do to mitigate that is to not give him everything in one hit, which is why I need to hide behind you. That way we can jerk him around because, when he doesn't get quite what he wants, you can shrug and blame your mystery supplier, me.'

I sat back somewhat stumped. This was a world in which ethics clearly had no place whatsoever. I clearly needed to toughen up or get out. How keen was I to get involved in 'jerking around' a man whom I suspect would have no hesitation in having me buried up to my neck in 'the sands of Araby'? Fortunately, at that moment, a shapely blonde in a black skirt and crisp white blouse approached, giving me a chance to think.

'Is everything to your satisfaction Peter?'

My companion nodded.

'Yes thanks Nicole, can you ask Dominic to bring us coffee and a bottle of schnapps? Oh, and put this on my tab will you?'

'Of course Peter, will that be all?'

'Yes thanks, for the time being.'

She smiled in a way that stirred more than my thirst for coffee and schnapps, and departed.

'You seem very well known here...' I ventured.

Peter smiled.

'I live here.'

'Really?' I gazed around with fresh eyes at my opulent surroundings, 'it must cost you a pretty penny...'

'It's not cheap, but they do me a deal as a long-term resident and I attract a fair few customers for them. Besides I don't have to pay a cleaner or a gardener. It suits me very well since I gave Patsy the boot.'

'Patsy?'

'My ex-wife. Came home one day and found her in bed with Jamila. Stood 'em next to each other and Jamila won hands down so poor old Patsy got the boot for her infidelity and I've been a single man ever since. Cheers.'

He raised the remains of his glass of wine and resumed:

'So have we got a deal then?'

I smiled back.

'No.'

'I beg your pardon?'

'I said no. You may think I'm a little unworldly, but I'm not as green as grass. For one thing you're too keen to close this deal so you've got to be trying it on. Besides I don't care how you assess risk. I've had the opportunity to assess Khoury in person and I really do not feel safe in his company. It's my balls on the anvil and, frankly it's a very uncomfortable feeling. Everything you've said simply goes to making it worse. Besides, if you can afford to live here, you don't need the cash as much as I do.'

This time Chisholm really grinned and even nodded in acknowledgement of my point.

'Jolly good, the last thing I need is a gullible idiot for a business partner. So what do you suggest?'

'I suggest you deal with the financial risk and I'll deal with Khoury and we split the profits fifty-fifty.'

I thought for a moment that he was going to come back at me with sixty-forty, but instead, after a thoughtful pause, he leant forward and filled the two shot glasses Dominic had just deposited on the table along with a bottle of schnapps. He handed one to me and raised the other.

'Fair enough old fella, you've got a deal.'

*

As I wound my way down the spectacular Gottardo Pass I was feeling distinctly jaded, despite the uplifting glow of the glorious autumnal sunshine. In fact, the glaring sunlight and vertiginous drops were only adding to my throbbing headache and general queasiness notwithstanding the tinted windows and feather-bed ride of the BMW Z4 Roadster that Peter had lent me. I spotted a roadside café up ahead and pulled in for a much needed pee and coffee break.

We had celebrated our new business partnership with several more shots of schnapps at the Hotel Glockenhof, and then departed for a nightclub in the company of Jamila and another dusky maiden, Adanna, whom she described as her sister. I wasn't sure if this qualified her as a blood relation or simply of African origin. I didn't give a damn. She was stunning. I decided on the spot that it was about time to put an end to my recent abstinence and, as it turned out, she raised no objection. The upshot of this was that I hadn't had a chance to sleep the schnapps off. Much the same had happened the following night.

Now, two days later, I was driving down to Turin on Peter's insistence. He had suggested that I had time to kill before showing my face back in Beirut and that it was important to have an alibi for my visit to Zurich. When I remarked that this seemed a little unnecessary, he pointed out that I had been followed off the plane on my arrival and tracked as far as the Bar Nocciolina, hence the sudden, dramatic pick up. Shocked, I enquired as to the nationality of my pursuer whom he informed me looked Arabic. I breathed a private sigh of relief. I didn't explain the reason for my enquiry, but the ghost of Detective-Sergeant Newcombe had just walked over my grave.

Peter went on to explain that, if Khoury asked, I should tell him that I had called in on an old colleague in Zurich who had contacts in the pharmaceutical industry and, after a couple of days R&R, he had referred me on to a contact in Turin. This contact was an international medical supplies broker who could supply everything I needed for both the field clinic and the general hospital. He gave me a name, Torino Farmaceutico Internazionale S.p.A, and an address in Turin that I could give to Khoury who would find out that it was a general trading company registered in Luxemburg and not a lot else. That would be the 'cut-out' between the two of us. The front man for this was a Mr Macari who had been warned to expect me.

It was just after one when I by-passed Milan and hit the autostrada westbound for Turin. By now the edelweiss and cow bells were history and I was locked in the unrelenting struggle for survival known as Italian driving. Given the excesses of the previous two days this was like sitting in the Hadron Collider listening to a Stradivarius being sawn in two. As I reached the outskirts of Turin, I decided that my frayed nervous system had had enough and pulled in at one of those ghastly motels that cater for reps and builders the world over. I booked a room for the night simply to have a relatively secure place to park Peter's BMW while I caught a taxi into town.

The office was on the second floor of a purpose-built block on a street called the Via Egeo; Egeo was presumably Italian for 'nondescript'. The bored receptionist directed me to the lift which opened onto a floor that accommodated a number of offices. Etched on the glass window of the third office I came to was Torino Farmaceutico Internazionale S.p.A. Pinned to the door below the window was an envelope addressed to me. It contained a note from Mr Macari explaining that he had gone to lunch and would be back around three unless I cared to join him. Apparently he could be found at the Ristorante

Baglioni which was 'best familiar to the taxi'. I cursed myself for dismissing my taxi, but decided there was no way I was going to hang around a faceless office block waiting for some bloody wop to finish feeding his face!

In fairness the restaurant was quite close by and was, indeed, 'familiar' to the driver summoned by the bored receptionist. As a result I found myself shortly in the company of my host Mr Macari. He treated me to a limp handshake and a 'Salve, salve' muffled by a mouthful of pasta, then returned to the task of enlarging his already ample girth. In the absence of any conversation I indicated to the waiter that I would have what my companion was having, and then set about a carafe of vino bianco to wash away the dregs of my hangover. Gradually I mellowed until even Macari's slobbering became tolerable.

Eventually, my host decided he was sufficiently gorged and licked his lips to check for any remaining morsels before dabbing them delicately with his napkin. He would have had greater success if he had licked the front of his shirt, but his double chins prevented that. He belched with an air of great satisfaction, and then treated himself to a swig of wine which he used partly to rinse his mouth with before swallowing.

Discouraged by this gross performance, and my own currently delicate digestive system, I picked at the creamy chicken concoction the waiter had deposited in front of me. Finally, my host deigned to speak.

'So you is 'aving the good journeys?'

In fairness, his English was better than my Italian, but not by a massive amount. Still, in the wider scheme of things, it would make life more difficult for any eavesdropping Syrians.

'Very good thank you.'

He nodded and lapsed back into silence, apparently satisfied that he had made an adequate contribution to the niceties. Was that it? The man was hardly the international commodities trader I had been expecting. He was more like some second tier Mafiosi gone to seed. The sort who turned up to beg favours of Marlon Brando in The Godfather. I won't attempt to render his almost impenetrable accent further.

'So those are your offices in Via Egeo?' I ventured, feeling obliged to take up the baton.

He shrugged.

'Sometime.' He pulled out a mobile and put it on the laptop beside him, then gestured towards them. 'This real office,' he added confidingly, and then sat back as if I was now conversant with his entire business operation. I began to appreciate that the challenge of communicating with Mr Macari was not confined to wrestling with his thick accent.

'Oh,' I said, at a loss for a response. A silence descended which he seemed quite impervious to, so I concentrated on my pasta for a while. When I ran out of that, I tried again. 'Mr Macari, do you happen to know why our mutual acquaintance Mr Chisholm felt it would be a good idea for me to visit you here?'

My companion signalled the waiter and after a rapid conversation which featured the word 'formaggio' – Italian for cheese if my memory served me right – finally deigned to reply.

'You must send the emails to this man Khoury from here. You are saying you meet me for business purpose which is good, okay? This must be from computer in my office you understand?'

'Why couldn't you have sent it on my behalf and saved me the journey?' I was suddenly rather interested in his response – I had not expected him to know or recall Khoury's name.

He shook his head.

'Not possible. 'He must see you are here.'

'How will he do that?'

'He will send spy. You must stay for two day so spy will see you here and tell his boss Khoury.'

'Oh, right, I see.' It was my turn to lapse into silence.

*

'D'you think that's him?'

It was three days after my arrival in Turin and we were sitting in the Ristorante Baglioni. Macari was about to consume yet another olive and I was about to lose yet another game of backgammon. He looked up from the board and followed my gaze across the room. He shook his head, but I persisted.

'How d'you know?'

'Khoury man here yesterday.'

'Really, why didn't you say?'

Macari popped the olive into his mouth and chewed it thoughtfully before spitting the stone on the floor and replying.

'You gone home before I go to office and check him out.'

'You didn't mention it this morning.' He nodded his agreement to this implied criticism, and then returned to studying the backgammon board as if I hadn't made it. Lugubrious was not the word!

I paused to watch him polish off the game, still baffled at

his consistent ability to win a game which appeared to depend largely on chance. I had 'A' levels in maths and physics for God's sake!

'So who's that then?'

Macari sat back from the table and glanced again at the man on the other side of the room.

'Dunno, maybe he is a customer of ristorante.'

The rolls of fat under his chin wobbled briefly as my failure to grasp the obvious amused him. For a moment I felt a strong urge to slip my fork under the table and watch his fat wobble as I stuck it in his thigh. To be honest, the pleasure of his company was wearing thin, limited as it was to sitting in his office playing backgammon and listening to him field phone calls, or sitting in the restaurant playing backgammon and watching him eat meals.

'So I'm free to return to Beirut?'

'Sure, you have seat on plane at eight-thirty tomorrow in morning.'

'Really, right, is there any reason why I couldn't depart today?'

My host shrugged regretfully.

'It is not so good. I am waiting for some information from Zurich.'

'What sort of information?'

'Some prices for medicines and things for you to show this man Khoury. This will make him very happy, yes?'

'Yes, certainly, I'm sure it will, and these will be ready for me by tomorrow?'

'Indeed this is so.' Macari nodded complacently and helped himself to another handful of olives.

I called for the waiter to bring the dessert menu. He held up a finger and tossed a curt 'un momento,' as he hurried across the room and presented the bill to a man in the far corner. I turned back to Macari then performed a perfect double take. My God, I knew the fellow! It was that creepy spook Parsons from all those years ago in Docklands. It couldn't be, but the harder I looked the more certain I became that it was. Gone was the 'Oxford don in an ill-fitting suit look', but it was him alright. What the hell was a random character from my dim and distant doing sitting in a poxy little cafe on the outskirts of Turin? The odds against were incredible!

Still, he was and I felt my temper rising rapidly. That particular episode had led to my divorce and imprisonment! Then again, I reminded myself that that had really not been Parson's fault; I had simply swallowed a red herring largely thanks to that wanker Roger. With an effort I got a grip on myself. Macari must have noticed my agitated condition because his eyes followed mine.

'So you know Mr Parson's?'

'Know him, too right I know him. The man owes me money and I'd like to know what the bloody hell he's doing here!' Suddenly the distinct paranoia I had felt throughout my trip had seized me by the throat. Who the hell was this man?

I threw down my napkin and made to get up but Macari grabbed my arm to stop me.

'Please be calm my fren'!',' he muttered.

'What,' I tried to prize his hand away from mine but he had me in an iron grip.

'We are family eh? I work with Peter Chisholm, you work

with Peter Chisholm and so does Signor Parsons. We are family. Family doesn't fall out.'

That took the wind out my sails completely. Macari knew this fellow and seemed to think we were all on the same side! After a pause, he let go of my hand. Seeing my confusion he took pity on me and decided to elaborate.

'Parsons is a contractor no? He does a bit of this and a bit of that for your intelligence services. He is, how do you say…non affiliati. Parson's works both sides of the fence, is only natural.'

Parsons had signed his bill and was leaving in our direction. Macari rose to greet him and enveloped him in a slobbering embrace. Finally, Macari broke his unhygienic hug and gestured toward me:

'Is my fren' Signor Tony.'

Parson's, smiling warily, stuck out his hand. I rose pointedly ignoring the gesture.

'I don't suppose you remember me Parsons…' I began coldly.

'On the contrary Mr Stamford, it is Mr isn't it and not Doctor?' his hand remained outstretched until, against my better judgement, I took it, 'I hear on the grapevine we now share a mutual acquaintance. No hard feelings about the Katya business. If it makes you feel any better we netted half a dozen politicians, chief executives, bankers, even one or two upstanding members of the clergy. You're in good company and if I might be so bold as to say you got off rather lightly, we milked some of them for exorbitant amounts; really made their eyes water.'

I was lost for words. The man seemed to think it was all a game! I finally managed to find my tongue and spluttered, 'was Roger party to all this?'

'Roger?' Parsons fished around trying to place the name. 'Oh yes, the bottom feeding solicitor from Barnes. Yes he was helpful. Took his cut as we knew he would. He wasn't party to the workings but brought us a steady stream of clients.' Parson's patted me on the shoulder. 'Good to see you on our side of the fence Mr Stamford, you're in safe hands with Peter, he'll make you a ton of cash. Hopefully, I'll see you around.' With that he gave me a friendly nod and strolled out of the restaurant.

*

I spent the evening in the motel bar sipping Diet Coke. I had consumed enough alcohol in the company of Peter and Mr Macari over the last few days to float a fleet of battleships and I suspected I was going to need a clear head over the next few days to conduct business with the menacing Khoury. Particularly if I did not want to end up buried in the remoter 'sands of Araby'. Besides I needed a clear head right now to try and assess my situation to-date.

To be frank, I was not entirely happy with it. True, I had apparently fallen on my feet in the light of my rejection by MSF. Better still, I had found a position which did not involve my return to the UK until I could be sure that I was not wanted for murder there. I had even managed a flit back into Europe and, assuming nothing happened at the airport tomorrow, I would appear to have gotten away with it. From here on I could hopefully leave Peter to handle things in EEC countries and stay beyond the reach of the long arm of the UK law. So, on paper, things were looking up, except that they weren't.

What was troubling me was the nature of the people I was doing business with. If first impressions were anything to go by, Khoury was an old boy of Beirut's leading borstal and my chums from the Ramzi Foundation were motivated more by their tax laws than humanitarian considerations.

If that wasn't bad enough, I was equally troubled by the people I had just recruited to meet their requirements. Fair enough, going back to my time in Standford, I was aware of Peter's somewhat chequered past, indeed it was partly what attracted me to him. If I was to stand up to the likes of Khoury, it made sense to have worldly people on my side. But how far could I trust him? I'd met him in prison after all and he still professed scant regard for the law or even conventional morality. In fact, especially conventional morality!

As for my latest acquaintance, Mr Macari, where did you begin with him? Did I even believe that ridiculous Mafia accent straight out of Central Casting? If ever there was a sleaze ball it had to be him, and yet Peter had entrusted me to his care. A little bird told me that I was in the process of being led by the nose into a world that I neither knew nor understood. In the presence of Macari I felt like the member of the audience who is selected by the conjuror to stand and look baffled as he pulls rabbits out of hats. The question was to what degree was I prepared to stand there marvelling at his dexterity?

The more I thought about it, the more I felt that, when I stepped into Peter's taxi in Zurich, I had crossed an invisible Rubicon, but unlike Caesar, I had no idea of what lay ahead. At least he only had to capture Rome!

In fact, I had no proof that Macari and I had even been

spied on. I only had his word for it. More importantly, how had I found myself back in a world where such a notion was even plausible? Past experience taught me that I was no good at this sort of thing, so why was I getting drawn into it again? But then past experience also taught me that we are not the masters of our own destiny we like to kid ourselves we are. My bitch of a late wife and her psycho lover had stitched me up more thoroughly than even they probably ever imagined and, as long as the ghost of D.S. Newcombe continued to haunt me, that would doubtless continue to be the case. In the meantime, I concluded, I had little choice but to go with the flow and hope that my new found business partners' interests continued to coincide with mine.

Finally, I ordered a large scotch to mix with the last of my coke. As nightcaps go, it was not a success.

13

It was just after nine the following evening when Talal met me off the plane at Rafik Hariri Airport. I was rather surprised at how glad I was to see him. I noticed with approval that he had swapped his chauffeur's uniform for a smart dark blue business suit, white shirt and grey silk tie. As my new Director of Finance he needed to look the part. He introduced me to his nephew Mahmoud who looked a little swamped in the aforesaid uniform and barely old enough to hold a driver's licence, but I let it pass. Despite the hour, we bypassed the Hilton and headed straight for the docks.

As we rode through the chaos of Beiruti evening traffic Talal explained the progress he had been making at his end. This had largely involved organising the import side of things under guidance from Peter via MSN while I was killing time in Turin. He was clearly greatly impressed by Peter's business acumen and savoir faire and positively blown away by what he could make out on-screen of Jamila.

Peter had already given me several tutorials back in Zurich on how I was going to need to conduct matters in Lebanon. These were all really aimed at controlling the power-play that he predicted would develop between Khoury and me. To this end he had explained that I needed an utterly reliable second-in-command who could be trusted to run the import of the medicines and equipment for the clinic and the hospital. He had been a little sceptical when I suggested Talal, but warmed to the idea as I explained how useful he had already been, his endless supply of relatives and his innate common sense.

When I mentioned his former military background, he really sat up and took notice. Did he still have any contacts there? How long had he been out? When I replied that I didn't know and pointed out that he was hardly likely to be able to recruit a force capable of opposing the sort of thugs Khoury no doubt had at his disposal, he shook his head impatiently and explained that it was all about front. Our people would not be there to oppose Khoury but simply to retain security under our control. If we already had security in place, Khoury couldn't infiltrate our set-up by insisting on 'helping' us by supplying his.

It made sense and, in fact, reminded me distinctly of the sort of power plays that used to go on at St George's except that those didn't tend to involve guns. I certainly recognised the jostling for control and status. Somewhat to my surprise, I found myself rather relishing the prospect.

The upshot of this was that Talal had been sent out on a recruitment/shopping spree and I was about to inspect the results. The car turned into the docks which were bathed in artificial daylight as trucks and forklifts trundled here and there between cranes, gantries and warehouses. Multi-coloured containers were stacked six or more high in endless rows. It was daunting but exciting to say the least.

His main shopping, under Peter's guidance, was the rental of a small bonded warehouse near Quay 14, away from the hubbub of what appeared to be a huge quay given over to containers. He explained that we were renting this from the port authority until our real needs could be assessed. In the meantime, this would be the place at which Khoury's minions would be given the chance to inspect and sign off the supplies for the field clinic and the hospital.

As we pulled up outside, I was immediately struck by the appearance of two plump, middle-aged men in uniform, one hefting a sturdy looking baton while the other struggled to control a particularly vicious Alsatian which clearly resented the short leash he held it back with. Talal explained that they were the front-line of our new security set-up. He had a brief chat with the two men who snapped smart salutes in my direction, then led me inside as they continued their patrol. I subconsciously christened them The Two Abduls.

Inside was pretty unremarkable. There was a certain amount of litter and junk courtesy of the previous occupants. Talal explained that workmen were turning up the next day to clear that. The only object of real interest was a standard shipping container which stood occupying the right-hand side of the centre of the room. It had obviously been treated to a new coat of yellow paint on which was emblazoned the legend Chisford Holdings International in white lettering on a dark blue disk – a logo Peter and I had arrived at after a great deal of drink-fuelled deliberation during my second evening in Zurich.

The door stood open and Talal explained how a full container would be parked alongside it and then the goods checked and transferred into it by customs and Khoury's men prior to its departure to whichever hospital it was intended for. A wooden flight of stairs ran up a side-wall of the warehouse to a first-floor office. We climbed them as Talal explained that this was where all the paperwork would be processed and duty and invoices paid prior to release of the goods. It all looked very neat and efficient. I briefly inspected the desks and new stand-alone PCs – Talal informed me that this made them much more difficult to hack – then made my way back downstairs.

As we drove out of the docks young Mahmoud again ignored the road that I imagined would take us towards the Hilton and turned left instead up the coast road. As we drove Talal explained that we were due to meet Dr Azzi in Arsal the next day to view the site for the field clinic. It wasn't across the square from MSF, but they wouldn't fail to notice us. Two days after that we were due to meet a whole delegation headed by Khoury to discuss the proposed site for the main hospital, details of which were waiting at the Villa. When I queried quite where or what the Villa was he smiled and simply answered that we would be there soon.

Shortly after we turned right away from the coast and up into the foothills through a couple of villages. We took another right, then a left, and followed a dusty track until we found ourselves driving alongside a tall white wall. Halfway along it we came to a pair of equally tall gates set into it. Mahmoud pointed a remote control device at them and they slowly swung open. We drove sedately into the grounds of an elegant, single-story, well-lit country residence replete with palm-encircled swimming pool. Talal turned to me with a grin.

'This is the villa.'

As I stepped through the patio doors into the luxuriously appointed lounge he explained that he had received an email from Peter instructing him to visit a Beirut estate agent. He was clearly expected and brought immediately out to view this place. All Talal had to do was ensure that it met the list of requirements that Peter had sent him. He emailed back to confirm that it did and the agent handed him the keys and asked him to sign a lease for a three month, renewable let. That was it.

The place was built in a sort of horseshoe with two residential wings and what I imagined would normally have been a central lounge/dining area in the middle with a large kitchen at the rear. I guessed that it was usually let as luxury holiday accommodation. Talal explained that he had allocated the right hand wing and the nearby outbuildings to the domestic staff and bodyguards he had been told to hire, whilst the left wing would house me and my personal staff when I was on site.

To be honest, I was not entirely surprised by my new home. Peter had explained back in Zurich that I would need a headquarters and, more importantly, a headquarters that would impress the likes of Khoury – hence the considerable retinue. However, I was impressed by the speed with which it had been located and secured. So far Peter was proving to be a man of his word.

Finally, after a brief supper of a local yellow cake which went very well with a glass of Sauterne, I announced that I was all-in and wished Talal goodnight and headed for my suite in the left wing. Too tired to unpack my valise, or even clean my teeth, I stripped off my clothes and dropped them on the settee in the sitting room, then headed though the door that had to lead into the bedroom.

As I walked in it dawned on me that the light was already on and, more importantly, the bed was already occupied. Lying on the white silk sheet, wearing nothing but a selection of brightly coloured African bangles on her upper left arm was Adanna. She sat up, putting a finger to her lips and held out what I recognised to be a postcard. Puzzled, I accepted it, noted the cityscape of Zurich on the front and turned it over. It read simply:

Thought you might need a secretary to attend to your needs.
Enjoy,
Peter.

*

The following day I slept a little later than planned thanks to a delightfully sleepless night. I finally headed out for a dip in the pool to wake myself up. If this was a taste of working with Peter Chisholm, I could definitely grow to like it.

Unfortunately, it didn't last long. I had just settled on a sun lounger to take a look through the sales literature for prefabricated hospitals that Adanna had brought with her when Talal joined me. A glance at his expression told me something was wrong.

'Good morning Talal.'

'Good morning boss...'

I held my hand up.

'Please, Talal, Tony not 'boss'. You are now a senior executive in my company and need to address me by my first name.'

'Sorry Mr Tony, I think we have serious problem.'

'Oh really, 'Tony', not 'Mr Tony'...'

'Yes, sorry, Tony...'

'That's better, how can I help you?'

'Mr Azzi has called to me. He says he must meet with you most urgently.'

'Why couldn't he call me?'

'He did not know you were back in Lebanon, but he says he cannot talk on phone. He wishes to meet with you most urgently.'

'Where?'

'In Arsal. '

'I see.'

I would have sat back to consider this if I hadn't been already reclining. I didn't 'see' at all. This was altogether most inconvenient.

'Well, what do you think? Did you get the impression that he was really serious?'

Talal shrugged.

'It is not easy to tell from the phone, Tony, but he sounded most worried indeed. He asks how soon you can meet him there.'

'Okay, we'd better go and find out what he wants. Ask Adanna to throw together some food for us, we'll breakfast en route.'

With a last wistful glance at the inviting blue pool, I headed in doors to dress.

Shortly after, the pair of us hit the road for Arsal. This time our preferred mode of transport was a brand new, black, four-door Jeep Wrangler with menacingly dark tinted windows. This, Talal explained, was again purchased on Peter's instructions and intended to carry us across the rough terrain we might expect to encounter on-site over the next few months. I suspected that it was equally intended to convey a tough, no-nonsense image to Khoury and his minions. We sat in the back as Mahmoud peered over the steering wheel to drive.

The Bekaa Valley was just as I remembered it though I thought I detected a lot more traffic on the highway, mostly military. As before, we turned right at Laboue village and here I definitely sensed more activity. As we drove past I could see 4x4's and lorries parked everywhere. We continued on towards Arsal, but now there were bulldozers working on either side of the road, clearing and levelling ground. I couldn't help noticing that the men doing the manual work were wearing army fatigues. Still, as Peter had pointed out, soldiers have always been used as cheap labour. Minister Khoury was clearly keen to get his hospital built.

Arsal itself hadn't changed much except for the worse. It seemed even more overcrowded than before if that were possible. Now Mahmoud had to nose the Jeep through seriously over-crowded streets past people who gazed dumbly at us as if wondering if getting out of the way was worth the bother. Even the children were too listless to play. They looked half-starved. Eventually we reached the square where MSF were located. Talal leant forward and said something to Mahmoud who continued past and carried along for a couple of blocks before turning left. A minute later we arrived at the area where Talal and I had pitched our tents what now seemed like an age ago. Now, however, I found myself confronted by a single-story, breeze block building in the process of having its roof put on. A taller, less complete building was going up behind it.

Azzi was waiting for us. As he hurried forward it was clear that something really was wrong. For one thing, that roof was partially built but there was no-one engaged in actually building it. For another, Azzi was not holding his hands out in greeting, he appeared to be wringing his hands in anguish. As he got nearer his expression confirmed this.

'Mr Stamford, sir, thank goodness for your rapid arrival. Please accept my apologies for calling upon you in this fashion, but a most terrible situation has arisen!'

The man looked so distressed I thought he was going to cry. I was used to breaking the bad news to bereaved relatives and telling people they had been diagnosed with terminal illness, but I had rarely seen anyone in such a state.

'Please, please, calm yourself! Can you tell me what has happened?'

'Yes, indeed sir. They have arrested Sheik Rezek!' This explanation caused him such distress that he paused to pound his temples with his knuckles.

'Who has arrested him? Why?'

'I do not know. His wife tells me they came for him in the night. They said they were Police and he was being arrested for the corruption and embezzlement.'

'Corruption and embezzlement of what?'

'I do not know. She says they read these things off a piece of paper then took him away. She was too frightened to understand.'

'And they didn't say where they were taking him?'

Azzi shook his head.

'No sir.'

'Do you believe there could be any truth in these allegations?'

'Most emphatically not, sir. I am knowing Sheik Rezek many years and he is most honourable fellow!'

From what I had seen of the 'silent sheik' I was less than convinced by this character analysis, but I kept my own council.

'Indeed, yes, I'm sure he is, and this must be most upsetting for you, but I hope you don't mind my asking why you have asked me to come here in order to tell me. It's not as if there is anything I can do to help...'

'Perhaps this is so, sir, but you are man of influence and you do business with Minister Khoury, so perhaps you might be able enlist his assistance. Minister Khoury is also a man of great influence.'

'I don't see how this is any of my business.'

'But do you not, sir? Do you not realise that, without Sheik Rezek's money, there will be no clinic in Arsal.'

'I'm sorry, I don't know what you mean.'

'I mean what I say sir. The agreement that was reached after you left our last meeting was that the Sheik would give the money for the building and running of the clinic and the Government would pay for the hospital. If Sheik Rezek is charged with these crimes, he will be unable to deal with such matters until he is proved innocent.'

Suddenly I felt the world rocking around me. This was not what I had envisaged at all. All I wanted to do was get back to being a surgeon. I was sick of screwing the wealthy witches of Hampstead under the guise of ministering to their minor ailments. I'd had enough of being put down by the likes of MSF for lack of a licence to practice, withdrawn thanks to a stitch-up courtesy of my late wife. I didn't mind helping Khoury and his cronies build a military hospital if it meant that I would get a chance to simply practice my chosen profession, but now even that was slipping through my grasp. I felt sick.

'Just wait there a minute,' I muttered, 'there is someone I need to talk to about this.' I turned and walked back to the Land Rover. As I did, I pulled out the Tripleton Enigma E2 phone that Adanna had brought with her, and switched it to secrecy mode. I had assumed the gadget was all part of the tough executive image that Peter was painting for me, but now I realised the practicality of it. I hit the only stored name on it which was his.

'Chisholm.'

'Hello Peter, it's Tony.'

'Hi Tony, what's the problem?'

'How did you know there's a problem?'

'Because that's what this phone's for, especially on secrecy mode.'

'Oh, right, I see, well as a matter of fact, there is a problem as it happens...' I explained what Azzi had told me. There was quite a pause before he finally spoke.

'Interesting, to be honest I expected him to come at this from a different angle, so we now know we have a cunning opponent on our hands.'

'Who are you talking about?'

'Khoury of course, who else?'

'But Azzi doesn't know who the kidnappers are. What makes you think Khoury's involved?'

'Well it's bloody obvious isn't it? From everything you've

told me Khoury has no interest in wasting time and money building a clinic for Syrian refugees. He probably hates the bastards and certainly would see them as an easy cover for spies and infiltrators.'

'So what's happened to the Sheik?'

'Fuck knows: probably tucked up in Khoury's office slurping sherbets and sharing a hookah – or even a hooker – with him right now.'

I did not share my business partner's apparent amusement at all this deviousness.

'Are you trying to tell me that Dr Azzi's wailing and gnashing of teeth is all an act?'

'Possibly.'

'Then he's a better actor than Lawrence bloody Olivier!'

'Who is to say he isn't? The ragheads have been wailing and gnashing their teeth ever since we dumped the Israeli's on them: they must be pretty good at it by now...'

'Oh for goodness sake Peter, will you take this seriously?'

'I am, but I don't have to take it humourlessly.'

'Right, well what am I supposed to do? Unless Azzi is lying about the contract, without the Sheik there is no way the clinic is going to get built.'

'I'm afraid you're going to have to do nothing for the time being.'

'I can't do that!'

'Of course you can. You don't know where the Sheik is, nor this contract which was apparently signed in your absence. What else can you do? Listen, Talal tells me you've got a meeting arranged on Thursday in order to thrash out a deal with Khoury and generally impress him with the way things are coming together. That will be your opportunity to ask him what's happened to the Sheik and who's going to finance your clinic if he can't.'

'Right, I see...'

'Oh, and Tony.'

'Yes?'

'Over the next couple of days you might like to spare a moment to ask yourself just how important the clinic really is to you...'

'What do you mean?'

'Well, I know you are keen to get back into surgery: it's your chosen profession and, besides, you wouldn't be human if you didn't want to give those snooty MSF bastards a poke in the eye. But bear in mind that you and I stand to make a packet out of the hospital, not the clinic, so don't forget to keep an eye on the main chance, okay?'

'Peter, hold it there! There is no way I am going to just walk away from a humanitarian crisis simply because some devious raghead, or whatever you call them, thinks he can twist me round his little finger! Do you understand me?'

'Yes, yes, Tony, steady down! I just want you to consider all the options, okay?'

'Yes, well I have and that's my final word on the subject, okay?'

With that I cut the call.

14

If I thought I would have a couple of leisurely days in which to weigh my desire to save lives against my desire to be rich and successful, then I was sorely mistaken; we had to prepare for Minister Khoury's visit. I barely had time to stop for food. It was like being a working surgeon again without the blood and guts. Not that that had ever bothered me, even as a junior. The plan was that he would inspect the warehouse at midday, and then proceed on to the Villa for lunch and spend the afternoon watching presentations from leading international hospital builders and suppliers.

Talal and Adanna set about sorting out the warehouse and preparing the Villa in anticipation of something approaching the significance of a royal visit. Talal ensured that the warehouse was cleared and cleaned up, and even repainted with our new corporate colours, whilst an impressive sign bearing the company's nomenclature was affixed across the front. Secretaries were brought in from a Beirut temp agency to occupy the upstairs desks and look busy. They were even given a brief training course in what to say if someone asked what they did. Adanna set about organising a feast at the Villa that Kubla Khan would have been proud of, whilst ensuring that the place was equipped with every visual and audio aid that the visiting company reps could possibly imagine a use for.

Along with overseeing all of this, I was left with the task of presenting a private summary of what we had heard from the reps, which would then be used to steer Khoury towards the hospital supplier of Peter's choice. That is to say the company who had promised us the most substantial kickbacks. We had gone over this in detail back in Zurich. When I had asked him if Khoury wouldn't be wise to this, he had laughed and said that Khoury would expect it. The business world, especially the Middle-Eastern business world, was fuelled by backhanders. Rather than appear hopelessly naive, I had chuckled knowingly.

The upshot was that it was down to me to persuade Khoury to buy a bespoke hospital from a company called Gortis Turnkey International and medical supplies and equipment from Torino Farmaceutico Internazionale S.p.A. When I asked him if the repulsive Mr Macari would be charged with the task of wooing Khoury on the 'meds and kit' front he laughed and assured me that one of his own people would be doing that and she was being briefed to fully satisfy any demands Khoury might make of her. I quickly assured him that I didn't want to know the details.

*

It wasn't until the evening before the big day that I found an opportunity to settle down beside the pool with my laptop. I took a swig of Chablis and then went into Google Chrome. I typed Ministry of Interior into the little box and clicked Search. It came up with the Ministry of Interior and Municipalities which described itself as dealing with a number of things including security. However, every time I tried to follow a link I found myself trying to read Arabic. I wasn't going to get far like that. I typed in 'Minister' instead of 'Ministry' and this time I found a bit of biography on Wikipedia for a man called Marwan Charbel. You could have transferred the information that it contained onto the back of a postage stamp: military background, Christian, in current office since 2011. It seemed he was particularly well-known for his anti-gay views and was generally just left of Ghengis Khan.

This was interesting. If he was Minister of the Interior then Khoury wasn't and yet they worked in the same building and both called themselves 'Minister'. So what was Khoury a minister of? When I typed his name into Google all I got back was a Beiruti apartment store and its offshoots. When I scrolled down further, the name Khoury popped up belonging to various individuals around the world, but none that resembled my Khoury. I was three-quarters of the way through the Chablis when I concluded that I was wasting my time. My Khoury clearly took considerable pains to avoid the public domain. Did Lebanon have the equivalent of our 'Ministers without Portfolio' or was he something more secretive than that? His resemblance to Saddam Hussein struck me as much nearer the mark than his resemblance to any of the characters I remembered from Yes Minister. He had a very plush office of his own and clearly wielded considerable power. I called Talal.

'Talal, it's Tony.'

'Yes Tony?'

'Are you still at the Villa?'

'Yes boss.'

I gave a mental shrug of resignation.

'Look Talal, if you can't call me Tony, call me sir, okay?'

I could almost hear a brightening in his voice.

'Yes sir!'

Why hadn't I thought of that before? The man had a military background.

*

The place was an absolute dive. Talal's cousin pulled aside the filthy old rug that served as the front door to the tatty building and we filed into the hazy darkness. The first thing that hit me was an over-powering, sickly-sweet smell. I had puffed on a joint and smelled joss sticks in my student days and it certainly wasn't that. Gradually my eyes became accustomed to the murky gloom as we made our way down a rubbish filled corridor. What little light there was filtered out of uncovered doorways to our right.

As we passed the first I peered in. The only illumination was a candle on a shelf in the corner. Men lay on filthy mattresses on the floor in what appeared to be states of semi-consciousness. The smell of what was clearly opium mingled with the sharper smell of urine and I noticed a communal bucket in the corner.

We got no further before everyone's image of a toothless crone hurried down the corridor and engaged Talal's cousin in rapid-fire conversation. She yammered on gesticulating as if in alarm. Perhaps she thought we were the drugs squad. We certainly didn't look like her regular clientele thank God!

Anyway, whatever her concerns, the cousin eventually succeeded in allaying them because, after an exchange of money, she turned and beckoned us to follow. As we proceeded further into the gloom the smell seemed to become ever more cloying and sickly. I found myself wondering about the possible effects of passive smoking in here. Did things still look normal? Did I feel a little weird? I decided the place was so abnormal and weird that I had no way of judging.

We turned into one of the open cells. It was occupied by two men sitting on mattresses and slumped against opposite walls. Both of them were completely lost to the world, and one of them was missing a leg. She gestured to the one with the stump. A few more words were exchanged then she scuttled off down the corridor.

'What do we do now?' I muttered to Talal.

'Now we must wait, sir.'

'How long?'

'She says maybe an hour, maybe two.'

'This had better be worth it.' I muttered as I pulled out a handkerchief and covered my nose and mouth to try and block out the smoky stench.

*

About three quarters of an hour later the man stirred and then cried out something unintelligible. The cousin grabbed him by the hair and slapped him round the face a few times. He reached into his pocket and produced a small bottle which he unstopped and shoved under the man's nose. Despite the general stench I caught a strong whiff of ammonia. The man tried to jerk his head away and then rolled over and began retching. Nothing came up: no doubt any money he had had gone on the opium not food. This passed after a minute or two.

The cousin lit a cigarette and passed it to him. He accepted it with pathetic gratitude and got it to his lips with hands that shook almost uncontrollably. The cousin then produced a hip flask of what I guessed was brandy and passed that to him as well. The man had hardly got it to his lips when it was snatched away. The man reached for it imploringly, but the cousin held it just out of reach and rattled off what I assumed was a question. I thought I made out the word 'Khoury'. The man paused for a minute as recognition dawned to be followed by an expression of absolute terror. He said something that sounded like pleading and lunged for the flask again, but the cousin was too quick and pulled it back out of reach. He repeated his question and this time after shedding several tears the man mumbled a reply. He was rewarded with another brief swig and so the interrogation began.

*

Talal and I picked up our drinks and headed for a table in the corner of the hotel bar. The place was one of many lining Beirut's southern coast road not far from the golf club. It wasn't plush but it was a world away from the squalid slums we had recently left. We had chosen it at random and had taken our time to see if anyone followed us in. Now, as we settled down, we were pretty certain that we had not been followed since leaving the opium den. Talal's nameless cousin had immediately slipped away up a back street upon leaving the squalid dump. Anonymity was a stipulation of his agreeing to help us.

I had no idea what to expect from this, but I sensed it was my best chance to learn things I would never find on Google.

I hoped to God Talal had been able to make sense of our informant's slurred, sobbing delivery.

'Okay Talal, how did Stump first meet Khoury?' Our choice of nomenclature for our opiated informant may seem a little callous but it worked in the absence of the man's real name which had not been forthcoming.

'He said they met as members of the Kataeb Regulatory Forces in 1976 under the leadership of Bashir Gemayel .'

'Who?'

'Do not ask me, I was not even born then.'

'Right, but didn't they teach you anything in history?'

'Yes but it depended on the political beliefs of the teacher.' I sat back, floored before we'd begun, but Talal grinned and continued. 'It is of no consequence. It is sufficient to say these people were the right-wing Christian forces who fought with the Palestinian Liberation Organisation in the Lebanese Civil War of that time.'

'Right, okay, so they were brothers in arms?'

'Yes, for a while, but it seems they fell out.'

'Go on.'

'He said they met in one of the units that took part in the massacre at the Karantina Camp.'

'Do you know anything about that?'

'Everyone in Lebanon knows of that.'

'Go on.' For some indefinable reason, this sounded interesting. Talal paused to gather his thoughts then began.

'Well, this is only what I was told by my father and my uncles but the PLO was attacking places all the time in East Beirut where the Christians were. It was very violent and then, bang, the Christians have enough and wipe out this big PLO camp. They kill over a thousand people, many civilians, women and children.'

'Did Stump describe his or Khoury's part in this?'

'Sure, he reckoned they were both there but Khoury was unit leader and he was only obeying orders. Every soldier will say this.'

I nodded my acceptance of this general truth.

'Okay, but did he describe exactly what they got up to, particularly Khoury?'

'Sure, if you believe Stump, Khoury was like a madman. Most of the guys just wanted to kill the enemy and rape some women, but Khoury kept shooting the kids and shouting 'Kill their future! Even his own soldiers tried to calm him down.'

'Is this why they fell out?'

'No, that came later.'

'What happened?'

'In 1976 was the attack on the Holiday Inn in Beirut which was another very famous part of the war. According to Stump his unit was trying to organise the escape of his people trapped in the hotel by the PLO. At this time the PLO discovered they were in control of Bank Street where all the big banks are, as the name says. The PLO called in the Italian Mafia to blow open the safes and then they rob millions of dollars. This was famous on the TV News all over the world.'

'The unit belonging to Stump and Khoury is doing a recce in a street near the hotel when a lorry comes around the corner carrying soldiers. The unit believes the lorry has come to attack them and they fight. They shoot the soldiers, but only Stump,

Khoury and two others survive. When they look inside, the lorry is full of gold. They steal it and drive it off to a place called Jounieh up the coast where they hide in a cave that Khoury knows. Soon they argue about whether they should share the gold amongst themselves or give it to their leaders to help the war. Khoury and one man wish to keep it, Stump and the other man wish to hand it over. Another fight happens. Stump's friend is killed and Stump is shot in the shoulder and the leg. Khoury and the other guy think he is dying and drive off. He never sees Khoury again for many years.'

'When thieves fall out, eh? What happened when he did see him many years later?'

'By the time Stump was found in the cave the wound in his leg had become bad and the doctors had to cut it off. He had no use in the army and for many years he became a beggar. He became very unwell and, during time in a hospital run by Christian nuns, he heard Khoury was a wealthy man and involved with the government. He thought perhaps Khoury would forget their falling out and feel pity for an old comrade. He persuaded one of the nuns to write a letter to Khoury asking for his mercy. He never received a reply, but when he left the hospital some men were waiting for him. They beat him badly and told him to leave Beirut and never come back. This made him despair and he began to take the opium which he had come to use for the pain in his stump all the time. The place where we found him is also good hiding place.'

I sat back.

'Thanks Talal, I think you've just told me an awful lot more about Mr Khoury than most people will ever know. It seems he takes a great deal of care to protect his privacy and now I reckon I know why.'

I sent Talal to the bar to freshen our glasses whilst I contemplated what I'd learnt. I didn't like it, in fact, I really didn't like it at all. It seemed that, if Peter had his way, we were about to try to negotiate a business partnership with a ruthless, homicidal maniac. On the other hand, given my current circumstances, I couldn't see any viable alternatives. I decided to wait and see what the following day would bring.

15

The big day dawned with frightening alacrity. Along with all my other duties I had somehow managed to find my way, under Talal's guidance, into Beirut and located a men's outfitters. It wasn't Jermyn Street but they stocked Hugo Boss so I managed to get myself kitted out in a mid-grey worsted number with a decent white shirt and navy/red striped silk tie. I could have been back on Harley Street.

Talal had to be summoned from the upstairs office where he was still rehearsing the secretaries as Khoury's cavalcade swept into view and proceeded in stately fashion down the docks towards us. I busied myself with the press, who had turned up in response to a press release from Khoury's office, giving ad hoc comments and posing for photographs to ensure I looked suitably important. Khoury's P.R machine was clearly well oiled. The first limo pulled up and a bunch of uniformed, body guards, wearing dark glasses, spilled out and took up a defensive posture around the second. They hadn't drawn their guns, but they were clearly itching to. Compared to them, The Two Abduls looked positively benign. Still, Peter had warned me of this back in Zurich.

'Open Day is going to be one long pissing competition, okay? Khoury is going to try to control and dominate from the moment he arrives. He'll turn up with a gang of thugs and there's nothing you can do about it because he's a Minister and commands a bodyguard by right. Your best bet, once he's seen the warehouse, is to suggest he might be kind enough to post them round the Villas perimeter to bolster your own security. He can hardly object and that way they won't be in your face all the time. Use Talal as your spokesman for the guided tour of the warehouse – make the excuse that they both speak the lingo. Talal has the status of Managing Director which is pretty senior and should enable you to stay more aloof.'

The chauffeur scurried round to open the door of the second limo for Khoury who emerged preceded by two men in black suits and followed by a shaven-headed, weasely-looking individual carrying a laptop. Khoury's Reactolites were pitched black. Again I was struck by his wasted physique. I stepped forward for the official greeting and posed mid-handshake with Khoury for the photographers. I then beckoned Talal forward and introduced him, which gave me a chance to step back and assess my visitor in bright sunlight. Out from behind his desk he was noticeably lacking in inches: if it came to a real pissing completion, I would be starting nearly a foot further up the wall. I couldn't help wondering if the size of his retinue was compensating for the size of his member. The sunshine also revealed pockmarks on his swarthy face; the comparison with Saddam Hussein shortly before he got the chop struck me again. He ignored Talal's out-stretched hand and turned to me, his face darkening quite literally.

'I deal only with the organ-grinder not his monkey!' he hissed.

I stood speechless, stunned by his rudeness, but thankfully, Talal intervened:

'If the Minister would prefer to discuss our operation with you alone sir, it would be most useful if I could go ahead to ensure everything is in readiness for his inspection...'

'Oh, yes, right Talal, certainly that would be a wise precaution. Fine, run along and we will be with you in a minute. Indeed, the Minister and I have much to discuss.' I watched Talal depart for a moment as I gathered my thoughts. I'd expected this bastard to be a handful, but I hadn't anticipated a disregard for protocol, or basic good manners, as crude as this!

*

The rest of the warehouse tour went off smoothly enough. Khoury was obviously satisfied that he had got in early with his 'nasty bastard' credentials and was now satisfied to nod his approval of our arrangements in a lordly fashion, much in the same way that my old nemesis, Chaudhuri, used to conduct his hospital inspections. He even paused to compliment The Two Abduls on their uniforms, just to reinforce his exclusion of Talal. I suspected that, like Chaudhuri, his egotism was counterbalanced by a generous streak of devious pragmatism.

There was a slightly awkward moment when he tried to quiz me on the computer system, but I immediately explained that Talal was in overall charge of IT and, since Khoury was still blanking him, the enquiry died there. Finally, we ran out of hands to shake and photographers to smile at and retreated to the cavalcade and our own cars for the next phase of the operation. This involved a stately ride to The Villa where lunch awaited us.

If Khoury had tried to impress us with the size of his retinue, Adanna fought back with the food. Two huge marquees virtually filled the front lawn, one to accommodate the presentations later, the other to host a feast of biblical proportions. Guests filed into the latter and set about a staggering variety of lamb, chicken and fish kebabs, and salads of all varieties. Fruit was piled high on tables for those who didn't fancy the rich, creamy desserts and waiters plied guests with drink at the flick of a finger. Finally, the last brandy was drunk, the last strong black coffee was swallowed, the last hookah stopped bubbling, and guests retreated to the other marquee for the presentations.

Throughout this extravaganza I played host to Khoury. It wasn't easy. Despite the sumptuous feast on offer, he ate sparingly, and, although he smiled and nodded ministerially, his eyes were always watchful behind his dark glasses. When I tried to steer the conversation onto the matter of the new hospital, hoping that it would inspire some animation, he leant towards me and muttered:

'Please, Dr Stamford, these matters are best left for private discussion. Even in Lebanon, we too have the directional microphones.'

'Right, yes, good point,' I muttered in reply, glancing round at the assembled guests. 'Sorry!'

I pretty much gave up trying after that and focussed on the food. I knew such things existed, but my knowledge of espionage was pretty much limited to the odd James Bond film on DVD. Was my guest an extremely cautious politician, or a paranoid nutcase? If he was the latter, was the condition a danger to those around him, in particular, me? Whatever the state of my guest's mental health, this latest version of 'speak when you're spoken to' allowed me to settle down for the presentations and discreetly observe his reactions. This was particularly important, Peter had explained, when it came to the presentation from Torino Farmaceutico Internazionale S.p.A.

He listened attentively enough as the various reps went forward and made their company presentations. Amongst the hospital suppliers, some majored on quality of design and build, others on speed of delivery and utility. The equipment and drugs companies stressed quality of materials, price and so on. He remained impassive throughout. It was only when the representative from Torino walked forward that he sat forward in his chair. To be honest, I couldn't blame him.

Even from the back, wearing a white lab coat, she set the pulses racing. The coat simply offset everything implied by the black seamed stockings and expensive, black leather heels below it. When she turned to the audience a hush fell that none of the other speakers had commanded. Her blond hair looked natural and her make-up was sensible, but she was so good looking that she hardly needed it anyway.

Khoury turned back and said something over his shoulder to the ugly, little, bald man with the laptop who had accompanied him out of the limo. I couldn't hear what he said, but I could guess. The Weasel, as I had already christened him, quickly closed his laptop and slipped out of the marquee. I looked across to the side of the stage where Talal was employing his bilingual skills as compère for the presentations. His eyes were fixed on me. I reached up and scratched my right ear; our fish had taken the bait.

*

We were sitting in the drawing room of The Villa and the press and reps and other guests had departed. God knows quite what arrangement the Weasel had come to with Peter's blond bombshell, but Khoury had the air of a man keen to get our present business matters over and done with quickly. Nevertheless, his libido was not going to override his negotiating instincts entirely.

'Please let me congratulate you, Dr Stamford, on the excellent way you have made your preparations for the building of our hospital.'

I nodded, cautiously, wondering what was coming next.

'Thank you, Minister.'

He went on:

'Indeed, we have seen today some most persuasive proposals from some most excellent companies. In particular, I am interested in the proposition placed before us by the gentleman from the company calling itself Gortis Turnkey International. This company seems most well equipped to satisfy our needs in the current situation.'

'I am pleased the Minister feels...'

He held his hand up.

'However, I cannot escape the belief that their price is considerably too high as is the case with this Torino Farmaceutico Internazionale.'

'Oh, I see,' I sat back in my chair as if this reaction had been entirely unexpected. 'Right, Minister, well I would point out that their prices are considerably lower than that of the other companies involved...'

'Indeed, this is so, but that does not make them low enough.'
I could feel his ego beginning to bristle even at this mild whiff
of opposition.

'I really cannot see them coming any lower...'

'Yes they will! If they want contract they will agree to my
terms!'

I looked up and gazed at the ceiling of the drawing room as
if gathering my thoughts.

'Perhaps, Minister, I can see an area of compromise that
would be satisfactory to all parties...'

'What is that?'

'Well, as I'm sure you will appreciate, given the current
situation in Syria and the friction it is creating with yourselves,
all the companies we have seen today, or indeed all others I
have spoken to, have made it clear that they are not prepared
to undertake any building work, or supply medicines or
equipment without payment upfront...'

'This is monstrous! Do they not respect my country's security
or integrity?'

'Of course they do Minister, while you are at peace, but that
is not their concern. You, yourself, have said that the purpose
of the hospital is to help you defend your eastern border should
the situation with Syria escalate. These companies are astute
enough to see that for themselves and have carried out their
own risk assessments.'

'Tell them this is not acceptable!'

'Unfortunately, Minister, I have already done that, but they
know that there are a limited number of companies in the
world capable of meeting your requirements and see no need

to give ground on this point.'

'Someone will give.'

'I'm afraid not, but we might be able to turn this to our advantage.'

'In what way?'

'Perhaps I could make a case to Gortis Turnkey International and Torino Farmaceutico Internazionale that we would expect a better price in return for upfront payment. After all they will be earning interest on that money which in other circumstances would have been earning money for you.'

'Khoury paused to consider my suggestion.'

'And you think they will agree to this?'

I shrugged.

'I cannot say, Minister, but I can ask. My only concern is that they may agree, but then save the money back by cutting quality...'

'Then it is your job to ensure this does not happen.'

'Of course Minister. Then I am free to put this proposal to them?'

'This is so.'

'Good, then I should have an answer for you within the next couple of days.'

He nodded his satisfaction and issued another command to the Weasel who had slipped back in behind him during our conversation. The man began issuing orders to the bodyguards in preparation for their departure. As Khoury appeared poised to depart, I addressed him again.

'Oh, one other thing Minister...'

He frowned slightly at this delay to his departure and

consequent encounter with Peter's bombshell.

'Yes?'

'It would appear that you finally agreed with Sheik Rezek that he would supply the funding for the clinic that we discussed at our first meeting. As I understand it, the Sheik has been arrested on corruption charges and is no longer able to honour that commitment.'

'I have heard something to that effect.'

'Yes, well I trust you appreciate that I only agreed to help you with the building of your hospital on the understanding that funds were made available for the building of my refugee clinic.'

'That is no longer my concern.'

'I'm afraid it is, because I have made arrangements that if you do not agree to fund it, third parties that you have no control over will immediately advise the companies you have seen today that you are not to be trusted. Oh, and if I disappear, or fail to call them at a prearranged time each day, you will be named in the international press as the person responsible.'

*

'I tell you Peter, the man's face went from green olive to black before my eyes – or maybe aubergine!' Adanna's exotic feast was clearly still on my mind as I tried to capture Khoury's complexion flushing with rage.

'What did he say?'

'Nothing, he just turned this alarming purple colour then turned on his heel and stormed off.'

'So you don't know whether he has agreed to deal?'

'No, not yet, though I expect we will hear something in the morning.'

'Right, then I expect you will be pleased to learn that he has. Congratulations old boy, we've got the hospital and you've got your clinic!'

'Really, how d'you know?'

'Jolanda was waiting for him in his limo when he stormed out.'

'Jolanda?'

'The blonde rep from Torino. By the time they got back to Beirut she'd extracted more than just a promise to calm down and reconsider out of him. The bodyguards had a right treat.'

'Right, I'm sure they did,' I paused, 'so you're not pissed off about me insisting on the clinic?'

'Not at all, all the more lolly for us! Still, I take my hat off to you; it must have taken a lot of bottle.'

'Not really, I've dealt with nasty little thugs like him before.'

This was more than simple bravado: I had accepted Peter's friendly lecturing with good grace up to now, but I was getting a little tired of my role as the 'new kid in school'. This had been my chance to prove I could mix it with the big boys and I had come out on top.

'Sure, and you've done a great job, but just remember, you're not in Britain now. Chaps like Khoury run on egomania and don't like losing. You're going to need to watch your step from now on.'

'What do you mean?'

'I can't say, but I'm quite sure he's not going to take this lying down. Stay savvy and, in the meantime, ask Talal to call me tomorrow when the first shipment arrives; there's a man he needs to talk to in Customs. Have a good evening and well done again.'

With that, my Tripleton Enigma E2 went dead. I shivered, suddenly aware of a chill in the Lebanese night. I had come down the garden in search of extra privacy. I started to make my way back through the debris of the party towards The Villa. The marquees had been struck, but the garden still needed a good clean up. With the guests gone, the place had an air of empty desolation. With Peter's caution still echoing in my ears, I suddenly felt distinctly lonely. What the hell was I doing here stuck in an unfamiliar, foreign country without the family I once kidded myself belonged to me? How the hell had I come to find myself mixed up with politicians who behaved more like Chicago gangsters? I glanced up as if the heavens could offer some sort of explanation. There were clouds gathered in the night sky that a month before had offered nothing but brilliant stars.

I lengthened my stride and told myself not to be so silly. I'd had a hectic and stressful day coping with things outside my usual ken. It was hardly surprising if my nerves were a little over-stretched. I knew perfectly well what I was doing in Lebanon. I was here to re-establish my reputation and status and, if possible restore my depleted finances, though that was my last priority. I was hardly badly off, just not where I had once been. This was my opportunity to put that right. By the time I climbed into bed and wrapped my arms around the waiting Adanna, the glass was half-full again. I was rather looking forward to the challenges of the next day.

*

It was, in fact, five days later when the gates of The Villa were swung open. I looked up from my poolside recliner where I had been killing time catching up on-line with recent issues of The Lancet. I watched as a black, Ford Lexus appeared and paused for the driver to talk to the guards. My phone rang.

'There is gentleman from Ministry of Interior to see you sir,' a disembodied voice from the gatehouse informed me.

'Okay, let him in.' I watched, briefly, as the car started its journey down The Villa's lengthy drive then closed my iPad and retreated through the patio doors to grab my jacket. Adanna appeared and went out to greet my visitor while I disappeared into the room we had converted into an office. I took up position sitting behind the large executive desk. A moment later Talal joined me and seated himself at the smoked glass table by the window. He opened a bulky file and spread documents in front of him. I opened the file on my desk and did likewise. Adanna buzzed through on my speakerphone:

'A Mr Roffe is here to see you sir.'

I winked at Talal.

'I'm a bit tied up at the moment Adanna, could you ask him to give me ten minutes then send him through.'

'Certainly sir.'

I sat back as Talal raised a fist in triumph. Peter had predicted that it would be beneath Khoury's dignity to show up in person and so it had fallen to Talal to track down the identity of the Weasel, whom he reckoned would take his lordship's place. I personally had been voting for the good Dr Azzi to be his chosen emissary, so I owed my new Managing Director a tenner.

We sat and chatted about where we would go for lunch once Roffe was out of the way until Adanna buzzed through again.

'Are you ready to receive your visitor now Mr Stamford?'

'Yes thank you Adanna, send him in please.'

'Certainly sir.'

On close inspection my visitor was an even more unprepossessing individual than first impressions had suggested. I was reminded of Max Schreck's rendition of the ghastly Nosferatu which I sat through at the cinema club back in my student days. Despite a Mediterranean complexion, he still managed an unhealthy pallor and dark, sunken eyes. I looked up from the file I was now studying and gestured to the chair in front of my desk without getting up to offer a handshake.

'Good morning Mr Roffe, how can I help you?'

The man was gazing round, obviously briefed to report back on our set up in detail. He stared at me in turn, before deigning to reply.

'Minister Khoury sends his warmest salutations and deepest regrets that he in unable to attend in person.'

I inclined my head.

'Please convey to the Minister that I am aware that he is a busy man and accept his apologies in the spirit in which they are sent. I take it that he has had an opportunity to study the terms of the contracts I forwarded to him from Gortis Turnkey International and Torino Farmaceutico Internazionale?'

'Indeed he has, sir.'

'And does he find them satisfactory?'

'He does sir.'

'Very good, so we can get them signed and instruct the companies concerned to proceed with construction and make arrangements for the shipping of supplies?'

'Indeed sir.'

'Good, and where do we stand with the completion of the clinic in Arsal?'

'Ah yes, sir, the clinic,' I thought I saw a sly smirk flit across his repulsive features, 'I am sure you will be pleased to learn that the charges against the esteemed patron of the Ramzi Foundation, Sheik Remek, have been disposed of and he has been released from custody and is therefore free and happy to resume his generous patronage of the clinic you desire to build.'

This little speech was clearly prepared in advance, so I pressed a little harder.

'Do you mind my asking quite who was making these charges?'

Again, that smirk.

'I am afraid that is information that I am unable to reveal sir. Perhaps it is sufficient to learn that the monies are restored?'

I sat back and stared at him to convey my displeasure at this evasion, but he was too ugly to look at for long. I had won the day so I decided to allow them their denial and nodded my unwilling assent.

'It would appear that it will have to be. Very well, if you would care to leave the documents with my colleague here, he will forward them to Gortis and Torino to be countersigned and then we can get the show on the road.'

16

We met Dr Azzi and the Sheik on site in Arsal the following afternoon. The Sheik nodded his acceptance of my somewhat ironic commiserations regarding his recent incarceration, looking remarkably unruffled by the harrowing experience. Azzi was beside himself with relief at the renewal of the project and, more than once when I happened to turn round, I caught him looking at me with what I fancied was a new-found respect. It did nothing to clarify just whose man he was, but I decided that a reputation for being able to look after myself was no bad thing in this country.

What did strike me was that the clinic was much nearer to completion than it had been at my last visit. I could even see truckloads of beds arriving. However the building behind it had progressed too. It now stood two storeys high! I asked Talal to have a quiet word with one of the workmen to find out when building-work had recommenced.

'He reckons five days ago boss.'

'Good work Talal, so the rest of the delay before Roffe's arrival was pure gamesmanship.'

Talal nodded.

'It is the Arab way. No Arab is happy to lose face, in particular a powerful man like the Minister. He will like to keep you waiting.'

I smiled.

'That's not exclusive to Arabs, Talal. That's true of powerful men the world over. Still with a bit of luck things will settle down now and he'll have other things to occupy his attention. Have you tracked down that architect yet?'

'Most certainly boss, he is over there.'

To call the man an architect was to put him on a throne when he didn't merit a foot stool! At best, he was a clerk from the Ministry of Works. He was puzzling over a sheaf of drawings when we joined him at a makeshift table made out of breeze blocks and an old door. He was plump, greasy and harassed, and not even a gaudy pair of red braces could detract from the dark circles of sweat under his armpits.

At my suggestion, Talal asked him to explain the proposed function of the buildings currently in evidence. After an exchange, which at one point became visibly heated, Talal explained that the man didn't know himself. He had been told that the use of the buildings was Top Secret, though these drawings had come from the Ministry of the Interior if that was of any assistance. He was just there to make sure the walls went in the right places and the roof went on the right way up. He had heard rumours that the smaller building was some sort of hospital. He had no idea what the bigger building behind it was for.

I had a nasty feeling I knew. This was the 'secure facility' that that bastard Khoury had been so insistent upon at our first meeting, but now it was three times the size of the 'hospital', in other words my clinic! If my memory served me right we had agreed on a modest interview block in which to vet possible Syrian infiltrators, not a scaled down version of the Russian Lubyanka!

'Ask him if the building at the back is what he was first ordered to build or has it changed.' Talal engaged in another exchange with our perspiring informant then turned back to me.

'He says it is very different. When they recommended work five days ago the first building, which was much smaller, was torn down and this erected from a different set of drawings. The men have been working day and night.'

'I see, thank you.'

I turned and walked away from the site to gaze out towards the Syrian border and collect my thoughts. Even in broad daylight I could make out distant figures trying to run the gauntlet and an occasional fighter flashed across the sky in pursuit. Things were getting worse.

Over the last few days waiting for Khoury's response to my ultimatum had left me plenty of time in which to watch the news and keep abreast of the deteriorating situation. Although the Syrian government was vehemently denying it, a news report had just come out talking about their use of chemical weapons against their own people. This was being confirmed by local news reports of increases in the number of refugees in towns like Arsal. Talal's interpreting skills were proving invaluable.

On the international front Mr 'Sincerity' Obama for the Yanks was talking about independent military intervention because even us Brits were suffering from cold feet, whilst the lizard-eyed Putin was being as obstructive as possible to keep the old East-West antagonisms stoked up. All in all, Syria was threatening to erupt as the latest US/Russian proxy war. That was the last thing I needed. I was here to rebuild my life, not get blown up!

Still, did that justify the new 'Lubyanka'? I didn't think so. No doubt the Ministry of the Interior did feel under pressure to gear up its border security, but that was not what was going on here. It was all too much of a coincidence: I clash with Khoury, he promptly rewrites our agreement, albeit a verbal one, by constructing this monstrosity. No, this was not about a greater security threat. This was intended to let me know who was boss.

I reached the end of the track and looked right. I could make out the MSF building a few blocks down the road. As always there were people milling around outside and vehicles of all sorts arriving and departing. God, how I envied them! There they were, no doubt stressed and exhausted, but safe. Not safe in the physical sense, but safe in the knowledge that what they were doing was worthwhile. Safe in the knowledge that they were fulfilling their vocations in life, not haggling and sparring with the likes of Khoury and his repulsive minions. Still what did it matter? I'd got my clinic even if it had to be built in the shadow of the Lebanese 'Lubyanka'. Perhaps I could now get on with the business of being a surgeon again.

*

That last, heartfelt wish was clearly not going to happen overnight; the clinic had to be completed, equipped and staffed, and that was no mean task in its own right. Added to that, I had the building of the main hospital to consider. In theory, it all looked pretty simple: Gortis Turnkey International had made their presentation to Khoury and he had agreed their price. The contract was between them and, in theory, having paid our kickback for fixing the deal, Gortis could now be left to get on with it. Only once the ground work was done and the building was in place would our interest reawaken in the shape of Torino Farmaceutico Internazionale S.p.A which Peter and I now owned indirectly via several shelf companies. Even then, Peter had assured me that all I needed to worry about was recruiting the medical staff and a Director of Administration, who would then recruit his own team to handle procurement etcetera. We would advertise it publicly, and then rig it to ensure that our man got the post. Peter already had a candidate lined up.

That was the theory, but, as Peter explained on the Tripleton Enigma E2 the following evening, in practice we needed to box very wisely indeed. For one thing the other companies we had invited to pitch for the contract would not have been too pleased to see their efforts come to nothing. Any whisper suggesting that the outcome had been rigged would fall on dangerously receptive ears, particularly given that his sources informed him that Khoury had more than his fair share of enemies in the Lebanese government. The last thing we needed was for him to be deposed.

He went on to explain that, with this in mind, he had arranged a 'discreet' meeting with a man called Swift who was the Project Director for Gortis, which is how, two days after the meeting with Azzi and the Sheik in Arsal, Talal and I were sitting in a conference suite back in the Hilton Habtoor Grand.

The meeting was 'discreet' rather than clandestine in the sense that we were not trying to pretend it did not take place.

We were already well aware of the cars that tailed us when we left the Villa. They made little effort to be unobtrusive, and we accepted that their presence was all part of Khoury's need to show us who was boss. The trick here, as Peter had explained, was to be perfectly open about the meeting, but arrange it in such a way that our pursuers had no time to do more than register that it was happening. That is to say, no time to set up bugs or deploy directional microphones.

To that end we were waiting for Swift to arrive directly from the airport where he had been collected by Mahmoud. Talal was sporting a rather smart black business suit which he had bought courtesy of the new company expense account, whilst I was back in the grey worsted. Following the limo's departure from the Villa, Talal and I had been collected by one of his relatives in a delivery van and dropped round the corner from the Hilton. We could not see out of the back, but our driver reckoned we were not followed, which meant that even if Mahmoud and Swift arrived with Khoury's minions in tow, it would take them some time to figure out that he was meeting us and no way of discovering why, or overhearing our discussion.

As Talal and I sat waiting for the knock on the door announcing our visitor, I found myself musing on how easily I had found myself slipping into this cloak-and-dagger stuff. This was a long way from the office politics of St George's and yet I found myself accepting and playing along with it as if it was all quite normal! I supposed that it was rather like finding yourself trapped in a suddenly occupied country. Circumstances could take you from a genteel comfortable existence to being on the run, or even herded into a concentration camp, in the blink of an eye. What did you do? History suggested that, if you didn't die, you adjusted. In fact, history was, if nothing else, an abiding testament to human beings' ability to adapt, like evolution itself. I had to admit that things were currently evolving in a way I was not entirely comfortable with, but perhaps that was just the unfamiliarity of the world I now found myself in.

*

The man who was shown into the meeting room by the bellboy was most certainly not what I had been visualising as a 'Project Manager'. I suppose I had built up an image of a burly, imposing individual in a hard hat, wellies and waterproof over an expensive suit and tie. The sort you see on advertisements for major, high-rise developments.

Mr Daniel Swift, by contrast was a slim, casually dressed individual of no more than average height. His slightly rounded shoulders suggested a life spent behind a desk, but that was belied by the vigour of his stride as he crossed the room to shake my hand. Close-up, there was a good sprinkling of salt in his black pepper hair which, along with his weather-beaten complexion, persuaded me that he was somewhere around his late fifties, perhaps early sixties even. What really caught my attention was his gaze. He had blue eyes that defined exactly what is meant when people describe eyes as 'piercing'; they seemed to look right into your thoughts and, more unsettlingly, find what they discovered there amusing. Almost disconcerted, I held out my hand.

'Tony Stamford, nice to meet you, Mr Swift.'

'Nice to meet you, Dr Stamford,' he replied as he shook my hand, 'or should I be callin' you 'mister'?' This was said in a soft Southern Irish accent, possibly from Dublin given Gortis' head office address on Google. I nodded my acknowledgement of his awareness of medical etiquette.

'Well, if you are asking whether or not I am a surgeon the answer is yes, so technically I'm a 'mister', but no-one seems aware of the distinction around here so take your pick.' I smiled to indicate my laissez-faire attitude to such protocol. He tilted his head as if considering the choice.

'I could indeed, but then it might be easier if I simply called you Anthony and you called me Daniel from the outset. Peter tells me you're not a man to stand on unnecessary formality.'

'Oh, right then, certainly, that's fine by me. I didn't know that you knew Peter...'

Those blue eyes seemed to sparkle with amusement at my confusion.

'Aye, I know Peter well enough, we go back years together.'

'Really, he never mentioned that. I had the impression that your firm was simply another bidder. I assumed you just came up with a better price than the other contractors.'

Swift chuckled.

'We did, but how d'you think we knew what that price should be? That's where Peter came in. Thanks to him, everyone thought they were offering the best price!'

'Oh, I see.' It was beginning to dawn on me exactly why Peter was worried that the losing bidders might be feeling rather touchy. Swift continued.

'Besides, it wasn't just price that swung it.'

'What d'you mean?'

'Didn't Peter tell you?'

'No, we haven't really spoken about this...'

'Oh, well, I'm sure I'm not leakin' any secrets now the deal's done. We offered that Khoury fella a statue in his swanky atrium.'

'You did what?'

'We offered the man a statue in the atrium of his pretty new hospital. That did the trick alright. We could have charged him double!'

I smiled my recognition of their tactics.

'Very good, but I hope you don't mind my asking who is 'we'?'

Swift looked surprised for a moment, and then replied: 'As far as Khoury is concerned, 'we' is Gortis Turnkey International of which I am Executive Director for International Sales, but when Peter brokered the deal with them he insisted on using me as the liaison between them and Khoury on the pretext that I had connections here. It was all bollocks but they were happy enough, particularly when he began talking about future contracts.'

'Why didn't Peter tell me any of this?'

'I don't know, but he doubtless has his reasons. I'm guessin' that he probably thought you could do without the extra pressure of knowin' it was rigged,' he paused thoughtfully, then added: 'He's a devious bastard that Peter Chishlom, in fact, the one thing I can definitely say about him after all these years is he's a hyper-devious bastard!' He nodded as if particularly satisfied with this character analysis, and then enquired abruptly: 'D'you mind?'

It took me a moment to register quite what he wanted to know if I minded. Then I realised he was holding up his laptop as if enquiring where to deposit it.

'Oh, right, forgive me. Please, let me introduce you to my Managing Director, Talal.'

I ushered him to the table where Talal had been waiting. A waiter came in with a tray of coffees while Daniel and Talal exchanged handshakes and pleasantries, but I noticed the Irishman was nowhere near as congenial with Talal as he had been with me. Did he dislike Arabs, had he recognised Talal as an underling, or was I the target of a charm offensive? Finally, we were settled at the table and, again, Swift took the lead.

'Right, gentlemen, as you may, or not be aware, I am due to meet this Khoury character tomorrow first thing and I want the complete and utter low-down on the bastard; everything from the size of his ego to the size of his sandals. Who wants to go first?'

Talal had already got his laptop set up, so I gestured in his direction.

'I believe Talal here has been doing some background research which may prove informative.'

'Very good, Talal, let's hear what you've got for us!'

Talal leant forward, adjusted the cursor and began to read through his notes.

'Okay, well this man's full name is Yasar Khoury. He states his birthday to be seventeenth of January, nineteen sixty-six, but this is disputable because his parents were both killed in that year by a bomb during Lebanese Civil War. This occurred in Tripoli. His parents ran a grocery shop. They were caught in explosion from a parked car. He was a baby left safe in the shop. I have newspaper cutting of this event.'

Swift nodded. 'Fine, proceed!'

Talal continued. 'The baby was taken in by the Maronite nuns and brought up as Christian until he ran away and joined the Brigade of the Lebanese Tigers at age sixteen. He fought well in Civil War and it appears he was most successful, soon becoming a senior commander. He also became wealthy and it is rumoured he made a lot of money trading hashish from Bekaa Valley. He was also said to have carried out assassinations on behalf of the leader Daniel Chamoun.'

This was the stuff Talal had garnered from old press cuttings following the business with his cousin. For some reason I did not want to share the murkier stuff we had learned then with anyone yet. I sensed it could turn out to be personally useful in my dealings with Khoury. Besides, I'd paid for it.

Talal glanced up at Swift, but he showed no reaction, so he continued.

'At the end of war in nineteen-ninety he seems to have joined General Security Directorate though I have been unable to find out in what position: this is very secretive organisation. From here, in 2009 he resigned and became a Minister in the Free Patriotic Movement run by Michel Aoun. It is believed he is the key emissary between the secret service and the government. It is believed that this is why he has survived several political battles including allegations of corruption involving the building of Beirut docks.'

This time Swift did react.

'Hmmn, that could be useful when Peter starts shipping

in the medicine and equipment. I take it nothing was found against him?'

'Most certainly not, sir. The newspaper concerned was sued for making these allegations and the editor was sacked.'

Swift grinned.

'Doesn't mess around does he? Sounds like a right nasty bastard. Did I understand you to say he is just a Minister?'

'Indeed, sir.'

'So he is not the actual Minister of the Interior?'

'No sir, that is another gentleman and they are rumoured to greatly dislike each other.'

'I see, so he has to watch his back?'

'Perhaps sir, everyone in Lebanese politics has to watch his back, however Khoury has a good friendship with our President, Michel Suleiman, who is also Maronite, and he has many good friends in the army. He is very powerful man.'

Swift nodded.

'Okay, good, anythin' else Talal?'

'No sir, that explains everything I have been able to find out.'

Swift turned to me.

'Anything to add to that Tony? What did you make of your dealings with the bugger?'

'Well, from what I have seen so far, I concur with everything Talal has said. He's a nasty ego-maniac and, as I'm sure Peter has already told you, we don't exactly see eye to eye.' Swift raised his eyebrows, as if slightly amused by my dig at Peter's puppet-mastery.

'Indeed, he did say something of the sort, but I prefer to hear things from the horse's mouth. Would you mind running over what he's done to upset you?'

I paused. In fact, I did mind. Not his desire to learn what I could tell him about Khoury, but rather the way in which he had swept in here and casually assumed command of the situation. Here were Talal and I 'reporting' to this complete stranger like a couple of prefects to the headmaster! What was worse I couldn't think of a way to redress the balance. Rather than sit here with my mouth open, I had to continue. I ran over our initial meeting in the Ministry and then the pomp and circumstance of his visit to the docks and the Villa. I described his reaction to my insistence of the completion of my clinic and the resultant rebuilding of the 'Lubyanka'. When I finished Swift, who had been leaning forward attentively, sat back with a chuckle.

'Sounds like you've pissed the bastard off good and proper. I take my hat off to yer!'

My annoyance of a moment before evaporated. I hadn't been expecting congratulations.

'Really, I rather had the impression I was meant to get along with the man. So you think this will all blow over?'

'I certainly hope not! As long as we've got the fucker plottin' and schemin' to do you down, Peter and I can get on with the honourable task of stitchin' him up. You've done an excellent job so far!'

*

As Talal and I exited the hotel I was still trying to decide whether I was pleased at having unwittingly pulled off an 'excellent job' or concerned that I was now the object of Khoury's malevolence.

It was therefore a moment before I realised that the limo was conspicuous by its absence. I glanced at Talal who was looking equally puzzled having phoned Mahmoud to collect us as the meeting came to its conclusion. Just as I was about to voice my puzzlement, an unwelcome voice spoke up behind me.

'Good morning Dr Stamford...' I turned to find myself facing the odious Roffe flanked by two burly minions in black suits. He stepped forward with an ill-concealed sneer. 'I regret to inform you, sir, that your vehicle has most unfortunately developed a problem in its engine. Thankfully one of my own drivers happened to be passing and has alerted me to this problem. I have taken the liberty of having the car removed to a government facility where it will be repaired courtesy of my employer Minister Khoury. In the meantime he asks that you might wish to join him for a cup of coffee at his offices as the repair will not take a great deal of time.'

The invitation was delivered with a finality which suggested that there was no point in asking how Khoury knew how long the repair would take. Nevertheless, I tried to find an exit.

'Really, there's no need to put the Minister to any trouble. We can take a taxi...'

'No sir, Minister Khoury would be most offended if you refused his hospitality. I must insist.' By now the two burly individuals were flanking us and the bulges under their jackets were clearly the products of more than simply body building. More importantly, we could hardly refuse without begging the question why? I shrugged.

'In that case, I would only too grateful to accept the Minister's kindness and generosity.'

17

The rattling of the antique lift was nothing compared to the rattling of my nerves as I again ascended to the top floor of the Ministry of the Interior building.

What the hell was this all about? Had they somehow managed to bug our meeting after all? If so what had they heard? I racked my brains trying to recall exactly what had been said and what might be construed as incriminating. As far as I could remember, no crimes had been admitted to, but anyone listening would have been left in no doubt that my relationship with my suppliers was considerably more intimate than I had led Khoury to believe. I also had a nasty feeling that the man would not take too kindly to hearing his career discussed in less than flattering terms or even that we had gone to the trouble of looking into it. Still, he was in the business of spying on people so he could hardly object when it was done to him.

Even as I straightened my shoulders, my defiance rang hollow in my ears. What was really troubling me was not so much his objection to being investigated, but what he might choose to do as a result of it. I had no doubt that, if I really incurred his displeasure, he could put me on a plane back to Britain at the drop of a hat. In fact, when I came to think about it, he could save himself the air fare and sling me in his charming new 'Lubyanka'. There was no-one at home, or here in Lebanon, who would raise any objection.

It was with such dark thoughts filling my mind that we

reached the door at the end of the corridor. Roffe knocked then opened it and beckoned me through. I glanced round but Talal's guards were now gripping him firmly by the biceps and not budging. He shrugged helplessly. I was on my own. I walked forward into the room.

Khoury said something in Arabic and the door closed behind me. Even Roffe was gone. Khoury was sitting behind his desk studying a piece of paper. There was no-one else in the room. I fleetingly wondered at this need for privacy, but was more relieved that I wasn't being greeted by men with truncheons. I really had talked myself into a funk. Khoury looked up.

'Good morning Dr Stamford, I trust your meeting with Mr Swift proved conducive to the construction of our new hospital?'

Christ, how did he know Swift's name? I paused and pulled myself together with a conscious effort. Of course he knew his name: he was the Minister of the Interior and Swift had just come through Customs! I told myself to calm down and get a grip.

'It's Mister, not 'Doctor', I'm a surgeon by profession,' I retorted to seize back some degree of self-assertiveness, even though it was dawning on me that his opening was considerably less hostile than I had anticipated.

'As you wish,' he assented with a dismissive wave of his hand. 'I trust you will accept my regrets for the breakdown of your vehicle and my assurances that this will be remedied most quickly.'

Despite an overwhelming urge to explain exactly how little I believed in the 'breakdown', which, if my memory served me right, had started life as a puncture, I decided to hold my fire. I needed to know just what this was about before I could risk throwing my weight about.

'Thank you Minister, your help in this matter is greatly appreciated. However, I am sure you have not given up your valuable time simply to offer me your reassurances?'

He studied me coldly for a moment then nodded.

'Indeed not, there are other matters of much greater importance that I wish to discuss with you.'

I raised my eyebrows even as my stomach sank.

'I see, please explain.'

He dropped the letter on his desk to indicate that it was the originator of the conversation.

'I am receiving this document from authorities in your country.'

'Yes?' My stomach turned over sickeningly.

'It makes some most serious allegations against you.'

The sickening dread now gripped my throat. 'I thought we'd been over that...' I muttered, thickly.

'Yes, but this is the formal extradition request from your government. It seems you have some most powerful enemies in your country.'

'You said you were willingly to shelter me in return for my help with your hospital.'

The bastard leant back and studied me dispassionately for an uncomfortable length of time. He was clearly used to taking his time over other peoples' suffering. When he finally spoke his reply seemed oddly tangential.

'Perhaps this is so, but tell me, my sources advise me that

before your imprisonment you were most successful surgeon in the world famous Hospital of St George?'

'Well, we call it St George's Hospital, but yes, that is true.'

He frowned slightly at the correction, but continued.

'Am I right to believe that in that place you were employed as the most senior,' he consulted another piece of paper on his desk, 'coloproctocologist'?'

'Coloproctologist, yes, that is true.' This time I corrected him, but didn't make a point of it. Given my current situation it was foolish to provoke him.

'I see, and am I right to understand that this means you are expert in the illnesses of the anus?'

'Well, the bowel and rectum in general. I am particularly well known for my work on the management of colorectal cancer.'

He nodded thoughtfully.

'This is good.'

'Really, may I ask why?'

'Because I wish for you to make examination of me.'

'Really?'

I stared at him in astonishment. This was probably the last direction I could have imagined this interview taking given recent events. I pulled myself together.

'I see, well that shouldn't be a problem, but do you mind my asking why you don't prefer to consult your own doctor?'

Khoury shrugged.

'Information is worth money, Mr Stamford, and the information that perhaps I am suffering from illness such as cancer is worth much money to my enemies. It would not be wise to trust too much a Lebanese doctor.'

'What makes you think you can trust me?'

'Because you stand to make much money and success from our hospital and I have the power to prevent this any time I wish to do so.'

I stood for a moment digesting this, but really there was no gainsaying it.

'I see, and when would you like me to carry out this examination?'

'I wish you to do it now.'

Perhaps it was something in his voice, but, for the first time since the meeting began, I looked him squarely in the eyes. In an instant I realised why this interrogation had lacked the aggression I had at first expected. I was no longer looking in the eyes of a tough and ruthless political fixer. I was looking in the eyes of a very frightened man, a man in need of my expertise.

*

'Thank you Minister. I'm sorry if that caused you any discomfort.'

The Minister's buttocks clenched involuntarily as I withdrew my exploratory finger. I briefly wondered if I was reawakening painful childhood memories: perhaps he was the product of an abusive uncle. It would explain a lot! I decided not to go there. I was a surgeon not a psychiatrist. He was probably just an out-and-out bastard. Besides I was preoccupied with a lot more than the 'nature versus nurture' debate. In fact, I was wrestling with a considerably larger question of professional ethics. Did I tell him that he was suffering from a nasty case of internal haemorrhoids, which was all I could detect, or did I allow him to continue in the misapprehension that the cause of the blood and discomfort was carcinogenic? I decided, given the wider issues surrounding my diagnosis, that a little medical prevarication was the order of the day. No coloproctologist worth his salt would be satisfied with an impromptu digital examination, indeed it was not unheard of for rectal carcinomas to be masked by haemorrhoids. I wouldn't be doing my duty if I didn't take the matter seriously and recommend further investigations. I made a decision: under the present circumstances it would only be professionally right and proper to make the bastard sweat.

I scrubbed my hand with distaste in the bowl of scented water he had provided in the absence of rubber gloves. Frankly, I didn't share Middle Eastern attitudes to personal hygiene, particularly when it was someone else's. When he had finished rearranging his clothing and was once more seated, I continued.

'I'm sure you will be pleased to hear that my initial examination has revealed that you are suffering from badly inflamed haemorrhoids which, while often very uncomfortable or painful, are quite easily treated, often without recourse to surgery even...' I paused to watch the look of immense relief spread across his face, then continued: 'however, that does not preclude the possibility of a rectal cancer. The conditions are quite separate and should not be confused...' I could have slapped him!

'What you mean?' he snarled, his face twisting with fear and anger. 'What is this thing you are saying?'

'Please, please,' I held my hands up to placate him as he appeared poised to lunge across his desk, 'I am simply saying that I have concerns about symptoms such as the blood in your stools and the abdominal pain you have described. I am only recommending that further tests would be advisable to put your mind at rest...'

'What sort of tests?'

'Well there are several that could be undertaken depending on facilities available and your need for discretion.'

'What you mean?'

'Well, for a proper diagnosis, there are several tests I would wish to carry out, all of which require the sort of equipment and pathology you would find in a general hospital, but which I have not purchased for the Arsal Clinic. The new hospital in Arsal will not be in operation for some time yet so, unless you are able to get yourself smuggled anonymously into a hospital in Beirut or Tripoli for tests, your desire for secrecy is a non-starter.'

'Why have you not purchased this equipment?'

'Because the Clinic is a trauma unit set up to deal with immediate injury not longer term illness. We have only just taken delivery of a couple of portable X-ray machines and we have no plans to acquire the sort of imaging facilities your condition requires.' If I was being a little presumptive about his 'condition', I felt the menace in his manner justified it. Besides, who would complain if I coaxed him into funding the best equipped front-line clinic in the Middle East? His fists clenched with frustration.

'How much are these things costing?'

I shrugged.

'I wouldn't know. Probably not a lot in the overall scheme of things. I could ask Talal to find out and look into delivery at the same time. I'm sure our suppliers could have it flown in to save time.'

Khoury unclenched his fists and sat back, much to my relief.

'This is better. What tests do you wish me to undergo?'

I would have sat back too, but I hadn't as yet qualified for the offer of a seat. An image of obsequious, mediaeval physicians gathered round the ailing monarch's bed flashed through my mind. It was time to assert a little authority here.

'Do you mind?' I gestured to a chair by the wall and, without waiting for his consent, crossed the room pulled it over to in front of his desk and sat down. I didn't hurry.

'Right, let me see,' I began, 'the first thing we will need is a blood test for anaemia. I can already see this from your finger nails and tongue, but these signs are not conclusive and certainly do not prove you have cancer. For a conclusive examination I would advise a colonoscopy backed up with X-rays. That would give me a complete picture of the bowel and reveal any other problems such as ulcers or polyps that could account for your symptoms...'

'What are these other problems?'

'Well, short of putting you through a crash-course in coloproctology, I don't see how I can answer that, but let us just say I need an overall picture of your bowels before I can decide what further steps need to be taken. I would also like to test you for diabetes...'

'Why do you wish for this test?'

'I wondered if you had it the first time I met you. The dark glasses suggest sensitivity to light and you look like a man who has lost a lot of weight rather than someone who is naturally thin. Have you noticed this?'

'Yes, I start to become thin when troubles start.'

'I see, well that could be stress and overwork, but men of your age often develop diabetes as a result of stress and it can be very dangerous, even fatal, if left untreated...'

'How long?'

'Sorry?'

'How long will these things take to be done?'

'That rather depends on how long it takes to acquire the equipment. As I said I need to talk to Talal about that.'

'And how long if I have got the cancer?'

'What do you mean?'

The Minister squeezed the words out through gritted teeth.

'How long do I have to live if this is your diagnosis?'

I studied him again. The anger was gone only the fear remained. Disease was one thing he couldn't control. The man responsible for the 'Lebanese 'Lubyanka'' was suddenly facing torture himself and he was not taking it well. In fact, unless I was very much mistaken, regardless of any physical condition he might be suffering from, the Lebanese Minister for the Interior was suffering from an acute case of hypochondria.

'I really cannot answer that without seeing the results of these investigations,' I replied calmly.

*

'Yes Peter, he's absolutely shitting himself to add to his discomfort!'

I heard Chisholm chuckle.

'Serves him right, he sounds like a real stinker from what

you've told me. Still, we've got him by the short and curlies now!'

'Sure, I'll have that clinic kitted out like the John Hopkins before you can say colostomy!'

Chisholm paused before replying.

'Yes, fine Tony, but I don't think you quite see the whole picture here. I think this calls for a Council of War.'

'What do you mean?'

'I mean I think you, Daniel and I should sit down and talk this through properly. You've just staked a claim to a potential goldmine.'

'Have I?'

'Certainly, look, is Talal with you?'

'Yes, he's right here...'

'Great, put him on. I need to talk to him about setting up a meet.'

'Okay, I'll hand you over now.'

Somewhat mystified, I passed the Tripleton Enigma E2 to my number two who was standing with me in the seclusion of the Villa's gardens. The evening was already drawing in thanks to my protracted meeting with Khoury.

I had expected Peter to be impressed with my news, but I hadn't foreseen a reaction like this. In fact, I had been so surprised by his enthusiasm that I had handed him over to Talal without seeking his advice on the question foremost on my mind. Perhaps it wasn't the question to preoccupy Peter, or, indeed, one that he could even provide a satisfactory answer to. But it was the question that was taxing me almost to the exclusion of everything else: who was the author of the anonymous letter that Khoury had shown me? I was being stalked and I wished to God I knew who by.

18

Along with the general 'ward fitness' of a working hospital surgeon, it would appear I had lost the sea-legs I had taken for granted as a competition sailor in my younger days. The chilly rain lashing into my face did nothing to ameliorate the nausea I was experiencing. Still, it wasn't every day that I found myself on a fishing boat, rolling around in a late autumn storm just outside Lebanese coastal waters. I peered over the side as the equipment I had ordered for Khoury's examination was passed up the ladder from the sleek cigarette boat moored alongside; the operation was taking longer than anticipated as the crew struggled to fend their pretty speedboat off the trawler's rusty hull. I made my way along the railing to join Talal who had got himself braced between the cabin and a set of bollards in order to capture the scene on a camcorder.

'What are you doing that for?' I yelled above yet another squall. Talal shrugged.

'Dunno boss. Peter tell me to.'

It was too windy to point out that he worked for me, not Peter, so I let it pass.

'Okay, well I've had enough of this. I'm going inside. Join me when you're done.'

As I turned towards the cabin, Peter clambered off the top of the rope ladder onto the trawler's deck with impressive agility for a man I put in his early sixties. I recalled his claim that the police would not have caught him in his younger days. He was kitted out in full, ocean racing gear topped off with a jaunty peaked cap and a wide grin. He was clearly loving this.

'Tony, how the devil are you?'

'Cold, wet and seasick to be frank, Peter: is this really necessary?'

'Of course old boy, don't think I'd drag you all the way out here for nothing do you? Come inside and I'll fill you in,' with that, he dragged open the cabin door, which was being held shut by the wind, and ushered me in.

I stood blinking in the bright light as the voice of my third companion in this adventure made a most welcome suggestion:

'Evenin' Peter, am I right in thinkin' you two would not be averse to joinin' me in drop of somethin' to warm the bones?'

Peter greeted this suggestion with caution.

'Certainly Dan, as long as it's not that fucking Raki stuff they drink in these parts. Bloody aniseed muck.'

'Come, come, Peter, you know me better than that! It's only Teachers but it'll warm the cockles. Here, bottoms up before I drink it for yer.'

With that, Swift, who had wisely dismissed the idea of leaving the warmth of the cabin to welcome our new guest, handed over a somewhat battered, leather-bound hip flask. Peter accepted it and took a generous swig before handing it to me. Despite the lingering nausea I did likewise and, to my relief, felt the fierce spirit brush the queasiness aside as it spread down into my stomach. Again, I experienced the uncomfortable impression that I was still the 'new kid in school' as Peter and Daniel shook hands and slapped backs. I took another swig.

After this initial exchange of pleasantries we found ourselves places to perch around the small cabin table. It was severely cramped, but that rather added to the somewhat 'Boy's Own' flavour of the adventure. We settled down and Peter assumed the chairmanship of the meeting.

'Right gents, Tony asked me a minute ago if this is all strictly necessary and the answer is 'yes it is' if we are to comply with Mr Khoury's wish that his treatment is carried out in complete secrecy. Like all men in his position, his enemies are his rivals in government and within his own department, real or imaginary. If we want him rubber-stamping our bills it is very much in our interest to feed his paranoia and pander to his whims.'

I suddenly felt a bit better about the rain and nausea; I could put up with a lot if it meant getting Khoury under our thumb! Peter turned to Swift.

'So Daniel, perhaps you would be kind enough to fill us in on progress with the hospital build?'

Swift nodded and turned the laptop he had opened on the table to afford Peter and me a better view.

'Certainly, Peter, perhaps it would be a good idea if I took it literally from the ground up?' Peter nodded his assent as Daniel called up a collage of photographs on screen and continued: 'These are just a few snaps I took of the ground works, but what they're showin' are the 'dozers levellin' off a decent patch of ground.' He clicked the mouse to bring up another collage. 'We're buildin' on a reinforced concrete slab for speed and this shows the mixers pourin' it. We've sited where the bedrock is really shallow and only put proper foundations under the part of the slab that'll bear the atrium. That's because it's made of glass and blocks so there's a bit of weight involved. The rest of it's made up of lightweight, prefab, bolt-together units. The slab will support them long enough for our purposes, so that's saved us a bloody fortune.'

Daniel passed round his hip flask for us to toast this good news. He took a tot himself then called up another collage showing a pool of water from various angles. He continued:

'As you can see here, we've also had a stroke of luck on the water supply front. There are natural springs in the area, so we are not havin' to ship it in.' He glanced at Peter. 'As we agreed, the objective is a quick in-and-out job, so this will save a fortune in time as well as haulage costs.'

Peter nodded his approval.

'Excellent. Any idea how much we've cut so far?'

Swift shrugged.

'Hard to say exactly, but I'm guessin' it could be in the region of twenty percent of the budget that that naughty Jolanda sucked out of Khoury.'

Peter chuckled his satisfaction: 'Not bad. How are the prefabs shaping up?'

'Fine, a good scrub and re-spray and they're good as new again. Once they're bolted together, you'll never know they've got history.'

Peter turned to me to explain.

'Bit of a stroke of luck on this one. Gortis had to repossess 'em from a charity in Ghana when the financial director did a bunk with the cash. As far as Khoury's concerned they're brand spanking new,' he grinned broadly, 'happy days!' He raised the hip flask in another toast then passed it to me.

I accepted the flask and took my swig, before handing it on to Daniel again. Despite the bracing effect of the whisky and the casual way in which the conversation was being conducted, I was feeling distinctly troubled. It was beginning to strike me that I was observing the machinations of what amounted to a substantial and carefully calculated fraud. Furthermore, I was not simply observing this; by my very presence, I was being drawn into it as a co-conspirator!

Before my faltering conscience decided to raise any vocal objections to this, another voice rose in my head to offer an alternative perspective. What was I worrying about? Surely, this was this just the real-politik of international business in action. Perhaps, in my naive, British, NHS, 'money-no-object' way, I had envisaged a gleaming new hospital built to meet Khoury's vision of a new city in western Lebanon, but that was hardly going to happen in practice. Wasn't I just listening to a rather cynical, clear-eyed explanation of the way these things come about in the real world, along with the corner-cutting and double-dealing that such ventures always involve? So what if a bullying thug like Khoury was going to end up paying through the nose for what would probably never amount to more than just a very expensive ego trip? I needed to wise up!

I reached this conclusion just as Peter turned to me with an encouraging grin.

'Fine, now Tony, I believe you've got some news for us that sheds a completely different light on our relationship with Minister Khoury?'

Peter and I had had no opportunity to discuss Khoury since our last phone call, so I was still in the dark as to why he seemed to be putting such significance on Khoury's hypochondria. Perhaps narrating the contents of the meeting would elicit an explanation. I turned to Swift and began with Talal's and my 'arrest'. When I finished, he turned to Peter with a slightly drink-induced solemnity:

'By Christ, pal, we've got the fucker's bollocks on the anvil!'

Peter clenched his fist and grinned his delighted agreement.

'Indeed, old boy; couldn't have put it better myself.'

I decided I'd had enough of being excluded from this moment of mutual self-congratulation.

'Excuse me...would anyone care to explain quite why my news is such a source of satisfaction?'

Peter turned to me with barely concealed impatience.

''Cause, from now on, anytime he hesitates to put his name to a new requisition order, you can tell him to find someone else to treat his cancer.'

'I beg your pardon?'

'If he won't clear our bills, you can withdraw your services?'

'I can't do that.'

'Why not?'

'Well it's wrong...I can't blackmail him into buying stuff from us on the basis that I won't treat him for a cancer that probably doesn't even exist!'

'Of course you can. You've not told him he's got cancer. Just the symptoms that indicate the possibility and you need to check it out. You've already done the donkey work. All you need to do now is string him along!'

'Yes, and what if he gets it checked out elsewhere and finds out that I'm exaggerating?'

'You're not exaggerating, just being cautious. Besides, you said yourself the man's a raving hypochondriac so he's always going to believe the worst. Don't worry about it!'

'That's all very well for you to say... you're sitting in your comfy office in Zurich while I'm sitting opposite a paranoid psychopath who already thinks it's clever to build a two-storey dungeon to intimidate me!'

Peter paused, and then glanced at me slyly.

'Not scared of him are you?'

'Yes, as a matter of fact I am!'

My companions sat there staring at me in tipsy surprise, while I sat there in horror. It was like one of those out-of-body moments I've heard survivors of 'near death' experiences describe. It was as if I was looking down on myself as I spoke. I had just heard myself admit to being scared; not scared of pain, or obvious danger, but of being scared to face a challenge, too scared to act. I had never admitted to being scared to face a challenge in my life!

Peter was suddenly very sober and serious.

'I see, well I'm sorry Tony. I had you down for sterner stuff than that, old boy. If you don't think you are up to...'

'No, I didn't mean it like that! Just give me a minute...I need to think!' I rose abruptly from the table and wove my way to the cabin door. I forced it open against the wind and shoved my way out into the squalling rain, desperate for air. I staggered to the side and threw up, barely remembering to clutch the rail as the ship rolled. I straightened up and took a better grip on the railing as the nausea cleared. I blinked hard to clear the rain or tears in my eyes, but I couldn't dispel the horrendous reeling bewilderment that was threatening to overwhelm my mind. I was clinging to my grip on reality as desperately as I was clinging to the railing and I was by no means sure that I could hang on.

Gradually the feeling passed to be replaced by dread. I knew this feeling all too well. It was the feeling of fearful confusion that defined my breakdown. The breakdown I thought I had left behind in Standford Hill Prison, the breakdown I had suffered at the hands of that bastard Ham, and my bitch of a wife, and my supposed best friend Roger. My God, was it coming back? What had that shrink in Putney called it? Acute Anxiety Syndrome; that was it! Perhaps it was like a physical injury, it healed, but it never went away entirely. It left a weakness that later stress could expose.

I stood breathing deeply, until the dread began to subside too. Okay, I had an Achilles' heel. Perhaps I was no longer fearless Tony Stamford, playboy surgeon and sportsman, but that didn't make me a coward. Alright, I was a bit scared of Khoury and his minions, but I had good reason to be. He was a powerful man in a country where I had no recourse to the sort of protection, let alone human rights, I took for granted back in England. At any moment he could accuse me of spying, or some other crime, and have me flung in an unmarked cell. I was still possibly a fugitive from justice back in Britain. My fears were based on very real concerns, not paranoia or residual Acute Anxiety Syndrome.

Still, what was I to do? I didn't want to go back to Britain and I didn't want to let Peter down. After all, it was me that had taken the project to him. He had thrown his weight behind it and, if it had turned out to be more stressful than I had foreseen, whose fault was that? True, I had not foreseen the questionable degree to which he would exploit the opportunity, but what did I expect? I had met him in prison for God's sake and, in fairness, he had made no secret of his aggressive attitude to acquiring wealth. No, I had no reason to complain about what he was asking me to do. The question was: had I got the balls to do it? The answer to that, given the episode I had just experienced, was, if I was really honest with myself, I simply didn't know. Still, there were two men sitting in that wind swept cabin waiting for me to walk back in with an answer. I had to make my mind up. I braced my shoulders and headed back through the lashing rain.

*

It was clear when I sat down that my companions had also been giving the situation more serious thought. The whisky flask was nowhere to be seen and Peter was looking concerned as he enquired: 'You okay?'

I grinned crookedly.

'Sort of...'

Peter continued:

'Don't worry about it, old boy. We've all been there: 'first night nerves', 'the hour before dawn' and all that. Nothing to be ashamed of, trust me.'

'It's not you I don't trust, it's him. The man's a bloody nutcase and he runs the asylum.'

'Sure, you're right but we're not suggesting you go in all guns blazing. Look, the man's paranoid about his enemies learning he's got cancer, so why don't you tell him that you've had a chat with your contact, Mr Macari at Torino Farmaceutico, and he has agreed to include your fees for treating Khoury in his invoice for meds and kit which has to be pre-paid anyway. All you have to do is tell Khoury that you reckon his treatment will take three months which is about all the time Dan and I reckon we've got in which to maximise profits before the whole situation goes tits-up. He'll never know how much we charge him for it because he's not going to want to see it broken down on invoices. That way we are in and out in twelve weeks max with Khoury's cash in the bank and he thinks you have done him a favour. Better still he won't have had time to really assess what we have sold him!'

Peter beamed his satisfaction at this elegant solution at me encouragingly, but now, as a semblance of clarity began to return, there was more than just my personal safety troubling me.

'Okay, Peter, that would certainly take some of the heat off me, but what exactly are you proposing to sell him?'

'Well, drugs and equipment. You know, as we've discussed.'

'Yes, but a minute ago you were celebrating the news that you were selling him a repossessed hospital as new and fit for purpose. Where are you laying your hands on the drugs and equipment, if you don't mind my asking?'

For the first time since I'd met him Peter looked decidedly shifty and I began feeling better for a little self-assertion.

'Well that depends on what the chaps in Zurich come up with. You pass your wish list to Macari, he passes it to me and I hand it on to the buying team. I've got half-a-dozen people working on it at the moment...'

'And where do they go to do their shopping?'

'Well I can't say off the top of my head. It's a huge market and they spend all day shopping around for the best prices.' He gestured expansively to indicate the impossibility of a precise answer.

'Come off it Peter, you almost live in that office in Zurich and you're trying to tell me you don't know where your teams are getting their supplies from? Pull the other one! Sure the drugs market is rich, but it's not huge. Not if you're working in the legal and above-board end of it. It's the counterfeiters, non-branders and outright hijackers that make up the numbers. So which part of the market do your buyers work in?'

'In the part that stands to make the most profit of course! Come off it Tony, I can go with you being worried about Khoury's psychopathic tendencies, but not about where we do our shopping. So we save ourselves a few bob buying unbranded meds and cheaper equipment than we invoice for, big deal! The big boys charge a fucking fortune for their fancy labels so let's make the most of it. When was it wrong to undercut in business?'

'That's not undercutting, it's counterfeiting and the big boys charge a lot because they pay for all the research...'

'So what, we're only in this project for the short term! Look, Tony, you're not the only one trying to rebuild here. Sure, I used my time in chokey to reshape things in Zurich, but it cost money and came with conditions. They didn't let me out for 'Good Behaviour', they let me out on the understanding that I stayed out of Africa, and arms dealing, and generally cleaned my act up.'

'Who's 'they'?'

'Interpol, primarily, but there are others which is why I don't want to show my face in Lebanon right now – nothing to do with this by the way.'

'Is that's why you keep talking about making a quick killing?'

'Exactly, I need capital. With a bit of cash in the bank I'll be clean as the vicar's vestments, but I need a leg up first, d'you see?'

I nodded. In fact I didn't see very much at all, but I had personal experience of just how hard it was to shake off the long arm of the law and Peter had a persuasive knack of making you feel that he was laying his cards on the table.

'So basically, you see this as a means to an end?'

'Exactly! That's all it stands a chance of being. Khoury will be dead of bum-rot, or back-stabbing, soon enough and, bear in mind, the country and his successor will still be left with a working hospital even if it will need new foundations in a year or two. In the meantime we will walk away with enough cash to operate completely above-board.'

'We?'

'Of course 'we' unless you have other plans...with Cameron and his chums dismantling the NHS there's going to be a killing to be made back in Blighty once we've finished here. You'll make the perfect front man!'

'Right, yes, of course.'

I tried not to show my delight, but I felt the sickening residue of Acute Anxiety Syndrome evaporate as abruptly as it had gripped me. I had a future. I was one of the team. True there was still the question of why the British Police wanted to talk to me, but suddenly that seemed negligible; Peter had dealt with Interpol for God's sake!

Did I mention Newcombe, or that fucking extradition request Khoury had waved under my nose? I decided no, I had done enough. I had established a reasonably non-life-threatening approach to handling Khoury and I had, at last, found myself something that, give or take an initial cashflow problem, had the makings of a new career. Most importantly, I had just caught a figurative glimpse of the white cliffs of Dover and they looked wonderfully inviting. I decided the details could wait until I was back on dry land before the sickening rolling of the trawler induced another kind of nausea.

19

I have no hesitation in claiming credit for the suggestion that Khoury undergo his treatments at the Villa. The idea came to me the following day as I rattled towards the top floor of the Ministry of the Interior in that rickety cage lift. I had briefly discussed possible venues with Peter before he transferred back to his cigarette boat, but I was feeling too queasy to really focus on the issue at the time. Now, with a key meeting with the Minister of Menace just minutes away, the choice of location was taking on alarming significance.

To say I found Khoury's office unsettling as a possible clinic was a distinct understatement. It was his turf and he controlled it right down to whether I was offered a seat or not. He decided which conversations were secretly recorded, and his guards stood outside the door. If I did not feel directly threatened, I certainly felt vulnerable and lacking control. Besides, there was nowhere obvious to hide the equipment I had ordered for his treatment from other visitors to his office. The place had drawbacks for him too.

The Arsal Clinic was just about ready, but again there were major issues with security if he wanted to keep his health concerns under wraps. I couldn't imagine him sharing his treatment with a bunch of common-or-garden refugees. There was the Lubyanka of course, but God knows what was planned for in there and I had no intention of finding out. I had no doubt that he was a hard bastard, but I suspected that even Khoury would baulk at receiving medical investigations to the accompaniment of screams from suspected agents provocateurs. Anyway, I wasn't going in there and that was final.

That only really left the Villa, unless he wanted to nominate an alternative venue altogether, but then locating and commandeering that would attract attention in its own right. No, the Villa made sense, but it was in the lift that I began to see just how much sense. I could use Khoury's paranoia to persuade him that it was the only plausible option; after all it was completely private and a perfectly natural venue in which we might choose to hold business meetings. Talal was bound to have relatives in the building trade who could convert one of the bedrooms into an office and an en suite bathroom would make an ideal examination cum treatment room. He could leave his guards outside the door if it made him feel better, but he would be guaranteed the secrecy he craved for his condition. From my point of view there would be no-one within miles who could question my diagnoses and, psychologically, it was all happening on my territory. I felt my spirits lift immeasurably as the guards at his office door patted me down.

Perhaps Khoury had already thought through the possibilities himself and his paranoia had won out without any prompting from me. Whatever, he began nodding before I had even finished outlining the suggestion. I explained that it would take a couple of weeks to complete the building work and make sure the equipment was all properly plumbed in and fit for purpose. In the meantime I had made arrangements for blood and urine samples to be shipped over to a private path lab in Switzerland for analysis. This was true, though the lab thought it was dealing with me working from Peter's address and their conclusions would be adjusted by me upon receipt to fit with my diagnosis. The paranoid fool seemed positively impressed with my security arrangements. I explained that I would personally call him with an appointment for him to visit the Villa to 'discuss hospital business' and learn his test results, at which time we could discuss a treatment plan.

With his personal issues out of the way, I took the opportunity to mention that I had begun drawing up a budget for medical supplies which Torino Farmaceutico Internazionale needed to start sourcing rather urgently. He did not seem particularly fazed when I told him I was already well into six figures in US dollars, so I suggested a down payment of two million to encourage them to get on with it. He simply nodded and replied 'I will see to it' then switched the conversation back to likely prognoses of his own condition. I patiently explained that there was no value in idle speculation and that he would simply have to wait for the results and our next appointment at the Villa. Unwillingly, he acquiesced and, with considerable relief, I found myself heading back down the corridor to the rickety lift.

*

With Khoury on ice and Swift handling the construction of the hospital, I was finally able to turn my full attention to my own pet project, the Clinic. By now my initial affront at MSF's pompous rejection of my services had rather faded, but my desire to get back to my calling as a working surgeon had, if anything, grown. To be honest I was finding all this skulduggery more stressful than exciting and I was yearning for the challenge of pulling the latex gloves back on and getting stuck in.

This of course had a significant effect on my lifestyle. For one thing, a daily round trip commute of nearly one hundred and sixty miles from the Villa to Arsal was out of the question. I was needed hands-on and in situ. I was effectively in charge of setting up a field hospital in a rapidly deteriorating refugee situation and that demanded a twenty-four-hour, seven-days-a-week working schedule. The flow across the border was becoming a flood as Syria was descending into all-out civil war and there were constant reports of cross border clashes and shelling between Syrian and Lebanese forces. People had already died in shelling in a village not far to the north of Arsal.

Not only was I desperately needed in Arsal, I also found myself vaguely repelled by the Villa, or rather the issues I associated with it. The Villa was where I worried about my past, and that letter Khoury had waved at me and, most importantly, Khoury himself and the dubious hospital we were building and kitting out for him. In Arsal I could immerse myself in work and forget all that. I rapidly made a decision to leave the Villa end of things to my new MD, Talal, and my secretary Adanna who were more than capable of liaising with Peter and Co in Zurich. I would only return to the Villa to treat Khoury which would be as infrequently as I could get away with.

This, of course, meant losing my right-hand man, but, shrewd as he was, Talal had no medical acumen and that was what this was all about. Regretfully, I explained the new arrangement whilst reassuring him that I would be back regularly and only at the end of a phone if he needed me. He took it well.

It also meant that Adanna was deprived of my services, but she was a modern lass and I had never given her any reason to see the relationship as long-term. I toyed with the idea of taking her out for a meal to break the news, but somehow the words never came and we ended up in bed instead. The following day I hit the road for Arsal and I decided en route that time and circumstances would break the news less painfully.

On my arrival in Arsal I planned to set about recruiting staff. I had vaguely assumed that, amongst the assorted nutters and misfits that had partially decamped from outside MSF as rumours spread of a new clinic opening, I would find a selection of sane, qualified people who, like me, had found their way to Lebanon with a desire to serve, but failed to meet with MSF acceptance for non-medical reasons. What I hadn't considered was how I was to set about identifying them.

I deliberately arrived late on a Friday evening with a view to dossing down in the new building for the weekend while I got my bearings and made an assessment of the facilities, medical supplies and equipment. Once I had a clear idea of those, I could then recruit people to utilise them to our best advantage. In practice, I was still lifting my holdall and medical bag out of the boot of my new BMW X5 when people started drifting towards me. I had to command the crowd to 'Get back!' as I pushed through them and unlocked the front door of the Clinic. I slipped inside slamming it shut behind me and hastily relocking it. I hadn't exactly been mobbed, more squeezed inside by weight of numbers. Some were apparently aspiring members of staff. Others were clearly refugees who had failed to find sanctuary elsewhere. Images of the lost souls wandering around liberated concentration camps filled my mind as I leant with my back to the door recovering.

Finally, I got a grip and straightened up. I don't consider myself as prone to wild imaginings, but the spectral crowd had quite unnerved me. Thank God I'd been wearing civvies! I dreaded to think what would have happened if I'd been positively identified as a doctor. Some of those people looked really desperate. Still, I had work to do. I couldn't help anyone without a base to operate from.

I looked around and found I was standing on a concrete floor in what could have been a single-storey warehouse. It was big, about a hundred feet to the far wall by a hundred-and-fifty feet wide. Along the left side, partitions had been erected to create five sizeable rooms presumably for use as offices and operating theatres. That was it.

Apart of course from all the piles of equipment still wrapped in polythene and boxes. At the far end I could see a roller shutter and tyre marks in the dust where lorries had backed in and dumped their loads haphazardly on the floor. Tyre marks! I bent down and examined the floor in the fading light. Just running my hand over it threw up a small cloud. Everywhere I looked the place was covered in a thin layer of fine sand no doubt mixed with dust from the concrete. How the hell was anyone going to operate with that stuff stirred up and floating in the air? Jesus, this place was going to take some sorting out!

I looked up and made out strip lighting suspended from the ceiling above me. I went in search of a means to turn it on. Sod's Law dictated that the junction box and switch were located in the far corner of the room at the far end of the place, but at least, when I threw the switch, to my surprise, the lights in the warehouse flickered and pinged into life. I tried the switch by the door in the room and they worked too. Unfortunately the additional illumination only served to further reveal the magnitude of the task ahead of me. Where on Earth was I to begin?

Cleaning, that was the first priority. There was no point even unpacking this stuff without a tolerably clean, dust-free environment to work in; anything else would be utterly self-defeating from the outset. I would phone Khoury first thing in the morning and tell him I needed an army of domestic staff to straighten the place out pronto. If he wanted a frontline clinic to sort out his refugee problem then he needed to come up with a lot more than some dusty shell on the edge of the desert! Just as I was beginning to rehearse my demands, another voice in my head reminded me that Khoury didn't particularly want a frontline clinic for refugees. Khoury wanted a swanky new hospital built well behind the lines with his statue in the atrium. In fact, Khoury couldn't care less about the clinic or the refugees, other than those who might turn out to be spies. In the real world, I could expect a more sympathetic hearing from Satan himself. Furthermore, I wanted Khoury in my debt, not the other way round. I didn't want to ask him for anything if I could avoid it. But how could I avoid it?

On the other hand, I couldn't clean up the fucking place on my own! I was a surgeon, not a skivvy for crying out loud and, more's to the point, it would take me a month even if I was willing to do it, which I wasn't. I sat down on a packing case and extracted a bottle of Evian from my holdall to whet my whistle whilst I tried to consider the problem calmly.

I needed manpower, but not from Khoury, so where from. Suddenly, as I sat sipping my water, an idea began to form. There was an army of helpers sitting just outside the front door. Not all of them were mad or bad, or even ill or injured. The majority, in fact, were women and children, along with the elderly, who didn't know where to go or what to do. Well I knew what they could do. They could earn their keep. Tomorrow I would sort out the able bodied and set them to work. One thing Khoury had agreed to was food and medical supplies, no doubt so that suspects could be kept alive for interrogation in the 'Lubyanka', so I did have something to bargain with. The only difficulty I could foresee was how to sort out the useful from the time wasters. If I could overcome that I had quite possibly found myself a body of domestics, the best of which might even be moulded into a rudimentary nursing staff. Only time could answer that, but it was a start.

*

'I need as many brooms, mops and buckets as you can lay your hands on along with gallons of bleach. I'm talking a hundred of each if possible, got it?'

It was six o'clock in the morning and I was on the phone to a rather bleary Talal.

'Sure boss, I'll do my best.'

'Fine, and get young Fadi on the road with them a.s.a.p, alright?'

'Sure, is everything okay there?'

'To be honest, it's a shithole right now, but I hope to recruit some help to get it cleaned up shortly. Can I leave that with you?'

'Certainly, I will call my cousin right away.'

'Good.'

I hung up without stopping to enquire which cousin specialised in janitorial supplies, then shovelled down the pot of honey and yoghurt that Adanna had prepared for me and donned my white coat and stethoscope. I rinsed the spoon in the sink I was temporarily using as a kitchen. Thankfully there was a sink with running water in each of the side rooms, though each bore ample evidence of the use the workmen who had installed them had put them to. I returned the spoon to my holdall, picked up my laptop, collected the keys and headed for the front door of the building.

The brilliant sunshine half-blinded me as I stepped out of the dingy building, nevertheless, I could make out an absolute sea of faces. The crowd of silent, seated people stretched back on either side of the approach road and off on either side of it for at least a hundred yards. As I appeared a ripple of comments and exclamations ran through the crowd and people began struggling to their feet. Before this could turn into another mobbing I raised my hands and spoke:

'Good morning everybody; does anyone here speak English?'

'Indeed, old fellow, I do!' came the instantaneous reply. I turned to face the owner of the rather plummy, German voice that had uttered it. A lanky man with wispy white hair and half-moon spectacles was already pushing his way to the front.

'Good and do you also speak Arabic?'

He stopped in his tracks.

'Arabisch? Nein.' The man looked most affronted.

'I'm sorry, I didn't explain myself properly. I need a translator.'

My first volunteer turned abruptly on his heel and waved his fist frantically at the crowd as if it were their fault that he didn't get the job, and then stormed off as best he could, given the people in his way. Another voice spoke up.

'I have okay English.'

I turned to find myself facing a middle-aged woman in a black skirt and white blouse with half a tattered blanket wrapped around her shoulders to serve as a shawl. Beside her an old man sat slumped in a battered wheelchair, unconscious or dead.

'Can you speak to these people for me? Is your voice strong enough?'

She nodded.

'I am teacher. I speak loud if it is necessary.'

'Good, please join me.' I gestured for her to come forward and the crowd parted to let her through. I took the opportunity to survey the throng with less dazzled eyes. Apart from the aspiring medics who had decamped from the square in front of MSF, all I could see were women, children and the elderly. There was not a man in sight. I began to make out stretchers on the ground; perhaps they were all injured, but that seemed unlikely. It was early and the Clinic was still caught in the shadow of the faceless 'Lubyanka' behind it. A chilling thought crossed my mind, but I shoved it aside and switched my attention back to my volunteer. Her face was haggard with exhaustion, but not unattractive. Still, such thoughts had no part to play in my current mission.

'What is your name?'

'My name is Barika Mussan.'

'Okay,' I nodded, 'from now on you are Sister Mussan, got it?'

'But I am not nurse...'

'That doesn't matter, nor is anyone else around here, but I'm putting you in charge of the clean-up operation and a title always helps. We'll worry about qualifications later. Tell them that my name is Doctor Anthony Stamford from Chisford Holdings. Tell them that Chisford Holdings is an international charitable, financial institution which builds clinics and hospitals in crisis situations. Tell them I need help to clean this place up and start treating people. Tell them I can give them food and treatment and medicine in return. Got that?'

She nodded a trifle uncertainly, but turned to the crowd and began to speak before turning back to me again:

'I am sorry, what is your name please?'

'Doctor Anthony Stamford and I am from the charity Chisford Holdings.'

She nodded and continued to a background of murmured whispers relaying her words back through the crowd. I recalled the game Chinese Whispers from my schooldays and wondered quite what the people at the back would end up being told. She turned and nodded that my message had been passed.

'Tell them that everyone able to help with the clean-up should come forward and line up outside the door of the Clinic for registration. Everyone who wishes to work in a medical capacity should return at midday to register, when they will be required to provide proof of their medical qualifications. Can you use one of these?' I held up my laptop. She nodded. 'Good, I'll set up a table by the door and leave it with a file open. Take the name and work qualifications of each person that comes forward and send them through to me.'

With that I turned and headed back into the Clinic to await young Fadi.

*

And that is how The Arsal Refugee Centre began. By the end of the weekend my gang of helpers had achieved a relatively clean and dust free environment and unpacked the beds, drips, and other paraphernalia. The following week we converted the side rooms into two sets of rest and operating rooms leaving the fifth room to be used as a sluice. Talal sent us a team of workmen, courtesy of a cousin, to knock up a hardboard partition for the right hand corner of the main room by the front door. This became a reception cum waiting room for new arrivals. They then built rows of single bed 'cells' along the right-side and rear walls for staff accommodation. I sent Khoury the bill.

It soon became apparent that Sister Mussan was an absolute God send: it never ceases to surprise me what a little responsibility will bring out in some people. The situation automatically brought out her womanly nursing instincts and, as any doctor will tell you, the rest is mostly common sense. More importantly, she was quick to spot any nursing aptitude in others and had no patience with slackers. She soon began to gather the makings of a pretty effective team around her. The rest were consigned to cooking and cleaning duties.

For my part, things turned out slightly unexpectedly. I had started with visions of never-ending surgery as I battled to save the wounded, but in practice I found myself dealing with a much lighter work load. We were inundated with sick people, some of whom had injuries from falls and the like, but very few with what might be called war wounds. Most were suffering from malnutrition, dehydration and exhaustion, along with emotional and psychological problems which were frankly not my field. I left those to Sister Mussan and the women.

My under-employment boiled down to the absence of men, especially fighting men. This hadn't changed since my arrival. Something was not making sense, but, for the time being, I could not see a way of getting to the bottom of it. Besides, I was busy enough as it was on the administration front and, truth be told, it was no bad thing. To be honest my theory that I would find a supply of surgical staff from amongst the misfits gathered outside MSF had fallen rather flat on its face. Over the week I interviewed some thirty applicants out of which only three emerged as even faintly viable candidates.

The most promising was Kaspar Winkler, the white haired chap from day one. He turned out to have a perfectly sound record as a general surgeon specialising in mastectomy and breast cancer and had worked in Dusseldorf and Cologne before spending many years at the Bürgerhospital in Frankfurt. The only problem was that, aside from his lack of Arabic with which I sympathised, he was seventy-seven going on seventy-eight at which age, with his wife dead of vascular dementia, he had decided to 'give his skill to the world'. It was very touching but, given our first meeting, I couldn't help wondering if his wife was the only member of the family touched by dementia. Besides, was he still up to the physical demands of a surgical day on the edge of a war zone? Still, beggars can't be choosers. I signed him up.

The second was a Welsh G.P, Carys Probyn-Rees, who had been struck off the register for 'Inappropriate behaviour with female patients'. Given the absence of male patients I had noted, she was going to fit in well. I put her in charge of triage and gave her a good talking to about maintaining professional standards of conduct which I had a nasty feeling had little impact. I could only hope that Arab women were as liberal minded as their men regarding same-sex relationships.

My third recruit was a Chinese called Mr Leung who explained painfully slowly that he was no longer employed there 'because of poritics'. Given the difficulty with which he pronounced that, I decided not to go any further into which part of the Chinese Communist Party he had offended. He, more or less, mimed that he was an anaesthetist, which I confirmed after an hour's hard work poring over his C.V. with the aid of Google Translator. Unfortunately, this was one vacancy I was desperate to fill because I couldn't operate without one. I consoled myself with the thought that he couldn't be any worse than some of the idiots I'd worked with back home. I'd just have to keep an eye on him.

Nevertheless, allowing for this disappointment and a plethora of other teething troubles, two weeks to the day after entering the building, I finished my hurried, early morning round and turned to survey my handiwork. Before me lay rows of neat beds with uniformed nurses scurrying around in attendance. Patients were being admitted at the front whilst others were being discharged through the doors at the rear for transport on to camps elsewhere in the country. For the first time since my world collapsed all that time ago back in England. I was wearing a white coat with a stethoscope round my neck and people called me Sir. It wasn't St George's in terms of facilities or even stimulating, entertaining colleagues, but then I equally I didn't have to put up with pompous little administrators like that arsehole Chaudhuri. Here I was boss and here I decided what went. I was still Mr Anthony Stamford MB,ChB, FRCS(Eng) and I had a hospital to work in. Against all the odds, I had won.

20

The summons to attend Khoury arrived the following day courtesy of the odious Mr Roffe.

I was actually inspecting the repairs I had made to the left shoulder of an old man who had been winged by a bullet in Homs the week before. God knows how they'd smuggled him across the border and kept infection at bay at the same time. He was obviously tougher than he looked and my handiwork was taking well. I reckoned twenty-four hours and he would be fit to ship out. It was just as well given the reports of violence coming across the border from the mouths of increasing numbers of refugees. It wasn't just rioting now; tales of people being hanged from lamp posts and being dowsed with petrol then set on fire in the street were becoming commonplace. It wasn't just the dark presence of Khoury in the back of my mind that was keeping my sleep to a minimum. Just as I was showing one of the trainee nurses how to replace the old dressing, I found the Weasel beside me.

'Ah, Mr Roffe, how nice to see you again. If you don't mind I'm a little busy for the moment. Could you give me a minute?' I might as well not have spoken. The vile creature reached out and gripped my arm to stop me working!

'Minister Khoury wishes for a discussion at your premises at Beirut. This is to be at nine o'clock tomorrow morning.'

I tried to withdraw my arm, but, to my annoyance, he obviously wasn't letting go. I was forced to turn and face him. The nerve of the bloody man!

'Do you mean the Villa?'

'Yes that is so. The Minister desires that you must meet him there.'

'But I don't even know whether the equipment I need to examine him with has arrived yet.'

'Then you must find out.'

'Okay, I'll get onto it. I should be able to let you know in a couple of days...'

'The Minister wish to know now.' I felt the grip tighten on my arm and found myself looking into a face that brooked no argument.

'Do you mind letting go of me...' I began, but he twisted my arm so hard I nearly gasped.

'The Minister wish to know now.' He simply repeated.

'Okay, okay, let me phone Talal to see if the equipment has arrived; there is nothing I can do without it.'

He nodded slowly as if considering this proposition. He released my arm.

'You phone him now.'

I brushed down my sleeve to try to reassert some kind of dignity in front of the nurse, then marched down the central aisle and out of the back door, pulling my mobile out as I went. Roffe followed hard on my heels. Outside I stopped and dialled Talal's number. I already knew the equipment was waiting at the Villa, it had arrived halfway through the previous week, but it was obviously in our interest to string Khoury along for as long as possible. I therefore went through the pantomime of hearing the good news before turning to Roffe.

'Talal informs me that it's all there and he should have

everything set up in a couple of days.'

'Tell him nine o'clock tomorrow.'

I stared at the odious bastard for a moment, weighing up just how far I could push this.

'And if that's not possible?'

'Then you have no more business here and perhaps you are put in prison.'

'But I have done nothing wrong...'

'Minister Khoury is to decide that.'

'I see. Well, the Minister is clearly very worried about his state of health. I'll see what I can do.' I turned and walked away as I spoke into the phone.

'Number's up Talal, he insists on nine o'clock tomorrow or else. Make sure everything's ready, okay. I'll call you back later.' I cut the call and turned back to Roffe.

'Okay, that's fine. Talal tells me they'll work over night to get things ready if necessary. Give the Minister my best regards and tell him I'll see him at the Villa at nine o'clock tomorrow morning.'

That sly smirk was playing around Roffe's lips as he turned to leave. He had won and, in doing so, had delivered a graphic reminder of just how precarious my situation was in his bloody country.

*

I watched Roffe depart then discarded my white coat, grabbed a few odds and ends, and spent ten minutes briefing Sister Mussan on the running of the Clinic over the next couple of days. Without more ado I jumped into the BMW and hit the road for the Villa. Much as I trusted Talal, I couldn't leave him to plumb in a load of hi-tech medical kit unaided and, besides, I needed to appear reasonably conversant with it myself. I normally left this sort of thing to radiologists and their ilk. I just hoped it all came with a comprehensible instruction manual written in English!

Truth be told I had been guilty of blocking out this impending meeting and not just because I was preoccupied with the setting up of the Clinic. As I raced through the Bekaa Valley, I now forced myself to confront my feelings. What emerged was a surprisingly throat-gripping wave of professional guilt. When I objectively considered what I shortly planning to do, it amounted to stepping completely outside the parameters I had always used to govern my professional conduct whilst ripping up the Hippocratic Oath and chucking it over my shoulder along the way!

It wasn't just that I was planning to lie to a patient, we doctors do that all the time as a matter of basic human kindness! It was the nature of the lie, or lies, I was about to deliver. We're all pretty expert at softening the blow from 'You'll just feel a sharp scratch' to 'You'll hardly notice the colostomy bag after a while', but that was not what I was planning right now. Right now, I was intending to tell a man he was suffering from a potentially fatal disease when, to the best of my knowledge, he wasn't.

Whenever the matter had tried to sneak into the front of my mind over the last fortnight, I had quickly quashed it with the thought that it was a white lie for the greater good: I was bending the truth, but as a means to secure the funding which would enable me to save countless lives. Better still, when, at the end of the day, I delivered a clean bill of health to Khoury, he would be as happy as any of the other people who had benefitted from my ministrations. Unfortunately, now, as I drove through the rain and darkness, I couldn't escape the fact that this amounted to nothing more than self-serving bullshit. Perhaps, if I had stood to gain nothing out of this personally, I could have made the case, but that was most certainly not true. The plan was to play on Khoury's health paranoia in order to sell him a second-hand hospital and a load of counterfeit drugs and stolen equipment. I was not sure of the latter, but nor was I born yesterday!

Still I had never planned to end up in this situation. I had never asked to be ripped off by my wife and her lover and unjustly imprisoned with my professional reputation in tatters. Nor had I asked to be harassed by the police on my release. Indeed, I had fought, despite all these setbacks, which I suggest would have floored a lesser man, to join MSF with a view to sharing my gifts with those in more desperate straits than I!

That was a good point, but it didn't really answer the fact that I was about to tell a monumental professional lie. But who was I about to tell it to? Aye, there was the rub! I was about to tell it to the biggest bastard I had met in my life, with the possible exception of Hamish Carmichael. A vision of the 'Lubyanka' lowering over my poor little clinic sprang into my mind unbidden. Did I seriously have no idea what was going on in that ghastly monstrosity? Like hell. It was an interrogation centre, a torture chamber, and I wouldn't mind betting that more suffering and misery were handed out in there in an hour than Khoury was likely to suffer over a couple of months being treated for an imaginary cancer diagnosed courtesy of his hypochondria!

I sat back in my seat feeling better. This was not the clear-cut, ethical world of the NHS, and even that was back-biting and Machiavellian when you scratched the surface. No, I had somehow found myself in a darker, more dangerous world where dogs ate other dogs and morality was utterly relative. If I wanted to survive and prosper I needed to get my head round the prospect of scaring the crap out of Minister Khoury.

*

'Ah, come in Minister. Please take a seat.'

I was sitting behind the mahogany desk I had purchased from a department store in Beirut. The office Talal's cousins had built for me was as accurate a replica of my old consulting rooms in Harley Street as my memory would allow. They had even converted the former bedroom's en suite bathroom into a small surgery by removing the bath and replacing it with a couch. I had decided that I would deal with him from behind my desk rather than give him the courtesy of meeting him at the front door. He sat down without demur, good. My phone rang.

'Excuse me.' I picked it up.

'He has brought two cars with six guards, boss.'

'Yes, lunch at one will be fine thank you Talal.' I hung up. That was good news, my guest had clearly understood that this needed to look to any casual observer like a regular business meeting not some clandestine encounter. I picked up a sheet of paper and pretended to read it though I already knew what it said off by heart. I had typed it on the word processor at three o'clock that morning. I passed it across to him to convince him of its authenticity, though I knew he would not make much sense of it.

'We've had the results of your blood and urine tests back and I'm afraid to have to tell you that, while they are far from conclusive, they indicate a need for further investigations.'

'What is this you are saying?'

'I am saying that one of the blood tests the path lab has carried out indicates a higher than normal PSA level. EN2 has also been detected in your urine. This is not in itself definitive but, coupled with what I was able to detect during the rectal examination I carried out, I'm afraid I have to tell you that it suggests the possibility of prostate cancer.'

'What is this prostate cancer?' His face was suddenly dark and his voice distinctly raised as he slapped the desk in agitation. He knew the word 'cancer'. I decided a bit of reassurance was in order before he blew his top.

'Well, as the name suggests, it is cancer of the prostate, a small gland responsible for the production of seminal fluid, but, as I say, this is not a definitive diagnosis and, even if it turns out that you have prostate cancer, there is no reason to assume that it is untreatable.'

On reflection this didn't sound as reassuring as I had anticipated, but then I doubted that my patient spent much time touring the 'Lubyanka' to put his victims' minds at rest.

Sod him.

'What is treatment?'

'Well, we have to establish beyond doubt that you are suffering from prostate cancer, but, assuming that is the case, there are a number of treatments available depending on how advanced the condition is...'

'What are treatments?'

'Please, Minister Khoury, would you let me finish? I appreciate that you are naturally anxious, but the diagnostic process takes time and we cannot formulate a treatment programme without it. First we will need a biopsy to confirm the early tests and allow us to see how advanced your condition may be.'

'What is biopsy?'

'A biopsy is the collection of a sample of cells from, in this case, your prostate. It is a simple, virtually painless procedure and can be done today. The sample will then be sent to the lab in Switzerland, assuming you still do not wish to use a Lebanese hospital, where, along with fresh blood and urine samples, it will be used to provide us with a TNM assessment. Without getting too technical, this will tell us if the cancer is a benign prostatic hyperplasia, in other words harmless, or malignant neoplasm, in other words dangerous. It will tell us if the tumour is confined to the prostate or has spread into the pelvis and other bodily organs. At the same time, if you turn out to have a malignant tumour we will be able to arrive at a Gleason score which will tell us how aggressive the cancer is.'

'You mean how long I am to live?'

'No, not at all. We haven't even established yet that it is a malignant cancer and, even if it is, we still don't know how serious it is. Once we know that, there are several treatments available which we can use to either cure the disease or manage it highly effectively. The treatment I will then propose will depend on which stage your cancer has reached.'

'What treatment is this?'

My voice rose in exasperation.

'I don't know yet! Chemotherapy, radiotherapy, open or laparoscopic surgery. It all depends on what the initial tests reveal.' Jesus, this was hard work! It was as if he was almost revelling in his own illness. I had had patients before who seemed to take an almost macabre interest in their condition, but never one who could have had me shot and disposed of with no questions asked if he didn't like my answers. At least this fascination had replaced his earlier fury for the moment. I took a deep breath and adopted a more practical approach: 'Now if you would like to join me in surgery I can proceed with your biopsy.'

*

I stood and watched from the patio doors as the ministerial cortège proceeded down the drive and out of the Villa gates. I couldn't help wondering where this was all going to end. Was I going to end up performing an unnecessary radical prostatectomy just to keep the man happy? Peter was right, it was all too easy conning a raving hypochondriac; he wanted to be told he was ill. The worry in Khoury's case was that he had the power and psychosis to kill me if he found out that I was lying and he wasn't! Still, a prostatectomy would probably leave him impotent which might reduce his aggression a bit and it would certainly reduce the probability of any more Khourys being born to inflict misery, so there was an upside. Jesus, where had my medical ethics gone?

As the gates swung shut, I reviewed the procedure to date. I had offered him a local anaesthetic but he had refused it. Perhaps he liked the feeling of things being inserted into his posterior or, more likely, he wanted to prove how tough he was. More fool him! I had inserted the ultrasound probe without ceremony and taken a good look at a healthy prostate before obtaining half-a-dozen superfluous cell samples. I privately hoped that my own prostate was looking as healthy as his! He maintained a steady stream of what I took to be Lebanese profanity throughout.

By now any guilt had evaporated in the glare of his foul mood so, to increase his discomfort and inflate my bill further, I informed him that the diabetes test had come back showing him as hyperglycaemic. I took more blood and went back out to my office while he squeezed out another urine sample. I took his temperature and checked under his eyelids for good measure. I maintained a neutral-to-grave expression throughout. Finally, I explained that, thanks to the need to use the Swiss path lab, we could expect the results in a week's time at the earliest. When he growled his displeasure, I pointed out that a local lab would be quicker if that was what he wanted. He frowned darkly but didn't object any further. I asked if he would like me to refer him to a diabetes specialist, but he insisted that I should treat him.

With my patient on his way back to Beirut, I retreated to

my old bedroom and changed out of my 'consulting' suit into a bather then headed for the pool to relax before I faced the journey back to the chaos of Arsal. I needed a chance to assess what had really gone on. Superficially, everything had gone according to plan. Before he departed I brought up the question of further funding for the Clinic and, more importantly, for the main hospital. He told me that from now on I should send all Clinic bills to Sheikh Rezek at the Ramzi Foundation and all hospital supply bills to him personally at the Ministry. I wondered privately quite what doctoring they were subjected to there, but was too polite to ask.

As I breaststroked up and down the pool relaxing, my mind began to clear. I was pleased with the way the meeting had gone, but not elated. In fact, the further I swam, the less elated I became. I tried to tell myself that no meeting with Khoury could ever leave me feeling completely comfortable, but I knew it wasn't as simple as that; something much deeper was troubling me and as I swam I gradually teased it to the surface of my mind.

I had reached the stage where every meeting with Khoury seemed to reinforce the air of menace that hung around the man. His surliness, the sudden darkening of his complexion as anger seized him: even his health paranoia which seemed to hint at a deeper more serious form of paranoia beneath. I was now completely convinced that I was dealing with a very dangerous man and, as I rolled that round my mind, I found myself wondering how I was going to get away from him.

That was it! That's what was troubling me: I was heading further and further into this dangerous conspiracy with no apparent exit strategy. That's what people who went into dangerous situations called it, an 'exit strategy'. Fine, I could see, and even agree with, the arguments that made me the best man for the job and, as far as I could see, this role had come about due to chance and circumstance. I had gone looking for Peter, not the other way round. My role had then evolved as need dictated. Nevertheless, I couldn't escape the fact that, if things went tits-up, I was the one left exposed to the wrath of Khoury in a way that neither Peter Chisholm nor Daniel Swift appeared to be! Was this just the fortunes of war or did it reflect the fact that they were clearly old partners in crime?

I tried to put that last thought aside. Peter and Dan's business relationship had no bearing on my circumstances, unless – and suddenly I was staring what was troubling me full in the face – unless they were planning to use me to take Khoury for everything I could wheedle out of him and then leave me to carry the can!

I floundered my way to the side of the pool and grabbed the rail, gasping for breath even though I was not the least bit tired. I hauled myself out of the pool and began pacing frantically up and down the poolside, at the same time gulping in air to try and control the panic that had seized me. They wouldn't do that to me would they? Dan, maybe – I hardly knew him – but not Peter, surely?

But why not? How well did I really know him? I'd met him in prison for God's sake, that was hardly a testimonial! What did I really know about him? True, I'd taken a pretty immediate shine to him and I fancied I was a pretty good judge of character, but, as a little voice was now reminding me, I had taken a pretty immediate shine to a certain Hamish Carmichael once, and he had ended up fucking my wife whilst I ended up in prison! Jesus Christ, was I being taken for a patsy again?

A bit more pacing and I began to calm down. Okay, perhaps there was no clear cut exit strategy yet, or perhaps Peter simply hadn't got round to discussing it with me. After all, we had only just reached the stage at which we could say that things were definitely going ahead! There was no need for me to panic or overreact. The one thing that was certain, the one thing that had come out of this last meeting, was that I needed to wise up and look to the future. It was no use relying on Peter or anyone else to rescue me from Khoury's clutches if he suddenly decided he didn't like my face. It was time to devise my own exit strategy. It was time to look after number one.

21

On my return to Arsal, life quickly returned to what I was rapidly beginning to think of as normal: a constant whirl of hospital management interspersed with emergency surgery of all descriptions. I had thought I maintained a hectic schedule in my St George's days, but it was nothing compared to this. I ate on the hoof and snatched sleep when I could. It was great. I was in command and in control. Even my surgical team began to meld into a more or less effective unit.

To keep Roffe off my back, I left it a couple of days then instructed Talal to call him and tell him we were expecting the biopsy results back from Switzerland in eight days time and to fix an appointment with Khoury at the Villa for then. Roffe didn't like it, but Talal pointed out that I didn't like his thuggish attitude and, without me, his boss was going to die. Did he really want to be responsible for the withdrawal of my services? That shut him up!

And so it might have remained, but for an incident that happened as I was returning late at night to the rather ancient, but serviceable, Nissen hut one of Talal's many cousins had come up with as lodgings for me. It was parked outside the back of the Clinic, in the shadow of the 'Lubyanka', slightly separate from the static caravans that housed Sister Mussan, Kaspar Winkler, Carys Probyn-Rees and Mr Leung.

As I fumbled with my keys in the darkness a voice spoke quietly out of the darkness.

'Well, well, if it isn't Mr Stamford the great London surgeon,

I want a word with you pal.'

I physically jumped with fright. I even raised my arm to ward off a possible blow. It wasn't just the shock of a totally unexpected voice coming out of the pitched darkness; it was the menace in its tone. He may have said 'pal', but that was clearly not intended as a term of endearment.

'Who are you?' I squeaked, to my annoyance. 'I warn you I'm armed,' I added unconvincingly.

'So am I,' came the chilling reply, 'and I've got the drop on you. Turn round, spread your legs and lean forward with your hands against the hut.'

I wasn't going to risk calling the man's bluff so I did what I was told and felt something hard dig in my back. I stood helpless, racking my brains for the identity of my assailant as he patted my pockets for my fictitious weapon. I knew that voice. I was sure I'd heard it quite recently. Suddenly, it came to me. The voice had been much more raised last time I heard it, but I had detected a faint, cultured Australian accent in the use of the word 'pal'. I was being held up by the MSF surgeon, King, by whom I had been so rudely ejected from the MSF surgery on my second day in Arsal!

'Still lying are we?' he commented as he finished his search and found nothing. 'Turn round.'

I did as I was told and watched as he replaced a piece of copper piping in his pocket.

'What do you want, King?' I demanded, a little more firmly now I knew I was not about to be shot.

'I want to know what the fuck you think you're playing at,' he snarled, his voice rising and his accent coming through more strongly, despite his attempt to maintain a whisper.

'I'm not playing at anything,' I retorted. 'I'm running this clinic and saving lives which is what I came to Lebanon to do.' I could see instantly what this was about. The man was clearly pissed off that I was proving to the world that his organisation didn't have a monopoly on humanitarian aid. Well fuck him, he should have taken me on board when he had the chance! I turned to the door and felt for the lock again. 'If you don't mind, I've had a busy day and want to get some sleep if that's all you've come to ask me...'

'It bloody well isn't, so you can wait right there! Have you any idea what trouble you've caused?'

'What do you mean?'

'Well, for a start, that bloody place wasn't there 'til you turned up.' He gestured back over his shoulder at the 'Lubyanka' with his thumb.

'That's got nothing to do with me...'

'Like fuck it hasn't! You turn up on our doorstep talking bullshit so we kick you out and suddenly, hey presto, that place gets built and you turn up in charge here. What shitty deal did you do with the Government to come to that arrangement, eh?'

'I haven't done any shitty deal and, besides, it's none of your business anyway.'

'Oh yes it is when people I've come halfway round the world to save are getting tortured and murdered in there before they can reach me!' Again he gestured over his shoulder at the menacing building.

'What do you mean?' There must have been a note of genuine

bewilderment in my voice because he paused and stared at me.

'You trying to tell me you don't know?'

'Well I know it's an interrogation centre to weed out spies and other undesirables from the genuine refugees...'

'Jesus pal, how fucking naive are you? That place would do credit to the Spanish Inquisition! Every Lebanese male coming across the border near here is taken there and tortured for information. They use the lot: beating, drowning, electric shock, and they don't stop until they've got everything.'

'What do you mean 'everything'?'

'What I say. They want to know the victims background, work and politics and any other information he can give them about the government and the rebels. The men we've spoken to think they might even be selling it back to the Syrian Government.'

'What men?'

'A couple have escaped and made it to us. They talk about an absolute hell hole. They escaped whilst being shipped out to be shot at some sort of death camp out there.' He pointed vaguely to the area I always referred to in my mind as no-man's-land.

'But this is impossible...'

'No it's not, its war. I've seen it in MSF missions all over the world and it's always the same.'

'I'm sure you have, but what actual proof have you got? How do you know these men were genuine? What's to say they weren't agents provocateurs sent to blacken the Lebanese government by some faction or other? Let's face it, you've got the ear of the World's press so who better to tell tales about torture to?'

'How do I know they were genuine? I treated their bloody injuries mate; that's how I know they were genuine. They didn't inflict those on themselves...'

'Yes, but they could have come from other causes and then been used as a cover story.'

'Do you really believe that?'

'Yes, no, I don't know. I'm just pointing out that there's more than one possible conclusion...'

Good God that sounded feeble! Why on Earth I was defending the goings-on in the 'Lubyanka' I couldn't imagine, but then, I suppose, they were, by implication, an attack on my own character and ethics. Suddenly all my misgivings about Khoury were crowding in on me. He had built a torture chamber and used me to lure victims towards it! King stopped and stared at me again for a moment.

'Okay, I can see why you don't want to believe it, so why don't you let me prove it to you?'

'What do you mean?'

'What I say. Meet me here tomorrow night at this time and I'll take you to see what's going on for yourself.'

'And if I don't?'

'Then I'm goin' to whisper into the ear of the World's press about just what a little shit you are.'

*

It was two o'clock the following morning when the knock on my door came. I grabbed the navy weatherproof I had had delivered direct from the Aishti department store in Beirut:

I didn't want anyone, even Talal, asking me what I needed it for. In fact, I needed it partly as a protection from the Lebanese winter weather, but, more importantly, I needed it as camouflage. King hadn't said where he was taking me, but I guessed that, if I was about to witness man's inhumanity to man, I didn't need to stand out from the crowd!

'Ready?' was all he said before turning on his heel and leading the way to the MSF Land Cruiser parked nearby. We climbed in without exchanging another word as we headed off down the new road that led back into Arsal.

Finally, I broke the silence as we turned off the made up road onto a track leading into the no-man's-land King had gestured to the following day.

'Do you mind telling me where you're taking me?' King kept his eyes fixed on the crumbling, pot-holed track ahead as he replied.

'Not at all, we're headed for an unofficial border crossing point.'

'Unofficial?'

'Yeah, both governments want to know who's coming and going so the refugees are encouraged to go through it on the promise of safe passage which is true enough until the Lebanese interrogators get their hands on them. The people you've seen coming out of the desert are the ones who don't fall for their government's promises and run the gauntlet. That's what that place behind your clinic is also used for. You're being used to pull in the refugees who don't trust the border crossings. They tend to be the most clued-up types. The ones most interesting to the government. That's why your place is where it is, so that the poor bastards head for you first. The men are picked up before they reach you. We used to pick some up by driving out there, but it's become too dangerous with the strafing planes and the Government insist we do it at our own risk.'

He glanced sideways at me for a reaction.

'Right, I see.' I replied, then shut up. What else could I say?

*

I stood beside the Land cruiser gazing down on the stream of humanity as it waded through the shallow river that was being used as the putative border. We were observing the crossing from a rise some fifty yards away. The area was floodlit by headlights from lorries on both sides. On our side I could see armed Lebanese soldiers sorting out the refugees as they waded ashore. There were trestle tables set up where officials appeared to be filling out forms much as officials do the world over. Even from that distance I could see that, as they were processed, the new arrivals were being sorted at gun point into male or female groups before being jostled and prodded into trucks. Images of old footage of the Jews being herded into concentration camps flashed through my mind as I watched in fascinated horror.

I forced myself to switch my attention to the Syrian side of the 'border'. On the other side of the river I could make out more men ushering people around at gun point, but they weren't in uniform. One of them stepped forward suddenly, raised a pistol to a man's head. The gun jerked and he buckled sideways to the ground. Two others dragged the body to one side.

'Who the hell are they?' I muttered half to myself.

'They're the Mukhabarat,' King quietly informed me. 'They started off as a criminal gang years ago and sided with the Government when the civil war began. They've sort of evolved into a particularly vicious secret service, though they're a law unto themselves most of the time. This is their idea of a good night out.'

I turned away.

'Is that it?'

'No, not quite, there's something else I want you to see. Jump in.' He got back into the driving seat and turned on the engine, so I had no choice but to follow him. We headed down the hill straight towards the crossing!

'Couldn't we see enough from back there?' I asked trying to conceal the alarm in my voice.

'No, that place is good for an overview, but I want you see our people in action on the ground. I'm not having you tell me this is ain't for real a second time. '

As we approached I began to realise what he was talking about. There were MSF Land Cruisers parked among the lorries which is why I probably hadn't made them out from the hilltop. Close-up, I could make out people in white coats and caps arguing with the guards and the officials. King pulled up and got out. Somewhat apprehensively, I joined him.

'Here, put these on,' he ordered. He handed me a lab coat and a white baseball cap with MSF stamped on it in orange. He pointed at the soldiers who were watching as the MSF people argued heatedly with the officials. 'The Lebanese diggers respect uniforms and that's the best we've got. They probably won't shoot you with those on.' I donned the cap and struggled into the lab coat which didn't want to fit over my weatherproof. Despite the ill-fit, I felt a ridiculous glow of pride at this token acceptance; he must have read my mind.

'I'll have those back when we're done here,' he remarked, coldly.

'So what do you want to show me?' I replied, equally coldly.

'I want you to see some real MSF people in action.'

I ignored the implied insult and followed as he walked off towards the trestle tables: I wasn't going to have him call me a coward as well as a liar! I caught up with him as he stopped some twenty yards away from the haggling. At that distance the soldiers' guns looked horribly real, but it was the way they waved them about and pointed them at people that was really unnerving.

'I didn't realise that MSF service included this sort of thing, I ventured,' in an attempt to sound casually interested in the alarming situation. King nodded his agreement.

'Can't say I've ever seen anything like it myself, but needs must. Most of these people are local MSF volunteers because they speak the lingo. Bloody brave people if you ask me. Several have been beaten up and one was shot a month ago.'

I decided not to open a discussion about how MSF could accept locals and turn down the services of a highly qualified surgeon. Besides, I knew the answer: I should have waited to get my licence back, but then Newcombe had put an end to that. Still, who knew where this would lead.

'So, apart from getting people beaten up and shot, what does this actually achieve?'

King gave me a hard glance before replying.

'Well, for one thing, it puts a curb on their behaviour. Since the shooting we point mobile phones back at their guns and record what's happening. They don't like that and it gives us some leverage.'

He was right. I had noticed MSF people holding up phones without registering the full significance of what they were doing.

'For another thing,' he continued, 'we've begun posting footage of this on Facebook to let the rest of the world know what's happening. That way we can shame the Government.'

I was about to ask him quite what he imagined my contribution to these efforts could be when I was distracted by a sudden commotion in the crowd of refugees queuing at the table nearest us. As I focussed properly I could see a young woman had broken away from the crowd and was half running, half stumbling across the rough ground towards us. She was only ten yards away and I could hear her crying out as she ran. A young soldier stepped forward and raised his gun. It was the strangest sensation, but her gaze and pleas seemed to be directed solely at me. I couldn't understand what she was saying, but I knew instinctively that it was a cry for help. I also knew that I couldn't stand there and watch her get shot in front of me.

Without thinking I ran forward. I don't suppose the guard had ever shot anyone in his life and, thankfully, he hesitated now, shouting something which was no doubt Arabic for 'Halt!' The delay gave me time to reach the girl interposing myself between the two of them and raising my hand as if that would fend off a bullet from the assault rifle I was staring down the barrel of. Whatever the effect of my raised hand, my shout of 'No!' delivered with all the command I could muster and backed up by my token MSF 'uniform', made him pause.

'No!' I shouted again, switching my gesture of 'Halt!' to a pointing finger of accusation. I glared into his faltering face across the thirty feet separating us. He didn't know what to do and, come to that, nor did I. I'd faced down angry patients and survived an assault by one, I had even emerged victorious from a vicious fight with my nemesis Hamish Carmichael, but I had never experienced a gunpoint Mexican standoff before, especially with a border guard who didn't even speak my language! How did I break the deadlock without panicking him into some impromptu action which quite possibly included shooting me dead?

Thankfully, fortune in the shape of a Lebanese officer chose to intervene. He emerged from the crowd, which by now had become a riveted audience, with a sharp command which made my adversary lower his gun immediately. I switched my finger to point at him and repeated 'No!' equalled forcefully then began to back away reaching back to keep the girl behind me. To my astonishment, he paused as if to double-check his estimation of the situation, then shrugged, turned on his heel and went back to supervising the officials. Without any further invitation, I grabbed the young woman and retreated back to King.

'Let's get out of here,' I muttered as I hurried straight past him heading for the Land Cruiser. He didn't argue: he jumped in the driver's seat and started the engine as I bundled our new companion into the back and followed him in. He pulled off an impressive wheel spin as we tore off into the darkness and I suddenly became aware that I was being held in a tight embrace. The young woman was clinging to me and shivering with what I assumed was fright. I gave her a gentle squeeze and an encouraging smile. For the first time I was able to closely inspect the benefactor of my lunatic valour. She was lovely. As she clung to me gazing up at my face with her deep brown eyes I felt like I hadn't felt since I got my first real kiss at the age of fifteen. I told myself to get a grip, but her beauty quite took my breath away. Jesus! As I gazed down at her she reached up and pulled my head down. Before I could react she parted her lips and engaged me in a slow, lingering kiss.

A quarter of a mile later King began to slow down as it was clear we were not being followed. He glanced back at me and then fixed his gaze on the road and spoke somewhat awkwardly.

'That was a pretty brave thing you did there, mate.'

I disengaged from the girl and shrugged.

'Someone had to do something,' I replied self-deprecatingly. Funny how I'd just become his 'mate' when I was a liar a few hours ago. 'Why do you think the officer let us go?'

'Because you were rescuing a female. It would have been a different kettle of fish if you'd tried to rescue a man. That would have been taken as an attempt to rescue a spy and we'd have all been shot. Still, good for you pal.'

With an effort I turned from the girl and stared silently out of the window into the darkness. I sat there in silence but my brain was not idle. In fact I was struggling with a very real quandary. King had proved beyond any reasonable doubt that Khoury was up to some serious villainy and he was clearly going to expect me to do something about it, though God knows what! He probably imagined that I could simply withdraw my services, but it was not as simple as that. If I decided to rock the boat, Khoury would stop authorising Peter's invoices and no doubt our bills to the Ramzi Foundation would be spiked as well. That was my generous pension fund vanishing off down the Swanee in short order and, much as I was enjoying my current role at the Clinic, I really didn't see it as any longer term than it took to relieve Khoury of as much cash as possible. I was realistic enough to appreciate that my efforts would soon be subsumed in the gathering crisis and I would probably end up being glad to get out of there in one piece. In the meantime, at least I was saving people's lives regardless of whether they were male or female.

Besides, there were questions of loyalty: I had offered my services to MSF they had told me to bugger off in no uncertain terms. In fact, it was King himself who had yelled it at me. Peter Chisholm, on the other hand, had befriended me in prison when I was at my lowest ebb and done more than anyone to set me back on the road to reality. When I'd gone back to him for help with the Clinic, he had backed me unhesitatingly. Admittedly his vision for how we should handle the situation had been less utopian than mine, but then he was a worldly businessman whilst I was a comparatively naive product of the British NHS. No, I owed it to Peter to do nothing to rock the boat we were sailing no matter how sorry I felt for the refugees.

So what could I say to this bloody Australian to get him off my back without losing face? After the rescue of the girl, he clearly had me down as one of the good guys and a part of me wanted desperately not to disillusion him. As I stared out into the darkness an idea began to form. At first it seemed ridiculous but, in the absence of any better ideas, I let it play. It was preposterous, but then he had some evidence to support the notion that I was more than just a humble surgeon and, try as I might, I couldn't see a catch in the story that could trip me up. Furthermore, if things panned out as I hoped they might, he'd never be any the wiser; just left with a good story to tell his grandchildren. I turned back from the window and studied him thoughtfully. When he became aware of my gaze, I spoke solemnly.

'Look, I don't know you very well but, from what I've seen, I think I can trust you. I want you to swear that what I am about to tell you will go no further, okay?'

King glanced at me and nodded.

'Sure.'

'I mean it. This is just between you and I, understood?'

'Yeah, understood.'

'Good, then I'm prepared to tell you a certain amount about my mission here.'

'Mission?'

'Yes, I'm on a top secret mission for the British Government.'

'What sort of mission?'

'Well I can't say too much, but I'm here to destabilise the work of a man called Khoury. He is the head of the Ministry of the Interior and an extreme right-winger. He is involved with a faction which stands to make a lot of money out of a war with Syria.' I paused to gather up some of the baffling strands of Lebanese politics that I had been pulling together over the last few weeks thanks to Talal and the constant TV coverage of the impending war. 'He has clandestine links with

the Lebanese Phalange and the Kataeb Party amongst others.'
That had to sound impressive. I hesitated, not wanting to over-
egg the cake, then decided what the hell and plunged on. 'He is
the man behind the scenes: the link between the Government
and the right-wing military. Our sources reckon the factions he
controls even plan to invade Western Syria if the civil war gets
completely out of control.'

King held up a hand to make me pause.

'Okay, but what has that got to do with me?'

I allowed myself a pregnant pause then spoke significantly.

'He is the man who funded the Clinic and that building
behind it.'

King took a minute to chew this over.

'I thought you were a doctor...'

'I am, but I have a military background. Once you become
involved with the more clandestine parts of the military, you
can always be called upon, if you know what I mean. When
they discovered that Khoury was planning to build a military
town out here in Bekaa, they asked me to take part in an effort
to discredit him. The plan was to infiltrate me into the country
as an MSF surgeon, but there was a fuck up in communications
and I wasn't reinstated with the GMC after a spell in prison as
part of my cover. It was you that spotted it and threw me out.'

'What do you mean 'discredit'?'

'Well we can't just shoot him. There are quite strict rules
about MI6 carrying out political assassinations believe it or not,
so the idea was to give his enemies enough ammunition to
attack him for major fraud. A bit like the FBI used the IRS to
nail Al Capone for tax evasion. It's an open secret that he's as

bent as a nine bob note: he made a fortune in the Civil War selling arms and smuggling hash, so he was bound to see the contracts to build his military town as a golden opportunity to feather his nest. Thanks to a massive stroke of luck, when you threw me out, I bumped into a couple of people from an organisation which was involved in his plan, a charity called the Ramzi Foundation.'

'I see,' breathed King, who clearly didn't see much at all.

'The vital thing is that we are nearly there. I have succeeded in getting myself recruited as the Medical Director for the town's new hospital and within the next few weeks will have enough evidence to prove that Khoury is stocking the place with stolen equipment and counterfeit drugs then charging his government top price for the goods. He's got plenty of enemies who will have a field day with that sort of ammunition. Once he falls, that monstrosity behind the clinic will be shut down and I was thinking of persuading the government to offer you guys the building as a proper base. It's bigger and more fit-for-purpose than the place you're in now.'

King braked and brought the Toyota to a halt. He turned and stared me in the face, his eyes bright with excitement.

'You serious about this?'

'Sure, you might even be able to turn that interrogation centre into something useful if you took the bars off the windows...'

He grabbed my shoulder and stared hard into my face. Finally he spoke:

'I guess I owe you a big apology mate. I had you wrong. I really had you wrong.'

22

She woke me just before dawn. It was a gentle, gradual awakening from a deep sleep. I was first aware of my face being kissed, soft, frequent kisses on my eyelids then my lips. As I opened my eyes to make sure I wasn't dreaming, I glimpsed the shadowy outline of her head before it moved lower and I felt the kisses on my chest. By the time she reached her objective I was awake in all senses of the word: it fleetingly occurred to me that I hadn't had the pleasure of Adanna's company for over a fortnight and the same thought was clearly occurring to the Old Chap!

Sometime later, she decided that things were coming to a head, if that's the right expression, and in one lithe movement shifted on top of me, reached down and guided me inside her. I reached up to caress her firm, young breasts and run my fingers through her long, luxuriant hair as it brushed and tickled my face in the darkness. Then I closed my eyes and concentrated on lasting as long as possible. Afterwards, she slipped out of my bed and disappeared back into the living room where I'd left her sleeping on the couch the night before.

I tried to doze, but there was no way I was going back to sleep after that. Besides, the light was seeping through my curtains and I was due for my early morning hospital round in an hour. I lay there and tried to make sense of this new development instead.

It was not until after my heart-to-heart with King, and the long silence that ensued, that the question of what to do with our passenger arose. We both agreed that there was no way we were going to hand her back to the Lebanese officials. That officer may have been indifferent to her escape, but captors don't usually tend to take kindly to people who evade their clutches. Besides we were curious to know why she had taken such a risk.

King, or Brandon as he'd now become, reckoned he could take her if the worst came to the worst, but there was no way he could keep an eye on her and she would probably get carried away in the tide of MSF patient processing. We both nevertheless felt that, until the episode at the border had had a bit of time to blow over, it was probably best if she could be sheltered somewhere. That left the Clinic, but that was heaving too and provided no more shelter than the MSF quarters. The only other place left until I could get her smuggled out to somewhere like the Villa was my Nissen hut. Brandon dropped us off at the Nissen and headed for home.

That was all discussed quite rationally and calmly without a hint of my ulterior motive. Much as I sincerely wanted to ensure arrangements were made for our passenger's well-being, I was also privately determined to see quite where that first heart-pounding kiss was likely to lead.

That, however would have to wait until later. When we arrived, the lateness of the hour and, no doubt, a considerable come-down from the earlier blasts of adrenalin had taken their toll. I simply pointed to the couch, arranged the cushions as pillows for her, dug out a blanket and nodded 'goodnight'. I had gleaned by now that the girl's grasp of English did not extend much beyond yes, no, please and thank you, though

Brandon had ascertained in the car that her name was Laila. I had headed almost drunkenly into my bedroom next door, stripped naked, crawled under my duvet and fallen straight into that deep sleep.

Now, this unexpected visit had cast an entirely new complexion on things. What was I to make of it? Did I even want it? After all, until half an hour ago, I was a dedicated, celibate surgeon devoted to saving lives. Suddenly, the celibacy part of my mission had lost its shine. There again, who had ever said that sexual abstinence had to be part of the deal? Certainly, the Clinic had demanded every last drop of my energy and concentration to start with, but things were now running pretty smoothly and I was a doctor not a monk!

So what did she want out of it? Was this just a thank you for saving her life, or did she want more? Was this a ploy to enrol me as her protector? I wasn't a fool: women have been using men for their own ends since Delilah did the dirty on Samson! On the other hand I couldn't forget that moment of eye contact as she ran towards me. It was as if we were already bonded, as if we were in some way made for each other. Had she made a run for it simply because she had seen me as a possible rescuer? It was a hell of a risk if that was all she had seen in me!

Before I could speculate further there was a tap on the door. After a slight pause, it was gently pushed open and she entered carrying a tray. She had obviously raided the kitchen because it bore a teapot and two mugs and a loaf of cheese and onion flat bread that one of the Syrian nurses had discovered I was partial to. She had also raided my laundry basket because she was wearing one of my shirts and nothing else. It was only held together by a single button.

She handed me the tray, then slipped into bed beside me. She retrieved it and poured the tea, then smeared a dollop of the local chickpea hummus I had recently developed something of an addiction to onto a chunk of the bread and held it up for me to bite. I sat back and discreetly inspected, or perhaps I should say adored her, as she fed me breakfast. She was lovely. In the light of early morning her hair was every bit as dark and luxuriant as I had imagined earlier. Her deep brown eyes made me want to melt and her smile, as she turned to offer me another piece of bread, left me weak. The only part of me that hadn't turned to jelly was the Old Chap who was beginning to behave as if I was sixteen again! She noticed and set the tray down on the floor before turning and undoing that single button.

*

I was in love. In retrospect it was all rather ridiculous, a middle-aged man and a young girl probably not even out of her teens, but, at the time, I simply did not care! She made me feel young and invigorated and so it continued over the ensuing days. She showed no desire to leave and I was desperate that she shouldn't. The language barrier was a help not a hindrance: we could just get on and satisfy each other's basic needs. It was wonderfully simple, something I had never experienced in my life. We couldn't argue if we wanted to and my token effort to ascertain her age was met with a puzzled shrug. My marriage to Elizabeth had always been mired in middle-class cynicism and my various affairs had always been tainted with the thrill of the deceit, the mock penitence and the lust of forgiveness. In comparison, this felt clean and honest in a way I had quite forgotten.

The demands of the Clinic, the underlying guilt of the conspiracy behind it and the menace of Khoury in the background all seemed to fade into insignificance. As far as I can recall, I functioned normally enough on the outside. I stuck to the hectic schedule I had been maintaining and the Clinic treated the female refugees and their children and their grandparents with steadily increasing efficiency, which was just as well as the demand for our services grew daily. What little time I had to watch the news only served to assure me that the situation in Lebanon had now turned to all-out civil war. I watched pictures of armed men dodging from doorway to doorway through the smashed streets of crumbling cities and I didn't care. Despite how I looked on the outside at work, a part of my mind was constantly replaying images of her: her smile, her hesitant attempts to speak English, the way her eyelids drooped as she reached up to kiss me. When I walked through the door of the Nissen hut after work her presence completely overwhelmed me.

*

The first thing to interrupt this blissful situation was the arrival of my next appointment with Khoury. I had my wits sufficiently about me to get Talal to phone to confirm the appointment. The last thing I needed was that vile creep Roffe turning up to remind me and laying eyes on Laila. No doubt I could pass her off as a servant, but that man gave me the creeps and I felt very protective, even secretive about her. I kissed her goodbye after a most delightful breakfast awakening and hit the road for Beirut and the Villa.

The set up was exactly as before. I waited for my patient in my 'Harley Street' office whilst Talal relayed details of his arrival from the gate. The only apparent change was an increase in Khoury's retinue which had grown to ten armed guards. They stayed outside as before so his paranoia was clearly not provoked by anything at my end.

I waited for him to get seated opposite me then looked up from the document I was studying.

'Ah, good morning Minister. You'll be pleased to know I have the full results of your biopsy here,' I held up the papers I had prepared. 'As you have probably guessed from what I have already told you, the news is not entirely what we would have liked, but, on the other hand, it is not indicating a situation which is untreatable...'

'What is it you are saying?' he snarled. The darkness was there instantly and he had risen to his feet as he gripped the desk. There was even more tension and aggression about him than last time.

'Please, please, there is no need to distress yourself! I am saying that the cancer in your prostate is unfortunately malignant but our tests indicate that it still very treatable. I have here your Gleason Score which tells me that your cancer is quite aggressive so we need to start a course of treatment fairly immediately, but that there is no need to panic. The growth has not spread beyond the prostate into the bones for example. It is currently confined to the two lobes...'

'What is treatment?' He hadn't sat back down, his face was black as thunder and his manners showed no sign of improvement.

Okay, if he wanted to cut to the quick, he could have it his own way.

'Well, under the circumstances I would recommend a course of radiotherapy with the option to proceed to surgery if that doesn't do the trick...'

'What is this radiotherapy?'

'It's a treatment using radiation to destroy the cancer...'

'How quick?'

'Well, I suppose a typical course would take about six to eight weeks...'

'This is no good!'

There was a crash as he raised his hands and slammed them back down on the table to make his point.

'I beg your pardon?'

'No good, six weeks. I do not have this time,' he snarled.

I leant back to make sure I was out of reach of his next point-making gesture and studied him. Jesus, this man really was on the edge!

'Minister Khoury, if you wish me to advise you on the procedures available to us, I suggest you sit down and calm down so that we can discuss your options in a civilised manner.' This was said with all the cold authority a lifetime in medicine could afford me. Thankfully it worked and he sat back down, though with the utmost ill-grace. As he took his seat again, things fell into place. The extra aggression, the impatience, the bigger bodyguard. This man was under a lot more pressure than when we had last met. Presumably of a political or military nature. I continued: 'If you don't mind my saying so, you seem rather stressed at the moment, Minister, but I'm afraid stress will not help your condition. In fact, it will only serve to exacerbate it if anything. I take it from your reaction that there is considerable urgency attached to your treatment?'

He nodded.

'This is so. The situation requires that I am made well immediately.'

Shit, this was the last thing I needed to hear! My plan had been to string him along by ordering radiotherapy which then involved the time consuming purchasing and installation of the necessary machinery etcetera. A couple of months of actual treatment on top of that would see his hospital built and Chisford Holdings supplying him with supplies and equipment at a handsome profit, with the added benefit of not having to remove his prostate for no reason. I could even use emetics to fake the side effects without filling him full of radiation. Now, this elegant solution was being swept aside by some sort of political necessity. I needed to think fast!

'Well, Minister, I am sure we all wish for that and I appreciate that the pressures of daily life all too frequently conflict with our health needs, but sometimes we simply have to set them aside. There is little point working hard if one will not live to reap the reward...'

'Fuck reward! There are things more dangerous for me than this cancer!'

I wasn't going to argue with him: he was best positioned to know! This really did put a different complexion on things, a little lecture on the importance of putting health before wealth was clearly a waste of breath here.

'Okay, right, I understand. Don't worry, there's no need to panic. There's another form of radiotherapy which I believe may be suitable in your case. It's called brachytherapy. It involves inserting radioactive metal seeds into the tumour inside plastic tubes and requires no machinery. If we use the high dose rate it will take about the same time as external treatment, but it only takes a day to prepare you and a few hours to insert the seeds. You can then carry on as normal, though you may experience some side effects.' Khoury was staring at me intently as I found myself fighting the urge to babble.

'Why did you not tell me this first?'

God this man was paranoid!

'Because, I suppose, the conventional equipment is readily available in the hospitals I come from and I am very familiar with it. However, if time is your priority, then brachytherapy is undoubtedly the way to go.'

'What are side effects?'

'Well, you certainly will not feel at your best during the treatment and you will possibly experience nausea and hair loss.' I toyed with the idea of mentioning impotence, but decided hair loss was as much as his ego could bear. By now I had also become gripped by the desire to bring this interview to a rapid end. Khoury had shot down my carefully constructed flight of medical fancy and I was now acutely aware that I was winging it. The thought of what he might do to me if he caught me in a lie was threatening to completely overwhelm my bedside manner.

'Why do you not do operation?'

'Because it may not be necessary, or even as effective as the course of treatment I have prescribed. It should be kept back as a very last resort.'

Khoury paused to stare at me as he made a mental calculation. Finally, he spoke with heart-stopping menace.

'Two weeks. You have two weeks for this thing to work. If not, you make immediate operation or I have you shot.'

*

I needed to think. I watched Khoury leave then gave Talal a couple of lists of supplies we needed at the Clinic. We talked over a few other practical matters as I changed out of my 'Harley Street' outfit back into my Clinic gear – cargo trousers for the extra pockets, tee shirt and white coat – the most practical gear for working in desert heat. I hit the road for Arsal as soon as was practically possible.

My route took me back through the traffic chaos of midday Beirut and before I knew it I was outside the Hilton Habtoor Grand where my Lebanese adventure had all begun. On the spur of the moment, I indicated and pulled into the forecourt: I was getting no thinking done battling through the cars, bikes and lorries competing in this congested version of the Dakar Rally!

I threw the keys of the BMW to a valet and headed up the steps and through into the lobby. The place was heaving. Men in business suits and Arab costume were shaking hands and murmuring, or shouting and gesticulating, across the whole spectrum of human communication. Film crews were jostling and fighting for space as they attempted to record them. For a moment I quailed at this apparent chaos, and then it hit me that this was precisely where I needed to be! I needed to find out quite what had lit Khoury's fuse so explosively. Short of spending a few hours in the viewers' gallery of the Lebanese parliament, this was clearly an ideal place from which to glean an update on the current political situation. In fact, its bars had televisions running English-speaking channels in several lounges, which made it an even better news desk from my point of view.

I battled my way through the lobby and was directed to a bar by a concierge. A further fifteen minutes and I finally got myself seated on a stool from which I had a view of a television offering rolling news with English subtitles. I ordered myself a large whisky and soda to minimise interruptions and set about figuring out quite what had got Khoury in such a paddy.

At first, this proved to be a considerable challenge as the program jumped from studio discussions to in situ reports then back to 'breaking news' type features. Nevertheless, I began to piece together a broad picture of how things had changed since my arrival God knows how many weeks ago. They had undoubtedly changed considerably for the worse; the footage shot in Syria itself showed cities that looked like World War Two Leningrad in the sunshine. Small wonder the work load was increasing so rapidly on my side of the border.

Quite what was happening on my side of the border was somewhat harder to make sense of. I ordered myself another whisky and soda as I attempted to piece it together: I had hardly touched a drop since Zurich and it was slipping down rather nicely. The problem, aside from the sub-titler's questionable grasp of English, was that, while it was clear that Lebanon was struggling desperately not to get drawn into all-out war, none of this was delving into the real politic I was interested in. It simply wasn't concerned with the corridors of power where the likes of Khoury lurked. It was like watching the Budget in order to understand the workings of the Treasury. I ordered myself another whisky and soda while I pondered this obstacle.

The barman was just passing me the soda siphon when a voice spoke behind me.

'Why don't you add a Bud to that, Doc?'

I turned, by no means sure that it was me who was being addressed, but nevertheless drawn irresistibly by a very sexy American voice. The owner didn't disappoint. She wore her blonde hair tied back in a ponytail under a tan cap, but you knew it was thick and wavy and the blonde did not come out of a bottle. Her eyes were startlingly blue and her teeth were dazzlingly white against her healthy, all-American tan. She looked in peak physical fitness, an impression enhanced by her skimpy white vest and a pair of hip-hugging khaki shorts. The Lara Croft look was completed by a practical, but no doubt expensive, pair of walking boots. Her warm smile assured me that I was her proposed benefactor. I nodded to the barman to confirm my agreement.

'I don't believe I've had the pleasure,' I began gallantly. Did I sound a little slurred? That was my third scotch and they were large ones...

'Indeed not, doctor...is that right? You are a doctor aren't you?'

'Well, surgeon actually, but yes that's my profession. What makes you ask?'

'Oh, curiosity really, it's just you look medical, but you're not exactly dressed like the doctors round here.'

I must have looked rather puzzled so she explained.

'I mean in Beirut. You know, your pants and stuff: you look like you belong in the desert not the city.'

'Oh yes, I see, very perceptive of you.' By now I was beginning to fully appreciate just how attractively her shapely breasts were fitting into that skimpy top which, added to the mellowing effects of my third large scotch, was beginning to turn this encounter into a most welcome departure from my earlier concerns about Lebanese affairs of state. She inclined her head at the compliment in a way that made me almost obliged to continue: 'I'm head of a medical refugee mission out near the Syrian border at a place called Arsal.'

'Wow, right out there on the frontline, huh. That must be kinda dangerous?'

I shrugged deprecatingly.

'Well it has its moments...'

'I bet it has...hey, I don't know about you, but I haven't eaten all day. How about I let you buy me dinner or, better still, why don't we go up to my room and order something up from there? The restaurants are packed out in here.'

Despite the disinhibiting effects of three large scotches a small voice at the back of my mind prompted a degree of caution.

'And why should I allow myself to be lured back to the room

of a highly desirable, but nevertheless completely unknown stranger?' I enquired with a certain worldly cunning.

She paused thoughtfully, and then grinned dazzlingly.

'Because I just adore stories of brave, handsome guys working in tough situations and, besides, doctors, particularly doctors in white coats, make me extremely hot.'

23

I awoke the following morning in an empty room, in an empty bed, with an orchestral headache. My mouth felt like the road to Arsal. I squinted my way to the bathroom to gulp down mouthfuls of water and empty a bursting bladder. I then crept back to sit on the side of the bed and ordered up a packet of paracetamol from room service. As I replaced the receiver, my eye caught a piece of paper on the duvet. On closer inspection it turned out to be a piece of hotel notepaper with a business card laid on top. The card read:

Rowan McBain
Freelance Journalist and TV Correspondent

There was a mobile number and an email address underneath. This brought hazy memories of the previous evening swimming uncertainly back into my mind's eye. I remembered sharing some canapé-type stuff along with a bottle of champagne, or was it two? This was the first alcohol I had consumed in weeks and, in hindsight, it had certainly done the trick! I remembered watching as those khaki shorts were enticingly lowered to reveal a skimpy pink g-string, which in turn was lowered to reveal what I believe our American cousins refer to as a 'Brazilian'. The lady obviously dressed for an exceptionally action-packed lifestyle!

What I couldn't remember quite so clearly was exactly what I had told her about my work at the Arsal Clinic or, more importantly, my wider objectives in Lebanon and, most importantly, my involvement in the medical import/ export business, Chisford Holdings. The words 'Freelance TV Correspondent' were making my blood run cold.

I certainly recalled telling her about the Clinic, but, as far as I could remember, only in the most general terms: I'd negotiated a deal with the Lebanese Government to help the overstretched MSF mission via a local Lebanese charity and was advising them on the building of a larger hospital to tackle the problem long-term. That took us up to the end of the first bottle of champers by which time things were getting distinctly hazy. I remembered trying to explain that Arsal was the genuine name of a border village not a vulgar nickname, in the same way that Mousehole in Cornwall was pronounced Mousel not Mouse Hole, but the other way round, or something like that. Anyway she seemed to find my explanation jolly amusing and it wasn't long after that that the shorts and g-string came off.

To be honest it wasn't one of my better performances. The booze certainly didn't help, particularly after the stress of my encounter with Khoury. When I did finally achieve a state of proper readiness, it was only thanks to her patience and generosity. Furthermore, rather to my surprise, I felt distinctly ashamed of my infidelity to Laila, an emotion I had never experienced in twenty-odd years of marriage to Elizabeth! More than that, I felt dimly I was being seduced for reasons more than simply sexual enjoyment, which was distracting to say the least. Nevertheless, fatigue, shame and suspicion aside, the unaccustomed drinking had drowned my distrust and that Brazilian had inflamed my lust.

Now, I simply could not recall what was said before I lapsed into unconsciousness for the night. With a nasty feeling that I was not going to like what I read, I picked up the piece of hotel notepaper. I was right. It read:

Good Morning Tony,
Got to run – press conference at 8.00. Great lay last night,
hope you enjoyed. Will see you in Arsal(?) for interview on
23rd as discussed.
Lots of love,
Rowan

Good grief! I did a painful mental calculation. The twenty-third was in three days time! I didn't agree to anything like that! But then a little voice in the back of my head told me not to be so sure. Another glimmer of the previous evening seeped through the shutters of my hangover; the bit that took place shortly after my athletic seductress decided I was spent and dismounted. As I hazily recalled she strolled au naturel over to the dressing table and returned rather breath-takingly with yet two more glasses of champagne, one of which she handed to me. I vaguely remembered her switching the conversation back to my work in Arsal, but I had absolutely no recollection of asking her to visit me there, nor any recollection of granting her an interview if she did!

Still, there it was in black and white and, even if I were to deny it, how did I go about doing that? It was simply her word against mine with no witnesses on either side thank God. If I called her and told her I had changed my mind, she would

318

want to know why and she didn't strike me as the sort to be fobbed off with an 'I'm too busy right now' type of excuse. I could hardly explain to her that I was involved in a hush-hush conspiracy to sell an overpriced, second hand hospital and a mountain of counterfeit drugs and equipment of questionable origin to a psychotic Lebanese Minister! How would that look on the cover of Time Magazine or wherever she flogged her articles?

Nor could I con her with some fiction about my working for the British Secret Service as I had done with the gullible King. She was a cynical journalist and an American to boot, so she wouldn't care less about exposing a secret British mission, even if it were true! She would have a field day with the story and I would be plastered all over the media, probably accompanied by loud denials from the British Government. Just when my whole purpose in life was to quietly string Khoury along with a bit of tactical misdiagnosis while we relieved him of his government's cash. Jesus, what had I been thinking of?

I retreated to the shower, sick to my stomach and it wasn't the hangover.

*

For the first time since my arrival in Lebanon, as I drove through the increasing militarised Bekaa Valley, my temples throbbing, I found myself desperately missing Britain. Not just the green and rolling hills of dear old Blighty. I was longing for a place where everyone spoke my language, where I had a legitimate job and a house on Wandsworth Common and some sort of respect and status. With an effort I reminded myself that had all fallen apart well before I left the White Cliffs behind. Unfortunately, that didn't make me long for the place any the less.

I forced my thoughts round to this latest eventuality in the hope that it had diminished along with my earlier, hung-over, amnesia, but the more I considered it, the more I wanted to kick myself. Why did I always feel the need to impress people? I could have just said I was an MSF doctor on a standard tour of duty, or better still passing through Beirut on my way home. She'd have let me buy her a drink then gone looking for someone more interesting. It wasn't as if I needed a screw!

Now, Christ only knew what was going to happen! Perhaps she would find a more interesting subject for her article, but a little bird told me that that was not too likely: if I had drunk enough to induce temporary amnesia, I had certainly drunk enough to induce a worrying looseness of the tongue and her note had a strikingly purposeful ring to it. Even so, did it matter that much? What could I have told her that could do any real harm? The mission was real, and so was the hospital, and so was my part in helping set them up!

But then that was all based on my false claim to work for MSF and behind that lay my lack of a medical licence and my time in prison back in the UK. If she caught a whiff of any of that and started digging she would find herself on the start of a trail leading to a Lebanese Minister who signed off large amounts of public money in return for his statue in a hospital atrium! Worse still she would unveil a whole raft of corruption and bribery which would eventually lead back to me!

What if I called her up and told her I was ill? That might delay things for a bit...but not for as long as I needed. On the evidence so far, she would turn up for a bedside interview if I was dying of Ebola and, besides, we doctors are meant to be immune to the diseases that afflict ordinary mortals. No, that was far too weak.

What would Peter suggest? I was only too happy to concede that he was considerably more worldly than I, but then I really didn't want to have to ask him. He had helped me out on more than one occasion and put a lot of time and resources into this project, so I most certainly didn't want to have to tell him that I'd ballsed things up at the first opportunity! No, that wasn't the way to go and I didn't feel that I knew Daniel Swift well enough to ask for a quiet opinion. I had the sneaking suspicion, nay conviction, that anything I shared with him would be rapidly shared with Peter anyway.

I toyed with the idea of simply upping sticks and disappearing off back to Britain, but the thought of what Inspector Newcombe might do to me put a rapid end to that option. There again, a murder conviction in Britain would probably be nothing compared to what would be done to me if Khoury discovered that I'd lied about his cancer, or lack of it. Jesus, what a choice!

What if I lured the bitch out into the desert under the pretext of showing her the border crossing and then killed and buried her out there in no-man's-land? I was a surgeon; it wasn't as if I didn't know where to insert a knife! But then what about her camera crew or whatever she was likely to turn up with? No, that was crazy, in fact, it was all getting rather crazy and I needed to calm down and think straight.

I took a deep breath and stared at the burgeoning town of Arsal as it appeared abruptly out of the distant haze. It didn't help. It just sat there looking dusty as I racked my brains for a solution but, short of putting back time, there was nothing I could do. I would just have to bite my tongue and pray that I heard no more from her.

*

'You did what?' Peter slammed his hand down on the cabin table so hard that I thought it would collapse. For the first time since I'd met him, I was seeing a glimpse of another Peter Chisholm. The tough, ruthless, former adventurer he clearly kept hidden beneath his usual, urbane, "Hail fellow, well met!" exterior. It was most unnerving.

'Well, as I say, I met this woman in the Hilton and one thing led to...'

'I know that. I just can't believe my fucking ears! You are telling us that you got yourself picked up in a bar and fucked by an American journalist and now you can't remember what you said to her? Jesus Christ, are your bollocks where your brains should be or what?'

'I didn't realise she was a journalist...'

'So fucking what! What did you think you were doing talking to anyone about our plans you bloody idiot?'

'I was pissed Peter. I'm very sorry, but I've been living under constant pressure for what seems like forever and it was the first time I'd had a drink since God knows when. I'm very sorry but it went to my head...'

'Never send a boy to do a man's job,' interjected Swift, unhelpfully.

'Why don't you fuck off?' I snapped. 'You're not dealing with a paranoid psychopath who can have you shot at the drop of a hat so you can shove your opinions where the sun doesn't shine!'

Swift was on his feet in an instant with both fists clenched.

'No fucker talks to me like...'

Thankfully, before things could get really out of hand Peter interjected: 'Shut up Dan and sit down! I need to think.' He rose abruptly and attempted to pace up and down the tiny cabin. He threw the door open in frustration and stormed out into the equally stormy darkness. The conditions were even worse than at our last meeting on Talal's cousin's trawler, so much for Mediterranean weather! I sat ignoring Swift and feeling sick: sick at my own stupidity and sick at the rocking of that damn boat.

Eventually, Chisholm returned. His expression was grim, so grim in fact, that Swift and I sat in subdued silence waiting for his pronouncement on out next course of action. Finally, he spoke.

'So this woman is turning up in Arsal tomorrow with a camera crew in tow, expecting to interview you about your work in Lebanon and how you came to be working for the Lebanese Government?'

I nodded. That was the gist of the email she had sent me earlier that day, two days after our meeting in Beirut. After much deliberation, I had concluded that my only available course of action was to own up to Peter, hence the hastily convened meeting on the boat.

'Okay, well assuming you're not pissed this time, or helplessly overcome by your rampant libido, what are the chances of your airbrushing over questions about funding and Chisford Holdings?'

'I don't know. It depends on what I've told her already...'

'And you can't remember that?'

'Well, perhaps...'

'No 'perhaps', can you or can you not recall the details of exactly what you told her?'

'No.'

'Right, then we need to get this operation wrapped up before she has a chance to get anything broadcast.'

'That's a bit dramatic isn't it?'

'No, unfortunately it is not. I told you from the outset that Chisford Holdings was my first step into legitimate medical services and supplies and I don't want it going tits-up before we've even begun. There are people watching me who could make things very difficult if I stray off their idea of the straight and narrow. Unfortunately thanks to your stupidity I'm going to have to wind this up simply because I dare not stick my neck out one iota.'

'Well perhaps you should have run this end of things instead of dumping it on an amateur like me.'

'I would have done but I have history in Lebanon going back to the Civil War so that wasn't an option. Besides, that has nothing to do with your decision to get pissed and fuck things up.'

I shrugged and turned away to stare at a bulkhead. There's

only so many times you can apologise. Peter paused to gather his thoughts then continued: 'Gortis Turnkey has been paid for the hospital and given us our cut, so we have wiped our hands there. I had planned to keep going on the supplies front, but we've made a fair few bob already and the last thing we need is for Khoury's enemies to get a whiff of corruption and start an investigation thanks to this bloody woman. Besides the political, and even the military, situation is worsening all the time. From what you've told me on the phone, this Khoury fellow looks like he's losing his grip.'

I nodded.

'True enough, he was in a right lather when we met the other day.'

'In what way?'

'Well, when I recommended the course of radiotherapy to string him along, he got extremely uptight and told me to forget it: I had two weeks to fix him up or he'd have me shot. I had to come up with some bullshit about brachytherapy to calm him down. He's expecting an operation in two weeks at the latest.'

Peter frowned.

'Not soon enough.'

'How d'you mean?'

'Well, we have to assume the worst. It would seem that you have told this woman something that makes her believe she is onto a story which justifies her travelling nearly a hundred miles with a camera crew with all the expense that entails. That means she thinks she's onto a story worth real money. We therefore have to assume that her next step after interviewing you will be to try to get to Khoury. Even if she doesn't succeed she will broadcast the fact that she can't as evidence of a cover-up. Either way, things will rapidly start to unravel between Khoury and us, and you will be slap bang in the firing line.'

I felt an icy hand grip my intestines.

'What are you saying?'

'I'm saying that, from what you tell me, this man Khoury is obviously a serious control freak and, probably quite justifiably, paranoid. He is not going to take kindly to an inquisitive journalist turning up, asking awkward questions and claiming to come from you, just when, by his own admission, he is more worried about his enemies than his cancer. That's what he said wasn't it?'

'Yes, he made that abundantly clear.'

'Right, well in that case he's so deep in trouble he's probably not worth doing business with any more, that or his paranoia is completely twisting his judgement which amounts to the same thing. Either way, we have to shut this down before she gets to him.'

'How do you propose to do that?'

'Well, first you're going to have to do your utmost to persuade her that your clinic is just some sort of humanitarian operation run by a local charity and that is all. Tell her they imported you direct from England to help with the refugee crisis and you had set up a clinic to help manage the overspill from MSF. Don't suggest any involvement with them beyond that, keep it simple. Tell Khoury that you've decided to bring his operation forward a week and a half, tell him there's been a balls-up over his test results or something...'

'That's really going to impress him!'

'Well it's about time you impressed somebody. It shouldn't be too difficult. After all it was him who was complaining about things taking too long. If you can get him under the knife within the next three or four days we stand a chance of getting our latest invoice paid and out of Lebanon before she has a chance to get to him, or go public about our involvement with him. She's not talking about a live interview so she'll need time to edit the piece and place it with a broadcaster. With a bit of luck we'll have him under the knife and out of action before she can even get to him.'

'And what happens when he comes round after the op?'

'What are you talking about?'

'Well, he's going to come round and when he does, she'll still be waiting with her film crew.'

'He won't come round.'

'Why not?'

Peter stared at me as if taken aback by my obtuseness, then spoke as if talking to a simpleton.

'Because you're going to kill him.'

'I beg your pardon?' I stammered, feebly.

'You heard,' he snapped, grimly.

*

Of course I had put up a fight at first, but Peter's logic was remorseless: if I'd kept the Member for Wandsworth zipped up this would never have happened. We could have got the new hospital very profitably stocked up to the gunnels with stolen kit and medicine then chosen a suitably discreet moment to slip away. Now we had an American newshound on our backs, hunting for an unusual story at a time when the public were getting bored of 'worsening situations' and 'streams of refugees'. That was my fault and I had to deal with it.

I put my foot down by pointing out that I was a surgeon and had dedicated my life to saving lives, not taking them, but he cut me short by pointing out that I ought to be more used to death than most people and, besides he was proposing little more than an oversight from which Khoury didn't wake up, not the shower scene from Psycho.

When I tried to dig my heels in by flatly refusing, he enquired just exactly how I intended to get out of Lebanon if a pissed off Khoury didn't want me to. There were road blocks everywhere and the road to Beirut Airport was closed as often as it was open. Khoury was the Minister for Internal Security for God's sake! He could stop me cleaning my teeth if he wanted to.

When I had suggested that I might simply up sticks and leave then and there – there was room in his speed boat for me, and Swift if he wanted to come – he laughed in my face and called me a pathetic coward. I had fucked things up and it was down to me to put things right. Swift was leaving quite legitimately in two days time as a member of the hospital construction team, having kept his side of the bargain. It was me who had fucked up and it was up to me to screw a last payment out of Khoury before things blew up in our faces. Besides it was cleaner this way. If Khoury died under the knife, this McBain bitch would have no story to pursue. We could then declare the Clinic too dangerous to continue with and shut it down. With no Khoury to answer to, it would be easy enough for me to join the stream of foreign aid workers and the like who were leaving the country in droves for healthier climes.

Finally, I had accused him of having planned to use me to murder Khoury all along, but he simply shrugged and replied that it wouldn't have been necessary if I hadn't rocked the boat. What was I being so sensitive about? This was as good as a war situation and people got killed in war. Given what we already knew about Khoury, I was doing the world a favour, particularly the world that lived in that 'Lubyanka' building I had described to him. What about those poor bastards? Think about how many more of them would die if Khoury lived.

Suddenly I was facing the charming, persuasive Peter Chisholm and my resistance was evaporating. I didn't have much choice anyway: it was obvious I wouldn't be joining him on the speed boat and my chances of getting out of Lebanon in one piece with Khoury as an enemy were nil. Despite the appalling nature of the favour I was being asked to do the world, killing the man looked positively attractive compared to the alternative. I nodded my agreement.

24

I got back to Arsal at crack of dawn on the Tuesday morning. Whether I liked it or not, I had an extremely tricky situation to deal with. First I had to pull the wool over this journalist woman's eyes and then murder the Lebanese Minister for the Interior, or whatever he called himself. The plan was to lure Khoury to a place where I could do the dreadful deed under the guise of a failed operation within the next three days. It looked simple enough on paper, but the more I thought about it, the trickier it became.

On my arrival in Arsal, I called in at the Clinic and went straight onto a ward round with Sister Mussan to catch up on the general state of play: we were overrun. Carys Probyn-Rees was clearly too exhausted to bother the nurses, whilst Kaspar Winkler looked like Old Father Time and Mr Leung appeared to be in the grip of his own anaesthetic. The staff in general looked like extras from The Night of the Living Dead. I concluded that, regardless of my dealings with Khoury, the time was rapidly approaching for the closure of the Clinic and, as soon as it was ready, a tactical withdrawal to the less frontline situation of the new hospital. Still, in the meantime it should supply Ms McBain with plenty of gruesome footage to occupy her attention.

That brought me sharply back to the question of her imminent arrival. She had confirmed in an exchange of emails that she would be arriving mid-morning which gave me an hour at most in which to sort things out. I looked around for where to begin, and then it hit me: there was nothing to sort out! If I wanted to show her a frontline clinic in crisis it was all there before me. All I had to do was give her the guided tour. I rescheduled several urgent cases for late afternoon surgery then retreated back to the Nissen and into the arms of Laila. I needed soothing more than sex, but she seemed to have the knack of providing both, so I was quite relaxed when she dismounted and went to fetch a tray of food for me.

*

I stood outside the front of the clinic maintaining the most welcoming smile I could muster as three Toyota pickups pulled up with a flourish of dust. Ms Mcbain jumped out of the passenger seat of the lead vehicle and strode forward, her Lara Croft image enhanced by a combat jacket, Ray-Bans and an authentically battered, cowgirl Stetson. In fairness, I had taken a moment to pay a little attention to my own image as a frontline surgeon, despite my limited wardrobe. I strolled forward to greet her in trainers, jeans, tee-shirt and lab coat with the obligatory stethoscope round my neck. With a bit of luck her camera crew would be too focussed on poor old me and my exhausted staff and dying patients to notice the 'Lubyanka' looming over the rear of the building.

She greeted me with an enthusiastic embrace which served to remind me of those marvellous breasts, despite the fog of alcohol prevailing at the time of my last encounter with them: they were the sort that wore a bra for decoration not support. With an effort I reminded myself that my purpose was to get rid of her at the earliest opportunity and sexual dalliance played no part in that pressing goal. Then again, perhaps a good seeing to might take her mind off the sort of things I wanted to steer her past? Even as the fancy crossed my mind, I dismissed it. Whatever else she was here for, it wasn't sex. In the sober light of day I knew her type from a mile off, sex was just a stepping stone to her ambition. She broke our embrace and stepped back to fully dazzle me with her smile.

'Tony, I can't say how good it is of you to agree to this...'

I refused to be dazzled.

'Yes, well, as you can see, the situation has deteriorated somewhat even since our meeting in Beirut so, as I explained in my email, I can only spare you a very limited amount of my time...'

'Sure, sure, I understand that. Don't worry, the guys are the tops when it comes to getting it in the can; we'll be in and out like a Magnum round. Why don't you show me round? I can take a look at the patients, then maybe we can find a quiet room for a quick interview. Larry and Joe here can follow us, while Carl and Ben take a tour outside to get a feel for the area. It sure looked rough as we were coming through the town.'

I stood there for a moment groping for a way to propose an alternative arrangement, but nothing would come. I was happy enough with the guided tour and the quick interview. I was a lot less comfortable with the thought of Carl and Ben roving around outside and inevitably pointing their camera at the 'Lubyanka'. Still, what could I do? I smiled my agreement and the tour began.

We had made it to the quiet room and I was busy dodging questions about our medical supplies when the cameraman called Ben walked in. He signalled to our cameraman to pause things then whispered something in Rowan's ear. She listened intently. 'Could you excuse us for a moment?' she asked me in a tone that implied no need for actual permission and accompanied the fellow out of the room. She was gone for perhaps a couple of minutes and when she returned her manner had changed noticeably. She frowned thoughtfully, and then turned to me.

'Before we continue recording this interview, there's something you might like to comment on off the record, Tony.'

What could I say? I nodded my agreement and smiled obligingly: 'Sure, no problem, fire away...' Did that smile hide my sick expression? I hoped so because I felt sure I was about to feel a lot sicker shortly.

*

'And you say this man threatened Carl and Ben with a pistol as he told them to leave?'

'Yes, he said that they were trespassing on Government property and he could have them arrested for spying if they didn't butt out pronto. Carl says he recognised him as the driver of the car that followed us from Beirut.'

'What did he look like?'

Rowan deferred to Ben.

'Creepy kind of guy, dark eyes and shitty teeth like a rat. Not so tall but stocky, bald and mean-lookin'.'

I nodded.

'Right yes, I think I might know the fellow...' I knew him

alright; it was Roffe to a tee! Before I could come up with a plausible explanation as to why he was threatening her staff with a pistol, Ms McBain the journalist cut in.

'Really, and do you know why he followed us from Beirut?'

'No, not at all, the county's swarming with secret service men...'

'So you recognise him and you know he's secret service, huh?'

'Yes well I said I might know him and that was off the top of my head...'

'Okay and might you know quite why he would appear to be guarding what looks like some kinda high security penitentiary? I mean what's a place like that doing right out back of a medical facility?'

Oh my God, this was going full-steam ahead into the territory I most wanted to keep hidden and all thanks to that fucking moron Roffe! I groped helplessly for an answer which might satisfy this unnervingly astute, nubile newshound. I held my hand up and addressed the group in general rather than have to meet Ms McBain's inquisitorial gaze too directly.

'Okay, okay, let me explain!' That brought me an expectant pause, but no explanation to offer. I took a deep breath and improvised. Somewhat to my own surprise, the bullshit flowed quite naturally: 'First off let me emphasise that I have no more knowledge than you regarding exactly what goes on inside that place. I have my suspicions but there is nothing I can prove and, as far as I'm concerned, it is my job to get on with saving lives in here, not prying into what goes on in there.'

Ms McBain was not impressed.

'Nuts Tony,' she interjected rather rudely, 'there ain't enough sand in this whole shitty country to hide your head in when it comes to that place!'

'That's because you're a journalist and it's you job to be inquisitive. I'm a surgeon, it's my job to heal the sick and wounded, not the problems that made them that way,' I retorted, secretly rather impressed at my own eloquence.

Ms McBain was less impressed.

'So do you know who that building belongs to?'

I shrugged as casually as I could manage; shit, this was creeping ever nearer to the territory I most wanted to avoid.

'No, not really...'

'Not really? Well, 'not really', who d'you think it might belong to?' Suddenly Ms McBain's manner was hard and alert. The irony was heavy and demanding.

'Well, my staff don't say much, but Sister Mussan tells me they talk about the Lebanese Ministry for the Interior.'

'That figures and, just out of interest, do you mind telling me who this building belongs to?'

I could tell from the gleam in her eyes that she thought she had me.

'I believe it belongs to the Ramzi Foundation, the charity I think I may have told you about back in Beirut.'

'Oh right, the charity that gets most of its funding from the Ministry for the Interior you just mentioned?'

'How do you know that?'

The bloody woman smirked.

'As you just said, I'm a journalist. It's my job to be inquisitive.'

Fuck me, what else did she know? What else had she dug

up since our last meeting? I fought back an alarming desire to panic and took a deep breath. The sort of breath you reserve for serious bullshitting.

'Look, you're right to suspect you are onto a story, but it's probably not as dramatic as you think. Yes this place is funded by the Ministry under the auspices of a man called Khoury and yes I believe that place at the back is an interrogation centre for Syrian refugees. But I met the head of the Ramzi Foundation, a Sheik Rezek and his sidekick, Dr Azzi, purely by coincidence and we agreed the building of the clinic well before I learned of their association with Minister Khoury. I thought I was working for the Ramzi Foundation and that is that. However, once I had signed a contract and recruited all my staff, things changed subtly. First they built the clinic as agreed then, without warning or any reference to me, that ghastly place was slung up behind us. What could I do? We were already saving lives. I couldn't simply down tools. When I demanded to know what was going on, it was made quite clear by Dr Azzi that Minister Khoury considered the clinic to be cosmetically useful but otherwise superfluous. If I wanted to create a fuss it would be shut down and those lives would not be saved. Since then I've kept my head down and got on with my job.'

I finished with a helpless, slightly pathetic shrug to emphasise my status as an innocent, indeed a victim, in all of this. Ms McBain and her crew eyed me with ill-concealed suspicion so I ploughed on.

'Look, Sister Mussan tells me Khoury is building a much bigger military hospital outside Arsal. They have already begun poaching our staff because they have received good basic training under my auspices and it won't be long before this place is shut down, maybe a week or two. How about you let me keep on saving lives until that happens and then I promise I will give you everything I can dig up on Khoury and that place out back in return. I've already decided that this country is getting too hot for comfort so I'll be getting out of here anyway.'

By now I was talking directly to Ms McBain and all eyes had turned to her. She cocked her head almost coquettishly on one side, clearly enjoying the moment. Finally she spoke:

'Okay, so what could you give me in two weeks time that you haven't given me already?'

I looked her straight in the eye.

'To be honest I don't know, but I have sources like Sister Mussan and I reckon Dr Azzi doesn't like Khoury as much as he feels obliged to pretend to. From everything I've seen and heard, I'm sure with a couple of weeks' grace I could set you on the path to a story that would really get the news agencies sitting up.'

I shoved my hands in my lab coat pockets and tilted my head back to indicate that I had made my best offer and the ball was in her court. She hesitated a moment longer and then smiled and nodded.

'Okay Tony, let's say we meet in two weeks time to discuss terms which will of course depend on what kinda story you've got to sell me...'

'Terms?'

'Sure, you get me the dirt on this Khoury guy and give me an interview I can sell, you're gonna expect a cut, but, If I've got to trust you not to skedaddle in the meantime, you can trust me to make it fair, okay?'

I nodded dumbly. Terms were the last things I had expected to be discussing, now or in the future, but my fortunes seemed to be holding. Unfortunately for her 'skedaddle' was exactly what I intended to do well before a fortnight had elapsed, but I reckoned Peter would compensate me for sacrificing my cut.

25

I dragged my thoughts back to the grim reality of the Khoury situation despite the sickness it induced in the pit of my stomach. It was time to get down to the real nitty-gritty.

I had a rough idea of how I might use a bit of medical hocus pocus to reel him in, but where to? The Clinic was no good. It was teaming with refugees and nurses. I could hardly see a Minister lowering himself to being operated on in there: it would be like Cameron being treated on the National Health! The new hospital was still waiting for the electricity to be connected and, according to Swift, they were still experiencing teething troubles with the plumbing. Both were brimming with potential witnesses to my crime.

What about the Villa? It was certainly private, which in theory would suit us both, though, if things went according to plan, me more than Khoury. It wouldn't take much for Talal's cousins to turn my examination room into a makeshift operating theatre and Khoury was used to the place. The paranoid fruitcake would feel as safe there as anywhere. No doubt he would turn up with a retinue of guards, but what could they do when I emerged from 'theatre' and announced their boss had died under the knife. Cutting up rough wouldn't bring him back and our own security would be on hand to face them down while they thought about it.

I turned this over in my mind and it began to fit better and better. What about staff? I could play the secrecy card up to a point in order to justify my lack of them, but he would still expect things to look like he was in an authentic medical environment. The right looking personnel would convince him more than anything else. The Clinic staff were no good. They looked half dead with exhaustion and, besides, they were all potentially dangerous witnesses from my point of view.

I could certainly use Laila as a theatre nurse. She had the lingo and could soon be coached into saying the right things to calm His Lordship. She only had to keep him calm until the anaesthetic took over. I put the image of her in a nurse's uniform out of my mind with a conscious effort and continued scheming.

Khoury had met Talal, so I couldn't use him, but I could use a few cousins in scrubs and masks as extras. They could even carry guns under their tops in case a stand-off arose with Khoury's thugs. That left me short of an anaesthetist/assistant surgeon. I felt reasonably sure that Khoury would fall for one man doubling up, but who? I was lying there picking at a bowl of olives when an idea began to form.

What about King? He certainly had the qualifications and experience to bring some real authenticity to the whole thing. I had seen him in theatre and he was clearly the real thing. But could he be persuaded to take part in an operation that would be tantamount to murder? He was a surgeon for Heaven's sake! But then that didn't make him an unswerving saviour of the sick: so was I. True, but I stood to lose a lot of money and perhaps my life if this didn't happen. What had he got to lose? Nothing.

Then I recalled the excitement with which his eyes had lit up as I swore him to secrecy and told him about my 'top secret mission'. Perhaps the idea wasn't so silly after all: he wouldn't be an MSF surgeon if he didn't enjoy a challenge and he was already convinced that Khoury was one of the bad guys. He didn't have to take part in the killing, he could simply turn up looking the part, administer the anaesthetic, and then leave the 'theatre' and the rest to me. I reckoned there was enough of the little boy in him to find the chance of a real life James Bond adventure irresistible. Even if he didn't, I reckoned he could be persuaded to keep it under his hat, so I wouldn't do any harm by asking him. I lay there for a while longer weighing up the pros and cons of this in my mind, then got up and walked through into the living room. I picked up my phone and dialled the secure number Khoury had given me for medical discussions. After a few moments he answered:

'Yes Doctor?'

I chose not to correct him and got straight to the point.

'Ah, Minister, I'm sorry to trouble you, but something has come to my attention which I feel you would wish me to discuss with you as a matter of some urgency.'

'Yes?'

'Well I'm afraid I have had a further report from the specialists who are reviewing your test results in Zurich.'

'What is this report?'

I could immediately hear the rising tension in his voice which presaged a violent fit of temper.

'I'm afraid I must warn you it is not good news...'

'Tell me quickly what is it!' This was a snarl.

'Well, Minister the review suggests that your condition is more advanced than initially thought. It has reached the stage we refer to as locally advanced prostate cancer, as opposed to the T stage two malignancy we had initially believed...'

'Who is responsible for this?'

'I beg your pardon?'

'Who is making this error?' His voice was thick with rage. I had to stand my ground before he decided I was to blame.

'Really, Minister, no-one is making an error! Blame God, or Allah, or your diet, but don't blame the people who are trying to help you. Assessing prostate cancer is a complex business and it is not being helped by your impatience. I know you are under pressure, but trying to lay blame on your consultants' shoulders will not help.'

'Someone will die for this!'

'Yes and it will probably be you if you don't calm down and listen to the course of action I recommend!'

There was the stunned silence of someone unaccustomed to being answered back. Finally he spoke more reasonably.

'What is it you must do?'

'Well, it seems evident to me that your treatment will have to reflect your personal situation in a way that we doctors would not normally expect to have to allow for.'

'How is this?'

'Well I imagine, given the current political situation and your position as a government minister, I do not have the freedom and time I would usually expect when handling this sort of tumour...'

'You have no time!'

'I rather thought as much, but cancer doesn't unfortunately care a jot for time and people's circumstances and there is nothing I can do about that. All I can do, if you wish, is carry out what is known as an open radical prostatectomy to remove your prostate gland and the surrounding infected tissues. That, coupled with continued brachytherapy is the best course of action I can recommend under the circumstances.'

'When is this?'

'As soon as possible, tomorrow or the day after...'

There was a long pause.

'This is so serious?'

'I'm afraid this is very serious,' I lied, hating myself but hating what he would do to me if he found out I had been cheating him more.

*

I met King late that evening outside the Nissen as before, but this time he didn't pin me up against the wall and this time I called him Brandon and he called me Tone in typical Australian fashion. I had deliberately chosen a late hour to add to the clandestine feel of the occasion. I first went through the rigmarole of swearing him to secrecy and then outlined the situation: I hated what I had been ordered to do, but my instructions came straight from MI6 headquarters on the Albert Embankment – I was drawing heavily on a dimly remembered James Bond film for this. I had never been asked to carry out a 'sanction' in my life – this came courtesy of that Clint Eastwood film about the mountaineer that I remembered from my school days. Still he seemed to appreciate a bit of 'trade' jargon.

I explained that my 'controller' (thank you John Le Carré)

had made it clear that this was an absolute priority which would save many innocent lives. I hastened to add that King himself was only needed to administer the anaesthetic and had no need to witness the dreadful deed itself. To my delight he was almost affronted by the suggestion that he didn't have the balls to see the whole thing through to the bitter end.

I explained as much as he needed to know about the Villa and informed him that I had arranged with Khoury to meet him there the following evening at midnight. I added that my second-in-command, Talal, was already setting up a makeshift operating theatre. I reassured him that we had the manpower and equipment to defend ourselves against Khoury's thugs if things went tits-up. He took this all in with the studied calm of a seasoned secret agent. We agreed that we would tell anyone that needed to know that we were off for an evening's R&R in Tripoli to throw a bit of a red-herring then turn left instead of right at the main highway. I had arranged for two sets of scrubs to be ready for us at the Villa so we would get changed there.

He asked how I planned to dispose of the body afterwards and I explained that I would simply dump it, figuratively, in the lap of his odious second-in-command Mr Roffe. The creep would be bound to be in attendance and, when I announced that things had gone wrong and his boss was dead, I would also be asking him what he wanted to do about it. I wouldn't be surprised if the answer was that he intended to step into his shoes, but that was not my business.

Would this Roffe bloke be up to this? King enquired. I shrugged coolly.

If he tried to duck out of the responsibility, I would then

give him the choice: either he made arrangements to dispose of the body first thing in the morning or I would announce the death to the world and let him handle whatever political fall-out resulted. According to the powers that be in London, the Khoury faction most definitely wouldn't want the latter. At first, they'd be left running around like a headless chicken by his demise. With their main fixer gone, their plans to exploit a political collapse in Syria would have no military muscle behind them. When they calmed down they would want his death stage managed with minimum fuss which could very well amount to the abrupt disappearance of the body all-together. They wouldn't want me making noises. At worst, we might be called upon, given our status as foreign doctors, to confirm that he had died in surgery due to unforeseen complications or some such.

We agreed that we would meet at the Nissen at eight the following evening which would still give us a couple of hours to get ready when we reached the Villa. Finally, I handed him a hip flask of brandy with which to toast our deal, then took a swig myself to seal our clandestine partnership.

*

It was a blessed relief when I finally got the old man into surgery. It was early afternoon and he'd come in earlier accompanied by his wife and assorted relatives who tried to set up camp around his bed. Sister Mussan drove most of them out but we could not get rid of his bloody wife who was determined to wail and gnash her tooth at anyone in hospital clothing. I was hurrying back from a toilet break after an emergency appendectomy when she latched onto me. It seemed like forever before I was able to detach myself thanks principally to the application of an arm-lock on the woman courtesy of Sister Mussan. I followed the trolley into theatre trying to assess the damage to my new patient in the absence of any reliable triage.

It soon became apparent that the poor old bugger had had his lower jaw blown clean off, perhaps by one of those bastards I saw killing people at the border crossing. I guessed the damage was caused by a bullet, the trauma was too localised for a grenade or a mine. Given the mess it had made I suspected it was the hollow-nosed variety that explode on impact. I recalled the uproar the Metropolitan Police had caused years before by shooting a Brazilian they mistook for a terrorist with these things. This war was paying no regard to the Geneva Convention.

I had long since ceased worrying about undertaking surgery that fell outside my particular field of expertise, but this really was new territory altogether. The big challenge was assessing what could be achieved given such limited facilities. Any form of reconstruction was out of the question, but I needed to assess what could be saved out of what was left and then figure out to what degree it could be used to create a stable platform from which my colleagues in a better equipped hospital might attempt to build. First off, what were my chances of leaving him with speech and the ability to eat? On close inspection, not much.

The bullet had entered just beneath the right hand molars on a slightly upward trajectory. Presumably the resistance of the inferior maxillary had exploded the soft-nosed bullet because it had shredded the tongue and blown away the entire left-hand temporomandibular joint. To all intents and purposes there was simply no jaw or tongue left. Someone had applied a wad of filthy padding to the stump of his tongue and he had been turned on his side to prevent him drowning in his own blood. A proper airway needed to be established and the whole trauma area needed cleaning up.

I was considering these issues when a hand gripped my elbow. Jesus Christ, it was Roffe again, but this time the vile bastard was interrupting an actual operation! I began to shrug him off, but I remembered it was futile, so I snapped: 'Come with me!' I stalked out of the theatre with the odious Weasel in close attendance.

'What is it now?' I demanded as we exited the building through the back entrance and I turned to face him. He paused for a moment with that air of smug amusement before replying:

'The Minister say your place no good.'

'What do you mean?'

He shrugged and slightly qualified the statement:

'The Minister say your place no good for operation.'

I paused trying to take this in.

'What do you mean? He doesn't want the operation anymore?'

He shook his head.

'He want operation, but not at your place.'

'For heaven's sake where on earth does he want it then?'

Even as I spoke an icy chill gripped my heart. Roffe didn't even reply, he simply raised his eyes to peer over my shoulder.

I knew without looking that the new venue was the building behind me, the grim Lebanese 'Lubyanka'.

I stood there speechless as Roffe regarded me enquiringly. The fear must have shown in my face.

'You no like?' he sneered.

I ignored the taunt.

'What is wrong with the Villa?'

He shrugged.

'Minister Khoury no say. He say operation happen here tomorrow night.'

I stared at the revolting little bastard, lost for words. As usual, Khoury had sent Roffe to do his dirty work. He stood there leering at me like Peter Lorre's ugly younger brother, exuding malice. At last I found my tongue:

'I can't possibly work in there. I need the right conditions. This is out of the question!'

He didn't argue he simply replied: 'Come!' He turned and led me to my nearby Nissen. He produced a key and unlocked the door; where the hell had he got that from? He entered and beckoned me in behind him. He turned and looked at me expectantly. I stood for a moment wondering what it was I was meant to react to, and then it hit me. She was gone. Laila was not there. The place was empty.

'What have you done with her?' I bellowed rounding on him with both fists clenched. He had clearly anticipated a strong reaction because he now held a pistol pointed at my belly. He gestured pacifyingly with his spare hand, and then spoke as if he was agreeing a trip to the shops:

'I take girl. You do good work I give you back girl, okay? You don't do good work, I kill girl, okay?'

I stood there speechless. What could I say? Did I hand over all control of the situation to this vicious thug and his paranoid boss, or did I make a stand and risk losing the first woman I had loved in years, possibly in my entire life? Who was to say that if I went into that hellhole I would ever come out alive? Roffe didn't wait for a reply.

'You will be here tonight at twelve o'clock with people for operation. If you not here, I kill girl myself.' He said this with unmistakeable relish, then turned and left the Nissen.

26

I went back to the old man with the missing jaw but I could no longer concentrate. Finally, I told the nurse to arrange an ambulance and ship him off to Tripoli. For all I knew that amounted to a death camp in the desert fifty miles down the road. I couldn't care less any more. All I could think of was Laila and that fucking building. What was happening to her in there? What was the place really used for? Fine, it was a straightforward breeze block construction, only remarkable for its lack of windows, but no one could tell me that prison buildings do not convey an air of menace, particularly if you believe they are being used for torturing the woman you love.

That brought me straight back to Laila again. She was probably in there right now and God knows what they were doing to her! I doubted they would let me go once they got me in there, so there was no real incentive for them to treat her decently. There were probably prison guards lining up to rape her right now! Was there even any point in putting myself in jeopardy for a lost cause?

What was I thinking about? I wasn't offering Khoury a one-off surgical procedure! This was just part of a treatment program which would have to extend over many months, or at least it would have done if he really had prostate cancer. Khoury wasn't a fool. He believed he needed long-term treatment and he trusted me to carry it out. He just wanted me to get on with it due to the political pressure he was under. This was just his thuggish way of asserting some control. I doubted very much if any harm would come to Laila as long as my services were needed...

And so it went on. I left the Clinic and went back to the Nissen. I just couldn't cope with the barrage of endless hospital trivia. I poured myself a hefty slug from the remains of the brandy, but had only taken a sip when I remembered that I needed to keep my wits about me. If Laila and I were to come out of this alive, I didn't need to be half-cut! I replaced the cap and tried a bit of pacing up and down, but each lap brought me back to the window from which I could see nothing but the Lubyanka. I threw myself on the bed and tried to force myself to think about what the evening would bring, but I couldn't focus on it. I began to get some understanding of what it must have been like for troops in the trenches waiting to go over the top.

Very gradually I began to focus on certain practical issues. For one, with Laila kidnapped, I needed a nurse to assist in Khoury's operation. After some thought, I decided Sister Mussan might be approachable. I could explain that Khoury was one of the good guys. He was building a much bigger hospital for the refugees and she would be needed to work there. It would help her case later if she was genuinely ignorant of the murder plot. Besides, I knew the signs, and she clearly worshipped the ground I walked on. I decided to approach her at seven that evening when the day shift finished and she went for her evening meal.

Brandon King presented a bigger, practical problem. It had remained an unspoken agreement between us that we met away from the MSF building and, in fact, kept our relationship secret in general. Neither of us had seen the need to formally agree this, it was just something that had grown out of the way we had got to know each other. Perhaps we didn't want loose tongues speculating about how we had gone from being enemies to being friends. Anyway, the upshot was that I had no means of discussing this latest development with him until he arrived at the Nissen at nine o'clock.

*

'So you wish for me to help to make this operation for Lebanese Minister?'

I nodded encouragingly, Sister Mussan was not turning out to be quite the push-over I had initially envisaged.

'Yes, just to help me prep him and keep him calm until the anaesthetic kicks in.'

'Why does he wish for operation in that building, not in proper hospital?'

I shrugged, trying to imply that this was normal procedure.

'The Minister has enemies, particularly in the current climate, and he does not wish people to know he is ill.'

'You ask me to do job here to save my people, not Lebanese people. I work very hard to do this for my people, but, perhaps I am not sure to this Minister. He has his own people.'

'Yes, but in helping make him well, you are saving your people because he is the man who pays for this clinic and will pay for the new hospital the refugees need so badly.' I gestured at the surrounding, open-plan hangar space; we were sitting in the area that passed for a staff restaurant and talking in subdued tones. She paused to digest this last point, and then changed tack.

'Why are there no men come here for treatment?'

That threw me.

'Well we do treat men here; your father for instance. How is he doing by the way?'

'Father is dead. He did not survive operation.'

'Oh, I'm very sorry...I didn't realise.'

'It is not your fault. He travelled many miles with wound and he was very old. You did the best possible.'

This was embarrassing. I had no recollection of operating on the old bugger at all, but then I couldn't remember everyone amid the chaos of those early days. Still, she seemed pretty stoical about it. Unfortunately, not stoical enough to let go of her initial point.

'Why do no young men come here?'

I paused and looked at her squarely in the eye. She was an intelligent woman and I clearly would get no cooperation by trying to fob her off on this point. Equally, I had already decided that the fewer people who knew about my murderous intentions towards Khoury the better, so the full-on 'James Bond' cover story I had sold Brandon was hardly helpful. In fact, it was better for her sake if she believed that my intentions towards Khoury were pure. I decided on a compromise approach.

'To tell you the truth, I simply don't know, but I've been asked by the British Government to try to find out.'

'How is this?'

'Well, this Minister Khoury is a very powerful man and he would know, or could find out, why so few men are arriving at clinics along this border. The British Government, along with other interested parties, is afraid that a very real breach of human rights is occurring and, if this is so, it intends to bring pressure to bear on the Lebanese Government to prevent it. It is hoped that I will be able to win Minister Khoury's confidence and find out more.'

I sat back rather satisfied with this diluted version of the Brandon cover story. She sat and studied my face intently for some moments then nodded.

'This is good for my people. Okay I help you. What must I do?'

*

King arrived punctually at the Nissen at nine o'clock. I had arranged with Sister Mussan to turn up at eleven. I didn't want her hanging round asking awkward questions longer than necessary. By then I would have had a chance to break the change of venue to King and hopefully persuade him to go along with it. The prospect of entering the 'Lubyanka', compared to the prospect of entering the Villa as I had described it to him, was a totally different kettle of fish. It didn't help that I was crapping myself at the thought of it as I set about trying to sell the idea to him. I decided that honesty, if that's the word, was the best policy.

'Ah, Brandon, come on in, grab a seat. Can I take your coat?'

'Don't we need to be making a move for Beirut?'

'Well, er, no actually. There's been a bit of a change of plan. Here, sit down. Let me get you a drink. What are you having?'

'I dunno, what you got?'

'Scotch and water's about the best I can do: that okay?'

'Sure, I guess so, thanks. What's this about a change of plan?'

I busied myself with the glasses and the drink as I answered over my shoulder.

'Well, I had a visit from Khoury's number two, a man called Roffe, earlier.'

'Oh yeah, what did he want?'

'Well, basically, he came to say there's been a change of venue.'

'A change of venue, why's that?'

'I don't really know. Roffe said something about the Villa not being secure enough. You've got to remember that Khoury is a certifiable paranoiac and I suppose the Villa could be vulnerable to a direct assault if his enemies found out he was there and out for the count on an operating table.'

King took a thoughtful swig and swallowed slowly before he spoke again:

'You don't think he suspects us of planning anything do you?'

I had been wondering the same thing myself almost constantly since parting company with Sister Mussan. I turned to face him with all the confidence I could muster.

'I'd be a liar if I told you that that was completely out of the question, but I've thought this over carefully and I really don't think so. If he thought we intended to do him harm, why would he bother to let me anywhere near him in the first place? He could have us, or at least me, deported or even 'disappeared' at the drop of a hat. No, I'm quite sure he doesn't suspect us. I reckon he simply wants absolute control and he's under a lot of pressure to get his treatment out of the way.'

King pondered this then asked the question I had been least looking forward to:

'So where's the new venue?'

I pointed out of the rear window of the Nissen: 'In that building over there.'

King turned a distinctly whiter shade of pale. He rose and walked over to stare out at the Lubyanka outlined against the night sky.

'Jesus, I've got kids, y'know,' was his first, shaky, comment.

'So have I,' I replied, neglecting to mention that, to the best of my knowledge, they hated my guts, 'but I really don't think we need to be put off by the appearance of the building. Khoury's going to need my on-going care and treatment for some time after the op so I reckon we're perfectly safe.'

King turned away from the window.

'I dunno mate. Look, I don't want you to think I'm a coward but, Jesus, how the hell are we going to get out of there if we kill him? I mean, the place is gonna be full of his people and they're hardly gonna be pleased when we announce their boss is dead. They'll lock us up for starters and who's to say they'll give a shit about how or why he died. They could simply shoot us on the spot no questions asked!'

I let King get his initial panic off his chest and then raised a hand to calm him down.

'I've thought about that, believe me, I've thought about that more than anything else and I reckon there's a way we can make sure that doesn't happen.'

'How?'

'We are not going to deliver the coup de grace, or at least not while we are there.'

'How d'you mean?'

'Well, for a start, his second-in-command, Roffe, is bound to be there and he is the most suspicious bastard on the planet, so we've got to assume that our every move is going to be scrutinised and our every word listened to from the minute we walk through the door. We need to use that to our advantage.'

King raised his eyebrows sceptically, so I continued.

'If Roffe sees an operation take place which does nothing to arouse his suspicions and, if anything confirms all his expectations, then he cannot refuse to let us go, so all we need to do is perform what looks like a radical prostatectomy, stitch his boss back up and announce that we'll be back when he regains consciousness.'

'So this Roffe man will just let us go leaving his boss unconscious?'

'He'll have to. I'll tell him we have to return to the Clinic to carry out biopsies on the tissue we have removed or something. The man's a bloody peasant; he has no idea what's involved and he's not going to obstruct me if I tell him it might kill his boss.'

'And in the meantime?'

'In the meantime we give Khoury a shot of insulin that would kill a horse while he's still under. He won't die immediately and it'll be virtually untraceable afterwards. We'll be long gone by the time anyone realises he's dead.'

'If the security's that tight, how are we going to smuggle insulin in?'

'We don't have to. I've already convinced Khoury he is diabetic. I had him tested for it when I first became his doctor and let his hypochondria do the rest. If Roffe queries the insulin, Khoury himself will back us up. You can confirm that insulin levels have to be adjusted whilst he's under anaesthetic, in fact, you can make a pantomime of doing just that while I muck around with his prostate. How can they argue? Barika will be the only nurse present and she's untrained so she won't suspect anything. As and when she finally realises he's dying, we'll be gone and she'll have no idea what to do. Nor will anyone else there.'

'Okay, so assuming we make it back out of the building, what then?'

'Well, my second-in-command Talal will be waiting outside with a fast car and plenty of armed relatives to see off the opposition if a problem arises and anyone tries to stop us. There will be a helicopter, courtesy of MI6, waiting in the desert ready to take me to a boat out at sea, next stop Zurich. I won't be coming back. You're welcome to come with me if you like, though, if anyone stands to take the blame, it will be me. Besides, you'll be pretty untouchable back in the bosom of MSF with no-one even sure that any foul play has taken place. Barika just has to play the dumb nurse and slip away in the confusion. According to HMG, the whole thing will be covered up by his cronies anyway.'

King paused a moment longer, torn between common sense and the opportunity to turn a routine MSF tour into the adventure of a lifetime. Finally, he grinned and nodded as the Aussie fighting spirit that had seen Anzacs die at Gallipoli in their thousands finally won out.

*

They hadn't even bothered to paint the grey, breeze block walls that formed the central corridor running the length of the 'Lubyanka'. Bare light bulbs were strung along the ceiling on exposed cables. The unswept floor was concrete dusted with sand carried in on shoes and boots. Occasional dark patches on the walls and floor could have been dirt or blood. It was impossible to tell in that light. I decided it was best not to speculate. I also decided not to speculate about the occasional screams and shouts that seemed to emanate from deeper within the building. To add to the generally intimidating atmosphere of the place we were escorted by a two-man armed guard.

The odious Roffe brought the procession to a halt about halfway down the corridor and opened a door on our left. The guards took up positions outside as he ushered us in. The room had clearly undergone an extremely thorough clean-up and stank of disinfectant. It was spacious enough to serve as a comfortable operating theatre though I dreaded to think what purpose it usually served. It was too big for an ordinary cell and the white-wash was freshly applied.

The surgical couch, equipment and lighting I had ordered were all set up in the middle of the room, while Khoury himself was sitting on a sofa in the far corner wearing a surgical gown. He looked pale and he didn't get up as I approached. I wondered if this was fear or the effects of the particularly radical bowel prep I had prescribed for him the day before: we doctors have many ways of dealing with obnoxious patients.

A man dressed in scrubs and a mask stood beside the couch.

His shifty eyes and hesitant body language exuded fear. I ignored him and addressed Khoury.

'Ah, Minister, good evening. I trust you are ready for your operation?' I didn't wait for a reply. 'If all goes well the operation should take one to two hours and you will probably regain consciousness sometime tomorrow. You should be fit to return to your office at the Ministry the following day where I understand you have installed a bed and made arrangements to be nursed.'

He peered up at me with dull eyes.

'These medicines you give have bad actions.'

I nodded with false sympathy.

'Yes, well unfortunately you wanted the operation done as a matter of urgency, and so we had to ensure your bowels were properly evacuated at short notice to avoid any risk of potentially catastrophic infection. I hope the experience wasn't too unpleasant.' I said this in the sublime certainty that it was. I had prescribed enough enemas and laxatives to evacuate Dunkirk!

I nodded at the man in the scrubs.

'I trust you appreciate that it would most inadvisable to undertake a complex operation such as this assisted by a complete stranger which is why I have brought Dr King here with me. I only work with strangers when I'm teaching and the pupils and the situation are properly controlled and backed-up.' This wasn't strictly true, but there was no way he could prove otherwise.'

Khoury frowned and waved a hand irritably.

'Dr Labaky is observer not surgeon,' he growled.

'Don't you trust me?' I enquired a little too flippantly.

'There is no need with Labaky observer,' he snarled. It crossed my mind that perhaps I had overdone the purgatives.

'Do you mind my asking quite what qualifications Dr Labaky has for such a role?'

'He is Doctor at University.'

That didn't help clarify things and I was suddenly uncomfortably aware of the need to keep third parties observers from witnessing the treatment of Khoury I had in mind; particularly observers who might turn out to be expert in the field.

'Doctor of what, flower arranging?' I demanded sarcastically. 'Just being a 'Doctor at University' is no qualification for assessing surgical competence.' I added. Khoury, however, was in no mood for contradiction.

'This man is observer and that is all!' he barked. 'You fail in your task and he will tell Roffe to kill you that is all!' He slumped back, apparently exhausted, and shut his eyes.

I glanced at King and gave him a reassuring wink to sustain his courage in the light of this latest twist in our situation then pulled back my shoulders. Very well, if he wanted my work observed, Labaky would observe a perfect prostatectomy carried out before his eyes and be none the wiser when the complications set in. With any luck he'd take the blame in my absence!

Before I could build further upon this determined optimism, I felt my elbow gripped in that insistent fashion unique to Roffe. There was no point in resisting, particularly now I knew he carried a gun. I was led over to a table with Labaky in close attendance. A pile of scrubs, still in their plastic, lay on it.

'Take off clothes!'

I stripped to my underpants, too accustomed to Roffe's piggish manners to protest at the lack of privacy.

'Take off all clothes!' he snapped. To quash any protest the odious little runt gave my pants a downwards yank. I stepped out of them with as much dignity as I could muster, drawing myself up to show the repulsive bastard what a decent male physique should look like. This was somewhat defeated by Dr Labaky's insistence that I opened my legs and bent over for a completely thorough inspection. 'Put on these things!' was all Roffe added, thrusting a packet of scrubs into my hand before turning to supervise Brandon and Barika.

27

I stepped back from the table and gestured for Barika to mop my brow again. I was sweating profusely despite the comparative coolness of the place. Khoury was anaesthetised, shaved, draped and prepped for an open prostatectomy. A catheter had been placed in his urethra to drain urine. He had also been treated to a rather unnecessary cystoscopy to kill a bit of time, but now it was time to get down to the real thing and I was running out of options.

The problem was that Labaky was proving to be a most distracting nuisance. It was like that rhyme: 'Big fleas have little fleas to bite 'em'. I was being bitten by Labaky, who in turn was being bitten by Roffe, all on behalf of Khoury, who had left orders for them to devour me if things went wrong. Obviously, Labaky had to be seen to be fulfilling his role as invigilator to keep Roffe off his back, but having him peering over my shoulder constantly was more than just distracting, it was a constant reminder that I was walking a terrifyingly high tightrope.

The problem was that I didn't know just how qualified he really was. Up to now I had done nothing to give him grounds for thinking there was anything amiss, but the time was fast approaching when I was going to have to reveal Khoury's prostate and remove cancerous tissue which, to the best of my knowledge simply did not exist. That was a tough one to get round if this man really was a doctor!

I glanced at him again. As usual he was shifting round trying to get a better view of what I was doing. Up to now I had pretty well ignored him, but now I studied him a little more closely. I had automatically put him in the enemy camp, but was that necessarily the case? He was undoubtedly going to do what the Minister for Internal Affairs told him to do out of fear for his life, but was there a way in which that could be turned to my advantage?

He hadn't said a single word to me, but that was quite possibly because he was embarrassed by his position. No doubt he realised that he had the power of life or death over me, so he was hardly likely to invite me for a cup of tea and a chat, even if the bizarre situation we found ourselves in permitted it. I didn't think our lack of communication was simply down to a language barrier: English was far too international for that, particularly in the medical profession. No, the more I thought about it, the more I concluded that embarrassment and fear were to blame.

I wondered if he had thought out the full implications of his current employment. Did he realise quite what a psychopath his current employer actually was? If he did, he should be wondering by now quite what his future held once his usefulness to Khoury had expired. Did he seriously imagine he would be left free to tell his friends and colleagues about this top secret operation that had taken place in some high security detention centre cum torture chamber in the back of beyond? If he was harbouring such doubts, now was the time to find out and exploit them. First off, I needed to break through our lack of communication.

It was time to prepare for the first incision which I had

already decided would be retro pubic. For that I needed Khoury head down/feet up. Given that the operating table was manual, I was justified in asking for help. I addressed my invigilator for the first time:

'The patient needs to be in the Trendelenberg Position so I'm going to need your help if you don't mind.' The man looked slightly taken aback at being addressed unexpectedly, but he didn't look thrown by the technical terminology. He nodded and looked down to locate the height adjusters on the table. Good, he spoke English and knew something about surgery. Together we rearranged Khoury's position. That naturally involved a few more words of question and agreement. Roffe stepped forward.

'No speaking! You work in silence!'

I turned to face him, drawing my mask down and myself up to my full height. I glared at him with all the authority I could muster and spoke with cold fury:

'Now just you listen to me and listen well, you little runt, because I don't intend to repeat myself! As long as we're in here, this is my operating theatre. I decide whom I wish to talk to and when. I decide what happens, when it happens and why it happens. If I decide I need assistance from this man, I get it and that is final. If you don't like it, I am out of here right now and you can explain to your boss why I left, that's if he lives to listen to you. Do you understand me?'

Roffe stood there nonplussed at my reaction, so I walked right up to him and bellowed in his face: 'Do you understand?'

He blinked as if adjusting to a bang round the head. For a moment I expected him to snap to attention and salute.

Perhaps thanks to his twisted frame, he half-bowed and nodded instead. I had guessed right, a bit of parade-ground Sergeant Major had done the trick. I turned on my heel and returned to the operating table.

It was a hell of a gamble, but it paid out generously. Not only did it push Roffe further back out of earshot, it also showed my new assistant that it was possible to stand up to these people. When I returned he was looking at me curiously and I was sure some of that look of fear had dissipated. He was still clearly on tenterhooks, but who wouldn't be, but he was looking at me now with what I sincerely hoped was respect. As I leant across the table to adjust the drapes, I muttered:

'I can get you out of here to safety if you are interested.' I glanced up at him to see if he had heard and understood what I said. His eyes had widened. I indicated Roffe with a backward roll of my eyes. 'Otherwise, yesterday, I overheard the Minister here,' I rolled my eyes downwards, 'instructing this thug behind me to shoot you immediately after the operation.' His eyes widened, this time with terror, but he contained his reaction to a glance at Roffe who was doubtless looking his usual revolting self. He looked away quickly.

'Please, how do you do this?' he whispered.

'You simply follow my lead and accompany me when I say we are leaving. You will tell him you wish to observe the tests I must do at my clinic while his boss is regaining consciousness. I have men outside and we won't be coming back. In return you have to back me up when I tell him that I have successfully removed a Stage Two cancerous growth from his boss's prostate.'

'He will let me go with you?'

'I don't know, but it's the best chance you've got. With his boss unconscious he is not quite sure how to handle me and therefore, by association, you. We need to make the most of his uncertainty. I think there's a good chance that he will insist on accompanying the three of us,' I nodded at King, 'to my clinic but, once we are outside, the forces I have waiting for us will swing the balance of power in our favour. Are you with me?'

'What is this man suffering?' he was staring down at Khoury.

'Nothing, but he is an evil man who plans to kill many people if we do not kill him first. All you have to do is tell this thug that I have performed a prostatectomy. I will do the rest. Do you agree?'

The man stayed for a moment longer staring down at Khoury's inert figure, no doubt trying to get his head round these developments and more importantly the limited options I had outlined. At last he glanced up.

'Okay, you must count me in!'

*

Labaky and I peered solemnly down into the open incision. The abdominal muscle was separated, the blood supply controlled and the prostatic capsule exposed for dissection. The only problem was that there was no cancerous tissue to remove. Roffe had clearly sensed that the operation was reaching a critical phase and had edged forward to get a view despite everyone's best efforts to exclude him. I had little choice but to rely on his medical ignorance.

'I think a total radical prostatectomy presents itself as our best option here gentlemen.' I announced to my motley team.

'Doesn't look like you've got much choice Tone,' agreed King convincingly, while Labaky nodded enthusiastic encouragement. Roffe glanced questioning at each of us only to be met with mutual, affirmative nods.

'Right, let's get on with it then. Can you check his levels Brandon? If you can pass the scalpel and forceps please Mr Labaky...'

Without more ado, we carefully removed our patient's prostate, discarded it along with a bit of extraneous tissue for good measure, then re-attached everything, allowing a lengthy delay for hemostasis, and sewed him scrupulously back up. If nothing else, it all took a convincing amount of time.

Finally, I stepped back from the table and peeled off my gloves as Barika mopped my brow again. I turned to Roffe:

'There you are then, job done. I just need to get those tissue samples back to the lab for analysis to ensure the cancerous spread has been contained...'

Roffe had his answer ready.

'You do not leave until Minister comes awake!'

So did I.

'Just you listen here, my man! If I do not get these samples tested within the next thirty minutes they will be useless and there will be no way of knowing whether your boss is still suffering from cancer. It has to be done immediately with the help of Mr King and Mr Labaky to speed it up or there's a very real possibility that the Minister might die of a secondary malignancy. If that happens, I have already made arrangements to tell the world that his death was the result of your stupidity and stubbornness!'

Perhaps I had underestimated his stupidity and stubbornness, or perhaps this bid for freedom was more transparent than I had hoped. Either way, instead of stepping back and gesturing politely to the exit, he stepped back and pulled out that bloody gun again.

'You no leave!'

I stood, stunned by this impasse, then took another deep breath and drew myself up to my full height again, but I never got the chance to deliver another broadside. As I opened my mouth, out in the corridor a deafening volley of shots rang out!

I stopped dead, stunned by this new development. I hadn't told Talal to attack the place. There were enough cousins to mount a convincing re-guard action, but never enough to mount a frontal assault. What the hell was going on?

Roffe was less uncertain, no doubt accustomed to outbreaks of armed conflict. Unfortunately he was convinced I was the cause of this surprise. Now the gun was pointed straight between my eyes. I raised my hands because that is what everyone does, but it didn't help. I couldn't help being transfixed by that whitening of the knuckles that everyone else notices. I was even more struck by the look of absolute hate in the eyes staring at me from behind them. It was all in slow motion and I even remember wondering dimly what I had ever done to make him feel that way. Was it a class or nationality thing?

The door crashed open and my thoughts were abruptly focussed as a bullet blew the back of Roffe's cranium off, hurling him into my arms. Thankfully, his gun flew away in the process. The next thing I knew, I was on my back, pinned to the floor by his corpse, with his brains spilling out onto my face. My desperate urge was to shove him away but, in a moment of clarity, I realised that would probably get me shot. With a superhuman effort I lay absolutely motionless, hardly able to breathe as his blood and brains spilled over my nose and into my mouth.

I lay like that for what seemed like eternity. Men rampaged around me and shots rang out; some at terrifyingly close quarters. I cringed waiting to be next, but a bullet never came and suddenly calm descended as a more authoritative voice arrived and began to instil some order. Suddenly Roffe was hauled off me and I was dragged to my feet. After a suitable interval of being pushed and shoved around I found myself, with my hands cuffed behind my back, standing in front of a man in civvies surrounded by soldiers. He was average height and middle-aged, but with an unmistakeable air of authority about him. He looked me condescendingly up and down, before enquiring with studied coolness: 'Who are you?'

I didn't know how on Earth to play this. Was this man for or against Khoury? A bad choice either way could clearly be extremely costly looking at the corpses around me. Along with Roffe, King and Barika were clearly dead. I thought I had caught a glimpse of Mr Labaky twitching as I was being shoved around, but corpses do that and it was hardly ideal circumstances for a Confirmation of Death. Khoury was being lifted unceremoniously off the operating table so there was no way I could form an opinion regarding his state of health. Not good if I had to make an off-the-cuff diagnosis. I tried to find some middle ground.

'My name is Anthony Stamford and I have been employed by Minister Khoury to perform a prostatectomy on him.'

The man smiled at me slyly.

'And why does our respected Minister of the Interior, Khoury, chose to employ a foreign surgeon to do the work of a capable Lebanese surgeon?'

This man was Western educated, possibly Oxford from the roundness of his vowels. He needed treating with caution.

'To be frank I don't know, but if I had to hazard a guess, I would suggest he did not want his political rivals to know he was ill.'

The man inclined his head in acknowledgement of my suggestion and then turned to gaze down at Khoury.

'Hmm, this is a most plausible explanation, but perhaps not as plausible as this man's contempt for the Lebanese people and all their achievements. This man is a wealthy Maronite who cares nothing for the ordinary people. No doubt you have been paid a great deal for your services. I have spent some time in your country and am well acquainted with the way men in your position exploit the sick through your private practices!'

His voice was rising and it was clearly not the time to enter into a debate about the UK health system, particularly one I had no chance of winning. This man clearly took a rather dim view of private practice.

'I believe I have been paid fairly for the work I have undertaken and, to the best of my knowledge, I have been paid out of Minister Khoury's pocket, not the public purse,' I countered. It was worth a try, but I didn't hold out much hope. By now he was glaring at me with a fury that made Roffe look downright matey.

'Then you are a fool! This man is a corrupt and self-seeking traitor and you are complicit in enabling him to continue his exploitation of the Lebanese people!'

Oh dear, I'd found myself one of the Hezbollah types I'd seen waving guns about on the News. He'd be waving his well-worn copy of The Koran in my face anytime now. I didn't stand a chance so, rather than provoke him further, or, worse still, encourage him to investigate the true nature of my financial dealings with Khoury, I clammed up. He walked slowly round me, looking me up and down. I studiously ignored him.

'What do you say to these charges?' he suddenly snapped.

I continued to look straight ahead in silence. He would find a way to twist anything I said against me so I wasn't going to give him any further satisfaction by appearing intimidated. He was only average height so this had the unfortunate effect of making him have to lean back to study my face. I say unfortunate because he suddenly chose to punch me hard in the solar plexus to correct this imbalance. As I doubled up, this triggered a further surge of indignation in the form of a flurry of punches to the head and face, one of which broke my nose with a crunch that sounded like a grenade going off in my head. I couldn't cover up with my hands cuffed behind me so I simply had to take it and spit out the blood that was running into my mouth.

He tired and backed off. I stayed doubled over in case it was just a breather. After several moments I glanced up, up but he stayed backed off. He was nursing his hand. With a bit of luck he'd broken his knuckle when he broke my nose. He snapped something unintelligible at the guards who grabbed me by my cuffs and yanked them up my back then marched me, with my nose almost touching the floor, out of the room and down the filthy corridor. Some way down they stopped, unlocked a door and shoved me through into a stinking, unlit room. As I stood trying to get my eyes accustomed to the darkness, I heard the door clang shut and lock behind me.

28

If the darkness was enveloping, it was nothing compared to the stench. It made it almost impossible to breathe as if my whole body was trying to reject the poisonous atmosphere. I began gagging in response. I held my breath but Mother Nature soon made me choose between suffocation and nausea so I adopted minimal, shallow breathing as a compromise. Gradually, my eyes too began to function as they identified a trickle of moonlight from a tiny, unglazed window high in the wall facing me and I began to adjust to that too.

There were other people in the room. I could just about make them out lying curled on the floor or sitting propped against the wall. I counted five in a room that measured no more ten foot square. That left a small patch in the far corner for me. With my hands still cuffed behind my back, I picked my way through the bodies, leant back on the wall and slid down into a squatting position. It took a moment for the revolting crunching sensation to register: I was crushing the cockroaches that lined the walls.

At floor level the stench was almost unbearable. I was unable to make out any form of latrine or even bucket and, from what I could see my cell-mates were in no fit state to use such facilities any way. The sand covered floor was apparently used for that.

In the feeble light it was impossible to discern much about my new companions. Only one appeared to be conscious and he just sat slumped against the wall, gibbering to himself and letting out occasional cries. The rest were either asleep or dead.

Given the assorted grunts, snores and moans, the latter did not, at least, apply to all of them.

There were manacles hanging from the wall beside me and, from the body positions of others, I suspected that that was the more usual form of restraint. I began to pray that come the morning someone would arrive to chain me up too: the cuffs behind my back were already agonising. They were no longer chaffing and I realised my wrists had swollen so much that they were now cutting in. The slightest movement set them on fire. The real pain however was in my shoulders, which felt like they had been dislocated as the guards used the cuffs to march me along. That was compounded by the constant waves of cramp that ran down my arms. I closed my eyes and thought fondly of HM Prison Standford Hill, Isle of Dogs.

*

I awoke to a crash as the cell door was thrown open. Yes, I had been asleep and yes, this really was not a terrible dream. I had slumped over onto my side and no longer had feeling of any sort in my arms and back. I lifted my head out of the stinking straw and peered up at the cause of the disturbance, gripped for an absurd moment by the thought that someone had come to tell me this was all a most dreadful mistake. I was greeted by a vision that dispelled that instantly.

The cell had gone from dark to dingy as the early morning light came seeping through the window. Still, it was sufficient to see the huge figure framed in the doorway. Those that remember the huge wrestler Big Daddy that my fellow students and I used to find so absurdly entertaining back in my student days will have some idea of this man's dimensions.

I recalled laughing along with my colleagues at the bald grappler's pantomime antics; I wasn't laughing now. This man peered around the cell at its prone inmates, and then bellowed something completely unintelligible. He appeared to be in a rage though no-one had said or done the least thing to upset him.

On closer, discreet inspection from my corner of the cell, the comparison with Big Daddy rapidly waned. True, both were bald giants, but, to the best of my recollection, Big Daddy was pallid, this man was swarthy, though it was hard to separate complexion from grime. More importantly, Dig Daddy's face was not covered by crazy, swirling tattoos and his eyes didn't burn with insanity.

He set about kicking his wards into consciousness as a skinny individual followed behind him slopping water over their faces from a metal bucket. They swallowed it greedily. Both wore grimy army fatigues. I braced myself for the army boots that were heading my way.

The kicks hurt, but they were fairly token by the time they reached me. I concentrated on swallowing the water which was clearly in short supply. The giant stopped after a few kicks, reached down with one huge hand and grabbed me by the front of my gown – yes I was still in my surgical gown! He lifted me effortlessly to my feet and held me upright as his companion produced a key and undid those dreadful cuffs. My arms flopped uselessly by my sides and, to my horror, I realised I was whimpering with gratitude and tears were running down my cheeks.

This seemed to amuse him enormously because he switched from Mr Angry to Mr Hilarity in an instant, bellowing with laughter as he pulled me up until our noses were nearly touching. Just as abruptly, his expression softened to something almost childlike. To my horror he stuck out the biggest tongue I have ever seen in a human mouth and very deliberately licked away my tears. Before I knew it his mouth was planted firmly on mine and it was quite obvious where that tongue was going next!

I can't say I actually recalled the title of that film, Midnight Express, but a memory of the scene where the young man bit his gaoler's tongue out flashed into my mind. Thanks to my profession I am far from squeamish, but that really did not appeal; for one thing that film was based on events that happened before anyone had heard of AIDS!

As a somewhat hopeless compromise I attempted a head butt. It was hopeless because he had me by the shirt front and, besides, my neck muscles, thanks to my recent cuffing, were barely able to support my head, let alone direct a forceful blow. Nevertheless, I managed something akin to an admonitory nod which tapped him on the nose. It didn't even produce a yelp, but it served to cool his ardour back down to ordinary rage. With a bestial snarl he lifted me clean off the floor and flung me back against the wall down which I slithered for the second time since my arrival. He clearly did not handle rejection well.

His colleague bent down and fitted the manacle round my neck. He threw some alternative clothing down beside me, and then hopped aside as his boss bent down and grabbed the chain. The man dragged me back up to nose to nose and snarled something which I instinctively knew translated as the Lebanese equivalent of: 'I haven't finished with you yet', and then he threw me back down on the floor again. As I watched the two of them exit the cell, the blood began to circulate back into my shoulders and arms and I began to scream.

*

Sometime later the skinny one returned on his own. My circulation had returned and I had donned the collarless shirt and beltless army shorts that clearly constituted standard prison issue. I recognised the psychology from Standford: no prisoner was to stand out from the crowd, particularly one that could be identified as a man of status, such as a doctor, by his clothing.

He was carrying a metal bucket and a stack of those dreadful white plastic beakers that drop down in coffee machines. When he reached me he handed me one and ladled some almost colourless, foul-smelling liquid into it which he clearly expected me to drink. Along with that came half a piece of rock-hard pitta bread. I stared at it for a moment, and then set aside my immediate revulsion. It presumably contained some degree of nutrition and God only knew when I might expect anything else. I lowered the collar of my shirt which I had been using to shield my nose and mouth from the ubiquitous flies and took a sip. It tasted every bit as disgusting as it smelt.

Breakfast over. I began a discrete survey of my fellow inmates. They all looked filthy and some were clearly carrying injuries though I had no way of telling if they were inflicted before or since arrival. The figure nearest the door lay absolutely motionless and had done so since first light. He or she seemed to attract an unusually large cloud of flies which would explain the growing stench of putrefaction that was threatening to overwhelm the pervasive smell of excrement. Given the heat there was no way of guessing a time of death but it had to be at least the day before.

I peeped more closely at my living cell mates. It was hard to tell given our shapeless uniforms, but the one opposite me and to my left appeared to be female. He or she was sitting elbows on knees and head in hands so the only clue was the long, tangled but luxuriant hair and the shapely, feminine arms and hands. Did this suggest that our accommodation was only temporary, or did my captors simply have no regard for even the most basic human dignities such as privacy between the sexes? On the evidence of what I had seen so far, I had a horrible suspicion that it was the latter.

Now I was becoming accustomed to the squalor of my surroundings I began to think about alternative accommodation. It was safe to assume that my fellow captors had already thought along similar lines with no success, so forming an escape committee and tunnelling out could be put right to the bottom of my list of options: the door looked fit for purpose, the window was too small to squeeze a dwarf through and the breeze block walls were clearly impervious to finger nails. It seemed my only really viable means of escape was to talk my way out. For that I needed to know who my captors really were.

I turned my attention to the man on my left: the window wall was on my right, so my options were restricted. I knew instinctively that raised voices would bring the guards and he was the only person in whispering range. I rolled over to within a foot of his back and whispered quietly, partly not to attract the attention of any guards outside, and partly not to scare him.

'Excuse me old chap, sorry to trouble you...' I paused for a response but none came. I reached out and tapped him on the shoulder. 'Excuse me, are you awake?' There was a long pause in which it even occurred to me that he might be dead; then he muttered a barely audible reply.

'Leave me.'

It wasn't encouraging, but at least it was a reply and, under the circumstances, I had no choice but to persist.

'Look, I'm sorry to trouble you, but there are a couple of things you might be able to help me with...' That didn't produce so much as a twitch of recognition; I needed a new approach. Perhaps a white lie would help.

'Listen carefully. I have a squadron of armed soldiers out there waiting for my signal from that window to tell them that it is the right moment to launch an attack on this place and free us. I will protect anyone who helps me make that signal.'

That worked! The man rolled over to face me his eyes wide. I put a finger quickly to my lips expecting an excited outburst, but his expression was intelligent and enquiring. I relaxed, then realised he would expect a cover story to support this claim. I decided to stick as approximately close to the truth as possible.

'Okay, listen, I am an English doctor, a surgeon, and I was sent here by my government and the Lebanese Government to carry out an operation on one of their Ministers. It appears he is a traitor working on behalf of the Syrian dictatorship. The plan was that I was to signal from a window on this side of the building when he was unconscious and a troop of soldiers would be sent in to arrest him whilst his security team was leaderless. That was meant to take place at noon today. In the meantime this place was attacked last night. I don't even know if the people outside know it has changed hands, it could have happened before they arrived, so I need to know who these new people are and what they're up to.'

The man looked surprised at my ignorance.

'These men are Lebanese fighters of the Hezbollah party. They are returning from my country where they have been working as mercenaries for the Syrian Government. Now they will surely kill me.'

'But aren't these people followers of Al Qaeda?'

'Maybe, but they are followers of money first. It is madness.'

'And who are you?'

'My name is Say'eed Homsi. I am engineer from Damascus. I bring my family here to escape the war, but Lebanese soldiers take them away at the border and bring me here. They beat me and say I am spy of Syria, but I tell them no I am just engineer. I just wish to save my family.'

'But the Lebanese soldiers who brought you here are not the same as the Lebanese Hezbollah soldiers who are in charge now?'

'This is so. Hezbollah soldiers have killed soldiers who first beat me; now they will surely kill me.'

'But why do two groups of Lebanese soldiers wish to kill each other and why do both groups want to kill you?'

The man mustered a prone shrug of despair.

'Lebanese politics is very complicated and no one likes refugees.' I nodded my dim understanding. Jesus, I'd grown up with the IRA and the cock-eyed politics of Northern Ireland constantly in the news, but that was kiddies' stuff compared to this!

At least I now had a rough idea who my current captors were. Apparently I was now in the hands of a fanatical, Lebanese, Shi'ite militia belonging to Hezbollah. From what I'd seen on the News over the last few years, my heart wasn't filled with optimism. As I sat pondering what else I could usefully ask him, a key grated in the cell door and it flew open. The skinny thug entered with two guards and marched over to my new companion. One guard produced a key and undid Say'eed's neck collar whilst Skinny kicked him in the ribs a couple of times. Apparently, despite our efforts at discretion, our discussion had been observed. Say'eed moaned pitifully as they dragged him unceremoniously out of the cell.

*

There was no way off keeping track of time, but it was probably a couple of hours later when the skinny one and the guards returned. Say'eed was naked and unconscious. They didn't even bother to manacle his neck. They just threw him down beside me and left. He landed face down and lay still.

I was sure I was being watched. What did my captors expect me to do? If I tried to help him, would I be similarly punished? Were they waiting for me to prove my claim to being a doctor by treating him? God alone knew, but I couldn't just sit there and do nothing. I edged up beside him and inspected his injuries more closely.

He had been beaten with appalling brutality. His back and buttocks were covered with wide wheals and gashes several of which were still bleeding. I donned a figurative surgeon's cap and studied his back with medical dispassion. At a guess, the wounds had been inflicted by a wide belt with a heavy buckle. The skin had even been punctured by the prong in several places. I took his wrist and felt for a pulse. It was weak and irregular. I noted the fresh sores on his wrists where he had presumably fought against some form of restraint as they beat him.

I continued my examination down his back until, as I reached his buttocks, I froze. All pretence at medical dispassion evaporated in horror. He had been beaten there as on his back, but the fluid there was not, as I had assumed, comprised solely of blood. Some of it was pink where it had mixed with blood, but some of it was white and viscous. For a moment I tried to convince myself that his torturers had spat on him, but I knew that was wishful thinking. I knew seminal fluid when I saw it. Say'eed had been raped.

I pulled away and sat back against the wall, my mind whirling. The first and most obvious conclusion was that there was nothing I could really do to help him: I had no water to bathe his wounds and nothing to dress them with. I toyed with the possibility of tearing a strip off my shirt and using spit instead of water, but I knew the action was futile and I found myself gripped by a strange paralysis. The full implications of this appalling brutality were beginning to hit home. Whoever had done this was well aware that I would be unable to treat it, so he wasn't asking me to prove my medical credentials. That left only one conclusion. This was a demonstration of what he had lined up for me.

I had no doubt as to the identity of the 'he' in question, that huge tongue and those mad eyes swam constantly into my mind, making my paralysis absolute. I sat cringing with dread. What on Earth had persuaded me to attempt that head butt? But then it was an instinctive, spur-of-the-moment reaction and there was no way I could have imagined its possible consequences.

And what was the final outcome of these consequences? These people were trained, experienced killers with clearly no bounds to their cruelty and depravity. They had no doubt grown up with war and all its savage diversions. They would know above all else that, in war, the wise man never leaves anyone to bear witness against him later, that is the blood-pact of comradeship. The giant and his comrades would have their way with me, and then they would torch the place, leaving it with me and my fellow prisoners inside.

I racked my brains for a solution. What could I say or do to persuade that man that I didn't deserve to be raped and murdered? Every time I asked the question those mad eyes raged at me, or mocked me, and the hopelessness of my situation smothered me. Terrible as it was I would have given anything to retreat into the terrifying bewilderment of my former breakdown, but that simply wouldn't come. I sat in the filth and squalor of that stinking cell, dimly wondering what on Earth I had ever done to bring me to such a sordid, wretched end, and waited for Fate to take its course.

*

The cell door opened with another crash; there had been several throughout the day as Skinny and the guards turned up to take other prisoners away. Unlike Say'eed, none of them had been returned which rather confirmed my belief that he had been used to torment me. This time the guards headed for me, ignoring Say'eed who had died a couple of hours before. It was now dark outside the cell window.

They unshackled my neck and dragged me to my feet, then shoved me out of the cell with a few encouraging kicks and punches. I would like to say I was beyond caring, but that wouldn't begin to describe my condition. I was simply too gripped with terror to resist. My heart was pumping so hard I could barely breathe and my legs were cold where the urine ran down them. It was simply uncontrollable.

I hobbled and cringed my way down the corridor, continually kicked, prodded and punched by the guards until Skinny called a halt outside another, nondescript door. The guards stationed themselves outside as Skinny stepped forward, grasped the handle, and threw it open with a dramatic flourish. I kept my eyes glued to the floor, unable to look at what lay ahead, as Skinny grabbed my shirt and yanked me through into the room. I paused, summoning every last ounce of will-power, and then raised my eyes to face the fate that awaited me. Sitting on a hard-backed chair next to the civilian who had arrested me, looking calm and phlegmatic as always, was Detective Sergeant Newcombe.

29

I stared at him stupidly, too dazed and surprised to take this in, unsure even whether to believe my eyes. Was this some absurd hallucination born out of fear and despair? I had lost my grip on reality before and knew the terrible tricks the mind could play when caught in extremis. On the other hand I couldn't imagine what would possess me to conjure up Detective Sergeant Newcombe as an alternative to the terrifying maniac I was expecting. Besides, if I was that lost to reality, how come I was speculating about whether or not I was hallucinating in the first place? Before I sank hopelessly into further existential conundrums, the object of my astonishment spoke up.

'Well, well, Mr Stamford, sir, it would appear we have been in the wars. I had hoped to say it was nice to see you again after all this time, but I didn't expect to find you in such a sorry condition.'

This was Detective Sergeant Newcombe alright. I'd recognise those lugubrious, mock-sympathetic tones anywhere. I straightened my shoulders as best I could and looked him in the eye.

'What d'you want?' I croaked.

He studied me in that irritatingly measured way of his, then spoke in his usual infuriatingly pedantic fashion.

'Well that very much depends on whether your disappearance from our shores signified a need for some private time in which to consider the very generous proposition I took the trouble to put to you at our last meeting, or whether it signified an unwillingness to involve yourself in helping your government with a project of considerable national, not to say international, importance. If it was the former then I want to discuss the renewal of our budding working relationship; if it was the latter, then I want to arrest you for the premeditated murder of Mr Hamish Carmichael and your wife Elizabeth.'

I groped for a reply.

'But I didn't do it. He died in a car crash on the A3. It was an accident. It was nothing to do with me. I was in prison at the time...'

Newcombe cut across me with, for him, considerable impatience.

'Really Dr Stamford, we've already been over this and prison is not an alibi.'

Despite my shattered condition I fought on.

'Yes, but you admitted yourself you need further proof and, besides, this is Lebanon, not London, to the best of my knowledge. A country that falls outside your jurisdiction.'

Newcombe inclined his head in acknowledgement of my point before continuing in his tediously pedantic manner.

'If you recall, sir, you asked me what I 'wanted', not what I 'intended'. The two things are not necessarily one and the same, though I would explain that the people I currently represent have the wherewithal to ensure that any evidence brought against you regarding that car crash would more than satisfy a British jury.'

Subtle distinctions between 'wanted' and 'intended' were as clear as mud to my battered psyche, but I fought on in the desperate certainty that this was not going to lead to somewhere

I wanted to go.

'And just how do you propose to get me back in front of this British jury?'

That would be simple enough to arrange bearing in mind that I have already reached an accommodation with our host here,' he nodded at my captor, 'regarding your removal, regardless of whether it concerns your extradition or your recruitment.'

'My recruitment?'

'Indeed, sir, the recruitment we discussed back in London, but that is not a subject it would be discreet to discuss under these particular circumstances, so I suggest it might be an appropriate moment to adjourn to your private residence across the way from here.'

'You mean we are free to just walk out of here?' I nodded rather unsubtly at the Hezbollah commissar, or whatever he was.

Newcombe greeted this with his usual smug self-assurance.

'Indeed, sir, I have come to an appropriate understanding with Mr Mansour here and we are free to go.'

'I thought he was a fanatical, anti-Western Moslem zealot...'

Newcombe frowned with some impatience.

'That he may be, sir, but he is also an Arab so he understands money. Perhaps we had best be going before he reconsiders.'

*

The caravan was much as it had been twenty-four hours previously, which only served to heighten the unreality of my situation. In a fifty yard walk I had gone from the very depths of degradation, dread and despair into the cosy home I had shared so comfortably with Laila over the last few weeks, or however long it had been. I wondered where she was now, but it was too awful to contemplate and I turned my thoughts to my own more pressing situation.

The walk from the Lubyanka to the Nissen also served to heighten my awareness of the physical damage I had endured in such a short time. I hurt in every part of my body from repeated kicking and punching. I was parched with thirst and sick with hunger and yet I felt sure I was running a fever. My soiled clothes were chaffing everywhere. Newcombe had to assist me over the step into the Nissen.

'Right sir, perhaps you would care to sit yourself down at the table whilst I make us both a nice cup of tea and we discuss your recruitment?' Newcombe nodded at the small dining table in the room that constituted the hut's kitchen cum dining cum lounge area.

'You can make us both a nice cup of tea if you want, but I'm not doing anything until I've cleaned myself up and dressed my wounds,' I croaked.

Newcombe turned to face me with the air of a man anticipating a confrontation.

'I'm afraid that won't be possible for the moment, sir. You see you are now my prisoner and, until I am satisfied that you have agreed to fully participate in the mission for which I have been sent here to recruit you, I am to not let you out of my sight.'

'If I'm your prisoner, where's your warrant?'

Newcombe reached into the inside pocket of his jacket and produced a piece of paper.

'It's right here as a matter of fact sir. I assure you it is all completely above board, but you're welcome to read it if you wish. I will also read you your rights if you wish, but I believe you've heard them before and it seems a bit of a waste of breath with no witnesses in the immediate vicinity.'

I waved the paper away. I was too weak to take in the written word.

'You can do what you like but I'm not discussing anything in this state. As I said earlier, we're outside your jurisdiction: that warrant counts for nothing.'

'It is true that we are outside my jurisdiction right now sir, but I have transport facilities and operatives on hand waiting to return you immediately to the UK to face the murder charges that await you there. You do not appear to have the men and resources you would need to prevent them doing so. Of course, if you prefer, they can escort you on your way to undertake the mission for which I have been sent here to recruit you instead.' He pulled out a phone. 'I can summon assistance right now if you choose to obstruct me.'

'But that's kidnapping!'

Newcombe shrugged solemnly.

'You may choose to call it that sir, but I prefer to use the term 'extraordinary rendition' as favoured by our American cousins.' He accompanied this with a self-satisfied smirk.

I mustered all my remaining reserves to wipe it off his face.

'In that case you had better get on with it. You can find someone else to carry out your damn mission and, while you're at it, you can explain to whoever you work for that they will have to stand the cost of fighting the best lawyers I can afford because you lacked the common decency to allow me a shit and a shave and something to eat!'

Newcombe stood gaping at this unexpected display of hidden reserves so, taxing or not, I drew on them further.

'Come on, make your mind up man! There's some pitta bread and honey in the cupboard which should help to pick me up. You can make that and put the kettle on whilst I get cleaned up, or there's no deal. Here, pass me that Paracetamol on the window-sill!'

I could see him wrestling with the alternatives I had put before him. Was I bluffing? Would I really risk returning to Britain to stand trial for the sake of a shower? On the other hand what harm could a little physical comfort do if he needed me to agree to carry out this mysterious mission? I suddenly realised I needed to know how far we could push each other. How much he needed me, not just how much I needed him. I was using the same psychology I had used on Roffe: the exploitation of a mind used to accepting and obeying orders, but Newcombe was from a less authoritarian background and no doubt somewhat more intelligent than Roffe. He still stood there weighing up the pros and cons of the alternatives I had given him, so I turned the screw again. I turned my back on him and limped, Quasimodo-like, through the door leading to the bedroom and adjoining bathroom. Newcombe paused a moment longer. What could he do: put me in an arm-lock, hit me with his warrant? He made his mind up.

'Alright, you've got five minutes and that's it,' he growled ungraciously. He turned and set about making tea and pitta with honey.

*

I sat back and held up a hand while I checked I was hearing correctly.

'Okay, wait a minute! Just let me see if I've got this right. You want me to go call Peter Chisholm and tell him that Minister Khoury is now dead and his killer, this Mansour character, wants to buy a nuclear weapon from him: are you fucking mad?'

Newcombe heaved a sigh of exasperation.

'No that's not what I have in mind. If you would just let me explain, sir...'

'I think you've explained quite enough thank you. You must be round the ruddy twist! I'm sorry but I don't do business with lunatics...'

'In that case, sir, I am arresting you for the premeditated murder of Mr Hamish Ross Carmichael on the night of...'

'Wait, wait!' I held the other hand up, to placate him. 'Let's not be hasty now. Peter isn't an arms dealer. This is ridiculous, we're setting up a medical supplies company together.'

'I see, and that's what you really believe is it, sir?'

'It most certainly is. Thanks to Peter I have successfully established that refugee clinic outside and a state-of-the-art hospital is coming on-line any day now, out in the desert, to handle more long term trauma cases.'

Newcombe gazed at me almost pityingly for a moment then heaved a patient sigh.

'Far be it for me to suggest that you have been a little naive in your dealings with Mr Chisholm, sir, but I'm afraid to have to tell you that his business activities are not entirely as he has led you to believe. In fact, I would go so far to say that he, in cahoots with his long-term partner in crime, Mr Daniel Swift, aka "Danny Boy", has taken you for a proper patsy.'

'What are you talking about?'

'Well, sir, let's just say an agent of the organisation to whom I am currently sequestered recently gained covert access to the warehouse in Beirut docks which I believe a company belonging to you and Mr Chisholm is currently operating from. Upon inspection of certain packing cases it was discovered that they contained goods more suited to the inflicting of, rather than the healing of, physical injuries, to whit a selection of mortar shells and other such military materiel. You may, or may not know, sir, that when you met Mr Chisholm in prison he was doing time for money laundering in regard to an armaments shipment transaction. Unfortunately Mr Chisholm is a wily customer and, at that time, we had only been able to prove a relatively minor tax allegation against him. Given the extent of his arms dealing we want him out of circulation on a much more permanent basis. You could be the lynch-pin in all of this.'

I wasn't willing to admit it, but I couldn't help hearing something encouraging in this. Still, I wasn't going to switch allegiances without some proper convincing.

'Yes, well actually Peter was quite open about his brush with the Law. I had the strong impression that your colleagues had been quite liberal with the truth in order to make their allegations stick and, furthermore, Peter assured me that the whole experience had been so traumatic that he would never risk being put in such a situation again.'

Newcombe raised his eyebrows in an expression of mock-surprise.

'Did he really, sir? Well I'm afraid you'll find that is an assurance the criminal is usually all too quick to offer anyone who will listen...'

'Yes, but it wasn't Peter who came looking for me to set up the Clinic. I tracked him down to Zurich and approached him for help with the Clinic. He had no way of knowing I'd come looking...'

'No, but if I recall from our surveillance, he gave you a card in case you decided to.'

'Well, he left me an address in case I had the chance to look him up when I came out. We were pretty good friends by the time he was released...'

'Precisely, that is exactly how people like him work I'm afraid, sir. It's like casting out fishing lines to them; sometimes they get a bite, sometimes nothing. He would have listened to your story and heard the tale of a man who had fallen from a position of status and power, a man who, it might even be fair to assume, felt a little aggrieved at the establishment, a man, perhaps, with a bit of a chip on his shoulder...'

'Alright, alright, I get the picture!'

'And he would have simply returned to his daily business, brokering dirty deals, and waited to see if you walked through his door one day.'

'Very well, and what about those plush offices and the buying and business team I saw. That wasn't set up for my benefit.'

'Certainly not, sir, Mr Chisholm is a man of style. He is not an out-and-out villain like Ronnie Biggs, he is a big-time deal maker, an entrepreneur. It's just he doesn't care which side of the Law a deal happens to fall on. He is solely motivated by money which unfortunately means he is drawn to the very high risk end of the market. That slick-looking team, or perhaps I should say gang, you saw working in his office in Zurich were trading commodities alright, it's just that at least fifty per cent of those commodities were stolen. In the week following your meeting, lorries carrying medical products started getting hijacked left, right and centre throughout Europe. Seems a bit of a coincidence don't you think, sir?'

'And that's probably exactly what it was. I don't suppose you've read Merton on 'self-fulfilling prophecy', have you? You should give it a go instead of trying to make evidence out of coincidence; besides, just suppose he helped himself to some gear that wasn't quite on the up-and-up, that's hardly trading in chemical weapons, is it? You people never give a man a chance. Have you any idea how difficult it is to get back on your feet after a spell in clink, especially with people like you on your shirt-tails trying to drag you back all the time?'

'Well sir, as it happens, I've never been in prison, at least not in the sense to which you are alluding, so I can only imagine. I've seen Merton on the telly, but I can't say I've read anything by him, so you've lost me there. What I can say is that we have reason to believe that your business partner Peter Chisholm saw an opportunity to use you as a front through which to open up links with a militarised faction within the Lebanese Government. A right-wing Christian militia represented at the political level by Minister Khoury.'

'We don't know if he was already aware of Khoury's organisation when you approached him, but it seems quite likely. Arms dealers like him are constantly sniffing around for deals and they are drawn to military hotspots like moths to a candle. Even if he wasn't, the moment you mentioned that you had contact with someone from the Lebanese Ministry for the Interior he would have been sitting up. It's a potentially lucrative powder keg he can't manage personally thanks to some villainy he perpetrated back in their terrible Civil War. But that wouldn't deter him. It was simple enough to establish if the Minister was interested in buying more than medical supplies through his chum Swift, particularly since you seemed to prefer spending your time tending to the wounded in your clinic out here in the back of beyond. Not surprisingly Minister Khoury, who is a sworn enemy of the Assad regime, jumped at the chance to buy weapons from him for his military people.'

Newcombe sat back having apparently delivered this entire summary in one breath. I hated to admit it, but, seen from his point of view, it was perfectly plausible that Peter had used me to get to Khoury and even, in doing so, 'taken me for a bit of a patsy', but then Newcombe would want me to think that if he was trying to turn me against my business partner. Frankly, I didn't know who the hell to trust anymore. In desperation, I returned to the absurd suggestion that had triggered my initial outburst.

'Okay, so let's suppose just for a moment that I accept that Peter has been supplying Khoury with arms as well as medical supplies behind my back. How the hell do you get from there to the idea that this character Mansour might want to buy a nuclear bomb and that Peter would have the wherewithal or inclination to supply him with one even if he did?'

To my disappointment, Newcombe looked distinctly unfazed by this challenging riposte. He paused to pick his words carefully before replying.

'I think sir, a little misunderstanding may have arisen here in regards to what you take me to mean by a nuclear weapon. I imagine, and correct me if I am wrong, that you take me to be referring to a missile of some sort. Perhaps the sort of thing you see on news reels of the old Soviet military parades. If that is the case, then I must apologise for conveying a rather misleading impression...'

'Yes, well there's no need. I read the papers and I am well aware that these things come in all shapes and sizes. I've heard of 'dirty bombs' and the like. I'm not entirely naive...'

Newcombe raised his eyebrows as if not entirely convinced on this last point, but contented himself with continuing: 'In that case, sir, you will appreciate that, in the modern, multi-facetted politico-military scenario a small nuclear device can make a sudden and very persuasive tool with which to hold a Government to ransom, allowing a small organisation to punch way above its weight...'

'Yes I see that, but what would Mansour do with such a device and how would Peter get his hands on such a thing?'

'In answer to your first question, that is anyone's guess. He could decide to use it as a weapon in the current, ongoing conflict or he could hand it over to Hezbullah for use in their wider terrorist activities. Given the international forces surrounding Syria, it is highly unlikely that he would get very far in any attempt to deploy such a weapon personally, but heaven know what damage his paymasters could do with such an item. More importantly, the powers that be want to strangle the supply at birth before fanatics like him can even contemplate such actions. That means putting an end to your chum Chisholm's activities.'

I opened my mouth to object to this sudden assumption of Peter's guilt, but he held up his hand.

'In answer to your second question, there have been nuclear weapons in circulation on the black markets ever since the downfall of the old Soviet Union. They're just sitting in mothballs waiting for the right buyer to come along. On recent evidence we have reason to believe that Chisholm has purchased ex-soviet materiel intended for gangsters in Somalia via a middle-man in Chechnya; a man called Dudayev operating out of Grozny to be specific. We know where he is getting the stuff, but we cannot crack his methods of distribution from there. Mr Chisholm knows precisely who to talk to alright.'

Dudayev? Grozny? Either Newcombe was a consummate liar, or this was all too specific to argue with. I changed tack again in desperation.

'But why do you think, assuming I believe a word of this, that I am the right person to attempt to broker such a deal?'

'Because Chisholm trusts you, even if he thinks you are a bit on the gullible side. In fact, he trusts you because he thinks you are a bit on the gullible side, sir. He thinks he's got you wrapped around his little finger. All you've got to do is convince him that everything was going ahead as planned for the operation until Roffe turned up and announced a change of venue, to wit that place outside. The operation was about to go ahead when Mansour turned up and staged his coup.'

'But why would Mansour use me? I'm a surgeon for God's sake! I didn't even know about these weapons.'

'Tell him Mansour set about interrogating Khoury regarding military supplies and, when he really got the thumbscrews out, in desperation Khoury told him about Chisholm and your connection with him. Then they killed him and told you to act as go between on pain of death. Tell him that Mansour wants to do some serious business. Say your next on the torture list if he doesn't agree to a meeting. Lay it on thick. Tell him Mansour insists on you as the go-between.'

'And what if he doesn't believe me?'

'Well, we'll be right behind you, of course, in case things don't work out...'

''Right behind me', eh? Well, from what you have told me so far, 'Right behind me' doesn't sound close enough. If Chisholm smells a rat, I can't see him hanging around for a friendly chat about why I've decided to stab him in the back.'

I saw a flicker of frustration cross Newcombe's face before he adopted his most persuasive tone.

'Look, sir, I'm not asking you to stab Mr Chisholm in the back. I'm just asking you to help us bring him to justice. If he agrees to supply Mansour with weapons, surely that will be enough to convince you that he is a truly dangerous, amoral man who needs to be stopped before he helps throw the Middle East into conflict on a catastrophic scale. All you have to tell him is that Mansour is in the market for a tactical nuclear weapon and wants you as the middle-man. Say he barely speaks English and won't leave Lebanon for fear of arrest. Chisholm will know the sort of thing he's after. If we're right and he buys the idea, you'll have helped capture a major international criminal. All you have to tell him that is that Mansour will take delivery of it using a fishing vessel. You can tell him you will send him the time, date and co-ordinates on that smart phone of yours. Once you've done that you're free to go.'

'And what if he doesn't buy the idea? What if you're wrong and he cannot supply this kind of thing, or smells a rat, or gets cold feet?'

'Then you're free to go anyway sir, but we're not wrong. He can supply this kind of thing alright. He'll move heaven and earth for this deal given the amount of cash it will involve. It's that very money which will also prevent him smelling a rat or getting cold feet. It's surprising just how blind people become in my experience, sir, when the old pound signs start obscuring their vision. Besides, if he doesn't buy the idea for some unforeseeable reason, you'll be in civilised Zurich and one-to-one violence is not his style. He'll simply show you the door, we'll have to think of another way to nail the bastard.'

I sat back and regarded him surprisingly steadily given my depleted physical condition. I let the silence hang and until it became slightly oppressive. This was my chance to cut a deal, probably the only one I'd get. Finally, I spoke.

'I have never heard such a load of utter cobblers in all my life,' I began as calmly as I could muster. 'Do you seriously expect me to believe that I am going to be able to stroll into the offices of a man you claim to be an international arms dealer, order a nuclear bomb on behalf of a terrorist and then walk away as if nothing has happened. If he's the villain you claim he is and he agrees to this, I'm going to know too much. Even if he doesn't bite, the very fact that I approach him with this proposal will prove that I know too much. He's hardly going to let me walk away with that kind of hold over him. My life won't be worth a fig. I'd be better off back in Standford!' My voice had risen somewhat.

'Yes sir, well I grant there is some risk involved...'

'Risk! We're not talking 'risk' here, Newcombe, we're talking immediate, physical danger. You're asking me to undertake a potentially fatal mission on the understanding that you will be 'right behind me' if I run into difficulties. Assuming I escape Zurich unharmed and you get your man, what's going to happen when he gets out of prison and comes looking for me then, eh? Answer me that!'

Newcombe was looking flustered for the first time since I'd met him. He paused as if wrestling with a difficult decision and then made his mind up.

'He won't be coming out of prison, sir,' he replied grimly.

'I beg your pardon. What do you mean?'

'He's given us the slip once too often and been responsible for the deaths of too many innocent people. If he is apprehended at sea in possession of a nuclear device it has already been agreed by the powers that be that it will be viewed as an act of war. The apprehending officers will therefore be sanctioned to use all appropriate force.'

'Speak English man! What is 'all appropriate force'? Are you telling me you are going to kill him?'

Newcombe nodded, but didn't speak.

'Well are you?'

He paused visibly struggling for a politician's evasion, but couldn't find the words.

'I believe you could put it something like that sir,' he answered lamely.

30

I stood alone amongst the olive trees in the empty gardens of the Villa remembering the vitality and excitement of the party we had once thrown to seal the deal with Khoury. The place was deserted now, just Newcombe nosing around inside in the way that coppers assume they have the automatic right to do. We had barely spoken since I had forced his intentions regarding Peter out of him. He had just insisted on having the last word by reminding me of the alternative, mandatory life imprisonment for murder if I let him down, no matter how tough things got. We had agreed that I needed to collect some personal effects and some smart clothes for my trip to Zurich from the Villa.

I looked again at my tranquil surroundings. The first glimmerings of a Middle-Eastern dawn were just warming the horizon much as they must have done two thousand years or so earlier when Christ stood alone in Gesthemane. He must have found himself in a very similar situation, surrounded by traitors and enemies, wrestling with the option to exercise divine power and take the easy way out, or face the agonising, mortal fate that awaited him. Should I too take the easy option and betray the man I called a friend, or should I face arrest and trial for a crime I still wasn't certain I had even committed? It was with some effort that I reminded myself that I was a rational man of science not a gullible subscriber to superstitious folk tales about a Palestinian rabble-rouser. Besides a nagging little voice at the back of my mind was reminding me that the betrayer of friends in the story was Judas.

At that moment Newcombe's voice startled me.

'Can I take it that we are ready to press on with this phone call sir?' He had emerged from the shadows.

'Oh, yes, right.' I pulled myself together and turned to face him. He pulled out a phone and handed it to me in the dim light.

'I think you've had enough time to rehearse what you need to say sir.'

'Indeed, you've been most generous,' I replied with an irony heavy enough to crush most men like a bug.

'Kind of you to say so sir,' he acknowledged blandly, thrusting the damn thing into my hand. I took it and dialled the number, surprised to note that my hands were shaking so much. It rang three times then an answer-phone cut in.

'Shit, wrong number, damn it!'

'Take your time sir, remember it's important you sound like your having a rough time of it.'

I knew that. I didn't need this bloody idiot to remind me! I took a deep breath and tried again. This time the phone rang twice and then Chisholm answered.

'Tony, hello, how come you're not calling on your usual phone?'

'I'm afraid it got lost.'

'Really? Careless of you losing an expensive bit of kit like that...'

Was he ribbing me? Did he sound suspicious? It was impossible to say.

'Yes, well, things have been a bit chaotic here over the last few days and I need to meet up for a chat. How are you fixed?'

'I take it it's not the sort of chat we can hold on this line?'

'No, not really. It's the sort of thing that would go down better over a beer in the Glockenhof's garden.'

'Sounds promising?'

'Sure. Listen, do you want to pick me up from that bar where we met originally?' I injected as much urgency as possible into this last suggestion.

'When?'

'Shall we say later on this afternoon?'

'This afternoon, that's pulling out the stops a bit isn't it?'

'Can't be helped, my new boss has leased a private plane for me.'

'New boss, eh? What happened to the Minister?'

'He didn't pull through, the cancer was too advanced. Look, I'll fill you in when I get there. Get your man to keep an eye out for me at the airport and then pick me up as before, okay?'

'Yes, sure, that should be no problem, see you then...'

'See you then.' I cut the call and hung up. I went to pass Newcombe back his phone, and then paused. 'I suppose I had better hang on to this now he thinks it's mine. I don't suppose it contains any hidden alarms or microphones does it?'

Newcombe regarded me darkly despite the brightening dawn.

'No sir, we have to assume he will treat you with the utmost suspicion and your person and personal effects will be subject to the most detailed examination. It wouldn't do to be caught carrying any tell-tales would it now?'

'No, certainly not, but then how will you know if he doesn't buy my story?'

'Don't worry, sir, I'll have a team of guardian angels right behind you all the way.'

*

'Herr Stamford?

I lowered the glass of beer I was sipping from outside the Bar Nocciolina. It was very chilly and I was rather underdressed for al fresco drinking in the Zurich New Year, but needs must. I noticed there was no sign of Chisholm at this rendezvous, just the burly individual who was opening the back door of a black Mercedes taxi for me.

'Herr Stamford, bitte!' he added insistently, shivering at the cold despite his body fat. He knew my name so he was obviously from Chisholm, but he was a lot less prepossessing than the staff I'd seen in the offices during my previous trip. Still, Newcombe had warned me to expect to be treated as highly suspect given the story I had to sell. Glad at least to get out of the cold, I deposited my glass on the table and accepted his invitation.

He drove quickly, zigzagging through back streets. Without even a sun in the overcast sky to give me a clue I hadn't got the faintest idea in which direction we were heading. I couldn't tell if this was meant to confuse me or shake off pursuers, but, if it achieved one thing, it succeeded in making me feel hopelessly alone. As far as I could see, Newcombe and his guardian angels were still sitting on the clouds I had just flown through.

We pulled up outside some rather run-down looking

apartments: the sort you don't see in the tourist brochures. My guest status had clearly taken a significant slide. My chauffeur opened my door with another bitte which seemed to be the extent of his conversation. He nodded me to a ground-floor door in the building which opened as I approached. He gestured me through with the air of a man who would just as happily shove me through if the need arose.

Inside, I was greeted by two more nondescript individuals: one wore jeans and one of those thick, woollen jumpers favoured by the alpine fraternity, the other wore jeans and a red and white, leather biker's jacket. On closer inspection, they were well-built and clearly fit, possibly ex-soldiers, the sort you wouldn't laugh at when they turned out in their Swiss Guard uniforms. I suspected that, when it came to inflicting pain, they were probably as well versed in human anatomy as I was.

I sensed more than saw that my surroundings were pretty run down and seedy: I couldn't take my eyes off my hosts who were inspecting me with cool indifference. I tried to reassure myself that they had no reason to cut up rough, particularly in a building where other tenants would hear the noise. But then how did I know that there were other tenants and, besides, it wouldn't be hard to silence me if that was their only concern. That cold feeling of utter loneliness got significantly worse.

The man in the leather jacket finally completed the tour of inspection he had taken around me and now he spoke:

'Strip, bitte!'

I had half been expecting this, but it still came as a shock. Shock or not, I decided it was best not to hang around for someone to help me. I took off my jacket and dropped it to the floor then began unbuttoning my shirt. As I removed each garment the man in the jumper collected it and methodically examined it, then he produced a small metal box about the size of a cigarette case. He pulled out an aerial and fiddled with some controls then passed it over each piece of clothing. Newcombe had been right to advise against being wired for sound.

Finally, I stood shivering with the cold in nothing but my underpants. I hesitated, but the man in the leather jacket simply nodded curtly for me to continue. I tried to convince myself that it was no different to stripping off for a shower after a game of rugger, but my situation told me otherwise, particularly when he reached into his pocket and produced a latex glove. There was no mistaking the gesture to bend over.

*

I sat in the back room where they had put me wrapped in nothing but a dirty, threadbare blanket. It was bloody freezing and I felt soiled if not actually raped. I kept telling myself that it was just part of a process designed to let me know who was boss. If Chisholm and his cronies were the sort of people Newcombe reckoned they were, they were going to want to be certain I was on the level and they weren't going to be fussy about the methods they used to find out.

As I sat trying to justify my immediate circumstances, another more insistent voice kept demanding to know what the hell I was doing there in the first place...I was a highly respected London surgeon for God's sake! How on Earth had I got myself involved in such a predicament?

The 'highly respected London surgeon' bit helped to rally me somewhat and I further reminded myself that, bizarre as my current circumstances were, it was all being undertaken on behalf of Queen and Country. Quite specifically on behalf of my earning the right to return to Queen and Country with the slate wiped clean and all possible charges of murder dropped. It may not seem a lot given the risks I was taking, but over the last few days I had come to realise that there was nothing I craved more in the world. Not only was I heartily sick of working in hot, insanitary conditions under constant threat of being overrun by lunatic militias, I was equally sick of the paranoia-inducing stress of scheming with Chisholm, lying to Brandon King and my staff at the Clinic, and fending off the likes of Khoury and Roffe.

My return to London was the final deal I had agreed with Newcombe before we left the Nissen for Beirut: a total amnesty in return for nailing Chisholm. No further allegations of murder and no criminal record, not even regarding my conviction for fraud and my stay in Standford prison. If asked by a prospective employer about the headlines at the time and my absence from hospital work up until now, I was simply to say that I had been engaged in secret medical research work for the Government. I was to give a telephone number where this would be confirmed to a legitimate enquirer.

When I pointed out that that would hardly restore me to the position I had once enjoyed, Newcombe had shrugged and replied that a man of my experience and qualifications should have no problem getting work given that I would be back on the Medical register. He even assured me that he had contacts who could cut through the GMC red tape as a little added sweetener!

At that point he produced a document which confirmed the deal in writing and went into various other things about The Official Secrets Act. By then I was too shattered and too gripped by the euphoria-inducing prospect of escaping the mess I was in and returning to England, to negotiate further. I read it through in a daze and signed on the dotted line. I couldn't keep a copy given where I was going, but he assured me in his bureaucratic way that it would be safe with him. For all I knew it wasn't worth the paper it was written on, but I decided to trust him. Probably because I so desperately needed to.

I had lost count of the number of times I had churned through these thoughts when Chisholm walked in.

'Tony, goodness me, what have these idiots been doing to you? I told them simply to check no-one had planted a bug on you! Here let me organise some clothes for you and sort you out a stiff drink, you look as if you could use one...'

'Fuck off Peter. I've come over here to offer you a deal worth a small fortune and this is how you treat me. Don't pretend this shit didn't come from you because you're suspicious about Khoury's replacement. I've a good mind to call it off right now and tell him you can't deliver...'

'Tony, Tony, calm down! You're right, I am curious to know what's happened. In my position, you'd be pretty curious too. I'm sorry if you've experienced a little discomfort, but at least we both are now assured of absolute privacy.'

'Yes, well you'd better make the most of it because, when I've delivered what I've come here to deliver, I'm out of here.

Mansour has paid me a fee to act as his messenger boy and that's it. I'm getting on a plane and I never want to see you or him again. You can sort out your own filthy deals and leave me out of it!'

Chisholm regarded me for a moment in mock alarm.

'My, my, we are unhappy: all a bit rich for your blood, eh? I had you down for sterner stuff; still you can only lead a horse to water...'

'I'm not interested in drinking from the same sewer as you. Give me some clothes then we can go somewhere decent to discuss this deal.'

Chisholm's eyes narrowed and I detected a spark of annoyance, but not as strong as the spark of greed I had detected a moment earlier when I mentioned the word 'fortune'.

'Very well,' he agreed, 'I'll get the boys to bring you in some clothes and we'll discuss things over dinner at the Glockenhof.'

*

We sat opposite each other in the vine-clad-arbour restaurant in the garden of the Glockenhof despite the cold which was, in fairness, pretty much chased away by the powerful blow heaters humming steadily in the background. A second hum was provided by the crowd of fellow diners surrounding us. Along with Jamila, I was pretty sure I recognised several other faces from my last trip to Zurich. It occurred to me that we were surrounded by Chisholm's people and I was observing a highly effective method of ensuring we weren't overlooked or overheard. As if to confirm this, Chisholm waited until the waiter had delivered the coffee and liqueurs we had ordered then produced a pencil and flimsy sheet of paper. He wrote on it and passed it across the table to me. It read:

Who is this new man?

I thought for a moment then wrote:

I believe he is a Hezbullah thug.

Chisholm studied my reply thoughtfully and then wrote:

What kit does he want?

I wrote:

He wants to buy some sort of nuclear weapon.

I handed it back. Chisholm read it and raised his eyebrows, but he didn't look astonished. He wrote:

What for?

I replied:

How would I know.

Chisholm read my reply then handed me his own:

Probably imagining some sort of dirty bomb. Be better off with gas – cheaper, easier to control and hide.

Gas? This was unexpected. To buy time I simply replied with a question mark. His answer said it all:

Chemical weapons. Tabun, sarin, VX etc. Just as effective and more reliable. Nukes discredited after Chernobyl survival rate. Chems cheaper – can release a demo dose to prove he's serious.

I sat back stunned at the casualness with which he discussed mass murder. Suddenly I felt rather good about what I was doing, though ten times more frightened: his openness did not augur well for my survival prospects. I desperately needed to stay calm and casual. I nodded as if agreeing to the sense of this and wrote:

Can I have my phone back? Will suggest this to him.

Chisholm read it and shook his head. His reply made my blood run cold:

Will deal with M in person. Call him to fix a meeting. Him and me alone on neutral territory. Suggest Cyprus. You stay here as my guest until deal is done.

Oh my God! The bloody man had gone straight to the worse possible scenario. If he spoke to Mansour my cover would be blown in an instant! I fought to keep my hand from shaking. I tried to convince myself the pencil was a scalpel and I was performing a routine op. Surprisingly it seemed to help because I managed to write an intelligible reply:

> *Sorry. M will only deal through me. Paranoid as hell and only trusts me. It is me or no deal. Final.*

I passed it back and stared resolutely at my de facto captor. He read it and sat thinking for a while, then pulled out the phone that had been confiscated from me by his thugs. He took the pencil and paper back and wrote again:

> *Is this thing encrypted?*

We swapped and I replied:

> *Sure and it's a direct line.*

Chisholm passed me the phone. This time he spoke:

'Okay, get him on it for me. If this doesn't check out you're dead.' He mimed the word 'dead' and gestured his throat being cut.

I took the phone and selected the number loaded into it for just this sort of situation. It rang and a voice sounding astonishingly like Mansour's answered:

'Hello Doctor Stamford. How is your trip?'

'It's going fine Sir. It's just the gentleman I have come to visit would like a quick chat with you. I'll just pass you over.'

I handed the phone to Chisholm, cringing inside. The man Newcombe had found to impersonate Mansour sounded authentic enough, but what if he said something that didn't add up? The consequences were unthinkable to yours truly! Chisholm didn't hang around getting to the point:

'How do you do Mr Mansour, is this line one hundred per cent secure?'

He paused to listen and then, apparently satisfied, continued:

'Fine, in that case I have advised Tony here that, for the project he has described to me, you should consider using chemicals as opposed to the alternative you are considering. I can assure you that I am happy to supply the sort of substances and equipment that will suit your needs.'

He paused for Mansour's reply then continued:

'True, but this method will allow you much greater control and invite much less interference from other outside parties. Look, you don't have to make a decision now. I will need to check out current market prices and availability for the sort of quantities needed to treat the areas under discussion. Once I have done that, we can discuss this method further and, if you approve, make arrangements for delivery. Tony will call you in three days time, okay?'

He listened a moment longer and then cut the call and handed me back the phone. As I took it he looked me coldly in the eye.

'Don't take this personally Tony. It's just I have survived this long by trusting absolutely nobody and that includes you. That means that, given the goods and sums involved, I will be making this trade in person and you will be coming with me as my insurance, so, if there is anything about this deal that doesn't add up, now's the time to tell me. You won't get another chance.'

I stared back as steadily as I could for a moment before replying: 'Are you telling me I'm your prisoner then?'

He smiled mockingly: 'Let us just say you are my particularly valued guest.'

*

In terms of comfort, there was no disputing the Glockenhof's superiority over the Lubyanka, but my elegant, spacious room was a prison cell nonetheless. This was reinforced by the presence of my earlier captors who were now stationed outside the door dressed in dinner suits. As far as the outside world was concerned I was doubtless an important guest and they were my bodyguards, but when I had tried to leave the room they blocked my way and, when I tried to push past, I received an abrupt jab in the solar plexus that had sent me back-peddling back into the room doubled over in pain. The door shut firmly as I tripped over a low table and sat down painfully on the expensive wooden floor.

On partly regaining my breath I crawled across the room to inspect the window as a second possible escape route. I gave that up without even bothering to see if it was locked: the building opposite told me I was on the fourth or fifth floor. There didn't appear to be a balcony outside, let alone a scenic lift, should I fancy some Bond-style high-wire escapology. Besides, I was a middle-aged man with a dislike of vertiginous situations.

I turned my attention to the contents of the room as a possible means of conveying my plight to the outside world. There was a writing desk but, with those guards outside the door, I lacked a carrier pigeon to make that effective. All electronic means of communication had been removed.

Defeated, I turned on the television and flicked through the channels in search of some sort of intelligent distraction. I gave up and tuned into the World News to watch Syria beating itself up. The place was in chaos as the UN postured over what it would do now that Assad had been caught using chemical weapons on his own people. Obama was brandishing his six guns whilst Putin's Russian Bear snarled at him and the rest of the world tried to perch on a fence that was swaying dangerously in the hot air of international opinion. Suddenly Syria was being talked about as the powder keg that could blow the situation from a proxy war into the real thing. With a sickening jolt of reality it suddenly hit me that a fanatic like Mansour passing Chisholm's chemical weapons to Hezbullah could be the spark that set the whole thing off. What I did, or failed to do now could have truly unimaginable consequences.

31

It was bizarre: three days in a gilded cage with only the World News and the regular arrival of gourmet cuisine to break the monotony. The availability of endless foreign language films, and football matches between teams I had never heard of, left me cold and sent me drifting off into the same old fruitless questions about what was happening and whether anything had gone wrong. Every time I tuned into the World News the crisis seemed to be getting worse. The reports from Lebanon gave the impression that it was hot on Syria's heels in terms of civil war. Even given my current perilous situation, I found myself thanking God I was out of there.

On the morning of the third day Chisholm accompanied my breakfast.

'Ah Tony, good to see you're up.' He sat down on one of the easy chairs and began helping himself to a croissant. 'Come on, tuck in, we've got a busy day ahead of us!'

'Well that makes a change. I thought you'd forgotten me!' Did that sound hearty or petulant? It didn't seem to matter.

'Yes, well sorry about that, but things have been a bit hectic. I've been out of the country most of the time.'

'Right, well it's probably best if I don't know where, but I trust things worked out to your satisfaction?'

'As well as they ever do with these deals. Anyway, it looks like I've got the kit at a price I can turn a profit on. All we've got to do now is convince Mansour that it will do the job for him. Eat up; it's time you made that phone call.'

I nibbled on a croissant, sick with anticipation. A conversation with the Mansour substitute opened wide the possibility of discovery but then what choice did I have? After a few moments I swilled down the bone-dry crumbs of pastry with a swig of coffee as Chisholm pulled out my phone, selected Mansour's number and then set it down on the table between us. It rang a few times; then that familiar voice filled the room:

'Hello Doctor Stamford, what news do you have for me?'

'I have good news for you Sir. I believe my friend can supply you with the goods you discussed with him last time if you have had a chance to decide if they will meet your requirements.'

The Mansour substitute paused for a moment to choose his words: he no doubt heard the echo of the phone on loud speaker mode.

'I am not quite sure of this new method Doctor Stamford, perhaps you have an opinion to advise me?'

'Well to be honest Sir, this is not my field at all. All I can say is that Peter assures me his suggestion will be highly effective without causing so much unnecessary damage...'

'Damage is no concern of mine! I only care for victory...'

As impersonators of fanatics go, Newcombe's man was top class. Even using this guarded double-talk we were instinctively employing despite the phone's encryption, he still managed to display a convincing volatility. I glanced at Chisholm who was listening with raised eyebrows. I tapped my forehead with a forefinger in the traditional gesture of madness and mustered a rueful grin. Chisholm nodded his agreement and gave me the thumbs up. I cut across the phoney Mansour before he let his thespian talents carry him away.

'Look sir, all I can say is that Peter here has a great deal of experience when it comes to the problems you are tackling. Much more than I. If he says a chemical treatment will do the job for you, then I would go with that. He tells me he has located a first class supplier but the man is impatient for a decision.'

Newcombe must have briefed the phoney Mansour well because he came back with characteristic arrogance: 'I do not care for this man's impatience! Fuck him. I will make the decision when I wish!'

'Certainly Minister, of course you will, but as a man of your experience will be aware, this is a market in which demand outstrips supply. As I understand it the chemical in question is particularly valued for its effectiveness and therefore much sought after. Surely you would wish to purchase the best product available?'

There was a long pause. This man was good. Finally he replied: 'Okay, how to proceed?' Before I could inform him that I hadn't a clue, Chisholm took over.

'Good morning Mr Mansour, I hope you are pleased with Tony's news?'

Mansour wasn't inclined to swap pleasantries.

'How much?'

'I beg your pardon?'

'How much money do you want?'

Chisholm gave me the thumbs up; we had our fish hooked! He clearly had no sense of the appalling amorality of the bait he was using! What shocked me more was that, for a fleeting moment, nor did I. I had been gripped momentarily by the thrill of the chase. His reply brought me back down to Earth quickly enough.

'I think it might be wise if we avoided discussing details such as money and delivery over the phone. I have an agent in your area right now. He could call in and go over such details with you face to face, his name is Talal.'

Talal! Since when had he worked for Chisholm? I thought he worked for me! But then, on reflection, I had left him in charge of the supply end of the hospital and clinic operation. Knowing Chisholm as I now knew him, Talal would have been an obvious person for him to recruit, and, if that was so, what the hell was going to happen now? I could hear the Mansour substitute hesitating at the other end of the phone. Should he agree to the meeting? More importantly, how could he not agree to it? It was a sensible suggestion. He paused a moment longer, and then replied.

'Very well, you send this agent. I will make agreement with him.'

*

Back in my gilded cage I retreated into a state of numb dread, largely consisting of dumbly watching the Middle East dissolve into anarchy courtesy of CNN or the BBC. This was occasionally broken by hopeless attempts to picture the outcome of Talal turning up at the Lubyanka to sell the real Mansour chemical weapons. Perhaps they'd shoot him out of hand and Chisholm would simply be left in the dark about his fate. That wouldn't be so bad. He'd have to press ahead with the trade without the failsafe of Talal's thumbs-up which he had so cleverly engineered, but I reckoned that greed would get the better of him and he'd do without that. A little voice reminded me that Talal had once been my close companion, comrade-in-arms even, but I dismissed it. He was a turncoat now.

But what if they didn't shoot him out of hand? Knowing Talal, he would talk his way past the minions and into the confidence of their leader in one easy breath. If that happened, one call to Chisholm would be enough to see me found floating face down in Lake Zurich before the day was out. Every time I got that far my brain shut down. My only hope was Newcombe and his guardian angels which filled me with dread not confidence. You couldn't fault the man for plodding persistence, but that was hardly a quality I needed right now!

True, my supposed allies knew there was a serious problem, but what could they do? Newcombe and I had hardly left the Lubyanka with a cheery wave and an invitation to pop back any time we liked. If the place was still in the hands of that gang of thugs, Newcombe would be made no more welcome than Talal.

Besides, even if the place was deserted when Talal turned up, what was Newcombe going to do with him? Up to now we had only needed to convince Chisholm, who had never met the man, over the phone! There was no way we were going to convince Talal meeting our substitute face to face!

There again, what if he didn't need convincing? Perhaps Talal was no turncoat after all. Sure, he had ended up working for Chisholm more than for me, but that was simply due to circumstances. We were old pals. We went back quite some way together. Perhaps when he realised that something didn't add up on the Mansour front he would pitch his tent in my camp, particularly if Newcombe got there in time to explain what was going on. To the best of my knowledge he shared no 'brothers-in-arms' history with Chisholm. For a moment I even felt a little guilty for distrusting my dear old friend.

Then another little voice in the back of my mind reminded me that the key word in all of this was 'if'. It was all wild speculation and guesswork. My fate now lay in other hands and without a crystal ball I could do nothing but wait. At that point my brain turned back to CNN, or the BBC, or whatever relentless, depressing crap was showing. The gourmet food sat on the table untouched.

*

'Get in the boat, Tony.' The command came from Chisholm. Thankfully the boat was not waiting for me at a jetty on Lake Zurich. It was sitting, twin-engines throbbing, at the water's edge of a sheltered cove in a sea that I was pretty certain constituted part of the Mediterranean. It was a souped-up racer of the sort Chisholm had used for our previous get-togethers on Talal's cousin's trawler. Two men had just finished very carefully loading an ominous-looking, black metal box on board. It sat suspended in some sort of small hammock affair in the middle of the floor.

I waded through the shallows and stepped over the side. Even in the moonlight I could see enough to appreciate that this machine was a real beast. I sat down in one of the two rear bucket seats with one of Chisholm's guards beside me. Talal and Chisholm sat in the two seats in front of us. The thug who had first worn the biker jacket was at the helm in a wetsuit; the rest of us had donned spray jackets and trousers. The engines moved from a throb to a growl and then a snarl as we pulled smoothly away from the shore and then accelerated across the bay and out into the open sea. That box hung, steady but menacing, in the narrow space between us.

I was now both literally and figuratively at sea. I had endured a nightmare of uncertainty for the best part of twenty-four hours according to the clocks on the news channels I kept flicking between. During that time I had quite seriously inspected the room for possible methods of ending it all. I can't say I wanted to die; I just wanted to end the sickening dread that was threatening to unhinge me. I don't know if hotel rooms are intentionally designed to minimise the bad publicity of visitor suicides, but thankfully I drew a blank. The windows didn't open, supposedly in deference to the air conditioning, and the kettle flex was too short to strangle a cat.

Finally, Chisholm and Talal walked through the door, but this did little to alleviate the uncertainty. True, they weren't accompanied by homicidal heavies, but nor did they volunteer any details regarding Talal's visit to the Lubyanka. Talal said nothing and, even allowing me a little understandable paranoia, seemed to pointedly avoid my eyes. Chisholm was simply abrupt:

'Okay Tony, time to go. The deal's going down tonight and it seems Mansour requires your presence to reassure him that it's all on the level.'

I had followed them out of my room and into the lift. We had climbed into the back of a windowless white van and sat in silence as it wove its way through the city. At the airport Chisholm handed me a forged passport in the name of James Carlisle. It was obviously a professional job because we went through customs onto a private plane. Some three hours later we touched down at a place called Marmaris in darkness. If my memory served me correctly we were therefore in Turkey. That made sense if we were headed for Lebanon. We climbed into another van and drove several miles down the coast to a deserted cove.

Nothing throughout my journey had served to reassure me. At first my heart had leapt at Talal's appearance. He was alive and Chisholm wasn't pointing a gun at him so presumably he had not blown the whistle regarding the phoney Mansour. According to Chisholm, the deal was still going down, so apparently Newcombe's subterfuge was still intact. But then what if this was a double-bluff? What if Talal had pretended to switch sides in order to talk his way out of Newcombe's clutches and then tipped Chisholm the wink? No, that didn't work: why would they still be going through the motions of going through with the deal if they knew it was a trap?

Jesus Christ, this was enough to drive me nuts! Indeed, how was I to know if it hadn't done just that? Was I relapsing into the nightmarish breakdown confusion I had suffered at the hands of Elizabeth and Ham? I simply didn't know anymore. What I did know was grim enough. I might not be in chains or held at gunpoint, but I was being kidnapped and taken to a secret rendezvous for the express purpose of selling a psychopath some chemical weapons. I didn't know who my friends were, but those who claimed to be were maintaining a very discreet distance. Furthermore, it was becoming increasingly apparent that they were considerably more interested in intercepting Chisholm and his ominous-looking, black metal box than they were in acting as guardian angels to yours truly! For the first time in my life I fully understood what was meant by the phrase 'to be at one's wits' end'.'

*

I sat in the bucket seat sick with tension as the boat swayed and bumped against the trawler's hull. Chisholm looked up from the laptop he had been studying intently, waiting for the email confirming the money transfer. He gave a thumbs-up to the winch man looking down from the deck of the trawler. The evil-looking black box rose from its hammock and began inching its way up the side of the boat, guided by out-stretched arms. How strong was it? What would happen if a larger-than-usual wave rocked the ship and dashed the damned thing against the unforgiving steel? I closed my eyes, but that didn't help. They opened again against my will and stared at the box until hands, oblivious to its deadly contents, reached out and pulled it in over the side.

That was it. If all had gone according to plan, we had just delivered the lethal cargo straight into the hands of Newcombe and his guardian angels and, presumably, any time now, a fleet of power boats would come speeding into view to arrest Chisholm and rescue me. The only fly in the ointment seemed to me to be the inevitable gap between my rescuers being sighted and their actual arrival. That would provide Chisholm with ample time to realise he had been betrayed and take his revenge. Clearly Chisholm's arrest stood head and shoulders above my well-being on Newcombe's list of priorities. Still, now I had some sort of picture of how things were about to unfold I could feel the numbing paralysis beginning to dissipate and a surge of fight-or-flight adrenaline kicking in. I felt oddly elated and ready for action as the speed-boat swung away from the trawler's side and began to accelerate off into the open sea.

I discreetly scanned the horizon for my rescuers, though no-one seemed to be paying me much attention anyway. Chisholm was punching the air and my guard and the helmsman were busy high-fiving each other as we sped away. Suddenly, one of them pointed and shouted something unintelligible. Something had glinted in the pre-dawn sky. It was a sparkling silver dot heading towards us just above the horizon and it was growing very fast.

Perhaps thanks to his years of experience in African wars, Chisholm recognised it, or rather its significance first. He shouted something at the helmsman who sent the boat veering to starboard. At the same time he reached inside his waterproof and pulled out a pistol. Perhaps it was the swerve to the right that prevented an entirely smooth draw, which was just as well because, when the gun did come free, he was turning it very deliberately in my direction.

His eyes blazed with fury as he raised the weapon, oblivious to the fighter jet closing on us from behind his back. His last words were: 'You fucking bastard!' as its canon began spitting. They would have been the last words I heard had I not been struck in the midriff by a flying Talal. I had risen instinctively to try to evade Chisholm and now, with a cry of 'Come on Boss!' Talal rugby tackled me clean over the side and out of the boat. Even as I flew backwards through the air I felt the mighty jolt of a canon round, but I felt no pain. Talal had taken the bullet for me.

As we sank in this bizarre embrace, a powerful surge pushed us further under. In desperation I began to kick for the surface detaching myself from Talal as we rose. I am not a strong swimmer and the last thing I needed was to be dragged down by a dying man! As I broke the surface I looked round for the boat, but it was gone. In its place floated shattered debris and, a few yards away I made out a body. Presumably a round had hit the fuel tanks and that extra surge was the force of the explosion. As far as I could see the only survivors were myself and, debatably, Talal.

As I began to gather my wits I realised that our return to the surface had been thanks to the air trapped in our water-proofs rather than any physical prowess on my part. Now I could feel that air seeping and being squeezed out by the buffeting waves. The suit was getting heavy. At present Talal seemed to be staying afloat, though he appeared to be unconscious. I wondered what sort of damage that bullet had done. Anyway first things first, I had to get out of the suit before I could devote any thought to helping him.

I kicked away my shoes and the water proof trousers, and then struggled out of the jacket, which left me floating in my pants and shirt. I looked around to assess my situation more carefully. One thing was obvious: it was well beyond my limited swimming ability to contemplate a bid for land. True I only had to swim towards the rising sun to get there eventually, but how long was eventually? I was sure Chisholm would have fixed a rendezvous well away from prying eyes given the nature of our cargo, and I was no Captain Webb.

As I bobbed up and down in the featureless sea, the grimness of my situation gradually sank in. At first it seemed the obvious thing was to stay put and hope for rescue. The pilot was obeying instructions from someone and he knew where that attack had taken place; ergo so did the people who had organised it. Someone would be out fairly soon to check for survivors, but would that someone be Newcombe and would he be planning to rescue any survivors he found? It would be a lot safer and simpler to ensure that there were no witnesses to what had amounted to a deliberate execution! Then again, Talal had deliberately tried to save me and, if he wasn't on Chisholm's side he was on Newcombe's: he was one of the guardian angels. If that was the case, perhaps they weren't as cynical as I feared. I gave up on this hopeless speculation and turned my attention to my saviour.

As I swam across the five yards of sea by now separating us I could see his face was twisting with pain. He wasn't dead or unconscious. Presumably, he was helping himself stay afloat to some degree, or perhaps, the air was more effectively trapped in his waterproofs. Something was enabling him to keep his face out of the water. I hesitated. A little voice in the back of my mind whispered caution. What had I been taught as a youngster all those years ago when I was training for my Bronze Medallion water lifesaving award?

Approach with caution. That was it! It was no use getting

yourself drowned trying to rescue someone else. I recalled in particular the emphasis the instructor had laid on the danger of approaching a drowning man who could quite possibly panic and drag you down with him, or tread you under in his desperation to stay on the surface. True, Talal didn't look particularly dangerous or panicked, but then I recalled the instructor warning how duplicitous a drowning man could be in his desperate desire for rescue. Furthermore, this was happening miles from anywhere in the middle of the Mediterranean, not in a six-foot deep swimming pool surrounded by lifeguards.

I stopped and trod water well out of arm's reach.

'Talal, Talal, can you hear me?'

This elicited no response. I stayed where I was and tried louder.

'Talal, Talal, can you hear me?' This time he opened his screwed up eyes. I adjusted my position so that we were rising and falling on the same wave. He got me in focus.

'Boss, boss, are you okay boss?'

'Yes, I'm okay. How about you, Talal?'

'I'm not so goo...' His face twisted so violently that it cut his words short as he gasped for breath. I almost reached out but stopped myself. Was this a trick to lure me in? I didn't think so, but then again, what could I do anyway? He had been hit in the back by a bullet at close range. It hadn't gone through him into me which meant that, unless it had missed me altogether, it had hit something like bone inside him and deflected. God knows what internal damage he was suffering from. If I had him on a table in a modern operating theatre I might stand a chance of saving him, but out here floating around in the middle of nowhere I stood no chance. I reverted to the standard medical stratagem in such circumstances: unwarranted optimism.

'Talal, Talal, can you hear me?' He opened his eyes again and nodded. 'Listen, there'll be someone along shortly. You're going to be okay. You're going to be fine. Do you understand?'

He tried to raise his head, but couldn't find the strength, it flopped back to the side. Instead he mustered a lop-sided grin, then a barely audible answer.

'You be fine Boss, you be fine...'

Suddenly his face twisted again and his head jerked back in a spasm of pain before slumping forward into the water. He hung motionless in the water making no effort to lift it out. Casting caution to the winds I swam forward, grabbed his hair, and lifted his head. His eyes were lifeless and face already had the pallor of death. I felt for the pulse in his neck but found nothing. I considered artificial respiration but what was the point; he needed state-of-the-art trauma facilities. I released him to drift away. My thoughts turned to the slim possibility of my own survival as the sun climbed higher in the sky.

32

As it happened I didn't have long to wait. The people who had organised the party were quick to clean up after themselves. They had stayed beneath the horizon while the plane did the dirty work, but now they approached cautiously in three black rigid inflatables. One of them detached itself from the others and headed for me, the others peeled off to inspect what was left of the boat. Two men, dressed in the sort of anti-biological/chemical, black outfits you see on documentaries about the SAS, reached over the side and fished me effortlessly out of the drink. I was obviously no threat.

With a tweak of the throttle we carried on over to Talal's floating corpse which they fished out likewise and laid in the bottom of the boat. The boats regrouped and headed off in what the sun told me was a roughly westerly direction. It was as unremarkable as that.

At first the speed and power of the boats made the rescue quite exhilarating, but soon the constant jarring as we bounced across the waves became tiring and mildly nauseating, a sensation unimproved by the solitude. As far as my rescuers were concerned I might as well not have been there. They hardly spoke to each other through their oddly menacing face masks, let alone me! I sat alone in the back of the boat with Talal at my feet, trying to focus on the battle with Newcombe that I suspected lay ahead. Maddeningly, each jolt seemed to dislocate my thoughts.

Finally, with the sun now directly overhead, I made out

something on the horizon that began to materialise into land. Given the direction we had been travelling in and the time it had taken, I guessed that it was Cyprus. I was aware that we still had military bases on the island so it made sense if I was still under the protection of the increasingly unpoliceman-like Inspector Newcombe and his guardian angels. We swung into a wide bay and headed towards what was clearly a very substantial military base. There was now plenty of air traffic overhead, transport planes and the like, and I began to pick out watch towers and antennae on the shore. Most of all I began to make out the grey, utilitarian concrete of military architecture the world over.

We pulled in at a small quay well away from the main areas of activity and I was ushered ashore and into the back of a waiting ambulance. No-one spoke. Given my lack of serious injury, I suspected the vehicle was intended as much to hide me from prying eyes and contain my curiosity as it was to hasten me to medical treatment. Nevertheless we pulled up outside some sort of medical facility where I was hustled through into a side-ward. I was gestured to undress and get into a pair of standard military-issue pyjamas. My captor collected up my old clothes without a word and departed.

I was now a prisoner of quarantine. It was remarkably like being one of Chisholm's 'particularly valued guests': I wasn't a prisoner, but nor was I allowed to leave. I would have bet good money there were armed guards outside the door if I had cared to look. The only significant difference was that my contact with the outside world had reduced from twenty-four hour TV News to a couple of battered, week-old copies of the Sun and The Times courtesy of News International's dedication to keeping 'our boys' informed of that oaf Murdoch's view of the world. With nothing better to do, I laid down on the bed and quickly fell asleep.

*

I woke up to the sound of the door opening quietly. I lay stock-still and opened my eyes a fraction to assess my visitor. It was Newcombe. He walked quietly over to my bed and stood for a moment watching me; then he turned and walked over to a nearby chair. He pulled it towards the bed and sat down. I lay motionless while I gathered my thoughts: the next few minutes could well turn out to be crucial in the overall scheme of things.

He pulled out a newspaper and unfolded it rather noisily. Damn him, I was trying to think! He glanced at the headlines and then folded the bloody thing methodically back up, rustling it even more. Jesus, how could that be so distracting? He sniffed then idly inserted a finger into his right nostril. He prodded around for what seemed like forever and then extracted a gobbet of mucus which he inspected thoughtfully before chewing it off the tip of his finger! Finally, he turned his attention back to me and spoke suddenly in that irritatingly self-satisfied manner of his.

'Well, well Mr Stamford, sir, it's good to see you've come through your little adventure in one piece.'

Damn it, the bloody man had known I was awake all along! Anyhow, if this was an invitation to engage in a little social pleasantry, it didn't work. I ignored him and continued struggling to get my thoughts in order. With a bit of luck, in a few minutes time he might not be so pleased to see me. He tried again.

'I'm sure you'll be pleased to know sir that your clothing has been thoroughly checked for any traces of chemical or biological contamination and there are no lingering traces of any form of pernicious residue to be found on them. You, yourself, now you are awake, will also be subject to a similarly thorough series of tests to ensure that...'

I sat up and held up a hand.

'Who are you, Newcombe?'

'I beg your pardon, sir?' I was pleased to note that I had startled him. I pressed on.

'I said who are you? Don't give me any bullshit about being a Detective-Inspector in the Metropolitan Police. I have just witnessed you organise and run an operation which falls way outside their remit.'

Newcombe frowned and paused to gather his thoughts before he spoke.

'Well, sir, I'm afraid you're wrong there. As I told you once before I am indeed officially a Detective-Inspector with the Metropolitan Police, but I am currently on secondment to a unit working closely with our security services and Interpol. This, I should add, 'top-secret' organisation is concerned with tackling arms trafficking to the Middle East which is currently in an extremely volatile situation. May I enquire as to why this is concerning you further?'

'Because as far as I am concerned the agreement we came

to regarding my return to Britain and my reinstatement as a medical practitioner is now null and void...'

To my considerable annoyance, the fool got entirely the wrong end of the stick.

'Oh, I see. Discovered a bit of a taste for the high octane stuff have we sir?'

'No I bloody well haven't, you idiot! Quite the opposite: I'm thoroughly sick of chasing round risking my life in order to satisfy your Boy's Own sense of adventure and the British Government's desire to meddle in wars that invariably back-fire on them. The sooner I see the last of this 'high octane' stuff, the happier I'll be, but it won't be on the pathetic terms with which you initially ensnared me!'

I had his attention now. His eyebrows were raised enquiringly and his eyes had taken on a coldness I had never seen in them before.

'Really, sir, and just what makes you imagine that I, or the people I represent, would consider, even for a second, any proposal to alter an agreement that was arrived at between us in mutual good faith?'

'Because I happen to have a recording of the entire conversation during which that agreement was arrived at.'

That stopped him. I could almost hear his brain whirring as he reviewed the discussion we had had back in my Nissen: his feigned surprise at my naiveté, his use of blackmail regarding the Aston, the proposition that I should persuade Peter to sell Mansour a nuclear device and, finally, his admission that he and his team had been sanctioned to murder him. That was the killer. He had admitted that that was their objective and it had come from the very top of the British Government. When he spoke again his usual lugubriousness had vanished completely.

'What do you mean? That's not possible!'

I tried not to smirk.

'I'm afraid it is. You should never have let me take that shower.' I saw real alarm in his eyes now and pressed on. 'I hid my phone in there when I got changed to accompany King and Barika to carry out Khoury's op. I didn't know how things would turn out, or who would turn up in my absence, and it was an expensive and possibly compromising piece of kit. When you let me in there to clean up I set it to record and propped it up against the bedroom wall under the bed next to the room we were in.'

'And what makes you think a mobile phone would be capable of picking up that conversation through a wall?'

'That was no ordinary mobile phone and the walls in that hut are paper thin. Besides I don't think, I know it did.'

'How do you know that?'

'Because all I had to do was dial a prearranged number to check it had been collected and that the recording had worked. If you recall I did just that in the garden at the Villa on the phone you yourself lent me. Remember the wrong number? The agreement with my contact, who shall remain nameless, was that if I dialled that and I got an answer phone, everything was okay. Most obliging of you.'

By now Newcombe's face was showing none of its usual phlegmatism. It was puce with what I diagnosed as barely controlled anger, no doubt at the realisation that he had been royally duped. He was visibly sweating and clenching his fists with what I adjudged to be something akin to what my colleagues in the psychiatric field call acute anxiety. Indeed, in a professional situation, I might well have recommended that he was referred to one of them. As it was I rather enjoyed watching the bastard crap himself.

'Who has the recording now?' he blurted abruptly. I sat back with a reassuring smile.

'Don't worry it's perfectly safe, though I should add that I have agreed with its current holder that he or she will auction off its contents to the world's press on the seventh day after it came into his or her possession unless he or she hears from me by prearranged code that I am well. That gives you, unless you've kept me here under some form of sedation, a few days yet in which to agree to my demands.'

'This is blackmail!'

I shrugged.

'Call it what you like. I don't remember you being unduly concerned about using my past to pressurise me into helping you.'

'And what makes you think, given that this is a secure military base and no-one even knows that you're here, that we won't use those few days to extract that prearranged code from you?'

I paused to study my opponent. His complexion was noticeably less livid and his expression was now more sly than panicky. This was starting to turn in a direction I really did not want to go in. I replied with studied calm.

'Because regardless of whether you hang me up by my thumbs, or shoot me full of that sodium pentothal stuff, you still won't be sure I've told you the truth until the shit hits the fan or nothing happens. I don't think you can afford to take that risk. Moreover, given the mood I'm in right now, I don't think your thugs could dream up anything sufficiently unpleasant to dissuade me from dropping you right in it up to your armpits. In fact I'm sorely tempted to do just that in order to teach you a lesson for having the gall to threaten me...'

Newcombe opened his mouth to interrupt, but I held up my hand for silence.

'... In case you don't quite see the complete picture let me explain. Either you agree to meet the very reasonable demands I am about to outline to you, or my accomplice will sell that recording to the highest bidder. The press would only thank us for such a story unsubstantiated, but they will pay a fortune for the proof of it. At the end of the day, it doesn't greatly bother me either way who compensates me for all the crap I've been through, but, call me patriotic or something, I suppose I'd rather save my government an awful lot of embarrassment and I'm sure you would...'

'You'll never get away with this!'

That was it! I knew I'd won, or at least I'd beaten Newcombe. His exclamation sounded pathetically hollow.

'On the contrary, I cannot see a single reason why I shouldn't get away with this. If you can organise an airstrike and a turn out by those chaps in black, I'm sure you can rustle up some petty cash to ensure the whole thing stays strictly between you and me and, of course, my anonymous assistant.'

'How do I know that will be the case? What's to stop you taking our money then still taking a copy to the highest bidder?'

'Because I am not stupid or greedy. I don't want to spend the rest of my days looking over my shoulder for your chaps in black on a debt collecting mission. All I want is to return to some sort of normality in the city and profession I once called my life. I want to do it with all the status and money I once enjoyed and without the need to keep looking over my shoulder in case you crawl out from under the skirting board. Is that too much to ask?'

Newcombe sat frowning at me as if trying to work out where the catch lay behind such a simple request. Finally, he obviously drew a blank and sat back like a bank manager behind an imaginary desk.

'How much do you want,' he enquired.

I paused thoughtfully, my head tilted back for me to gaze at the corner of the ceiling in order to do some serious mental calculations. Needless to say I had done these a thousand times already during my incarceration, but I didn't wish to appear overeager. At the time of my divorce from Elizabeth when everything was getting divvied-up the working figure had been some five million plus the house, but then there was inflation to take into account and besides there's the old adage: the more you charge the more they think you're worth. I didn't need to undercut myself. Finally, I withdrew my gaze from the corner of the ceiling and turned it on Newcombe.

'Ten million pounds,' I said coldly.

*

Newcombe walked back into my room and seated himself as before. He had been gone almost three hours, but I was as cool as a cucumber. I'd sat through enough hospital budget meetings to understand delaying tactics.

'I'm sorry about the wait Sir,' he said in a tone that made it quite clear he wasn't. 'I'm sure you will understand your proposals are somewhat above my pay scale...'

'I'm sure they are,' I interrupted abruptly. 'What is the answer from those for whom it isn't?' He looked startled by my tone. This was the first time since we met that the boot was on the other foot.

'Right Sir, well I've talked it through with the powers that be and their initial response is that there is no way that they could agree to the sum you are asking...'

I opened my mouth to speak but he held up his hand.

'However, under the circumstances and given the hardships you have endured in helping us with the completion of the mission, they are willing to offer a sum in the region of six million pounds sterling.'

This time I did speak.

'Okay, well you can tell you superiors that, in the time you have kept me waiting, I too have been considering my initial sum and it has now increased to twelve million.'

Newcombe gaped helplessly for a moment and finally found some words.

'But you can't do that, you're meant to meet me in the middle!'

'I'm not meant to do anything you expect of me anymore. You can phone your boss back and tell him my answer then we'll see if this can't be handled sensibly.' Newcombe looked stunned for a moment and then rose to leave the room. I held up my hand this time. 'You can call him from here, right now, to convince me you're not pissing around, or the price goes up again.' To my private delight he sat obediently back down. I watched as he fished out a mobile and dialled. He spoke quietly for a moment as I pretended to gaze out of the window at the concrete wall next door. Suddenly he held out the phone to me.

'My boss would like a word with you Sir.'

I took the phone, ready for a battle royal.

'Yes, Stamford speaking.'

A rather 'Hail fellow!' voice replied.

'Mr Stamford, how do you do Sir! Name's Wright, John Wright.'

That struck me as extremely unlikely, but I couldn't resist the obvious reply.

'Not my Mr Wright I suspect!'

'Ha, ha, very good Tony! Don't mind if I call you Tony, do you? Make things a lot more friendly while we sort this out?'

'I don't see anything that needs sorting out, but 'Tony's' fine if you wish.'

'Good, okay, now let me see, a bit of a problem with the cash what...yes, well to be frank the money's not a problem if you're happy to stick at ten.' He paused expectantly.

'I don't see why I should...'

''Cause ten's my ceiling and, besides, you were okay with it half an hour ago so what's the harm?'

I paused to consider his offer. There was no need to rush. After a further thoughtful study of that dull concrete wall I nodded. I held out my hand:

'If that's a concrete offer you've got a deal.'

I announced with a smile.

'Fair enough, provided my other demands are met.'

'Good, excellent, now about your other demands...'

'What about them?'

'Well there's only one that's causing a problem...'

'And what is that?'

'Your job, you say you want your old job back but at a hospital other than St George's.'

'Correct.'

'Well I'm afraid that's simply not possible old chap.'

'Why not? I'm a highly qualified, indeed world-renowned coloproctologist who will have a medical licence to practice by the time I get back.'

'True, absolute true, no problem with that, but the one thing we cannot promise is a vacancy. That is down to individual hospitals and, given the economy, vacancies aren't two-a-penny these days. However, don't think we haven't been busy on your behalf...'

'What d'you mean?'

'Well we wondered if all that blood and guts was still necessarily your bag, I mean, surely a chap needs a break from being up-to-the-elbows in that sort of thing.'

This time I really did pause. To my astonishment he had hit on something that had been niggling at the back of my mind too. Thinking back I had found myself asking on more than one occasion whether a change of employment might not come amiss. Each time I had dismissed it as exhaustion thanks to the battleground that constituted my recent surgical environment and then gee-ed myself up with the thought that I was working on the front-line of my profession. Now, these thoughts came flooding back. Too true, I was due a break! I'd done my bit and, now I really thought about it, I wasn't sure just how much I fancied a return to the more formal, disciplined environment of theatre in a top London hospital come to that!

'Go on,' I replied cautiously.

'Well we've got something here that might suit a chap like you down to the ground. It's still in medicine, but a chance to take a real break...'

'What kind of break?'

'Well an absolute doddle really. How would you feel about working in private industry?'

'I would consider it...I had a lucrative private practice back in London.'

'Fine, just the job, well there's a smashing non-executive directorship that's just come up with a multinational based near St Bart's.'

'What do they do?'

'Heaven knows, allsorts, pharmaceuticals and stuff. Anyhow you won't have to worry about that. You just have to show up when needed and dispense a bit of wisdom. Bloody sight more cash than the NHS.'

'How much?'

'I think a little bird whispered eighty grand in my ear and that's for two days a month. I believe there are expenses on top and they may be willing to pick up your old NHS pension if you smile nicely.'

'I see, well I'd need some time to think about it...'

'Why don't you think about it on the plane home to Blighty, then you and I can find somewhere quiet for you to put your moniker on a copy of The Official Secrets Act.'

'Rather keen aren't you?'

'Keen? No, not at all. Just keen to tie up the final loose ends on this job and glad to see a fellow patriot justly rewarded. Come on, how about it?'

'Let me think a moment.'

I lowered the phone taking care not to show a flicker of emotion to Newcombe as my brain worked nineteen-to-the-dozen trying to spot a catch. Finally, I lifted the receiver back up to my ear and nodded my agreement to the impassive concrete wall.

'Fair enough, tell Newcombe here to give me my own phone back so I can do a bit of online shopping then you can book me on a flight back to London.'

Also by
MIKE ADLAM:

The Rent Man

The Stamford Trilogy:
Malpractice
Sharp Practice
Out of Practice

 ponymous

MALPRACTICE

By Mike Adlam

Wealthy, philandering surgeon Tony Stamford seems to have the world at his feet until an embarrassing email from a recent conquest, Katya, proves the final straw for his long-suffering wife. But is she as long-suffering as she seems, and who really is Katya? As Stamford's life begins to unravel he finds himself lost in a world of mirrors, no longer certain who he can trust and doubting the value of his very existence. Stripped of everything he once owned, he embarks on a battle for his freedom and even sanity which can only end in death.

Sharply satirical and disturbingly dark, Malpractice takes a scalpel to the vanities of the medical profession and, in doing so lays bare the deceits and cruelties to which desperate people will stoop.

'A no-holds-barred, pull-out-all-the stops, breathless tangle of a thriller full of dark comedy...A heck of a good read'
Amazon.com

'An outstanding comic novel...Tony Stamford, philandering surgeon, is a masterpiece of grotesque invention'
Bookbrowse.com

'Darkly comic, beautifully paced, the novel is crammed with an almost Dickensian sense of atmosphere and turbulence, yet blessed with the deftness of Waugh. Full of great moments, it also succeeds in being momentous'
Goodreads.com

'Brilliantly entertaining and consistently outrageous, Adlam's brand of salacious humour spills out a tidal wave of manic delight'
Metro

'Sharp Practice is...admirably plotted, full of vitality, a novel that is truly comic, and, like all true comedy, also disturbing'
Literary Journal

THE RENT MAN

By Mike Adlam

Swansea is just one British port in the grip of the ruthless Rent Man Gang. Police and Customs are baffled by the fear and secrecy which surrounds their international drugs and male prostitution racket. Charlie Llewellyn is a local sculptor with a shaky cash flow, a taste for the beer and a divorce battle with the Bitch from Hell. But who are the men behind this brutal gang and why has Charlie really moved back to Swansea?

When a young male prostitute is murdered and Charlie commits suicide, the scene is set for one of the most original and gripping thrillers in years. At times hilarious, at times terrifying, The novel draws us through the trials and tribulations of everyday life into the dark, psychotic underworld of the brutal Rent Man Gang.

Riven with deliciously black humour and the almost touchable caustic atmosphere of decaying urban Wales. Mike Adlam's ability to create rounded characters makes his book, despite its dark subject matter, a breath of fresh air. There is indeed humour here, and characters to return to, but really The Rent Man is about thrills. And as the novel barrels triumphantly towards its unexpected but satisfying conclusion, it's in this respect that it delivers.

'I have read all of Stieg Larsson. I have read most of Jo Nesbo. They are spare, violent, and inhabit the sort of landscape most of us would prefer to avoid both physically and in imagination... Mike Adlam has transposed the reality of that type of darkness to Swansea and has done it in the most convincing manner'
Dai Blatchford, bestselling author of 'A Touch of Pigskin'

'An excellent thriller...unfolding at breakneck pace, with convincing settings and just the right blend of likeable and hateful characters'
Bookbrowse.com

'Part thriller, part mystery, and all action. Thriller writing doesn't get any better than this'
Metro

'A cunningly constructed action thriller...Adlam's narrative surges along with great power; the story is terrifying...grips you to the end'
Literary Journal

'Gripping in the way John Buchan, Len Deighton and John le Carre are. The writing is superb. A 100% copper-bottomed, no quibble guarantee of enjoyment. The excitement and danger are desperately well done'
Amazon.com

'A high octane adrenaline-raising thriller lifted well above the ordinary by sharp dialogue, well-drawn characters and elegant prose'
Goodreads.com

THE FINAL MILE

By Cal Smyth

The Final Mile is a biting social commentary of both the jobless hordes and the glitzy, gold-plated world of dirty deals and fat cat cronyism.

A man who has lost everything. Push him a little further. And he's going to fight back... Ryan Morgan is a good guy, a family man who runs his own business and lives by the rules. But when his business is liquidated, his house repossessed and his wife leaves him, Ryan starts to question the system. For years, the rich have ripped us off. It's time someone made them pay. Seeking payback, Ryan treks cross-country through a broken Britain menaced by an economic crisis. With nothing left to lose, Ryan cuts a brutally sweet swathe through the murky greed and corruption of bankers, CEOs and politicians whose skewered morals and hypocrisy have crippled a nation.

A stunning tale of morality and justice in which a simple, honest man is transformed into a killer, The Final Mile depicts a moral turnaround in the vein of TV's Breaking Bad. A story ripped from the headlines of tomorrow's newspapers.

'A resonant wish-fulfilment thriller that is cinematic and sparse genre writing at its very best. With nods to Richard Stark, Elmore Leonard and George Pelecanos, Cal Smyth has written a tale of revenge that challenges and entertains in equal measure: a blazing read that burns off the page, righteous indignation rippling through every heart-stopping moment'
Amazon.com

'Amoral, frighteningly violent and...portrays with deadpan brilliance the soul-less bankers who wheel and deal, exploit and thrive like rats in present-day Britain'
Goodreads.com

'A powerful and chilling story. The plot is convincing in every detail, the characters are entirely believable'
Metro

'Smyth's new thriller is a triumph...Suspenseful and elegant...a thoughtful, frightening story'
Literary Journal

'The Final Mile is, thankfully, fiction...it is five days since I finished reading the novel and it is still rumbling around in my head'
Bookbrowse.com

A TOUCH OF PIGSKIN

By Dai Blatchford

Piers Prideaux's promising career at an Oxford College is brought to an abrupt end following the intervention of a new master, one Sebastian Slope. It is not quite as simple as that, matters in Oxford never are. In defending himself Prideaux is directly responsible for Slope being sacked, arrested and jailed for fraud. Years later Slope returns to Oxford and it becomes clear that he is bent on revenge.

Slope is the leader of a group of dangerous men who are descended from an ancient Cornish secret society known as the Spriggans. Prideaux is forced to go on the run with his oldest best friend William Radleigh de Beaune, aka Billy Bones, an aristocrat fallen on hard times. As Slope pursues his deadly obsession anyone associated with Bones and Prideaux is in great danger.

Pigskin is a wise, quite surreal, philosophical meditation on the business of living, but with a witty and whimsical undercurrent, full of oddball characters and even odder secret societies.

'Cross Inspector Morse with Monty Python and you might get some idea of a book that, reduced to its pure essence, is a read and a half all the way... a dark and brilliant surreal thriller. Dai Blatchford has written a glittering, fantastical, cunningly contrived novel that leads the reader down a labyrinth of fear and dread. Rich with humour, character and incident'
Amazon.com

'A brilliant book, barmy and barnacled with the grotesque'
Metro

'A Touch of Pigskin is a first novel not only of tremendous promise, but also of achievement, a minor masterpiece...a mighty imagination has arrived on the scene'
Literary Journal

'A dazzling performance by Blatchford...a delightful display that marries the gusto of an international thriller with a collection of fascinating esoterica...stunning'
Bookbrowse.com

'Enthralling...there's no denying the bizarre fertility of the author's imagination: his brilliant dialogue , his wicked humour...'
The Literary Supplement

'Blatchford's the kind of writer who makes you want to nag your friends until they read him so that they share the pleasure'
Goodreads.com

www.ingramcontent.com/pod-product-compliance
Lightning Source LLC
Chambersburg PA
CBHW032139270626
47172CB00009B/398